GIRL GENIUS®

AGATHA HETERODYNE & THE VOICE OF THE CASTLE

A Gaslamp Fantasy with ADVENTURE, ROMANCE & MAD SCIENCE

Story by Kaja & Phil Foglio
Pencils by Phil Foglio
Colors by Cheyenne Wright

AIRSHIP ENTERTAINMENT

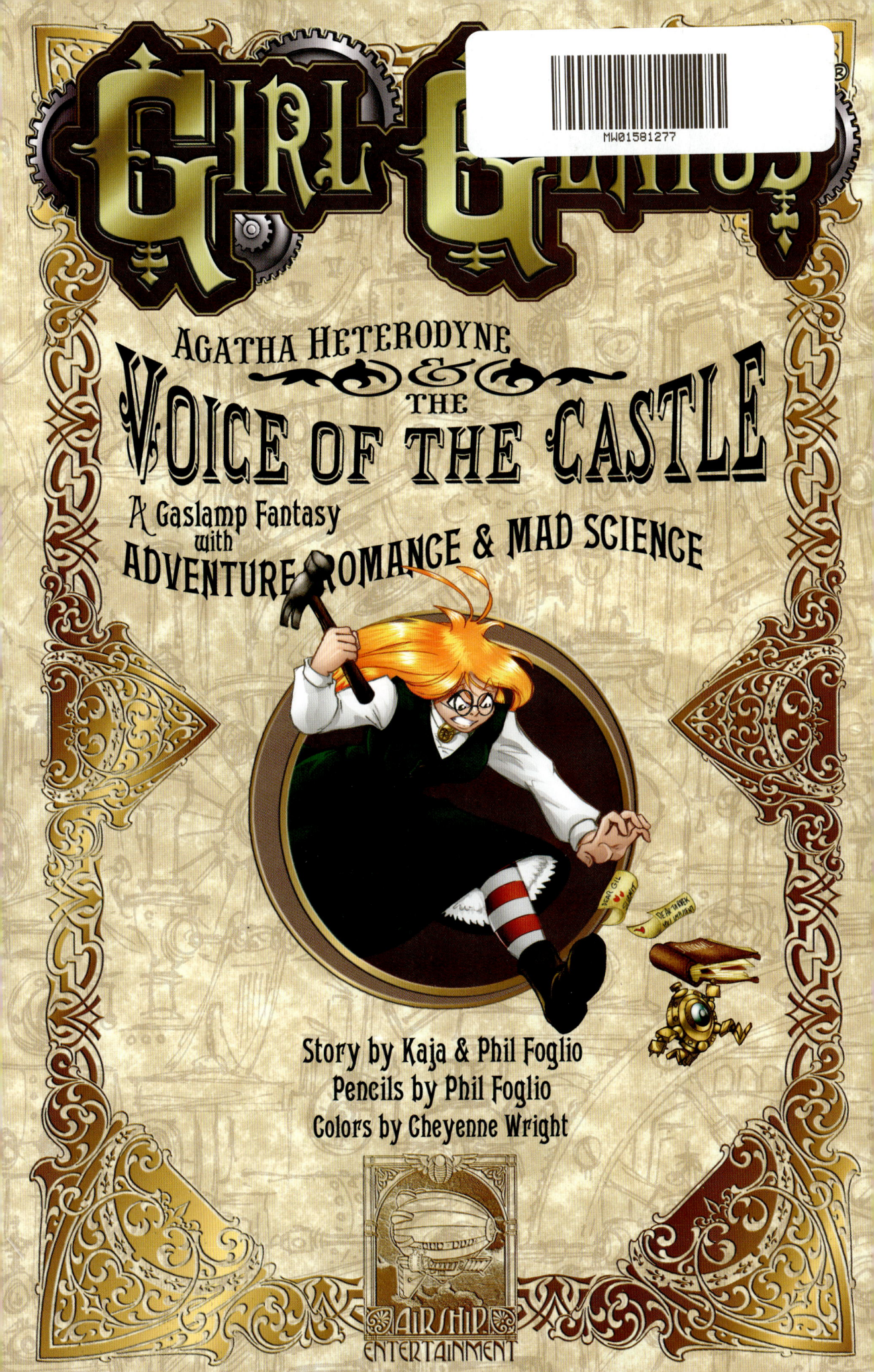

OTHER BOOKS FROM AIRSHIP ENTERTAINMENT AND STUDIO FOGLIO

Girl Genius® Graphic Novels

Girl Genius Volume One:
Agatha Heterodyne and the Beetleburg Clank

Girl Genius Volume Two:
Agatha Heterodyne and the Airship City

Girl Genius Volume Three:
Agatha Heterodyne and the Monster Engine

Girl Genius Volume Four:
Agatha Heterodyne and the Circus of Dreams

Girl Genius Volume Five:
Agatha Heterodyne and the Clockwork Princess

Girl Genius Volume Six:
Agatha Heterodyne and the Golden Trilobite

Girl Genius Volume Seven:
Agatha Heterodyne and the Voice of the Castle

Other Graphic Novels

What's New with Phil & Dixie Collection

Robert Asprin's MythAdventures®

Buck Godot, zap gun for hire:
- *Three Short Stories*
- *PSmIth*
- *The Gallimaufry*

Girl Genius® is published by:
Airship Entertainment™, a happy part of Studio Foglio, LLC
2400 NW 80th St #129 Seattle WA 98117-4449, USA

Please visit our Web sites at www.airshipbooks.com and www.girlgenius.net

Girl Genius is a registered trademark of Studio Foglio, LLC. Girl Genius, the Girl Genius logos, Studio Foglio and the Studio Foglio logo, Airship Entertainment, Airship Books & Comics & the Airship logo, the Jägermonsters, Mr. Tock, the Heterodyne trilobite badge, the Jägermonsters' monster badge, the Wulfenbach badge, the Spark, Agatha Heterodyne, Trelawney Thorpe, the Heterodyne Boys, Transylvania Polygnostic, the Transylvania Polygnostic University arms, the Secret Cypher Society, Krosp, Castle Wulfenbach, Castle Heterodyne and all the Girl Genius characters are © & ™ 2000-2008 Studio Foglio.

All material ©2001–2008 Studio Foglio. All rights reserved. No part of this book may be reproduced in any form (including electronic) without permission in writing from the publisher except for brief passages in connection with a review.

This is a work of fiction and any resemblance herein to actual persons, events or institutions is purely coincidental.

Story by Phil & Kaja Foglio. Pencils by Phil Foglio. Main story colors by Cheyenne Wright. Selected spot illustrations colored by Kaja Foglio and/or Cheyenne Wright. Logos, Lettering, Artist Bullying & Book Design by Kaja. Fonts mostly by Comicraft– www.comicbookfonts.com.

This material originally appeared from February 2007-December 2007 at www.girlgenius.net.
The short story Personal Trainer first appeared in May of 2006 on www.girlgenius.net.

Published simultaneously in Hardcover (ISBN 978-1-890856-46-5)
and Softcover (ISBN 978-1-890856-45-8) editions.

First Printing: May 2008   PRINTED IN CHINA

This volume is dedicated to Rachel "Sparks" Blackman. Without your heroic efforts on our behalf, we would have been doomed indeed.
Thank you so very much!

Kaja Foglio

Professor Foglio (of Transylvania Polygnostic University) recently undertook a research expedition to the Lost City of Thrindockle, where Agatha Heterodyne is rumored to have once bought a very nice hat. Following several old maps, garbled accounts from past adventurers, and a curious jade compass said to point to the inner sanctum of the main temple of the Spider Queen of Thrin, she finally discovered the city: hidden beneath a suburb of Antwerp. For a time, she lived among the high priestesses, conscientiously documenting their intricate rituals and arcane, science-confounding secrets; but soon became bored, stole the jeweled eyes of the temple idol, hacked her way past the hordes of giant guardian spiders, and caught the first train back to the University.

Phil Foglio

Professor Foglio is Co-Chair of TPU's Department of Creative History, specializing in the early life of Agatha Heterodyne. He was recently sandbagged when he was informed that, in order to keep his office, he had to teach at least *one* class every decade. His final series of lectures, entitled: *"A History of the Jägermonsters: Six Secrets of the Heterodynes"* was listed in the catalogs with an unfortunate printing error. As a result, so many students signed up that the course had to be offered multiple times in order to fill the demand. The lecture series was a stunning success, earning Professor Foglio the highly coveted "Most Beloved Teacher of The Year" award, and the even more coveted assurance of the University board that he would *never* be made to lecture *ever again*.

Cheyenne Wright

Professor Wright has been enhancing the adventures of Agatha Heterodyne for several years now. In that time, he has developed and added new devices and techniques to his art, resulting in a forced move out of the ruined tower he occupied in the north quadrant of Transylvania Polygnostic University. He has now relocated to a subterranean lair where he has access to, as he puts it: "Almost *infinite* supplies of *pure dark.*" Contemplation of this statement has caused several of TPU's theoretical physicists to lose sleep at night, as they have begun to worry about what might happen if the Professor has miscalculated and, by mistake or design, uses up *all* the dark. In an effort to let them sleep easier, we have taken special pains to reduce or eliminate all night scenes in this volume.

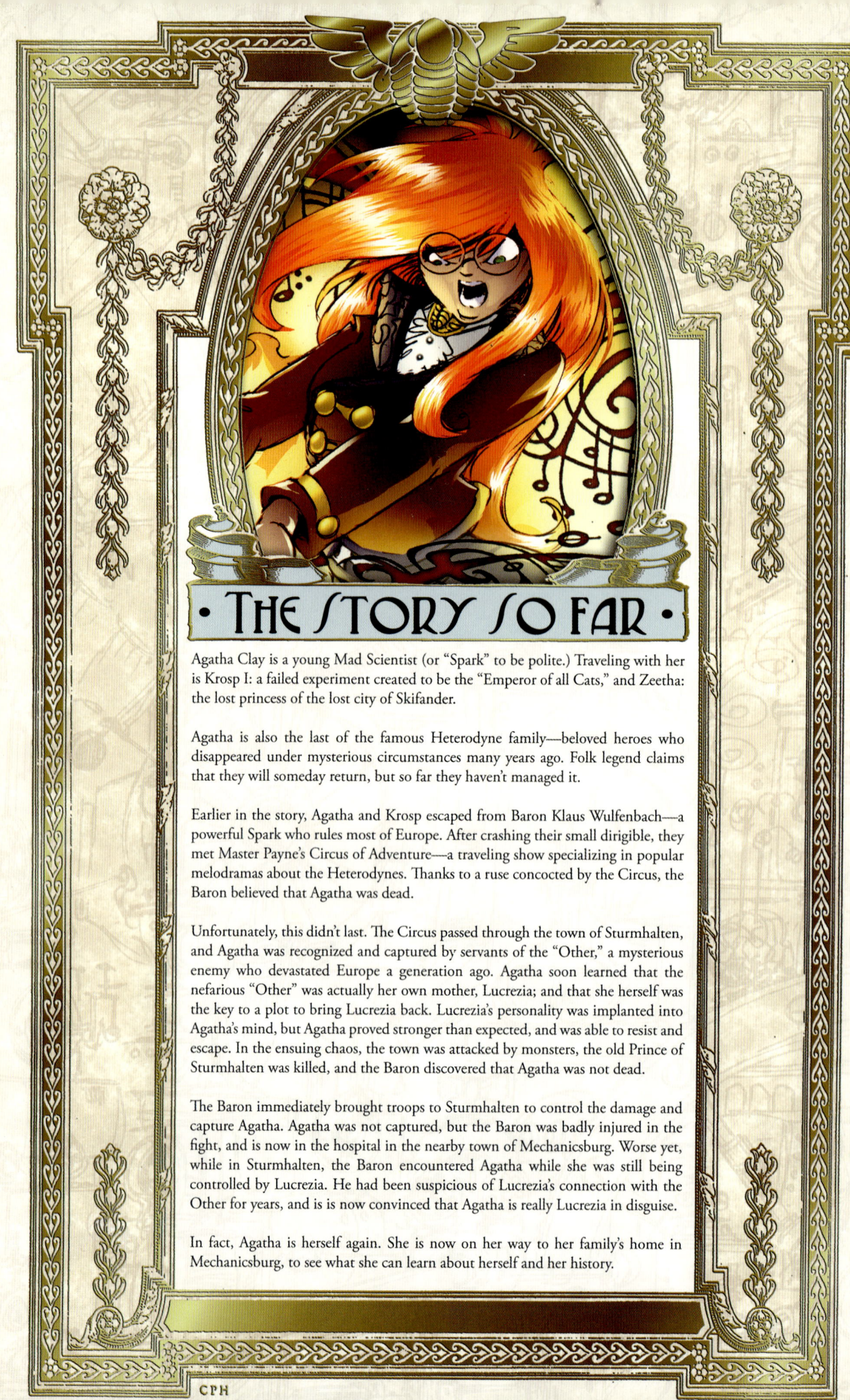

• THE STORY SO FAR •

Agatha Clay is a young Mad Scientist (or "Spark" to be polite.) Traveling with her is Krosp I: a failed experiment created to be the "Emperor of all Cats," and Zeetha: the lost princess of the lost city of Skifander.

Agatha is also the last of the famous Heterodyne family—beloved heroes who disappeared under mysterious circumstances many years ago. Folk legend claims that they will someday return, but so far they haven't managed it.

Earlier in the story, Agatha and Krosp escaped from Baron Klaus Wulfenbach—a powerful Spark who rules most of Europe. After crashing their small dirigible, they met Master Payne's Circus of Adventure—a traveling show specializing in popular melodramas about the Heterodynes. Thanks to a ruse concocted by the Circus, the Baron believed that Agatha was dead.

Unfortunately, this didn't last. The Circus passed through the town of Sturmhalten, and Agatha was recognized and captured by servants of the "Other," a mysterious enemy who devastated Europe a generation ago. Agatha soon learned that the nefarious "Other" was actually her own mother, Lucrezia; and that she herself was the key to a plot to bring Lucrezia back. Lucrezia's personality was implanted into Agatha's mind, but Agatha proved stronger than expected, and was able to resist and escape. In the ensuing chaos, the town was attacked by monsters, the old Prince of Sturmhalten was killed, and the Baron discovered that Agatha was not dead.

The Baron immediately brought troops to Sturmhalten to control the damage and capture Agatha. Agatha was not captured, but the Baron was badly injured in the fight, and is now in the hospital in the nearby town of Mechanicsburg. Worse yet, while in Sturmhalten, the Baron encountered Agatha while she was still being controlled by Lucrezia. He had been suspicious of Lucrezia's connection with the Other for years, and is is now convinced that Agatha is really Lucrezia in disguise.

In fact, Agatha is herself again. She is now on her way to her family's home in Mechanicsburg, to see what she can learn about herself and her history.

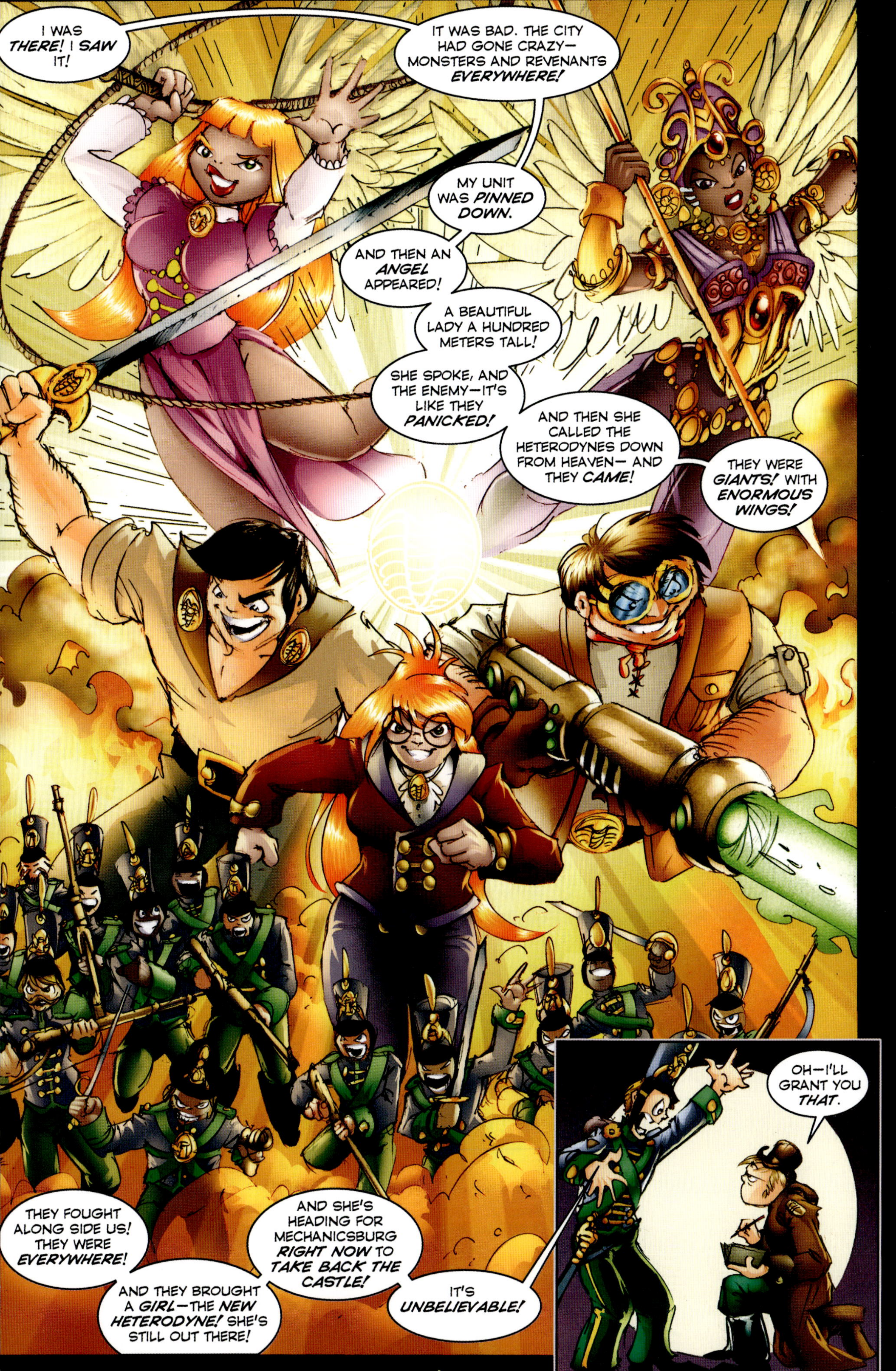

I WAS THERE! I SAW IT!
IT WAS BAD. THE CITY HAD GONE CRAZY— MONSTERS AND REVENANTS EVERYWHERE!
MY UNIT WAS PINNED DOWN.
AND THEN AN ANGEL APPEARED!
A BEAUTIFUL LADY A HUNDRED METERS TALL!
SHE SPOKE, AND THE ENEMY—IT'S LIKE THEY PANICKED!
AND THEN SHE CALLED THE HETERODYNES DOWN FROM HEAVEN— AND THEY CAME!
THEY WERE GIANTS! WITH ENORMOUS WINGS!
OH—I'LL GRANT YOU THAT.
THEY FOUGHT ALONG SIDE US! THEY WERE EVERYWHERE!
AND THEY BROUGHT A GIRL—THE NEW HETERODYNE! SHE'S STILL OUT THERE!
AND SHE'S HEADING FOR MECHANICSBURG RIGHT NOW TO TAKE BACK THE CASTLE!
IT'S UNBELIEVABLE!

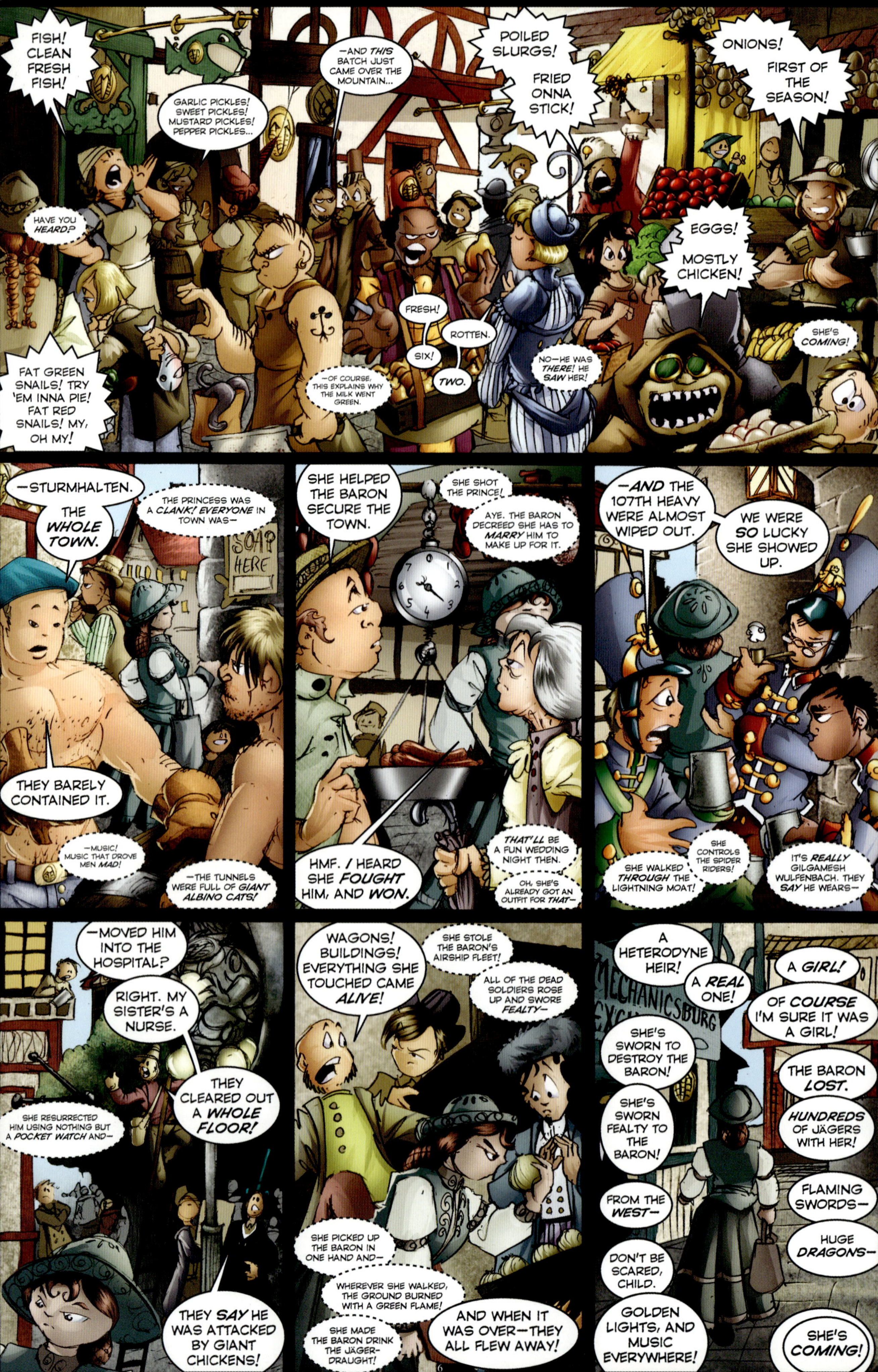

FISH! CLEAN FRESH FISH!
GARLIC PICKLES! SWEET PICKLES! MUSTARD PICKLES! PEPPER PICKLES...
—AND *THIS* BATCH JUST CAME OVER THE MOUNTAIN...
POILED SLURGS!
FRIED ONNA STICK!
ONIONS!
FIRST OF THE SEASON!
HAVE YOU *HEARD?*
EGGS!
MOSTLY CHICKEN!
FRESH!
SIX!
ROTTEN.
TWO.
—OF COURSE, THIS EXPLAINS WHY THE MILK WENT GREEN.
NO—HE WAS *THERE!* HE *SAW* HER!
SHE'S *COMING!*
FAT GREEN SNAILS! TRY 'EM INNA PIE! FAT RED SNAILS! MY, OH MY!
—STURMHALTEN.
THE *WHOLE TOWN.*
THE PRINCESS WAS A *CLANK! EVERYONE* IN TOWN WAS—
SOAP HERE
THEY BARELY CONTAINED IT.
—MUSIC! MUSIC THAT DROVE MEN *MAD!*
—THE TUNNELS WERE FULL OF *GIANT ALBINO CATS!*
SHE HELPED THE BARON SECURE THE TOWN.
SHE SHOT THE PRINCE!
AYE. THE BARON DECREED SHE HAS TO *MARRY* HIM TO MAKE UP FOR IT.
HMF. *I* HEARD SHE *FOUGHT* HIM, AND *WON.*
THAT'LL BE A FUN WEDDING NIGHT THEN.
OH, SHE'S ALREADY GOT AN OUTFIT FOR *THAT—*
—*AND* THE 107TH HEAVY WERE ALMOST WIPED OUT.
WE WERE *SO* LUCKY SHE SHOWED UP.
SHE WALKED *THROUGH* THE LIGHTNING MOAT!
SHE CONTROLS THE SPIDER RIDERS!
IT'S *REALLY* GILGAMESH WULFENBACH. THEY *SAY* HE WEARS—
—MOVED HIM INTO THE HOSPITAL?
RIGHT. MY SISTER'S A NURSE.
THEY CLEARED OUT A *WHOLE FLOOR!*
SHE RESURRECTED HIM USING NOTHING BUT A *POCKET WATCH* AND—
THEY *SAY* HE WAS ATTACKED BY GIANT CHICKENS!
WAGONS! BUILDINGS! EVERYTHING SHE TOUCHED CAME *ALIVE!*
SHE STOLE THE BARON'S AIRSHIP FLEET!
ALL OF THE DEAD SOLDIERS ROSE UP AND SWORE *FEALTY—*
SHE PICKED UP THE BARON IN ONE HAND AND—
WHEREVER SHE WALKED, THE GROUND BURNED WITH A GREEN FLAME!
SHE MADE THE BARON DRINK THE JÄGER-DRAUGHT!
AND WHEN IT WAS OVER—THEY ALL FLEW AWAY!
MECHANICSBURG
A HETERODYNE HEIR!
A *REAL* ONE!
A *GIRL!*
OF *COURSE* I'M SURE IT WAS A GIRL!
SHE'S SWORN TO DESTROY THE BARON!
THE BARON *LOST.*
SHE'S SWORN FEALTY TO THE BARON!
HUNDREDS OF JÄGERS WITH HER!
FROM THE *WEST—*
FLAMING SWORDS—
HUGE *DRAGONS—*
DON'T BE SCARED, CHILD.
GOLDEN LIGHTS, AND MUSIC EVERYWHERE!
SHE'S *COMING!*

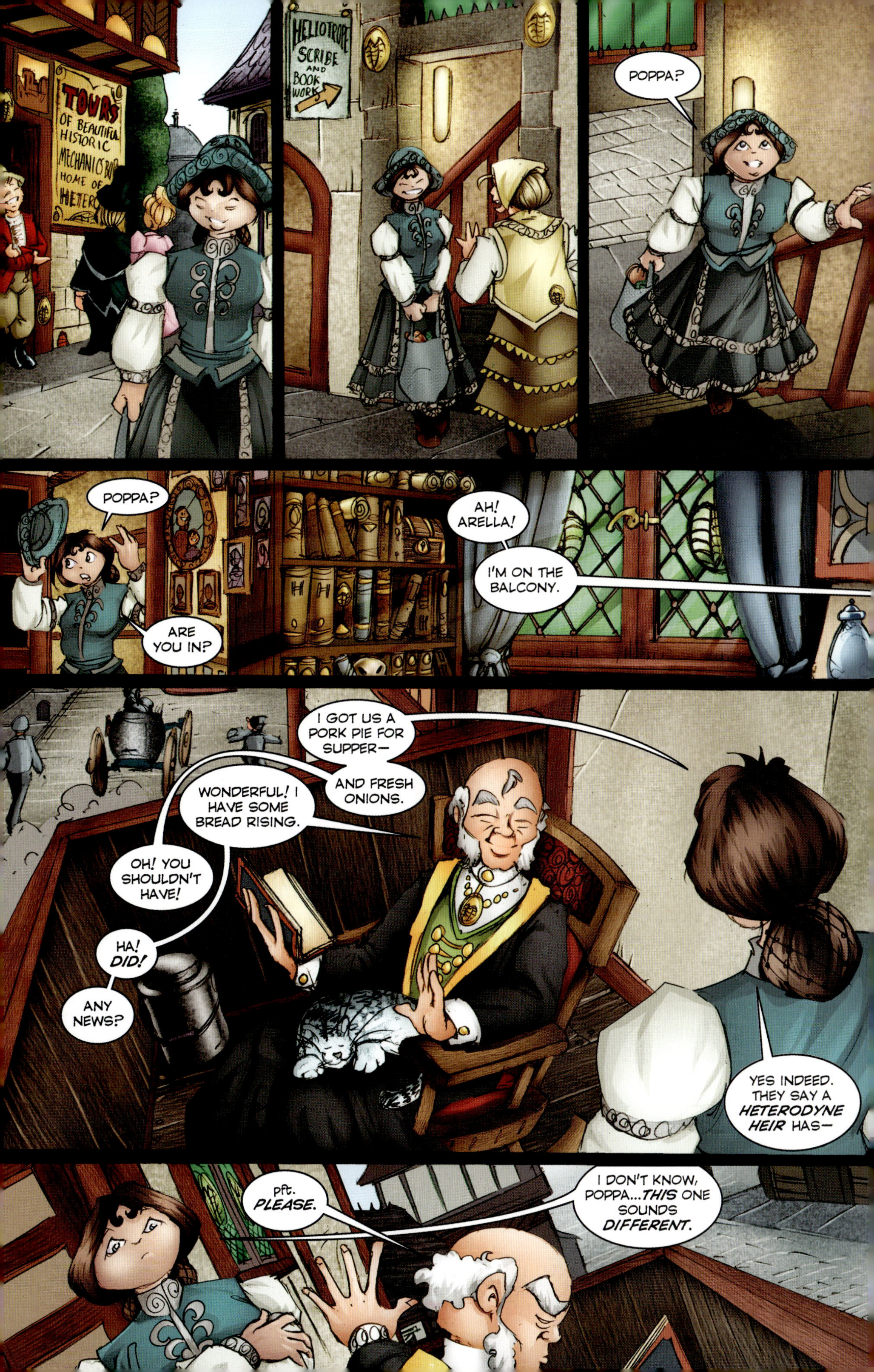
HELIOTROPE SCRIBE AND BOOK WORK
TOURS OF BEAUTIFUL HISTORIC MECHANICSBU HOME OF HETER
POPPA?
POPPA?
ARE YOU IN?
AH! ARELLA!
I'M ON THE BALCONY.
I GOT US A PORK PIE FOR SUPPER—
AND FRESH ONIONS.
WONDERFUL! I HAVE SOME BREAD RISING.
OH! YOU SHOULDN'T HAVE!
HA! *DID!*
ANY NEWS?
YES INDEED. THEY SAY A *HETERODYNE HEIR* HAS—
pft. *PLEASE.*
I DON'T KNOW, POPPA...*THIS* ONE SOUNDS *DIFFERENT*.

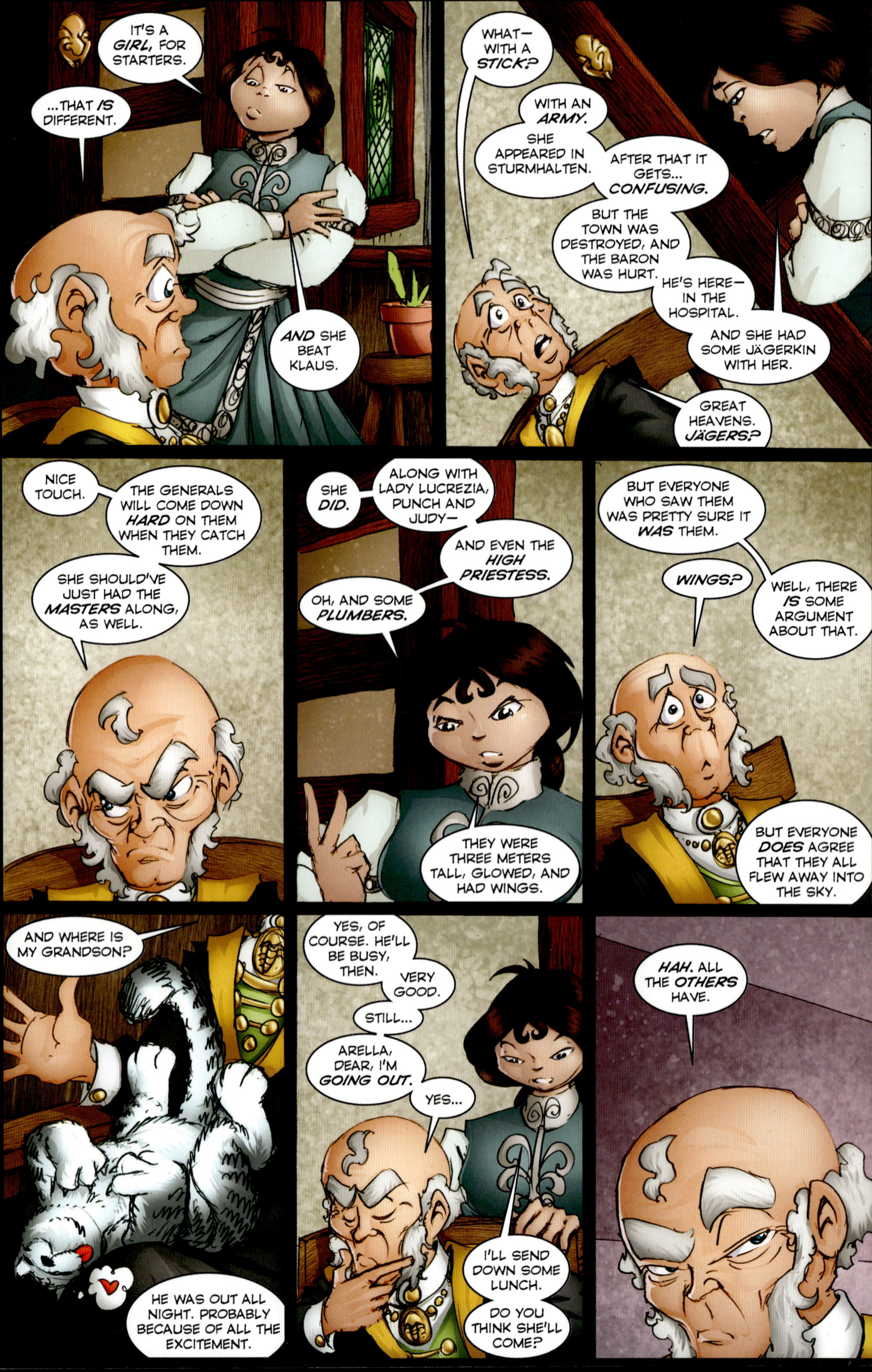
IT'S A GIRL, FOR STARTERS.
...THAT IS DIFFERENT.
AND SHE BEAT KLAUS.
WHAT—WITH A STICK?
WITH AN ARMY.
SHE APPEARED IN STURMHALTEN.
AFTER THAT IT GETS... CONFUSING.
BUT THE TOWN WAS DESTROYED, AND THE BARON WAS HURT.
HE'S HERE—IN THE HOSPITAL.
AND SHE HAD SOME JÄGERKIN WITH HER.
GREAT HEAVENS. JÄGERS?
NICE TOUCH.
THE GENERALS WILL COME DOWN HARD ON THEM WHEN THEY CATCH THEM.
SHE SHOULD'VE JUST HAD THE MASTERS ALONG, AS WELL.
SHE DID.
ALONG WITH LADY LUCREZIA, PUNCH AND JUDY—
AND EVEN THE HIGH PRIESTESS.
OH, AND SOME PLUMBERS.
THEY WERE THREE METERS TALL, GLOWED, AND HAD WINGS.
BUT EVERYONE WHO SAW THEM WAS PRETTY SURE IT WAS THEM.
WINGS?
WELL, THERE IS SOME ARGUMENT ABOUT THAT.
BUT EVERYONE DOES AGREE THAT THEY ALL FLEW AWAY INTO THE SKY.
AND WHERE IS MY GRANDSON?
HE WAS OUT ALL NIGHT. PROBABLY BECAUSE OF ALL THE EXCITEMENT.
YES, OF COURSE. HE'LL BE BUSY, THEN.
VERY GOOD.
STILL...
ARELLA, DEAR, I'M GOING OUT.
YES...
I'LL SEND DOWN SOME LUNCH.
DO YOU THINK SHE'LL COME?
HAH. ALL THE OTHERS HAVE.

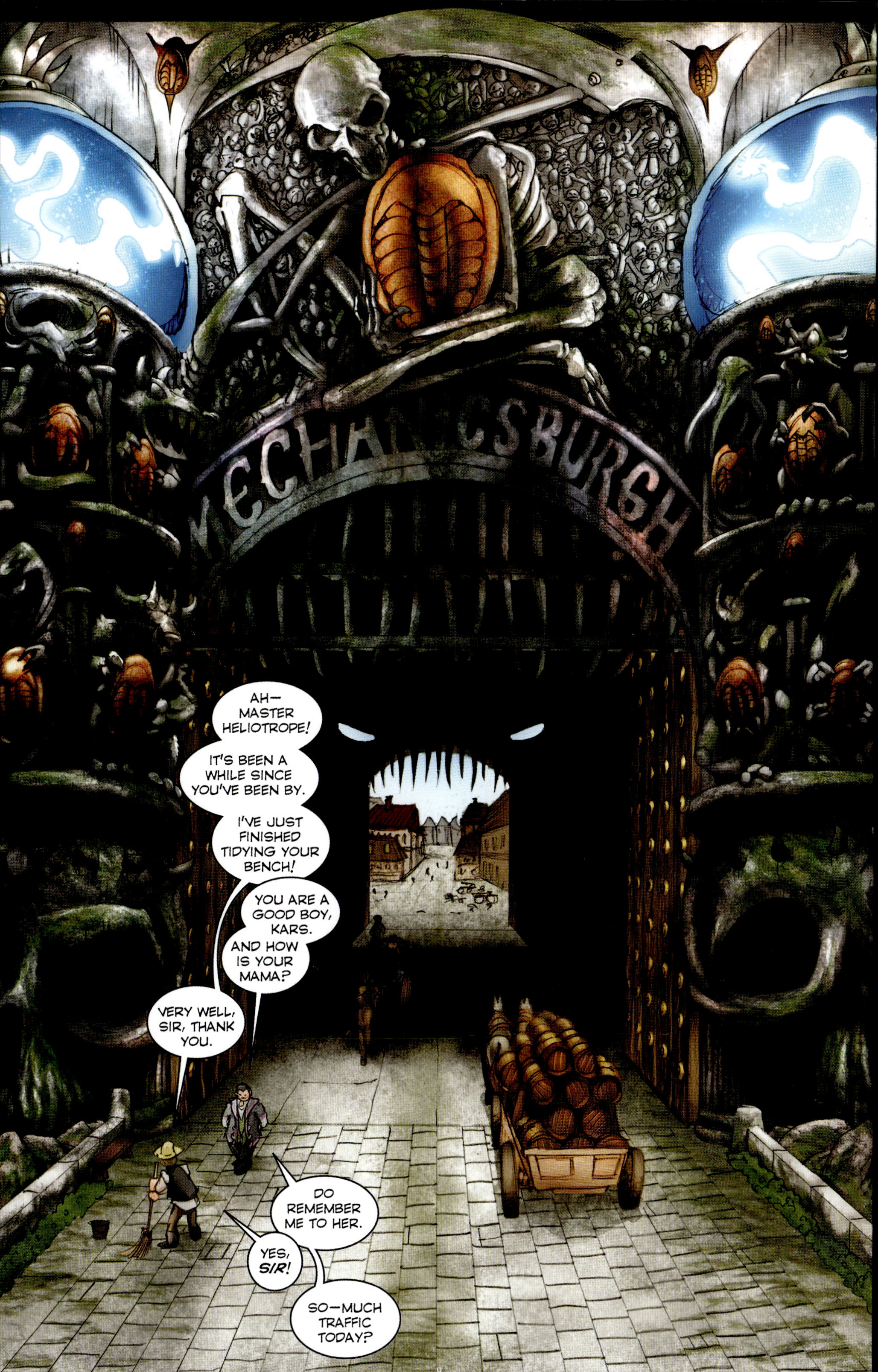
MECHANICSBURGH
AH— MASTER HELIOTROPE!
IT'S BEEN A WHILE SINCE YOU'VE BEEN BY.
I'VE JUST FINISHED TIDYING YOUR BENCH!
YOU ARE A GOOD BOY, KARS.
AND HOW IS YOUR MAMA?
VERY WELL, SIR, THANK YOU.
DO REMEMBER ME TO HER.
YES, *SIR!*
SO—MUCH TRAFFIC TODAY?

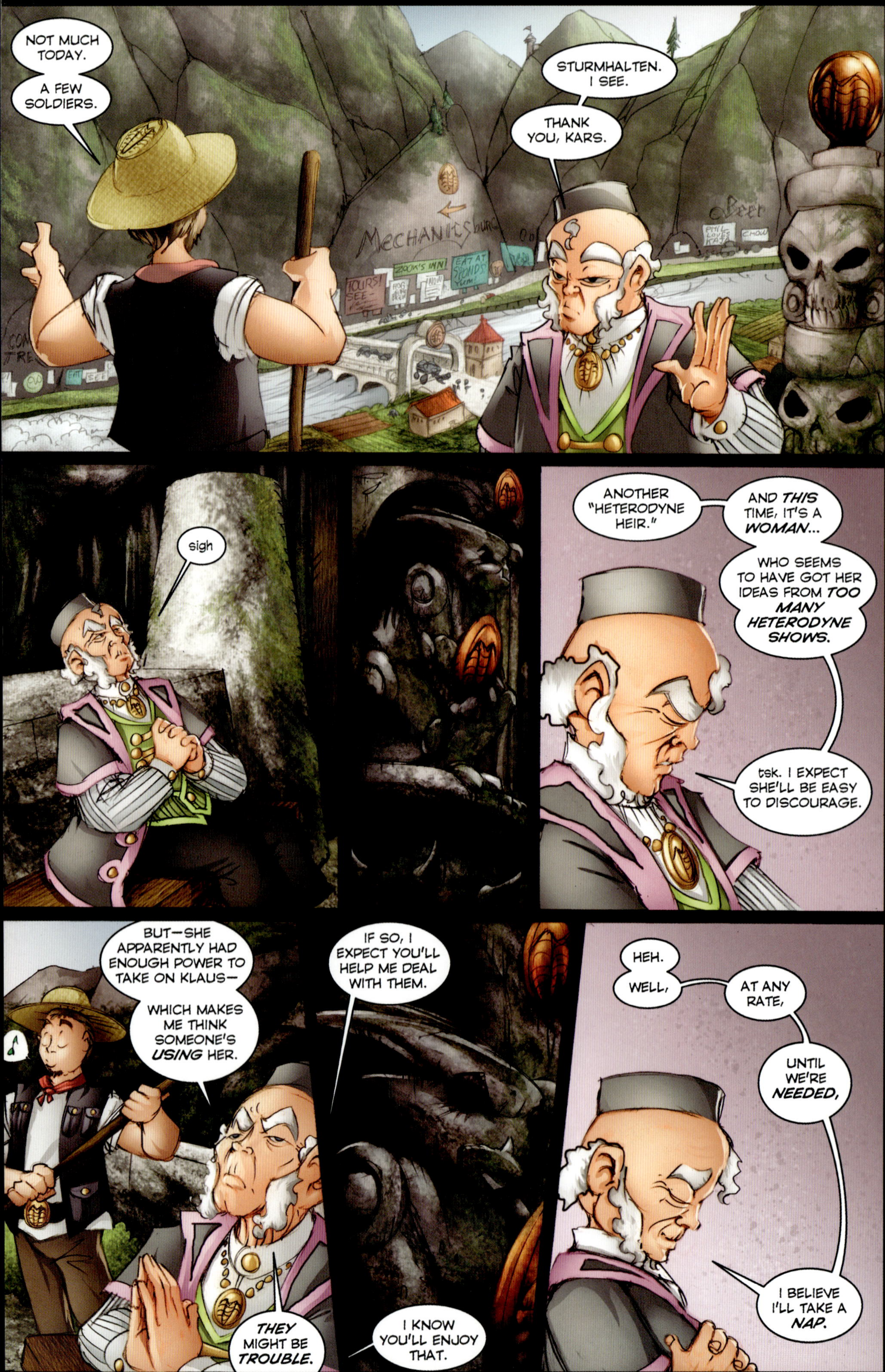
NOT MUCH TODAY.
A FEW SOLDIERS.
STURMHALTEN. I SEE.
THANK YOU, KARS.
Mechanicsburg
ZOOK'S INN
EAT AT
TOURS! SEE
Beer
CHOW
sigh
ANOTHER "HETERODYNE HEIR."
AND THIS TIME, IT'S A WOMAN...
WHO SEEMS TO HAVE GOT HER IDEAS FROM TOO MANY HETERODYNE SHOWS.
tsk. I EXPECT SHE'LL BE EASY TO DISCOURAGE.
BUT—SHE APPARENTLY HAD ENOUGH POWER TO TAKE ON KLAUS—
WHICH MAKES ME THINK SOMEONE'S USING HER.
THEY MIGHT BE TROUBLE.
IF SO, I EXPECT YOU'LL HELP ME DEAL WITH THEM.
I KNOW YOU'LL ENJOY THAT.
HEH.
WELL,
AT ANY RATE,
UNTIL WE'RE NEEDED,
I BELIEVE I'LL TAKE A NAP.

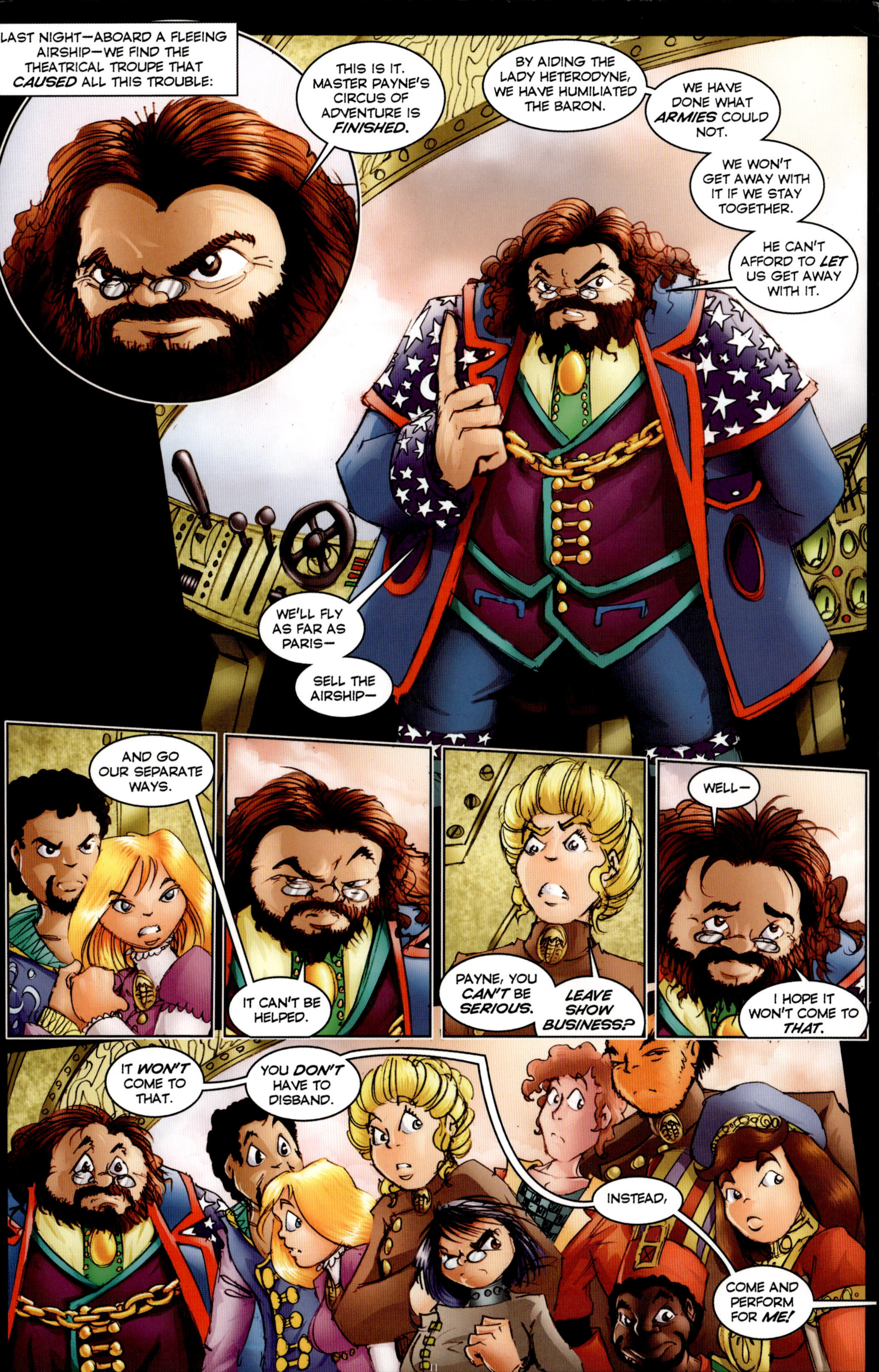
LAST NIGHT—ABOARD A FLEEING AIRSHIP—WE FIND THE THEATRICAL TROUPE THAT *CAUSED* ALL THIS TROUBLE:
THIS IS IT. MASTER PAYNE'S CIRCUS OF ADVENTURE IS *FINISHED.*
BY AIDING THE LADY HETERODYNE, WE HAVE HUMILIATED THE BARON.
WE HAVE DONE WHAT *ARMIES* COULD NOT.
WE WON'T GET AWAY WITH IT IF WE STAY TOGETHER.
HE CAN'T AFFORD TO *LET* US GET AWAY WITH IT.
WE'LL FLY AS FAR AS PARIS—
SELL THE AIRSHIP—
AND GO OUR SEPARATE WAYS.
IT CAN'T BE HELPED.
PAYNE, YOU *CAN'T* BE *SERIOUS.*
LEAVE SHOW BUSINESS?
WELL—
I HOPE IT WON'T COME TO *THAT.*
IT *WON'T* COME TO THAT.
YOU *DON'T* HAVE TO DISBAND.
INSTEAD,
COME AND PERFORM FOR *ME!*

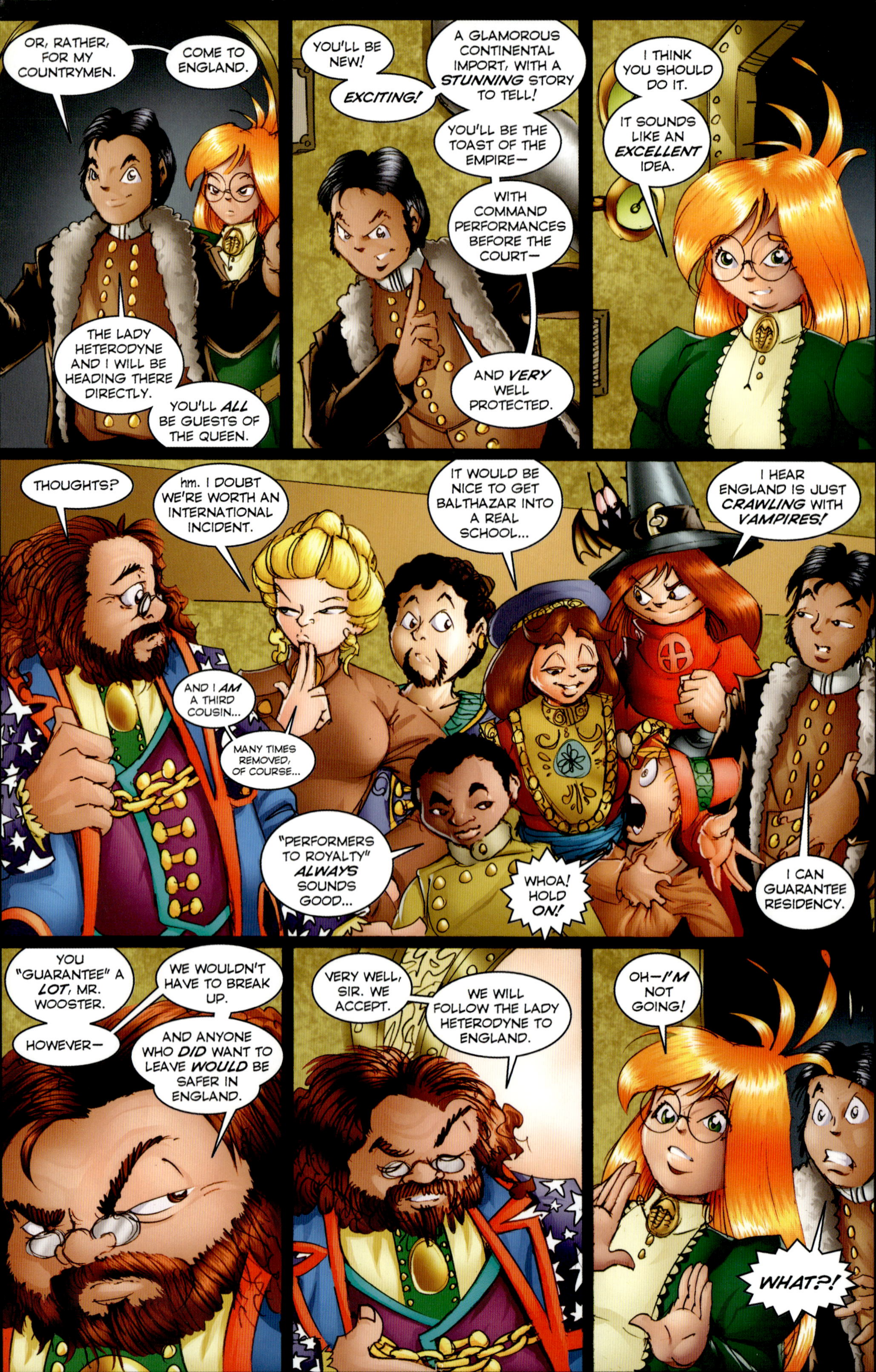
OR, RATHER, FOR MY COUNTRYMEN.
COME TO ENGLAND.
THE LADY HETERODYNE AND I WILL BE HEADING THERE DIRECTLY.
YOU'LL ALL BE GUESTS OF THE QUEEN.
YOU'LL BE NEW!
EXCITING!
A GLAMOROUS CONTINENTAL IMPORT, WITH A STUNNING STORY TO TELL!
YOU'LL BE THE TOAST OF THE EMPIRE—
WITH COMMAND PERFORMANCES BEFORE THE COURT—
AND VERY WELL PROTECTED.
I THINK YOU SHOULD DO IT.
IT SOUNDS LIKE AN EXCELLENT IDEA.
THOUGHTS?
hm. I DOUBT WE'RE WORTH AN INTERNATIONAL INCIDENT.
AND I AM A THIRD COUSIN...
MANY TIMES REMOVED, OF COURSE...
"PERFORMERS TO ROYALTY" ALWAYS SOUNDS GOOD...
IT WOULD BE NICE TO GET BALTHAZAR INTO A REAL SCHOOL...
WHOA! HOLD ON!
I HEAR ENGLAND IS JUST CRAWLING WITH VAMPIRES!
I CAN GUARANTEE RESIDENCY.
YOU "GUARANTEE" A LOT, MR. WOOSTER.
HOWEVER—
WE WOULDN'T HAVE TO BREAK UP.
AND ANYONE WHO DID WANT TO LEAVE WOULD BE SAFER IN ENGLAND.
VERY WELL, SIR. WE ACCEPT.
WE WILL FOLLOW THE LADY HETERODYNE TO ENGLAND.
OH—I'M NOT GOING!
WHAT?!

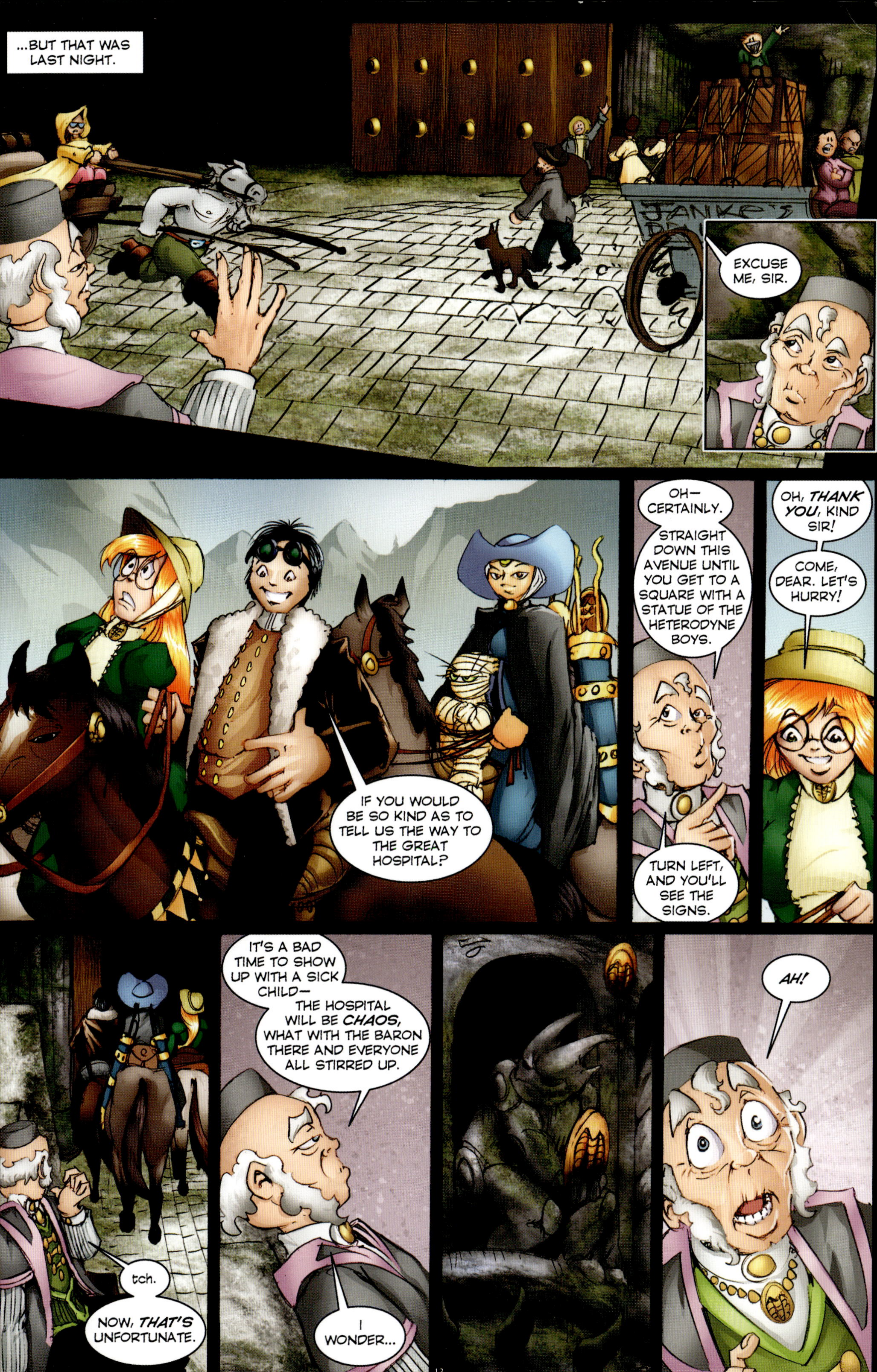

...BUT THAT WAS LAST NIGHT.
EXCUSE ME, SIR.
IF YOU WOULD BE SO KIND AS TO TELL US THE WAY TO THE GREAT HOSPITAL?
OH— CERTAINLY.
STRAIGHT DOWN THIS AVENUE UNTIL YOU GET TO A SQUARE WITH A STATUE OF THE HETERODYNE BOYS.
TURN LEFT, AND YOU'LL SEE THE SIGNS.
OH, *THANK YOU*, KIND SIR!
COME, DEAR. LET'S HURRY!
tch.
NOW, *THAT'S* UNFORTUNATE.
IT'S A BAD TIME TO SHOW UP WITH A SICK CHILD—
THE HOSPITAL WILL BE *CHAOS*, WHAT WITH THE BARON THERE AND EVERYONE ALL STIRRED UP.
I WONDER...
AH!

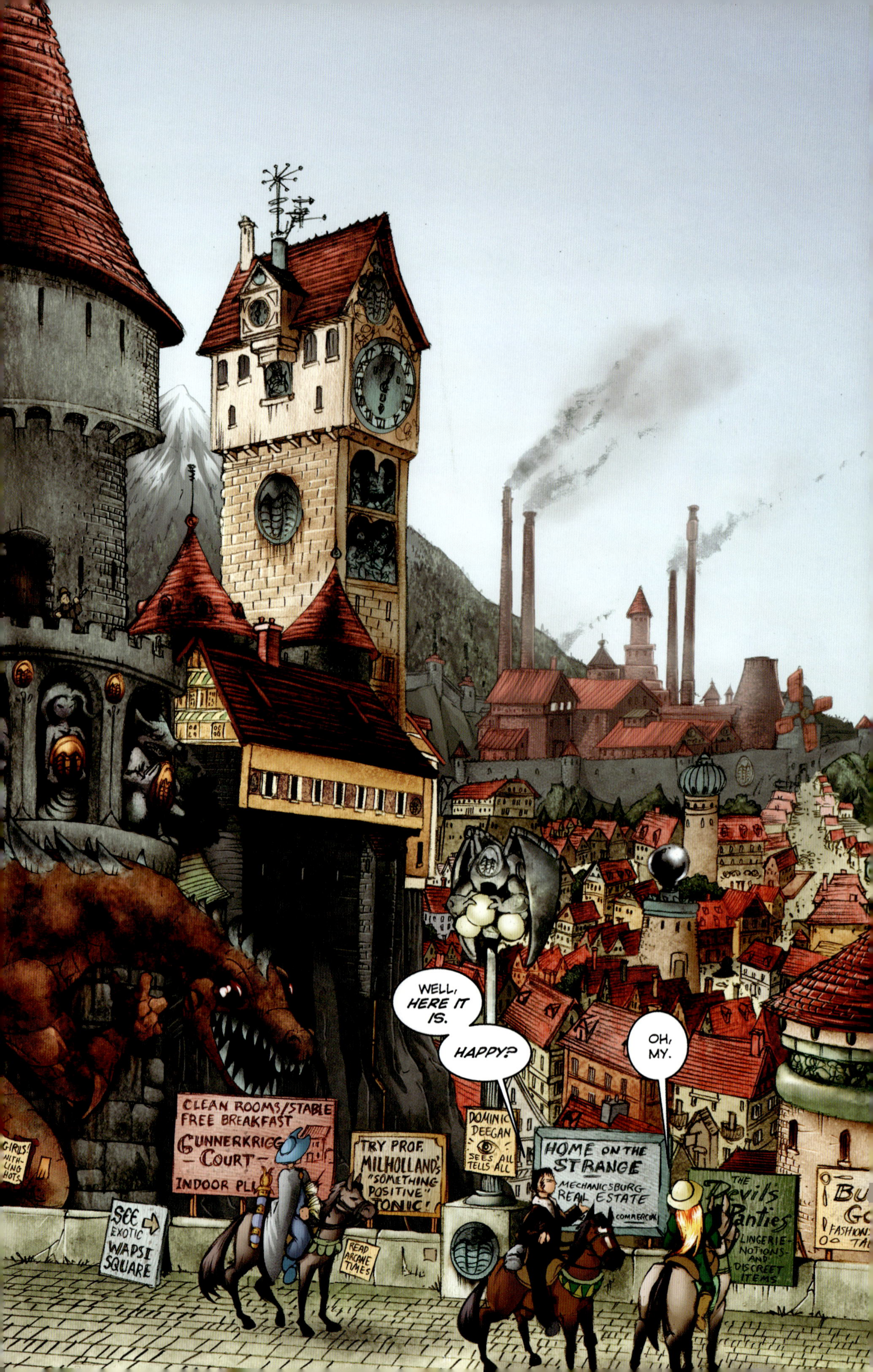
WELL, HERE IT IS.
HAPPY?
OH, MY.
GIRLS! WITH- LING HOTS
CLEAN ROOMS/STABLE FREE BREAKFAST
GUNNERKRIGG - COURT -
INDOOR PL
SEE EXOTIC WAPSI SQUARE
TRY PROF. MILHOLLAND'S "SOMETHING POSITIVE" TONIC!
READ ARCANE TIMES
DOMINIC DEEGAN SEES ALL TELLS ALL
HOME ON THE STRANGE
MECHANICSBURG REAL ESTATE
COMMERCIAL
THE Devil's Panties
LINGERIE - NOTIONS - AND DISCREET ITEMS
FASHION

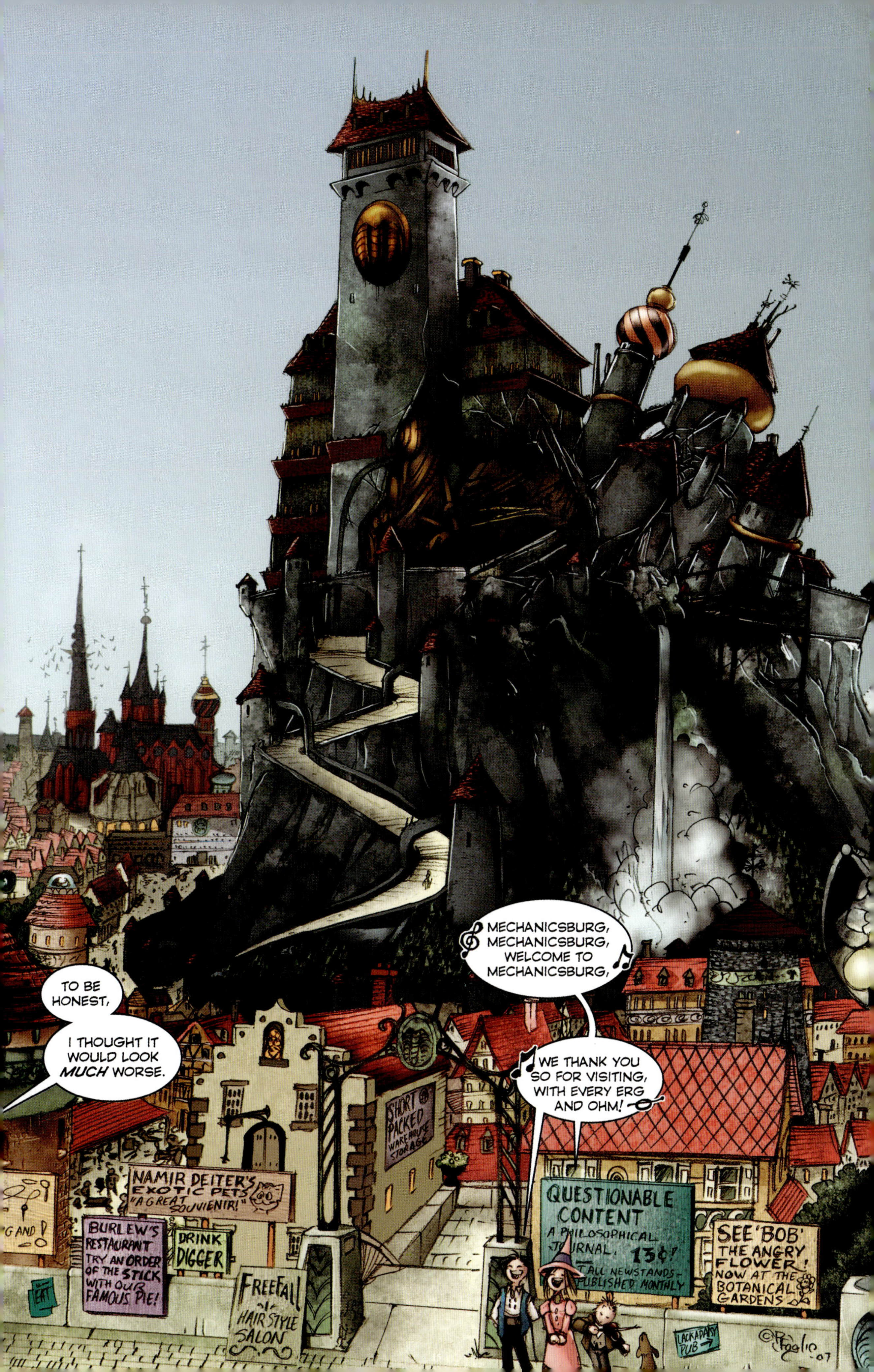
TO BE HONEST,
I THOUGHT IT WOULD LOOK *MUCH* WORSE.
MECHANICSBURG, MECHANICSBURG, WELCOME TO MECHANICSBURG,
WE THANK YOU SO FOR VISITING, WITH EVERY ERG AND OHM!
SHORT PACKED WAREHOUSE STORAGE
NAMIR DEITER'S EXOTIC PETS "A GREAT SOUVIENIR!"
G AND !
BURLEW'S RESTAURANT TRY AN ORDER OF THE STICK WITH OUR FAMOUS PIE!
DRINK DIGGER
EAT
FREEFALL HAIR STYLE SALON
QUESTIONABLE CONTENT A PHILOSOPHICAL JOURNAL. 13¢! ALL NEWSTANDS - PUBLISHED MONTHLY
SEE 'BOB' THE ANGRY FLOWER! NOW AT THE BOTANICAL GARDENS
LACKADAISY PUB →
©Pfoglio -07

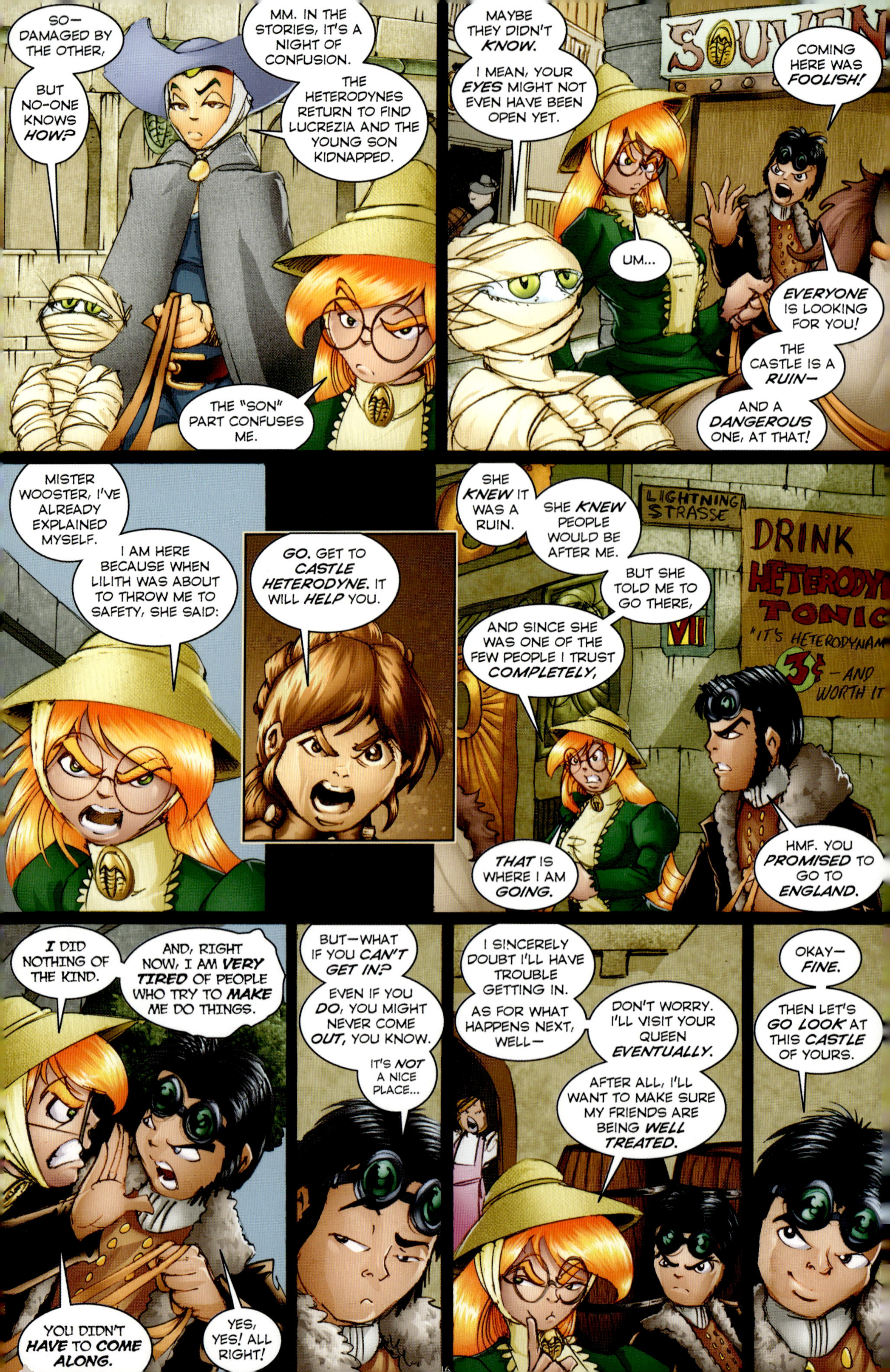
SO— DAMAGED BY THE OTHER,
BUT NO-ONE KNOWS HOW?
MM. IN THE STORIES, IT'S A NIGHT OF CONFUSION.
THE HETERODYNES RETURN TO FIND LUCREZIA AND THE YOUNG SON KIDNAPPED.
THE "SON" PART CONFUSES ME.
MAYBE THEY DIDN'T KNOW.
I MEAN, YOUR EYES MIGHT NOT EVEN HAVE BEEN OPEN YET.
SOUVEN
COMING HERE WAS FOOLISH!
UM...
EVERYONE IS LOOKING FOR YOU!
THE CASTLE IS A RUIN—
AND A DANGEROUS ONE, AT THAT!
MISTER WOOSTER, I'VE ALREADY EXPLAINED MYSELF.
I AM HERE BECAUSE WHEN LILITH WAS ABOUT TO THROW ME TO SAFETY, SHE SAID:
GO. GET TO CASTLE HETERODYNE. IT WILL HELP YOU.
SHE KNEW IT WAS A RUIN.
SHE KNEW PEOPLE WOULD BE AFTER ME.
LIGHTNING STRASSE
DRINK HETERODYNE TONIC
"IT'S HETERODYNAM
3¢ — AND WORTH IT
BUT SHE TOLD ME TO GO THERE,
AND SINCE SHE WAS ONE OF THE FEW PEOPLE I TRUST COMPLETELY,
THAT IS WHERE I AM GOING.
HMF. YOU PROMISED TO GO TO ENGLAND.
I DID NOTHING OF THE KIND.
AND, RIGHT NOW, I AM VERY TIRED OF PEOPLE WHO TRY TO MAKE ME DO THINGS.
YOU DIDN'T HAVE TO COME ALONG.
YES, YES! ALL RIGHT!
BUT—WHAT IF YOU CAN'T GET IN?
EVEN IF YOU DO, YOU MIGHT NEVER COME OUT, YOU KNOW.
IT'S NOT A NICE PLACE...
I SINCERELY DOUBT I'LL HAVE TROUBLE GETTING IN.
AS FOR WHAT HAPPENS NEXT, WELL—
DON'T WORRY. I'LL VISIT YOUR QUEEN EVENTUALLY.
AFTER ALL, I'LL WANT TO MAKE SURE MY FRIENDS ARE BEING WELL TREATED.
OKAY— FINE.
THEN LET'S GO LOOK AT THIS CASTLE OF YOURS.

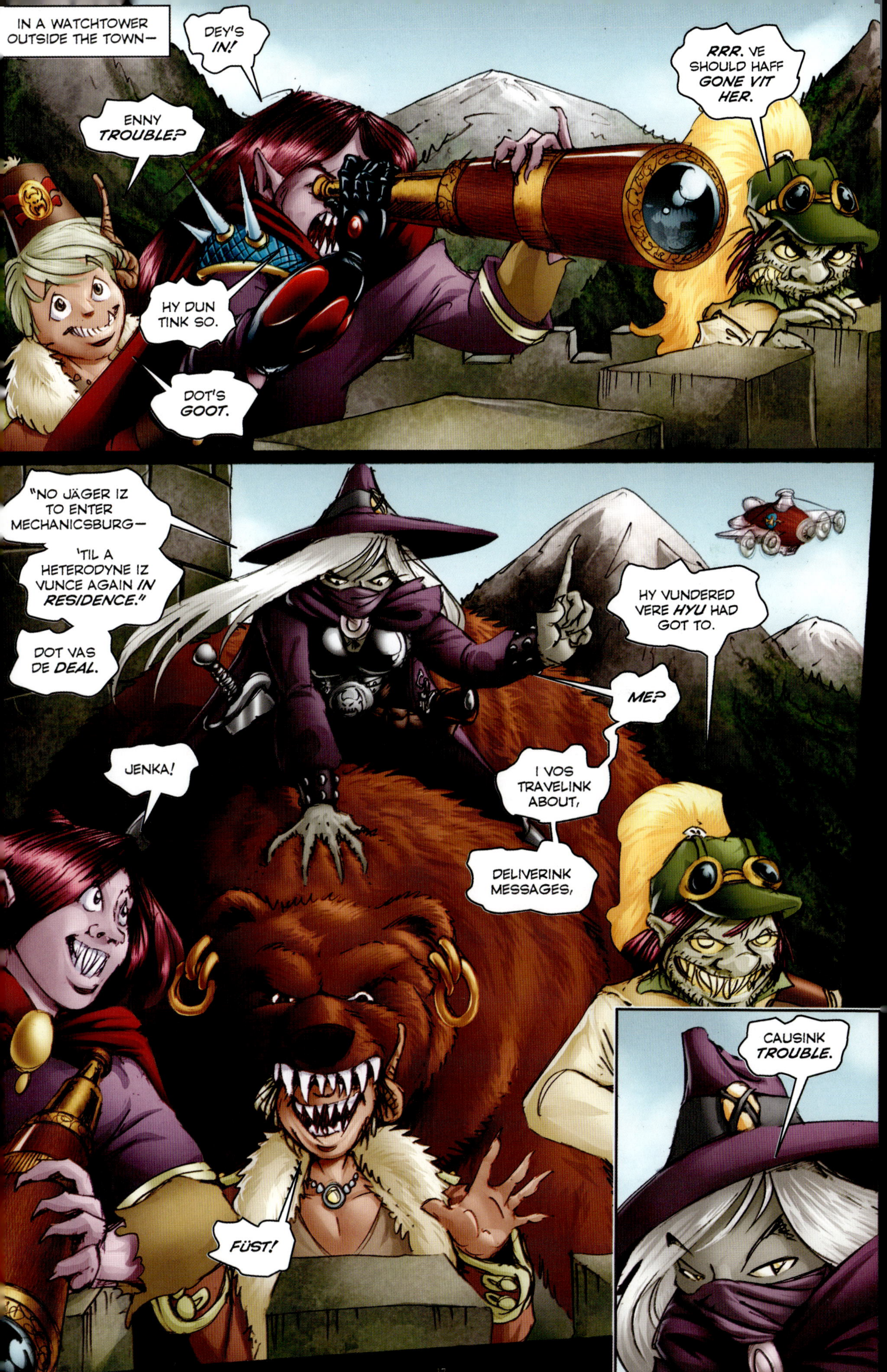
IN A WATCHTOWER OUTSIDE THE TOWN—
DEY'S *IN!*
ENNY *TROUBLE?*
RRR. VE SHOULD HAFF *GONE VIT HER.*
HY DUN TINK SO.
DOT'S *GOOT.*
"NO JÄGER IZ TO ENTER MECHANICSBURG—
'TIL A HETERODYNE IZ VUNCE AGAIN *IN RESIDENCE."*
DOT VAS DE *DEAL.*
HY VUNDERED VERE *HYU* HAD GOT TO.
ME?
JENKA!
I VOS TRAVELINK ABOUT,
DELIVERINK MESSAGES,
FÜST!
CAUSINK *TROUBLE.*

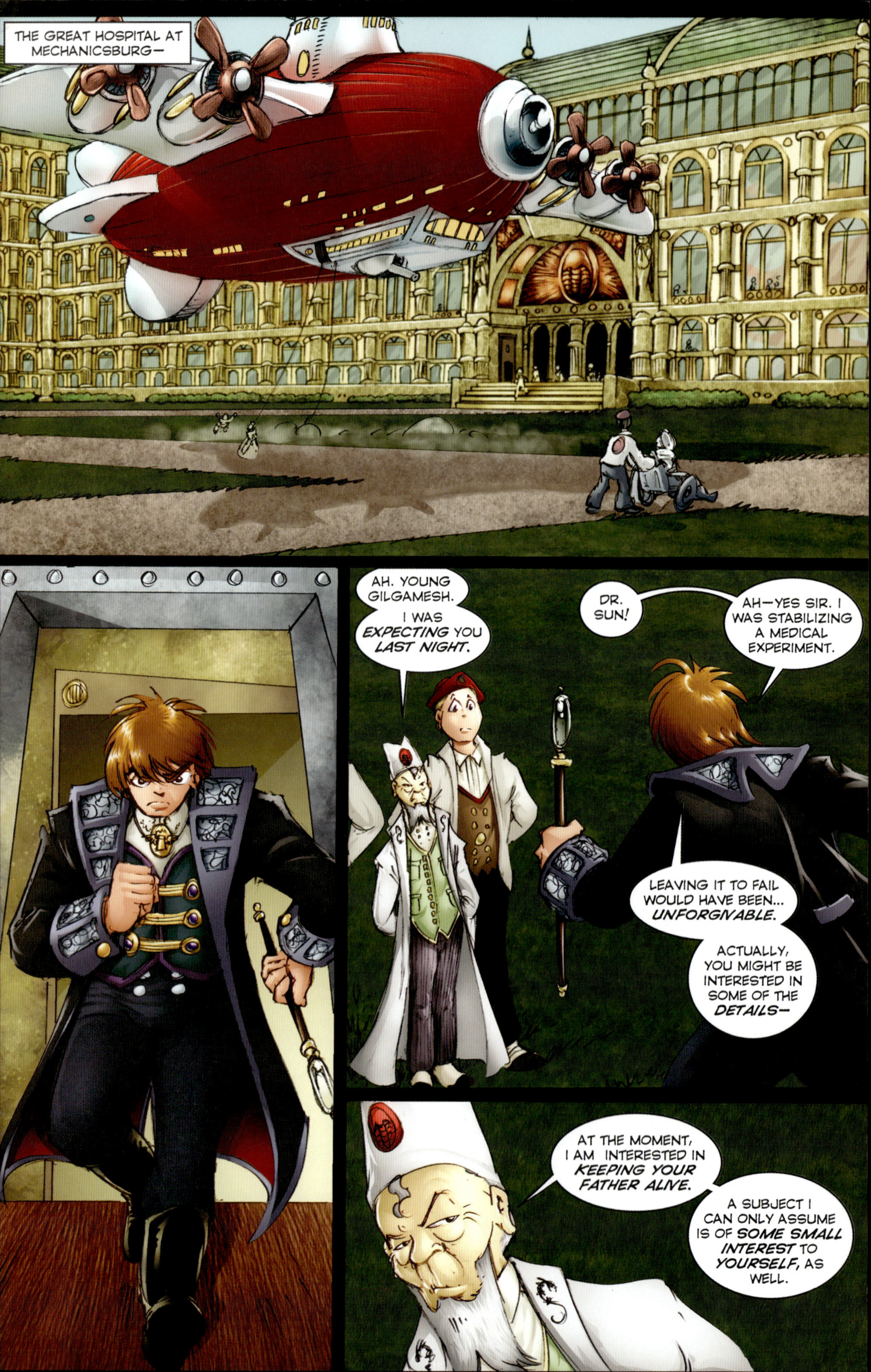
THE GREAT HOSPITAL AT MECHANICSBURG—
AH. YOUNG GILGAMESH.
I WAS *EXPECTING* YOU *LAST NIGHT.*
DR. SUN!
AH—YES SIR. I WAS STABILIZING A MEDICAL EXPERIMENT.
LEAVING IT TO FAIL WOULD HAVE BEEN... ***UNFORGIVABLE.***
ACTUALLY, YOU MIGHT BE INTERESTED IN SOME OF THE *DETAILS—*
AT THE MOMENT, I AM INTERESTED IN *KEEPING YOUR FATHER ALIVE.*
A SUBJECT I CAN ONLY ASSUME IS OF *SOME SMALL INTEREST* TO *YOURSELF,* AS WELL.

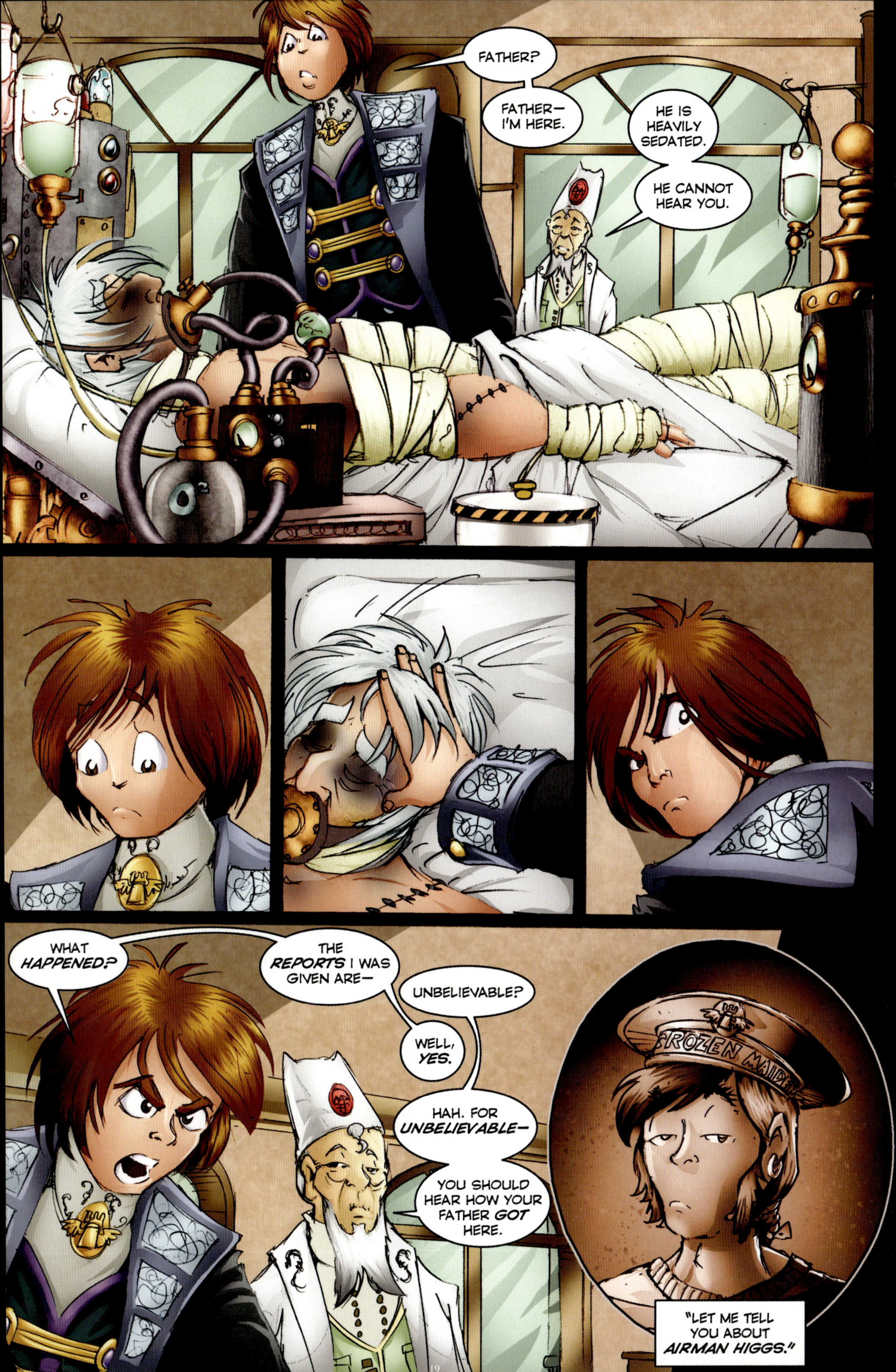

FATHER?
FATHER— I'M HERE.
HE IS HEAVILY SEDATED.
HE CANNOT HEAR YOU.
WHAT *HAPPENED?*
THE *REPORTS* I WAS GIVEN ARE—
UNBELIEVABLE?
WELL, *YES.*
HAH. FOR *UNBELIEVABLE—*
YOU SHOULD HEAR HOW YOUR FATHER *GOT* HERE.
FROZEN MAIDEN
"LET ME TELL YOU ABOUT *AIRMAN HIGGS.*"

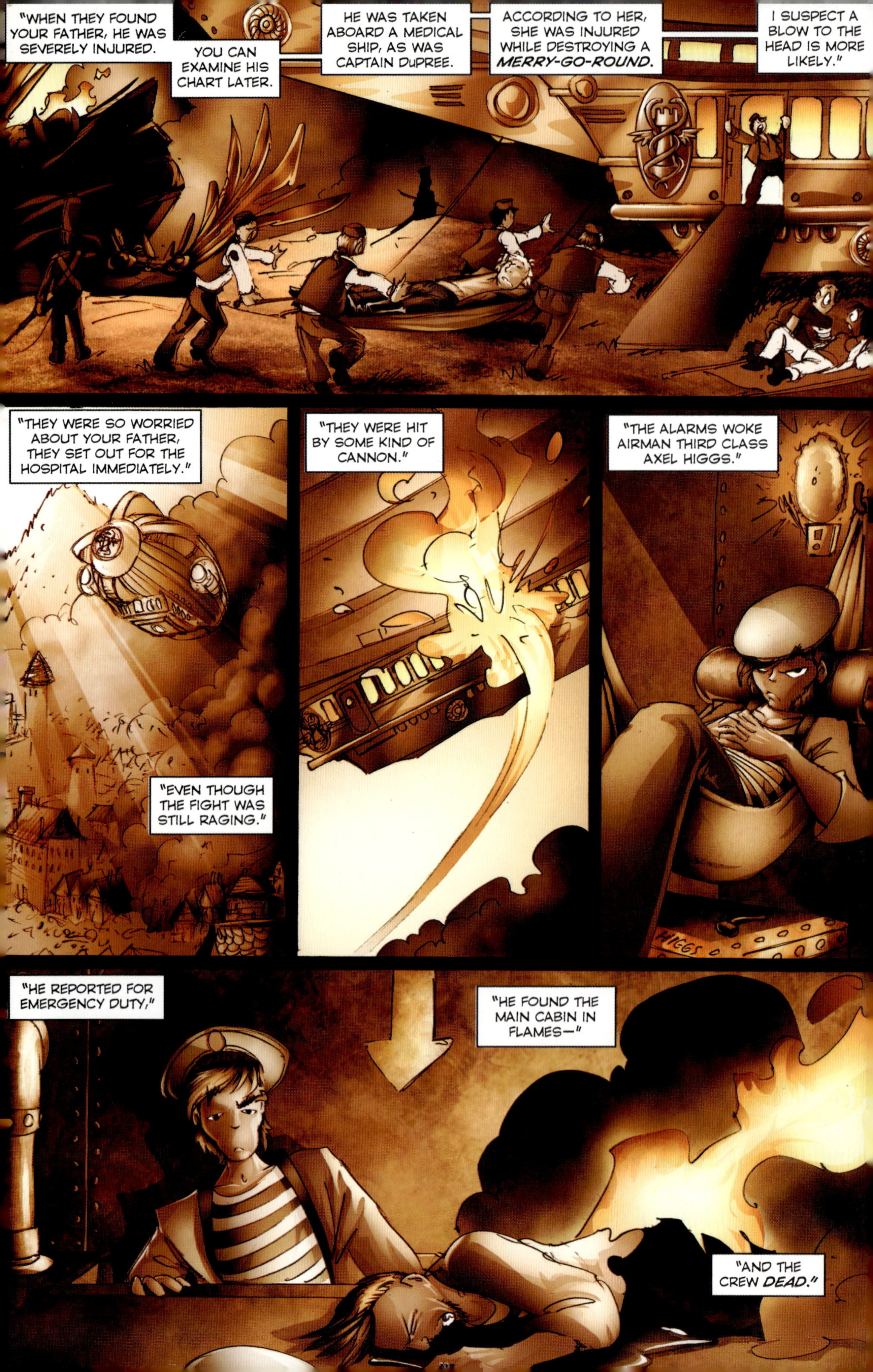
"WHEN THEY FOUND YOUR FATHER, HE WAS SEVERELY INJURED.
YOU CAN EXAMINE HIS CHART LATER.
HE WAS TAKEN ABOARD A MEDICAL SHIP, AS WAS CAPTAIN DuPREE.
ACCORDING TO HER, SHE WAS INJURED WHILE DESTROYING A *MERRY-GO-ROUND*.
I SUSPECT A BLOW TO THE HEAD IS MORE LIKELY."
"THEY WERE SO WORRIED ABOUT YOUR FATHER, THEY SET OUT FOR THE HOSPITAL IMMEDIATELY."
"EVEN THOUGH THE FIGHT WAS STILL RAGING."
"THEY WERE HIT BY SOME KIND OF CANNON."
"THE ALARMS WOKE AIRMAN THIRD CLASS AXEL HIGGS."
HIGGS
"HE REPORTED FOR EMERGENCY DUTY,"
"HE FOUND THE MAIN CABIN IN FLAMES—"
"AND THE CREW *DEAD*."

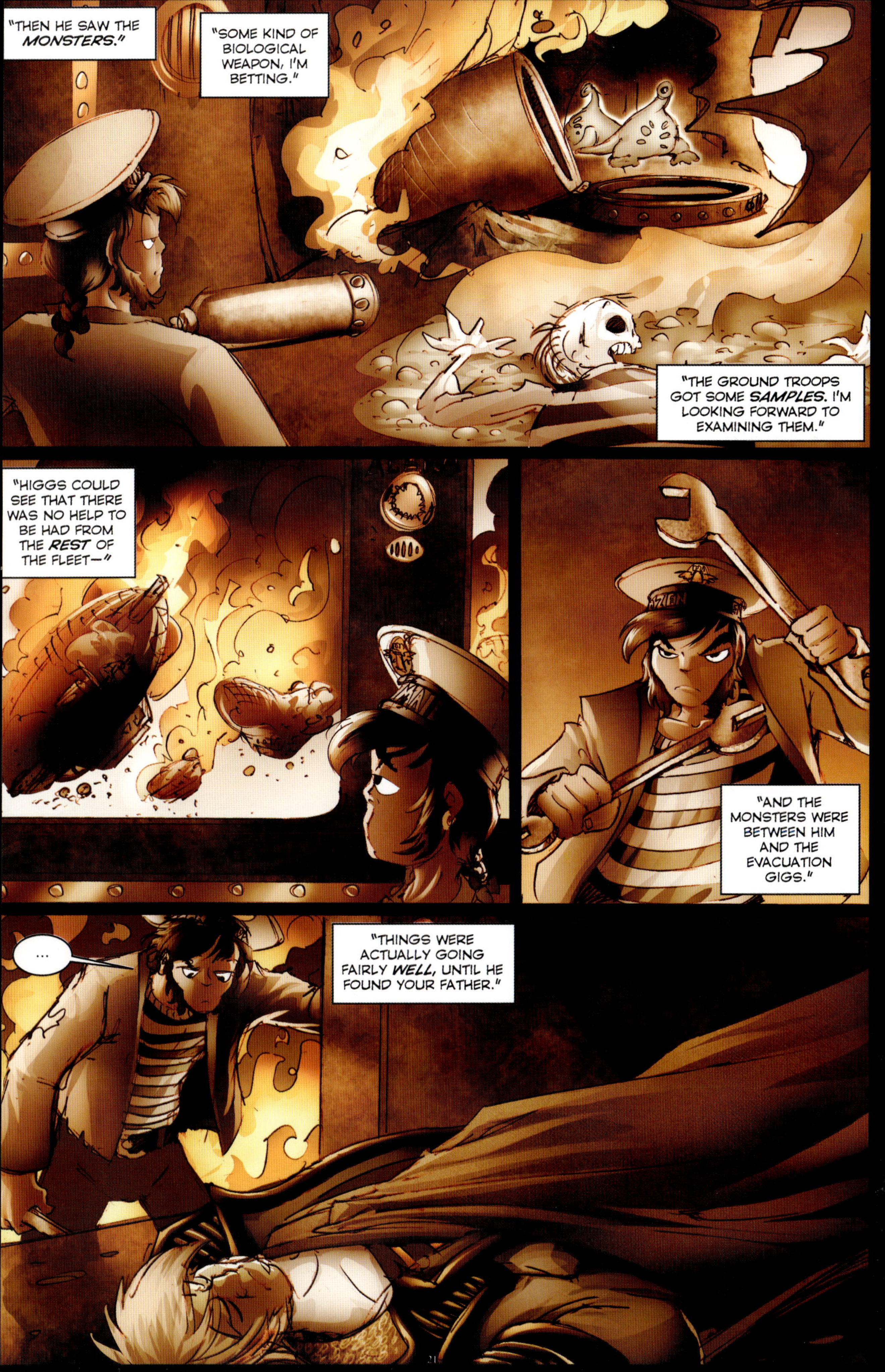
"THEN HE SAW THE *MONSTERS*."
"SOME KIND OF BIOLOGICAL WEAPON, I'M BETTING."
"THE GROUND TROOPS GOT SOME *SAMPLES*. I'M LOOKING FORWARD TO EXAMINING THEM."
"HIGGS COULD SEE THAT THERE WAS NO HELP TO BE HAD FROM THE *REST* OF THE FLEET—"
"AND THE MONSTERS WERE BETWEEN HIM AND THE EVACUATION GIGS."
...
"THINGS WERE ACTUALLY GOING FAIRLY *WELL*, UNTIL HE FOUND YOUR FATHER."

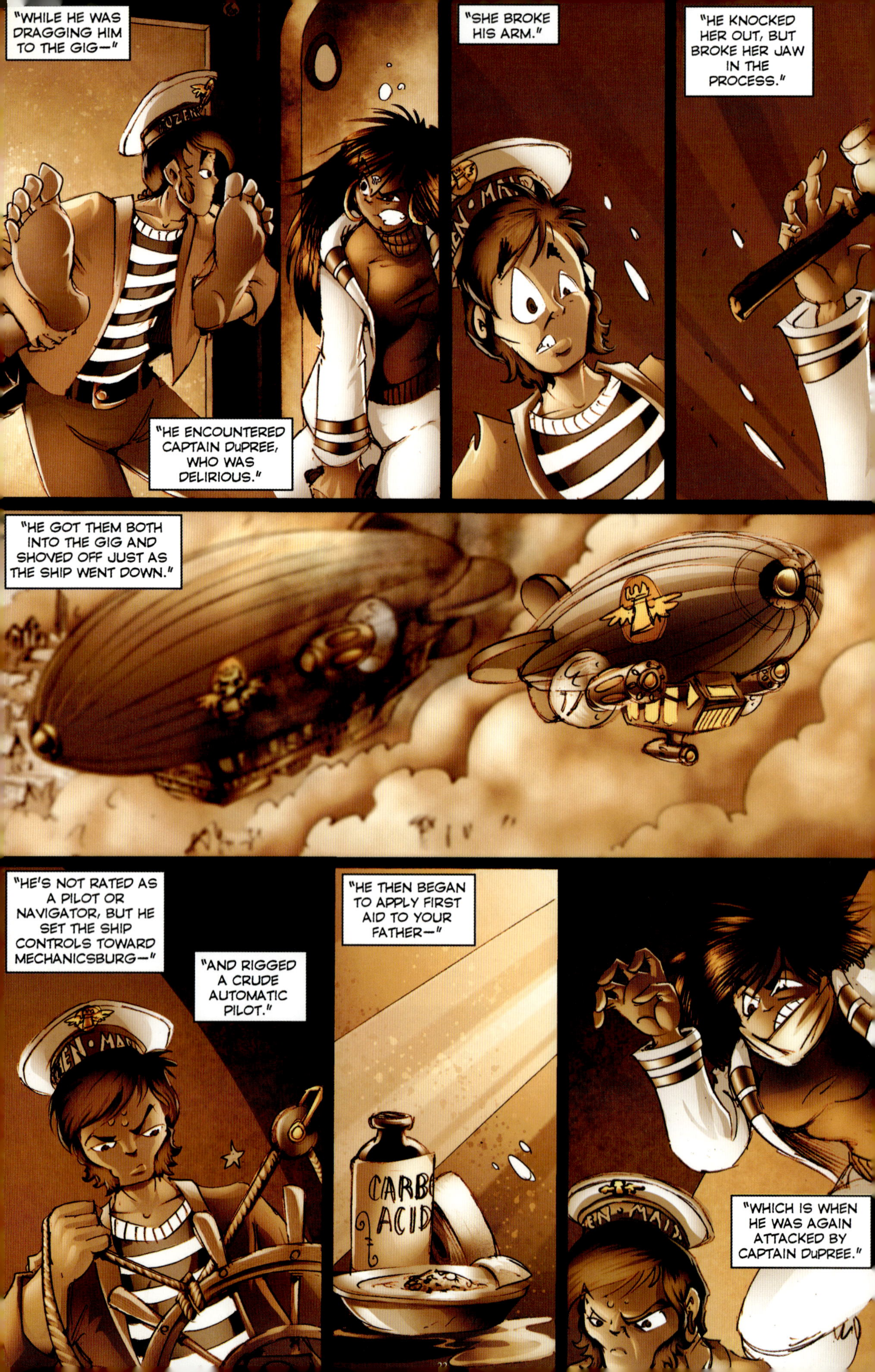
"WHILE HE WAS DRAGGING HIM TO THE GIG—"
"HE ENCOUNTERED CAPTAIN DuPREE, WHO WAS DELIRIOUS."
"SHE BROKE HIS ARM."
"HE KNOCKED HER OUT, BUT BROKE HER JAW IN THE PROCESS."
"HE GOT THEM BOTH INTO THE GIG AND SHOVED OFF JUST AS THE SHIP WENT DOWN."
"HE'S NOT RATED AS A PILOT OR NAVIGATOR, BUT HE SET THE SHIP CONTROLS TOWARD MECHANICSBURG—"
"AND RIGGED A CRUDE AUTOMATIC PILOT."
"HE THEN BEGAN TO APPLY FIRST AID TO YOUR FATHER—"
"WHICH IS WHEN HE WAS AGAIN ATTACKED BY CAPTAIN DuPREE."

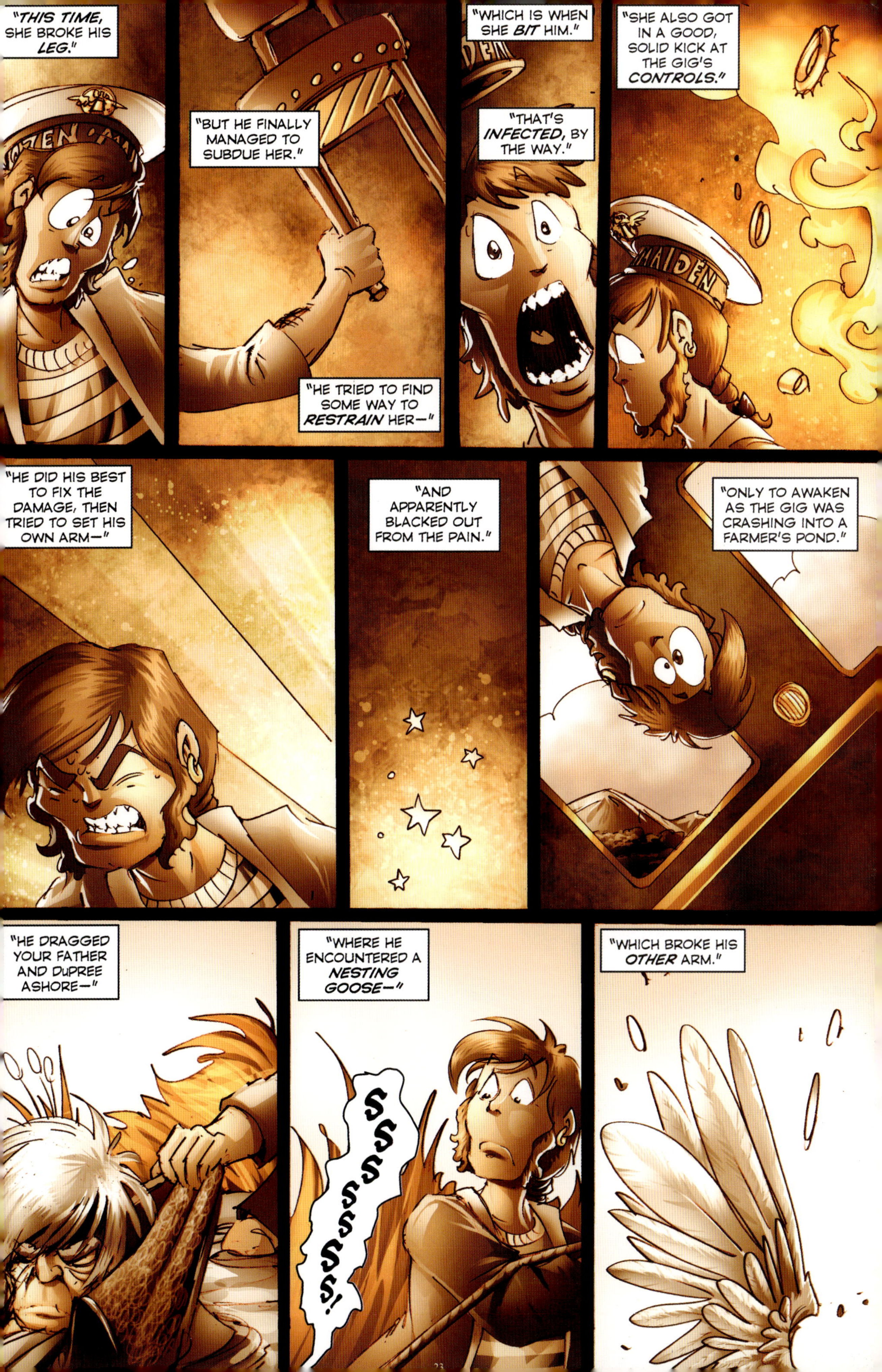
"THIS TIME, SHE BROKE HIS LEG."
"BUT HE FINALLY MANAGED TO SUBDUE HER."
"HE TRIED TO FIND SOME WAY TO RESTRAIN HER—"
"WHICH IS WHEN SHE BIT HIM."
"THAT'S INFECTED, BY THE WAY."
"SHE ALSO GOT IN A GOOD, SOLID KICK AT THE GIG'S CONTROLS."
"HE DID HIS BEST TO FIX THE DAMAGE, THEN TRIED TO SET HIS OWN ARM—"
"AND APPARENTLY BLACKED OUT FROM THE PAIN."
"ONLY TO AWAKEN AS THE GIG WAS CRASHING INTO A FARMER'S POND."
"HE DRAGGED YOUR FATHER AND DuPREE ASHORE—"
"WHERE HE ENCOUNTERED A NESTING GOOSE—"
SSSSSSSSS!
"WHICH BROKE HIS OTHER ARM."

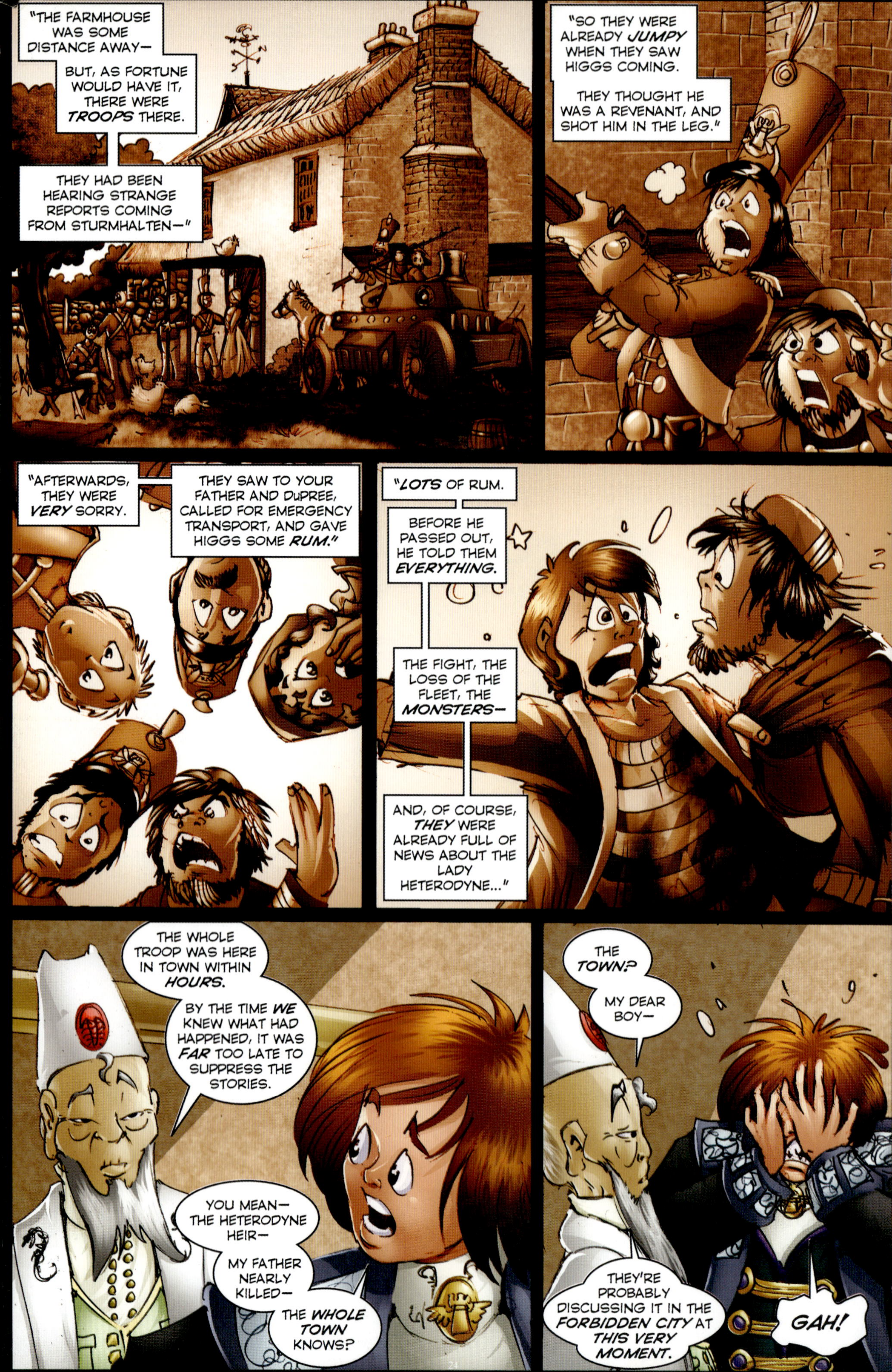
"THE FARMHOUSE WAS SOME DISTANCE AWAY—
BUT, AS FORTUNE WOULD HAVE IT, THERE WERE *TROOPS* THERE.
THEY HAD BEEN HEARING STRANGE REPORTS COMING FROM STURMHALTEN—"
"SO THEY WERE ALREADY *JUMPY* WHEN THEY SAW HIGGS COMING.
THEY THOUGHT HE WAS A REVENANT, AND SHOT HIM IN THE LEG."
"AFTERWARDS, THEY WERE *VERY* SORRY.
THEY SAW TO YOUR FATHER AND DUPREE, CALLED FOR EMERGENCY TRANSPORT, AND GAVE HIGGS SOME *RUM*."
"*LOTS* OF RUM.
BEFORE HE PASSED OUT, HE TOLD THEM *EVERYTHING*.
THE FIGHT, THE LOSS OF THE FLEET, THE *MONSTERS*—
AND, OF COURSE, *THEY* WERE ALREADY FULL OF NEWS ABOUT THE LADY HETERODYNE..."
THE WHOLE TROOP WAS HERE IN TOWN WITHIN *HOURS*.
BY THE TIME *WE* KNEW WHAT HAD HAPPENED, IT WAS *FAR* TOO LATE TO SUPPRESS THE STORIES.
YOU MEAN— THE HETERODYNE HEIR—
MY FATHER NEARLY KILLED—
THE *WHOLE TOWN* KNOWS?
THE *TOWN?*
MY DEAR BOY—
THEY'RE PROBABLY DISCUSSING IT IN THE *FORBIDDEN CITY* AT *THIS VERY MOMENT*.
GAH!

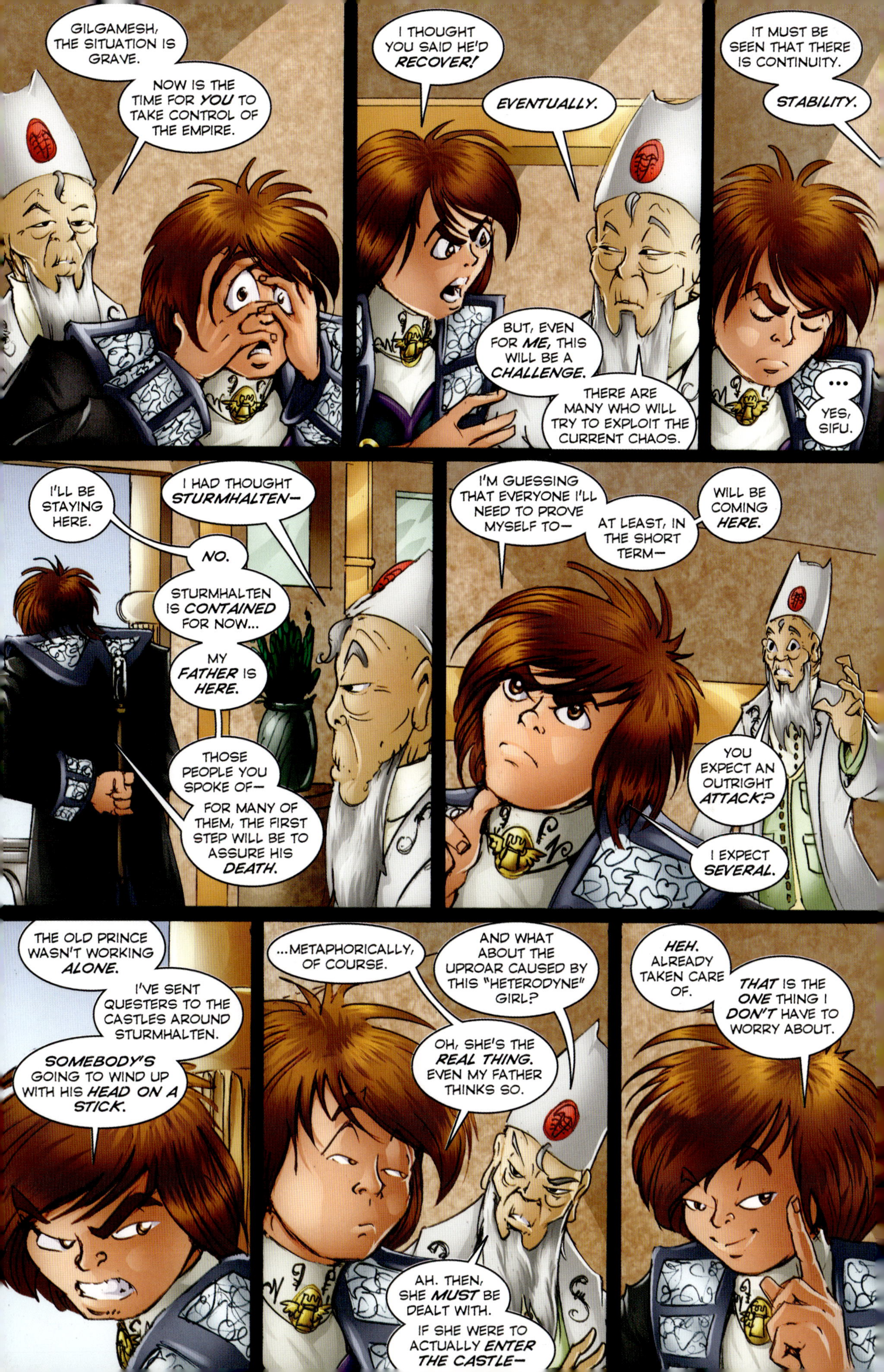
GILGAMESH, THE SITUATION IS GRAVE.
NOW IS THE TIME FOR YOU TO TAKE CONTROL OF THE EMPIRE.
I THOUGHT YOU SAID HE'D RECOVER!
EVENTUALLY.
BUT, EVEN FOR ME, THIS WILL BE A CHALLENGE.
THERE ARE MANY WHO WILL TRY TO EXPLOIT THE CURRENT CHAOS.
IT MUST BE SEEN THAT THERE IS CONTINUITY.
STABILITY.
...
YES, SIFU.
I'LL BE STAYING HERE.
I HAD THOUGHT STURMHALTEN—
NO.
STURMHALTEN IS CONTAINED FOR NOW...
MY FATHER IS HERE.
THOSE PEOPLE YOU SPOKE OF—
FOR MANY OF THEM, THE FIRST STEP WILL BE TO ASSURE HIS DEATH.
I'M GUESSING THAT EVERYONE I'LL NEED TO PROVE MYSELF TO—
AT LEAST, IN THE SHORT TERM—
WILL BE COMING HERE.
YOU EXPECT AN OUTRIGHT ATTACK?
I EXPECT SEVERAL.
THE OLD PRINCE WASN'T WORKING ALONE.
I'VE SENT QUESTERS TO THE CASTLES AROUND STURMHALTEN.
SOMEBODY'S GOING TO WIND UP WITH HIS HEAD ON A STICK.
...METAPHORICALLY, OF COURSE.
AND WHAT ABOUT THE UPROAR CAUSED BY THIS "HETERODYNE" GIRL?
OH, SHE'S THE REAL THING. EVEN MY FATHER THINKS SO.
AH. THEN, SHE MUST BE DEALT WITH.
IF SHE WERE TO ACTUALLY ENTER THE CASTLE—
HEH. ALREADY TAKEN CARE OF.
THAT IS THE ONE THING I DON'T HAVE TO WORRY ABOUT.

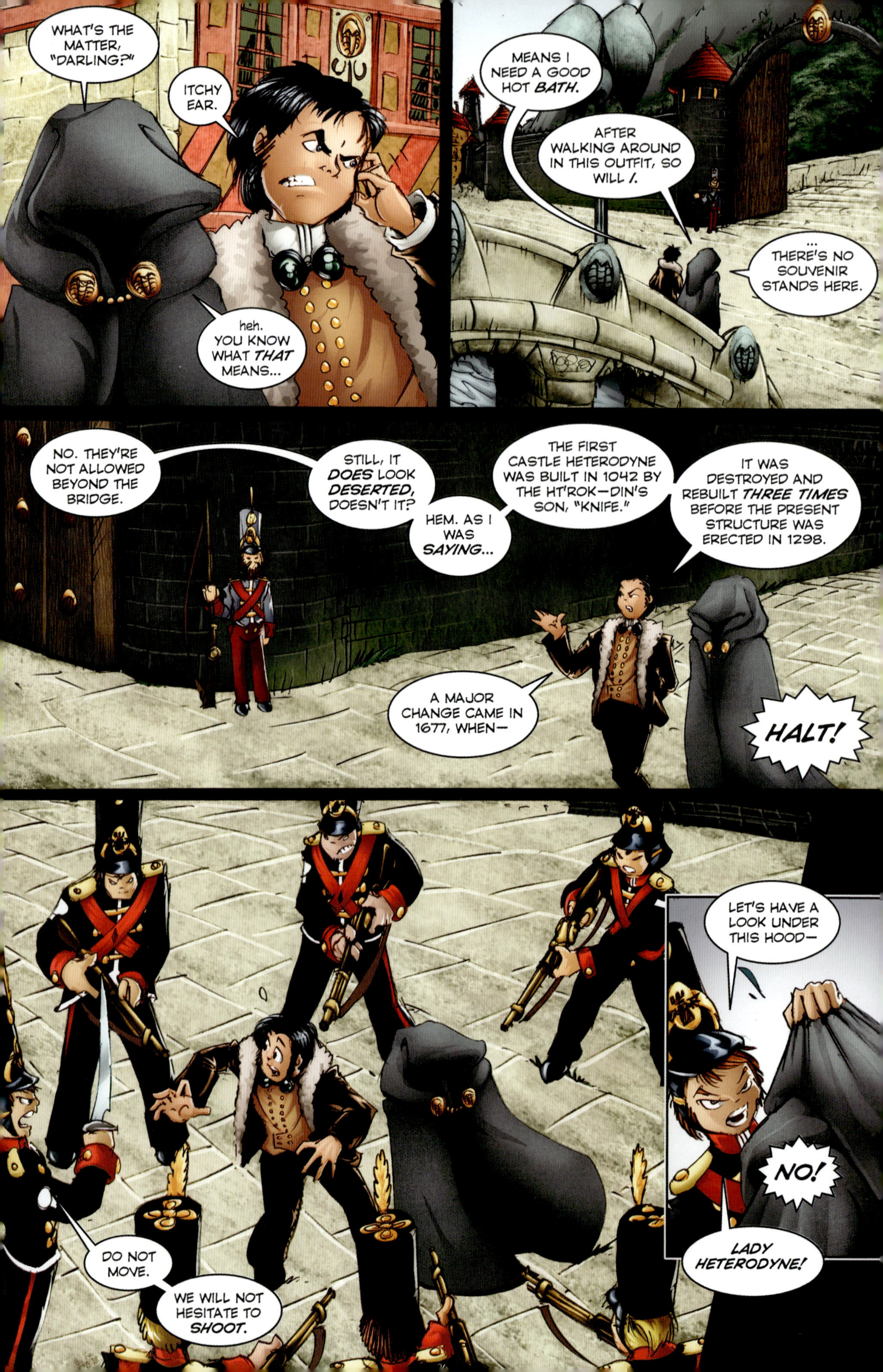
WHAT'S THE MATTER, "DARLING?"
ITCHY EAR.
heh. YOU KNOW WHAT *THAT* MEANS...
MEANS I NEED A GOOD HOT *BATH*.
AFTER WALKING AROUND IN THIS OUTFIT, SO WILL *I*.
...THERE'S NO SOUVENIR STANDS HERE.
NO. THEY'RE NOT ALLOWED BEYOND THE BRIDGE.
STILL, IT ***DOES*** LOOK ***DESERTED***, DOESN'T IT?
HEM. AS I WAS ***SAYING...***
THE FIRST CASTLE HETERODYNE WAS BUILT IN 1042 BY THE HT'ROK—DIN'S SON, "KNIFE."
IT WAS DESTROYED AND REBUILT ***THREE TIMES*** BEFORE THE PRESENT STRUCTURE WAS ERECTED IN 1298.
A MAJOR CHANGE CAME IN 1677, WHEN—
HALT!
LET'S HAVE A LOOK UNDER THIS HOOD—
NO!
LADY HETERODYNE!
DO NOT MOVE.
WE WILL NOT HESITATE TO ***SHOOT***.

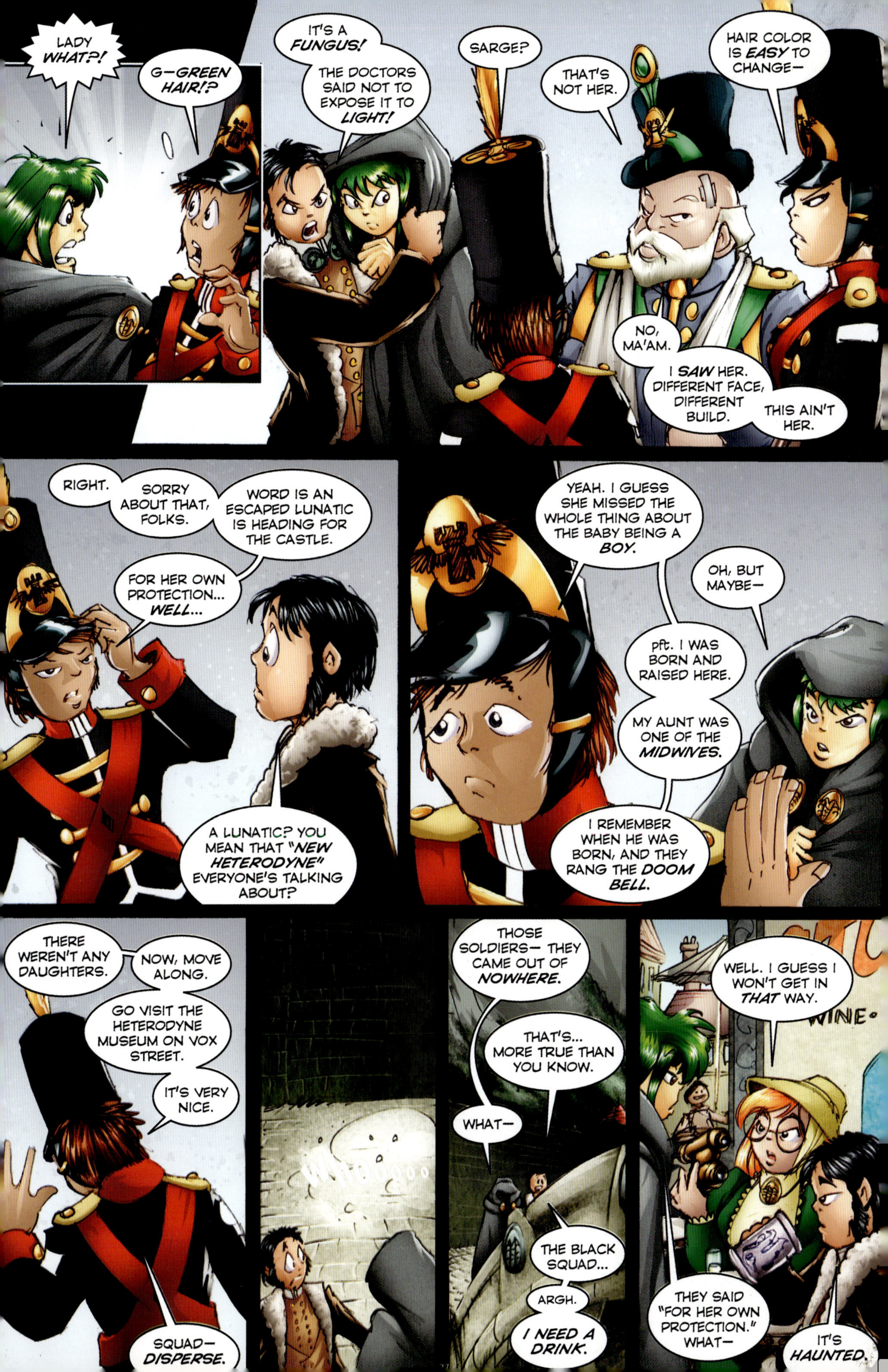
LADY WHAT?!
G—GREEN HAIR!?
IT'S A FUNGUS!
THE DOCTORS SAID NOT TO EXPOSE IT TO LIGHT!
SARGE?
THAT'S NOT HER.
HAIR COLOR IS EASY TO CHANGE—
NO, MA'AM.
I SAW HER. DIFFERENT FACE, DIFFERENT BUILD.
THIS AIN'T HER.
RIGHT.
SORRY ABOUT THAT, FOLKS.
WORD IS AN ESCAPED LUNATIC IS HEADING FOR THE CASTLE.
FOR HER OWN PROTECTION... WELL...
A LUNATIC? YOU MEAN THAT "NEW HETERODYNE" EVERYONE'S TALKING ABOUT?
YEAH. I GUESS SHE MISSED THE WHOLE THING ABOUT THE BABY BEING A BOY.
OH, BUT MAYBE—
pft. I WAS BORN AND RAISED HERE.
MY AUNT WAS ONE OF THE MIDWIVES.
I REMEMBER WHEN HE WAS BORN, AND THEY RANG THE DOOM BELL.
THERE WEREN'T ANY DAUGHTERS.
NOW, MOVE ALONG.
GO VISIT THE HETERODYNE MUSEUM ON VOX STREET.
IT'S VERY NICE.
SQUAD— DISPERSE.
THOSE SOLDIERS— THEY CAME OUT OF NOWHERE.
THAT'S... MORE TRUE THAN YOU KNOW.
WHAT—
THE BLACK SQUAD...
ARGH.
I NEED A DRINK.
WELL. I GUESS I WON'T GET IN THAT WAY.
WINE
THEY SAID "FOR HER OWN PROTECTION." WHAT—
IT'S HAUNTED.

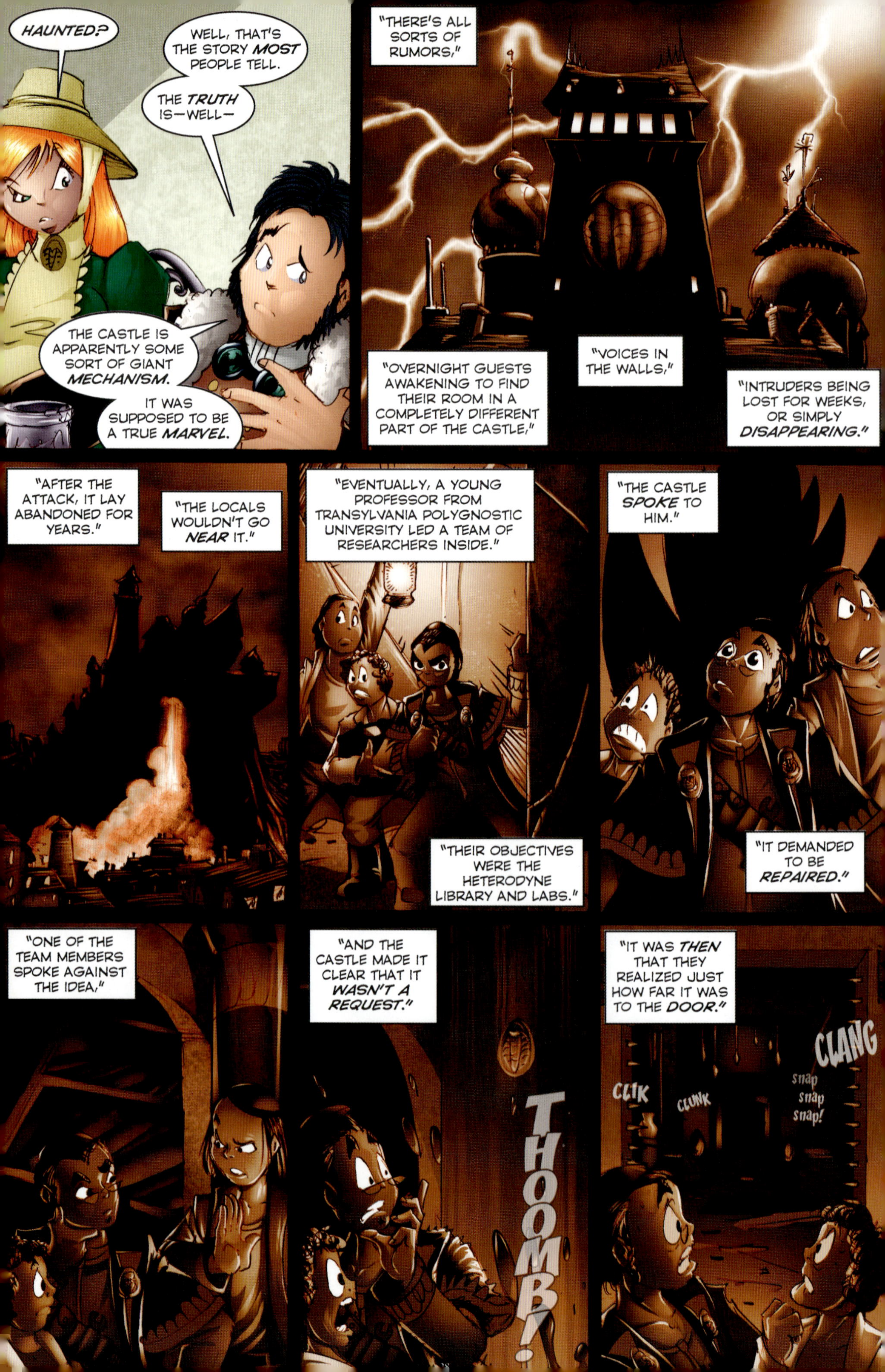
HAUNTED?
WELL, THAT'S THE STORY MOST PEOPLE TELL.
THE TRUTH IS—WELL—
THE CASTLE IS APPARENTLY SOME SORT OF GIANT MECHANISM.
IT WAS SUPPOSED TO BE A TRUE MARVEL.
"THERE'S ALL SORTS OF RUMORS,"
"OVERNIGHT GUESTS AWAKENING TO FIND THEIR ROOM IN A COMPLETELY DIFFERENT PART OF THE CASTLE,"
"VOICES IN THE WALLS,"
"INTRUDERS BEING LOST FOR WEEKS, OR SIMPLY DISAPPEARING."
"AFTER THE ATTACK, IT LAY ABANDONED FOR YEARS."
"THE LOCALS WOULDN'T GO NEAR IT."
"EVENTUALLY, A YOUNG PROFESSOR FROM TRANSYLVANIA POLYGNOSTIC UNIVERSITY LED A TEAM OF RESEARCHERS INSIDE."
"THEIR OBJECTIVES WERE THE HETERODYNE LIBRARY AND LABS."
"THE CASTLE SPOKE TO HIM."
"IT DEMANDED TO BE REPAIRED."
"ONE OF THE TEAM MEMBERS SPOKE AGAINST THE IDEA,"
"AND THE CASTLE MADE IT CLEAR THAT IT WASN'T A REQUEST."
THOOMB!
"IT WAS THEN THAT THEY REALIZED JUST HOW FAR IT WAS TO THE DOOR."
CLIK
CLUNK
CLANG
snap
snap
snap!

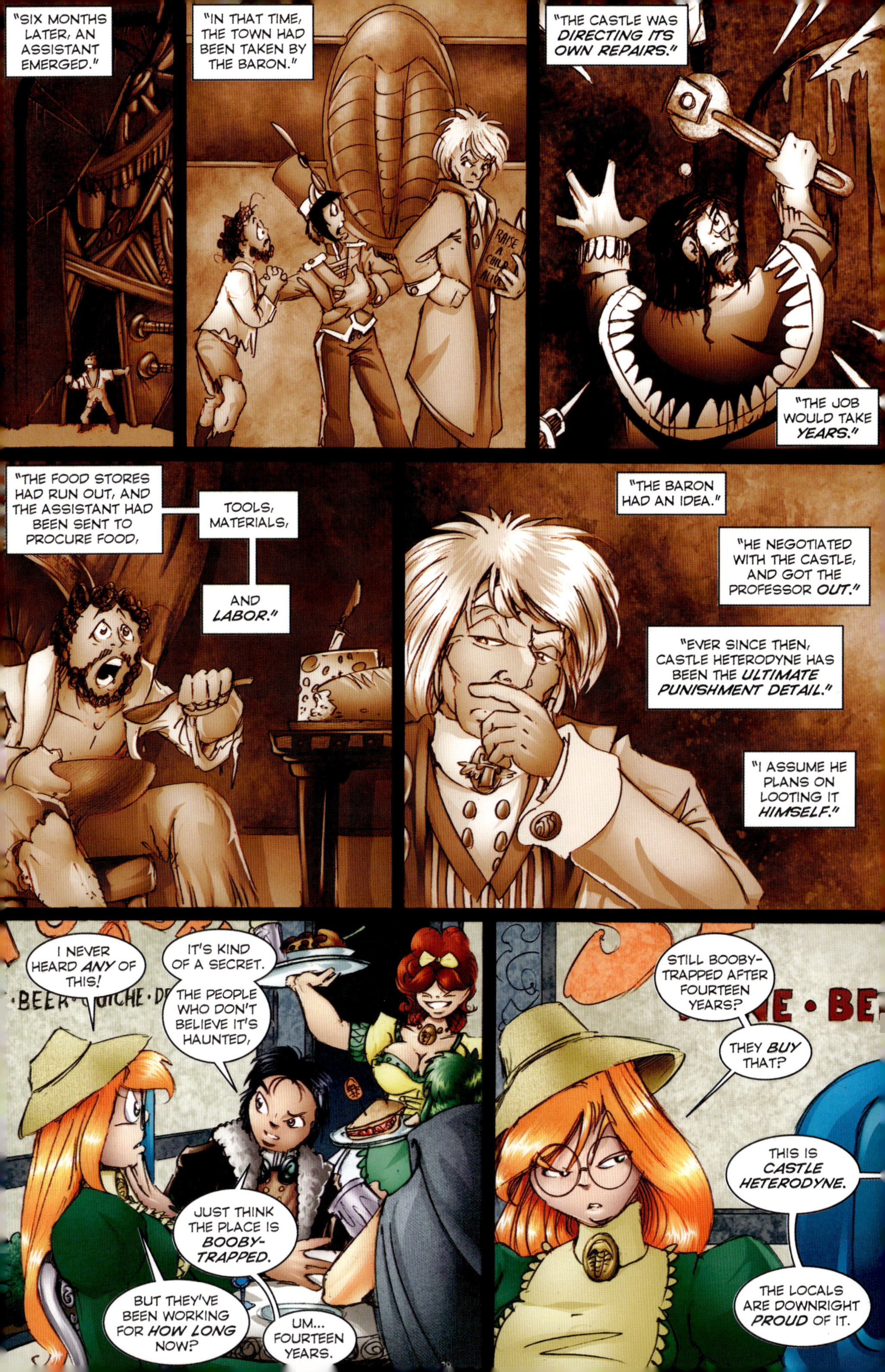
"SIX MONTHS LATER, AN ASSISTANT EMERGED."
"IN THAT TIME, THE TOWN HAD BEEN TAKEN BY THE BARON."
RAISE A CHILD ALIVE
"THE CASTLE WAS *DIRECTING ITS OWN REPAIRS.*"
"THE JOB WOULD TAKE *YEARS.*"
"THE FOOD STORES HAD RUN OUT, AND THE ASSISTANT HAD BEEN SENT TO PROCURE FOOD,
TOOLS, MATERIALS,
AND *LABOR.*"
"THE BARON HAD AN IDEA."
"HE NEGOTIATED WITH THE CASTLE, AND GOT THE PROFESSOR *OUT.*"
"EVER SINCE THEN, CASTLE HETERODYNE HAS BEEN THE *ULTIMATE PUNISHMENT DETAIL.*"
"I ASSUME HE PLANS ON LOOTING IT *HIMSELF.*"
I NEVER HEARD *ANY* OF THIS!
IT'S KIND OF A SECRET.
THE PEOPLE WHO DON'T BELIEVE IT'S HAUNTED,
JUST THINK THE PLACE IS *BOOBY-TRAPPED.*
BUT THEY'VE BEEN WORKING FOR *HOW LONG* NOW?
UM... FOURTEEN YEARS.
STILL BOOBY-TRAPPED AFTER FOURTEEN YEARS?
THEY *BUY* THAT?
THIS IS *CASTLE HETERODYNE.*
THE LOCALS ARE DOWNRIGHT *PROUD* OF IT.

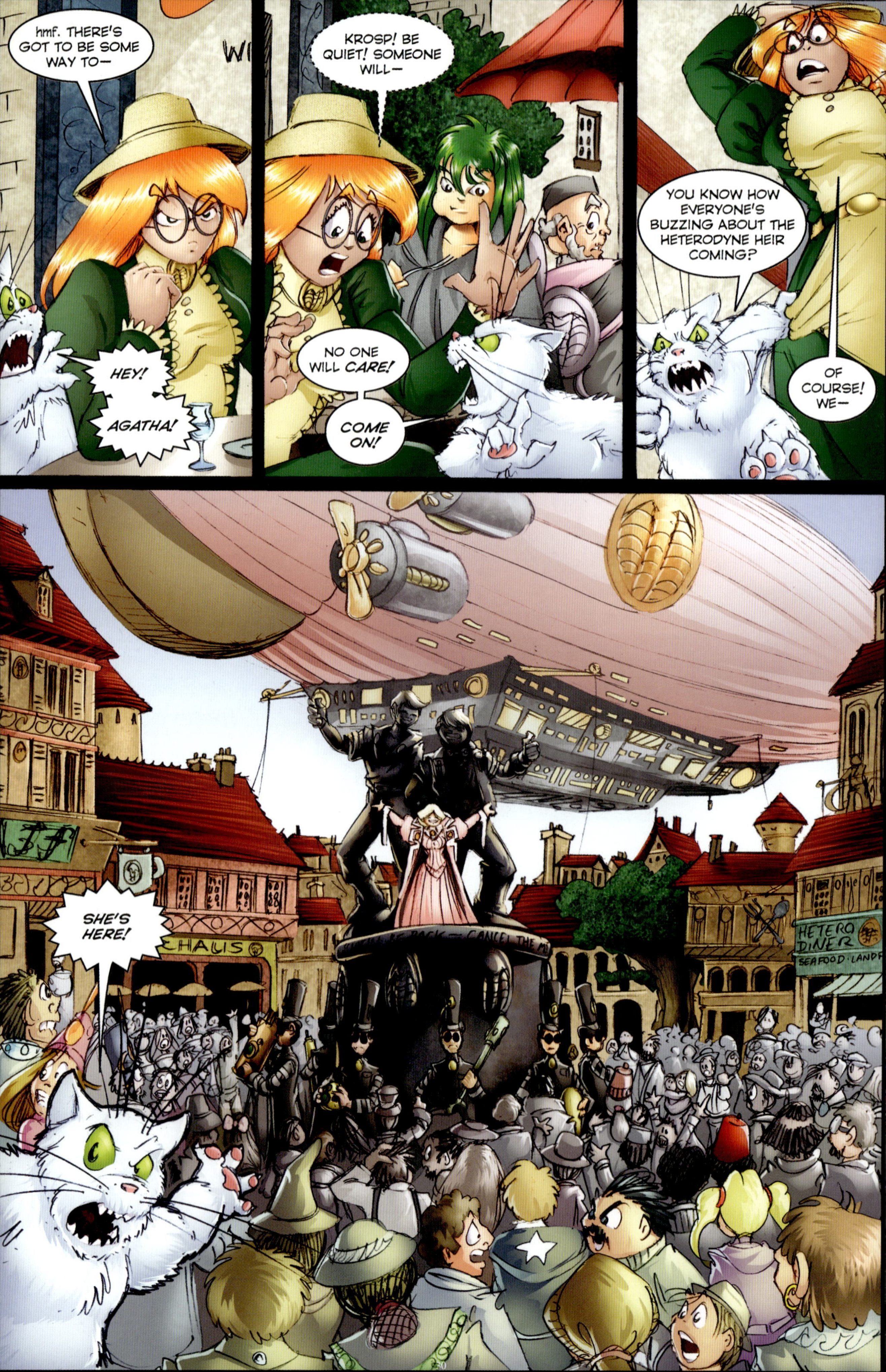
hmf. THERE'S GOT TO BE SOME WAY TO—
HEY!
AGATHA!
KROSP! BE QUIET! SOMEONE WILL—
NO ONE WILL CARE!
COME ON!
YOU KNOW HOW EVERYONE'S BUZZING ABOUT THE HETERODYNE HEIR COMING?
OF COURSE! WE—
SHE'S HERE!
HETERO DINER
SEAFOOD

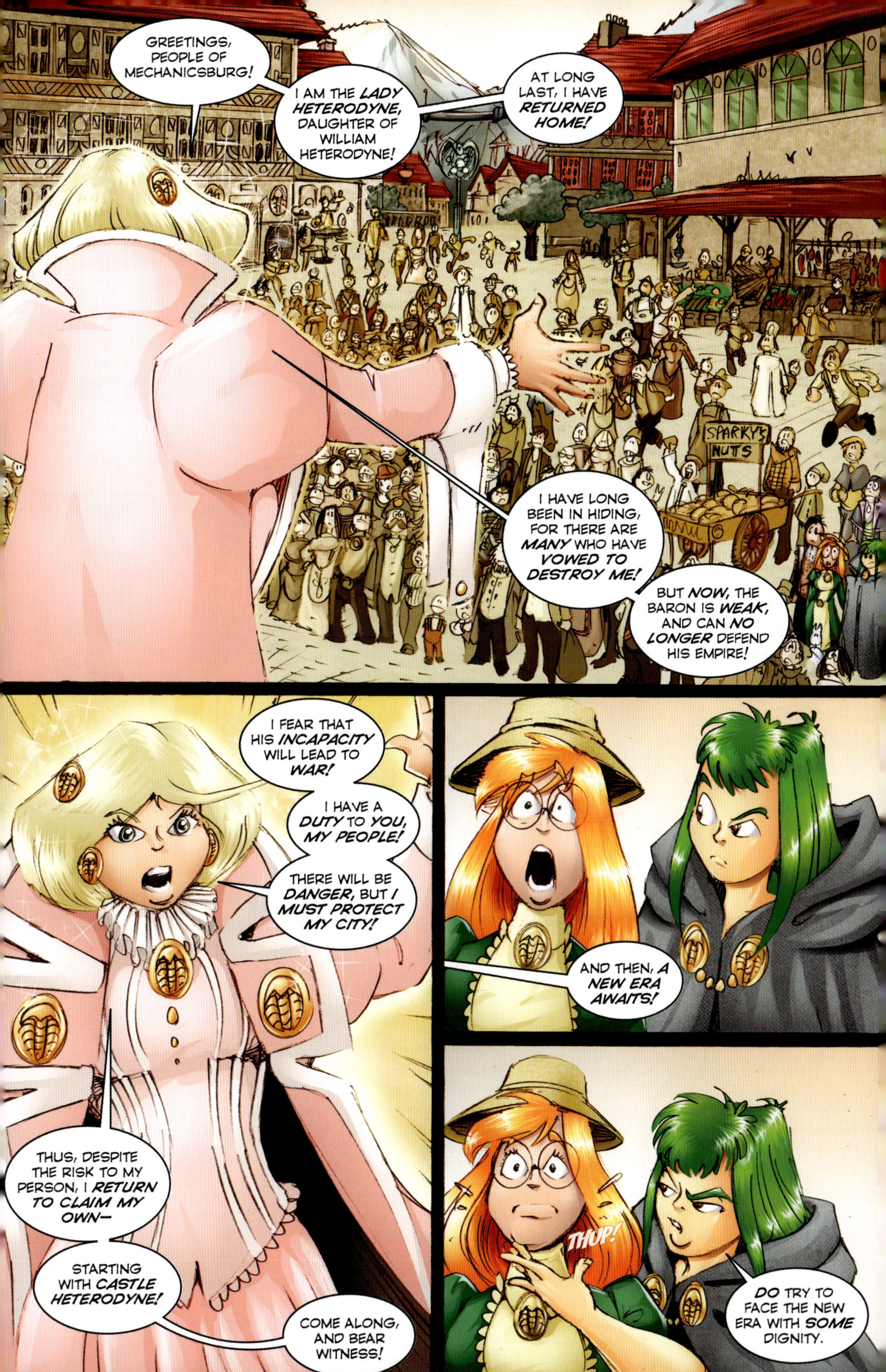
GREETINGS, PEOPLE OF MECHANICSBURG!
I AM THE *LADY HETERODYNE,* DAUGHTER OF WILLIAM HETERODYNE!
AT LONG LAST, I HAVE *RETURNED HOME!*
SPARKY'S NUTS
I HAVE LONG BEEN IN HIDING, FOR THERE ARE *MANY* WHO HAVE *VOWED TO DESTROY ME!*
BUT *NOW,* THE BARON IS *WEAK,* AND CAN *NO LONGER* DEFEND HIS EMPIRE!
I FEAR THAT HIS *INCAPACITY* WILL LEAD TO *WAR!*
I HAVE A *DUTY* TO *YOU, MY PEOPLE!*
THERE WILL BE *DANGER,* BUT *I MUST PROTECT MY CITY!*
THUS, DESPITE THE RISK TO MY PERSON, I *RETURN TO CLAIM MY OWN—*
STARTING WITH *CASTLE HETERODYNE!*
COME ALONG, AND BEAR WITNESS!
AND THEN, *A NEW ERA AWAITS!*
THUP!
DO TRY TO FACE THE NEW ERA WITH *SOME* DIGNITY.

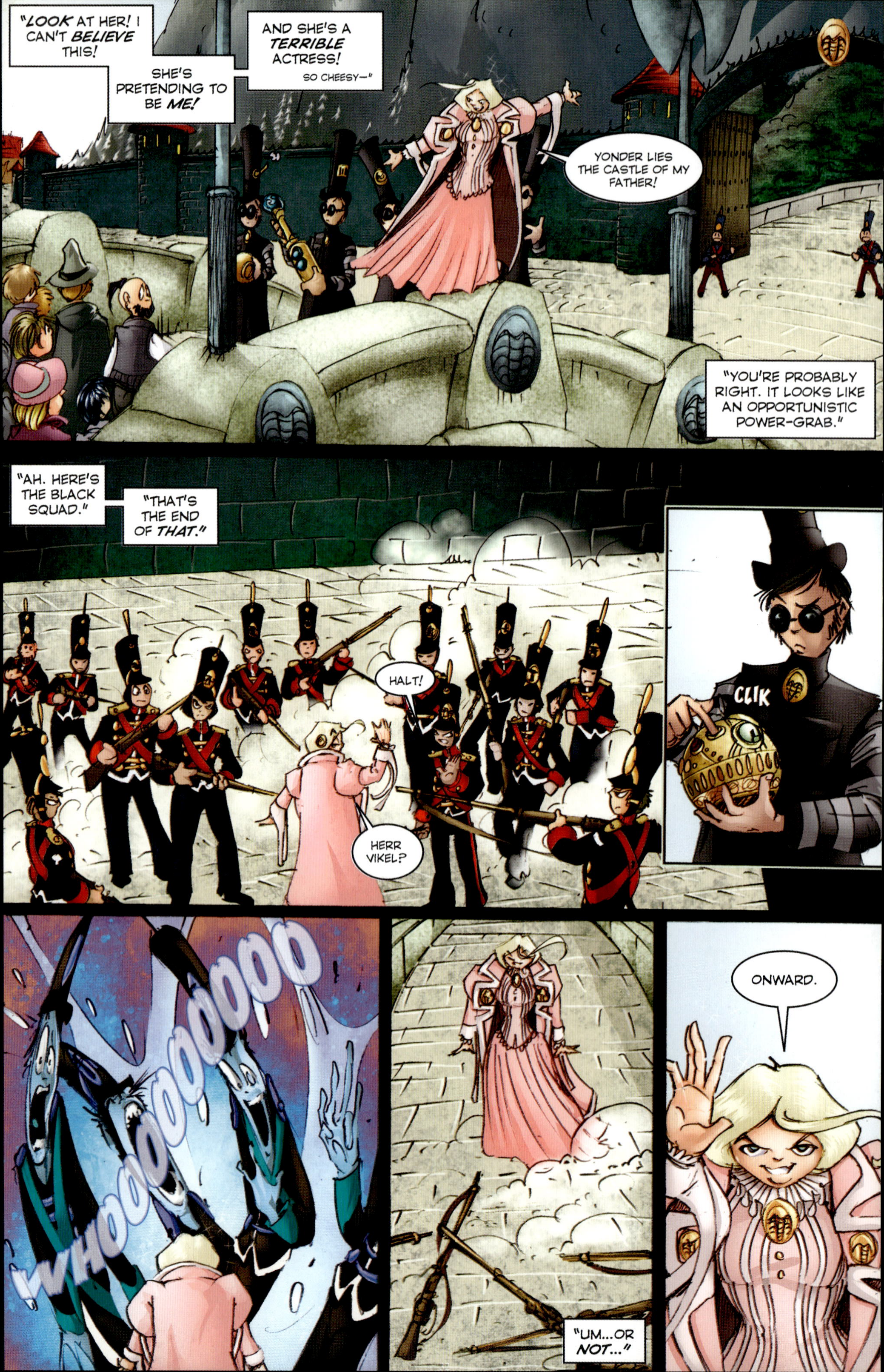
"LOOK AT HER! I CAN'T BELIEVE THIS!
SHE'S PRETENDING TO BE ME!
AND SHE'S A TERRIBLE ACTRESS!
SO CHEESY—"
YONDER LIES THE CASTLE OF MY FATHER!
"YOU'RE PROBABLY RIGHT. IT LOOKS LIKE AN OPPORTUNISTIC POWER-GRAB."
"AH. HERE'S THE BLACK SQUAD."
"THAT'S THE END OF THAT."
HALT!
HERR VIKEL?
CLIK
WHOOOOOOOOO
"UM...OR NOT..."
ONWARD.

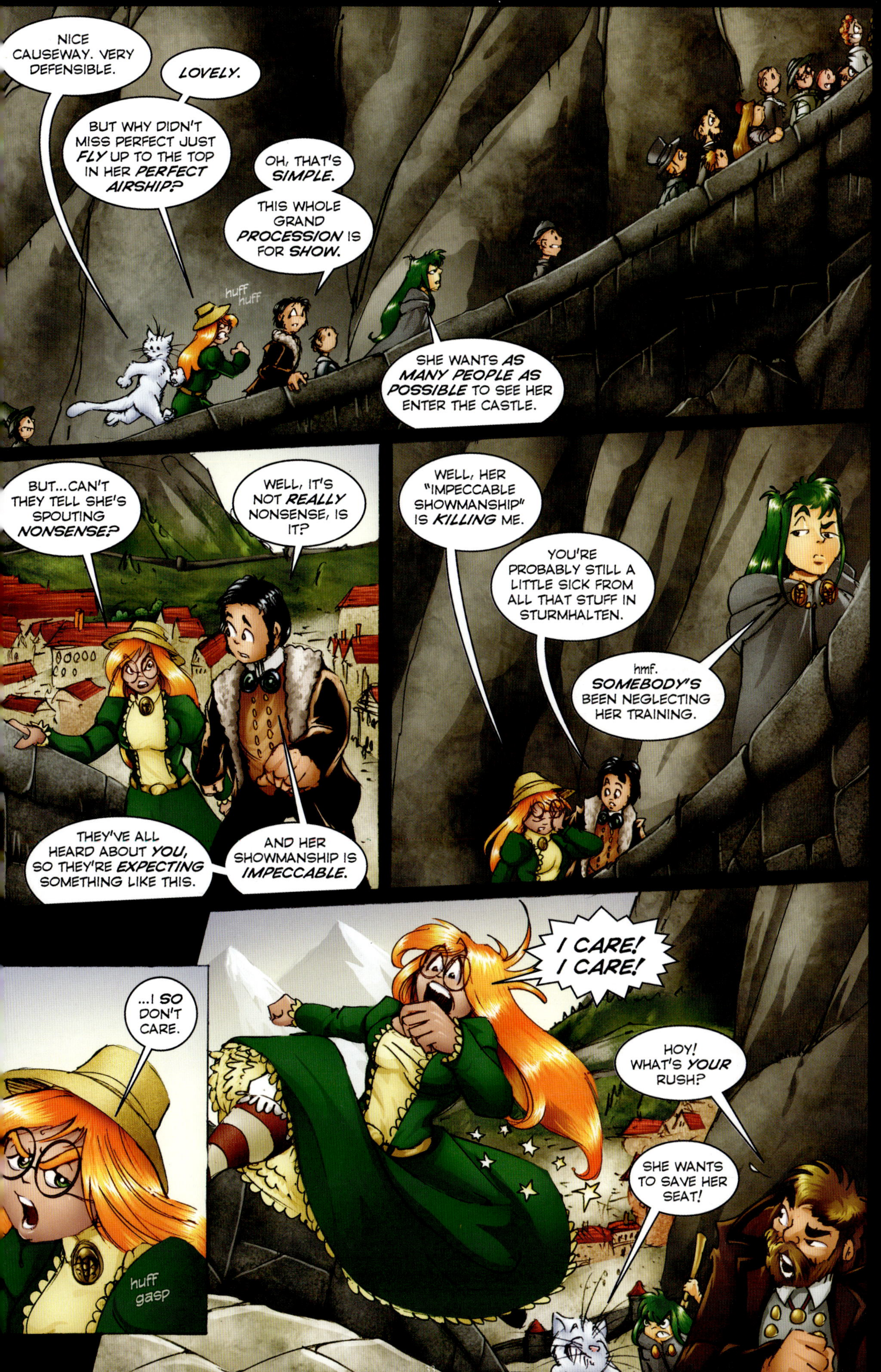

NICE CAUSEWAY. VERY DEFENSIBLE.
LOVELY.
BUT WHY DIDN'T MISS PERFECT JUST FLY UP TO THE TOP IN HER PERFECT AIRSHIP?
OH, THAT'S SIMPLE.
THIS WHOLE GRAND PROCESSION IS FOR SHOW.
huff huff
SHE WANTS AS MANY PEOPLE AS POSSIBLE TO SEE HER ENTER THE CASTLE.
BUT...CAN'T THEY TELL SHE'S SPOUTING NONSENSE?
WELL, IT'S NOT REALLY NONSENSE, IS IT?
THEY'VE ALL HEARD ABOUT YOU, SO THEY'RE EXPECTING SOMETHING LIKE THIS.
AND HER SHOWMANSHIP IS IMPECCABLE.
WELL, HER "IMPECCABLE SHOWMANSHIP" IS KILLING ME.
YOU'RE PROBABLY STILL A LITTLE SICK FROM ALL THAT STUFF IN STURMHALTEN.
hmf.
SOMEBODY'S BEEN NEGLECTING HER TRAINING.
...I SO DON'T CARE.
huff gasp
I CARE! I CARE!
HOY! WHAT'S YOUR RUSH?
SHE WANTS TO SAVE HER SEAT!

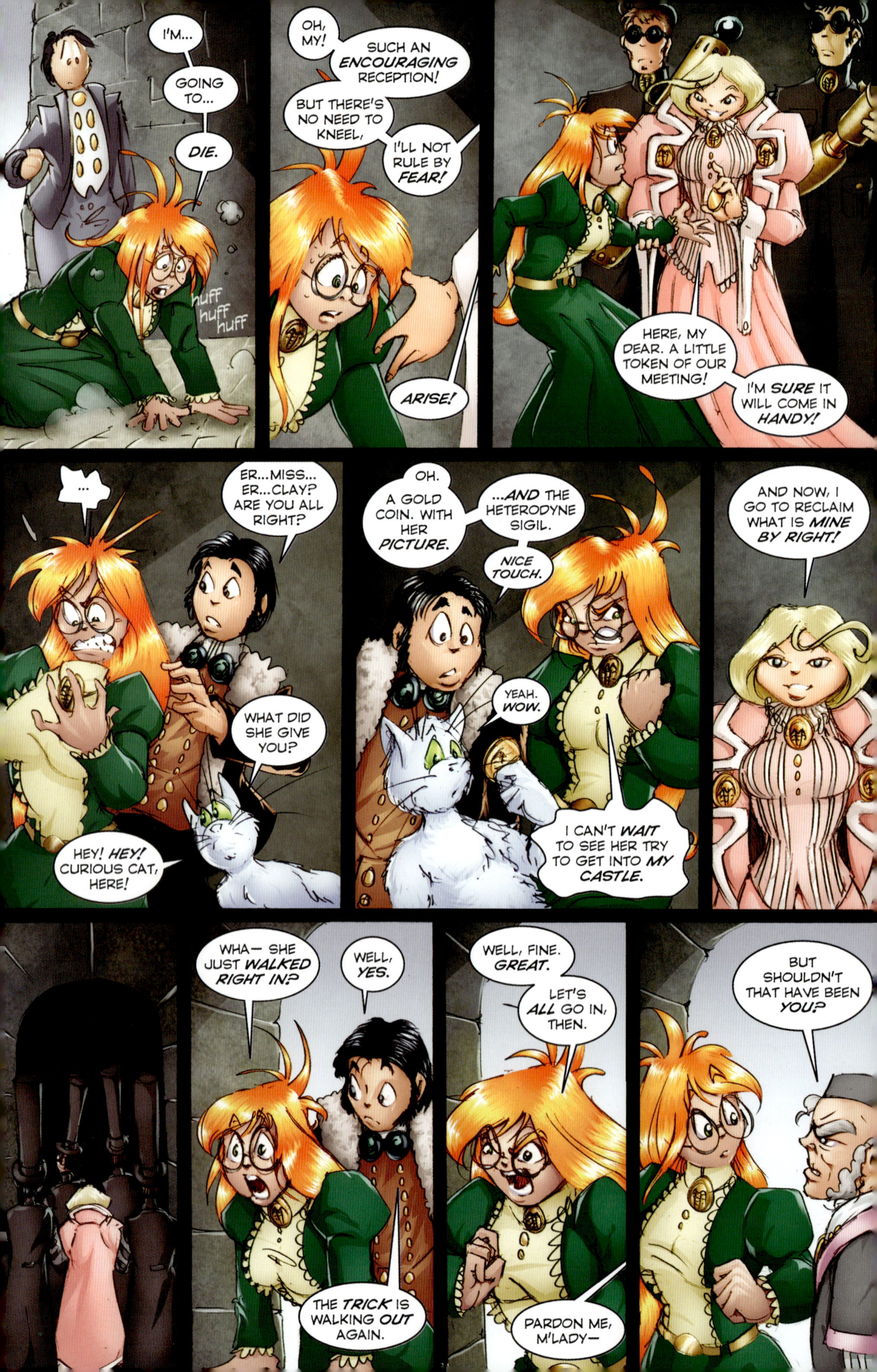
I'M...
GOING TO...
DIE.
huff huff huff
OH, MY!
SUCH AN ENCOURAGING RECEPTION!
BUT THERE'S NO NEED TO KNEEL,
I'LL NOT RULE BY FEAR!
ARISE!
HERE, MY DEAR. A LITTLE TOKEN OF OUR MEETING!
I'M SURE IT WILL COME IN HANDY!
...
ER...MISS... ER...CLAY? ARE YOU ALL RIGHT?
WHAT DID SHE GIVE YOU?
HEY! HEY! CURIOUS CAT, HERE!
OH.
A GOLD COIN. WITH HER PICTURE.
...AND THE HETERODYNE SIGIL.
NICE TOUCH.
YEAH. WOW.
I CAN'T WAIT TO SEE HER TRY TO GET INTO MY CASTLE.
AND NOW, I GO TO RECLAIM WHAT IS MINE BY RIGHT!
WHA— SHE JUST WALKED RIGHT IN?
WELL, YES.
THE TRICK IS WALKING OUT AGAIN.
WELL, FINE. GREAT.
LET'S ALL GO IN, THEN.
PARDON ME, M'LADY—
BUT SHOULDN'T THAT HAVE BEEN YOU?

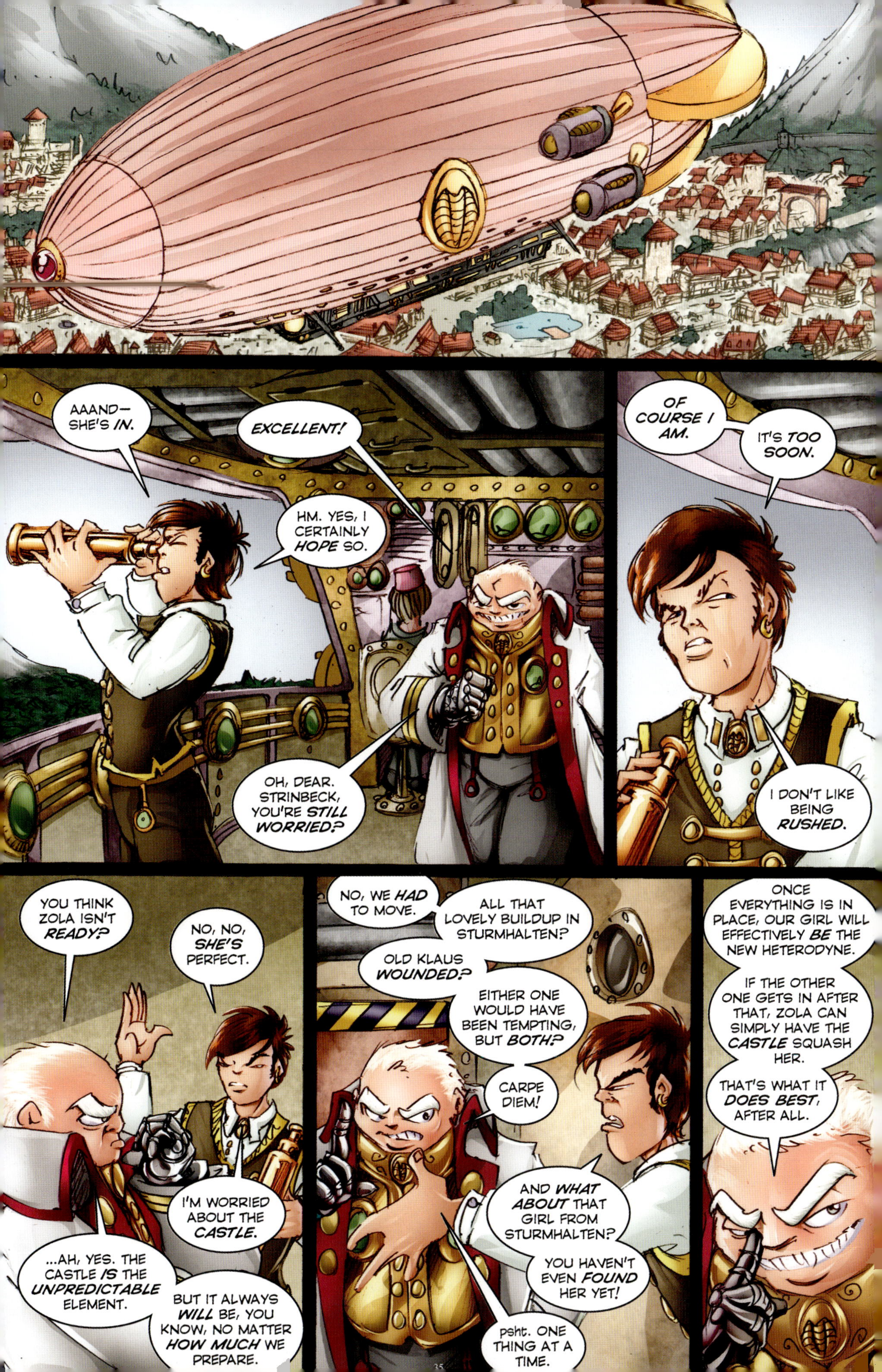
AAAND— SHE'S IN.
EXCELLENT!
HM. YES, I CERTAINLY HOPE SO.
OH, DEAR. STRINBECK, YOU'RE STILL WORRIED?
OF COURSE I AM.
IT'S TOO SOON.
I DON'T LIKE BEING RUSHED.
YOU THINK ZOLA ISN'T READY?
NO, NO, SHE'S PERFECT.
I'M WORRIED ABOUT THE CASTLE.
...AH, YES. THE CASTLE IS THE UNPREDICTABLE ELEMENT.
BUT IT ALWAYS WILL BE, YOU KNOW, NO MATTER HOW MUCH WE PREPARE.
NO, WE HAD TO MOVE.
ALL THAT LOVELY BUILDUP IN STURMHALTEN?
OLD KLAUS WOUNDED?
EITHER ONE WOULD HAVE BEEN TEMPTING, BUT BOTH?
CARPE DIEM!
AND WHAT ABOUT THAT GIRL FROM STURMHALTEN?
YOU HAVEN'T EVEN FOUND HER YET!
psht. ONE THING AT A TIME.
ONCE EVERYTHING IS IN PLACE, OUR GIRL WILL EFFECTIVELY BE THE NEW HETERODYNE.
IF THE OTHER ONE GETS IN AFTER THAT, ZOLA CAN SIMPLY HAVE THE CASTLE SQUASH HER.
THAT'S WHAT IT DOES BEST, AFTER ALL.

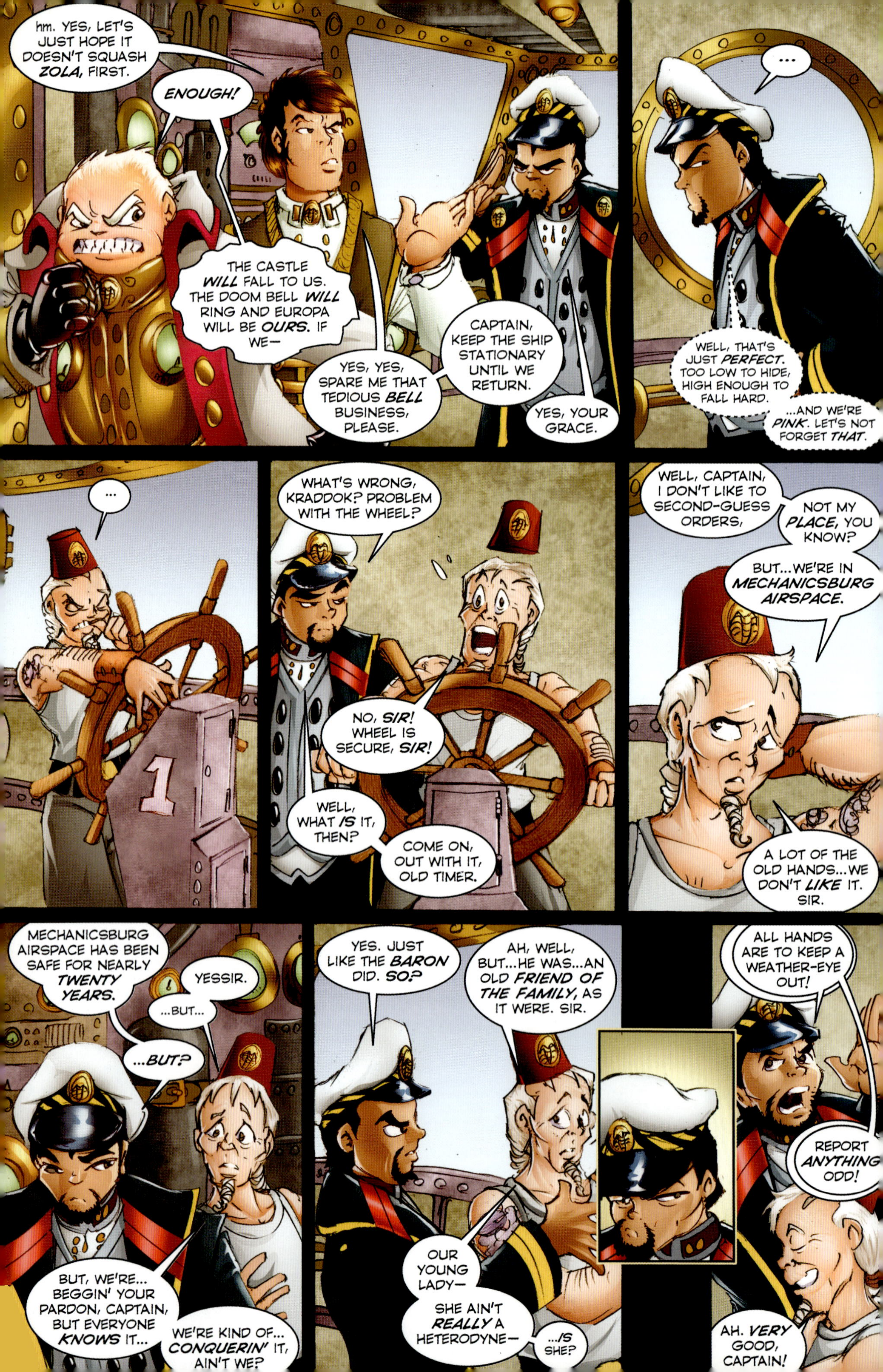
hm. YES, LET'S JUST HOPE IT DOESN'T SQUASH ZOLA, FIRST.
ENOUGH!
THE CASTLE WILL FALL TO US. THE DOOM BELL WILL RING AND EUROPA WILL BE OURS. IF WE—
YES, YES, SPARE ME THAT TEDIOUS BELL BUSINESS, PLEASE.
CAPTAIN, KEEP THE SHIP STATIONARY UNTIL WE RETURN.
YES, YOUR GRACE.
...
WELL, THAT'S JUST PERFECT. TOO LOW TO HIDE, HIGH ENOUGH TO FALL HARD.
...AND WE'RE PINK. LET'S NOT FORGET THAT.
...
WHAT'S WRONG, KRADDOK? PROBLEM WITH THE WHEEL?
NO, SIR! WHEEL IS SECURE, SIR!
WELL, WHAT IS IT, THEN?
COME ON, OUT WITH IT, OLD TIMER.
WELL, CAPTAIN, I DON'T LIKE TO SECOND-GUESS ORDERS,
NOT MY PLACE, YOU KNOW?
BUT...WE'RE IN MECHANICSBURG AIRSPACE.
A LOT OF THE OLD HANDS...WE DON'T LIKE IT. SIR.
MECHANICSBURG AIRSPACE HAS BEEN SAFE FOR NEARLY TWENTY YEARS.
YESSIR.
...BUT...
...BUT?
BUT, WE'RE... BEGGIN' YOUR PARDON, CAPTAIN, BUT EVERYONE KNOWS IT...
WE'RE KIND OF... CONQUERIN' IT, AIN'T WE?
YES. JUST LIKE THE BARON DID. SO?
AH, WELL, BUT...HE WAS...AN OLD FRIEND OF THE FAMILY, AS IT WERE. SIR.
OUR YOUNG LADY—
SHE AIN'T REALLY A HETERODYNE—
...IS SHE?
ALL HANDS ARE TO KEEP A WEATHER-EYE OUT!
REPORT ANYTHING ODD!
AH. VERY GOOD, CAPTAIN!

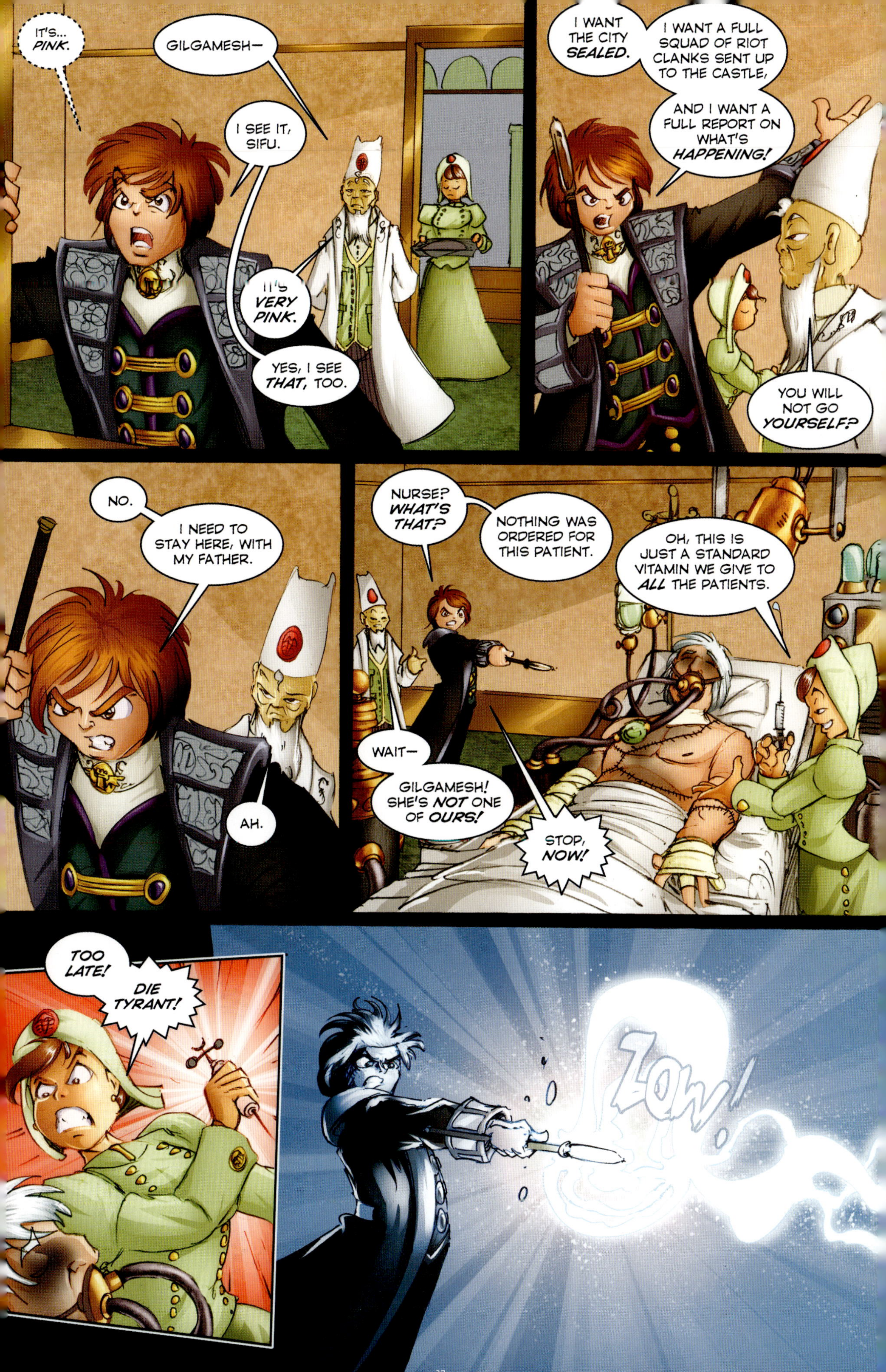
IT'S... PINK.
GILGAMESH—
I SEE IT, SIFU.
IT'S VERY PINK.
YES, I SEE THAT, TOO.
I WANT THE CITY SEALED.
I WANT A FULL SQUAD OF RIOT CLANKS SENT UP TO THE CASTLE,
AND I WANT A FULL REPORT ON WHAT'S HAPPENING!
YOU WILL NOT GO YOURSELF?
NO.
I NEED TO STAY HERE, WITH MY FATHER.
AH.
NURSE? WHAT'S THAT?
NOTHING WAS ORDERED FOR THIS PATIENT.
OH, THIS IS JUST A STANDARD VITAMIN WE GIVE TO ALL THE PATIENTS.
WAIT—
GILGAMESH! SHE'S NOT ONE OF OURS!
STOP, NOW!
TOO LATE!
DIE TYRANT!
ZOW!

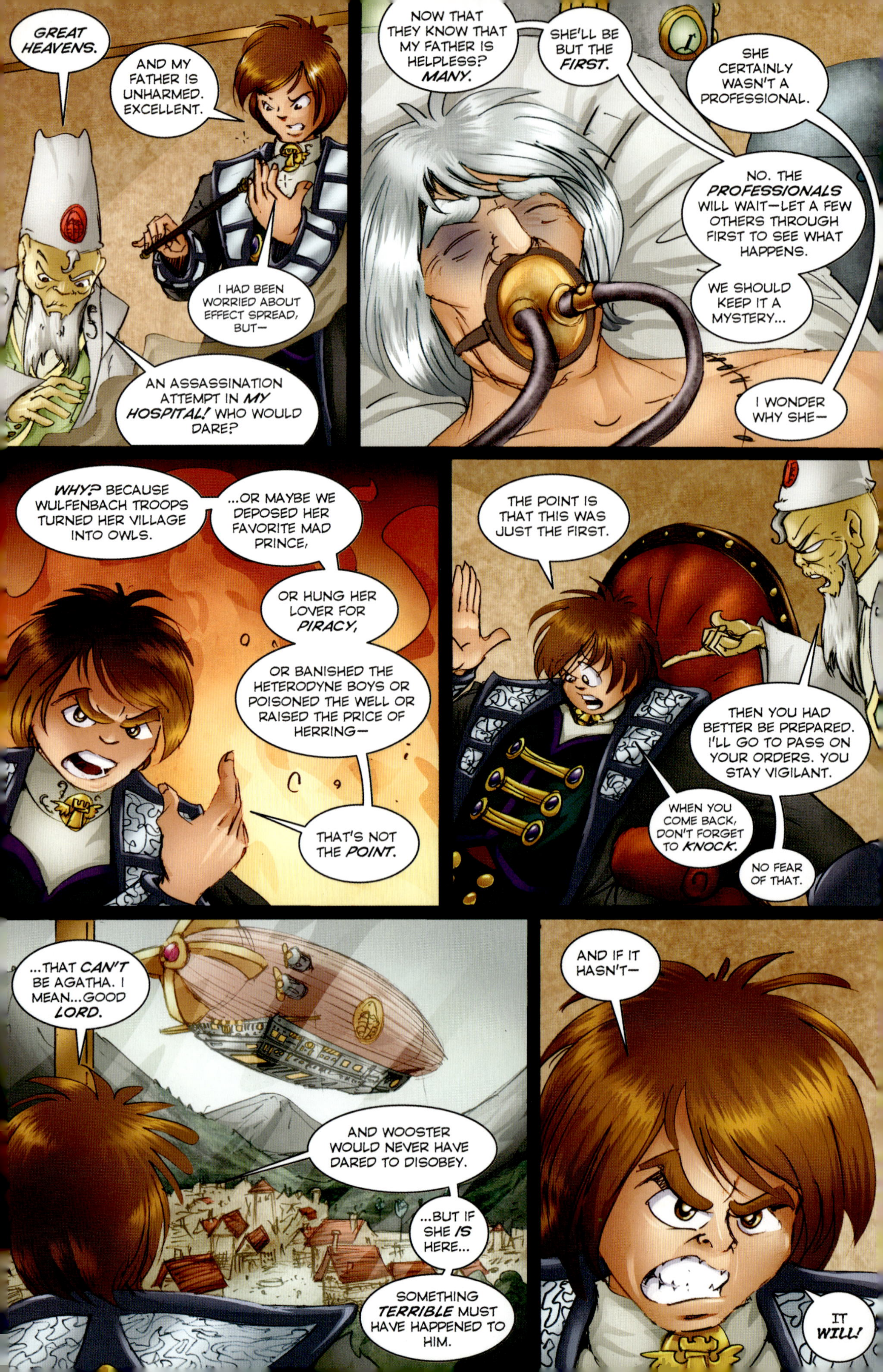
GREAT HEAVENS.
AND MY FATHER IS UNHARMED. EXCELLENT.
I HAD BEEN WORRIED ABOUT EFFECT SPREAD, BUT—
AN ASSASSINATION ATTEMPT IN MY HOSPITAL! WHO WOULD DARE?
NOW THAT THEY KNOW THAT MY FATHER IS HELPLESS? MANY.
SHE'LL BE BUT THE FIRST.
SHE CERTAINLY WASN'T A PROFESSIONAL.
NO. THE PROFESSIONALS WILL WAIT—LET A FEW OTHERS THROUGH FIRST TO SEE WHAT HAPPENS.
WE SHOULD KEEP IT A MYSTERY...
I WONDER WHY SHE—
WHY? BECAUSE WULFENBACH TROOPS TURNED HER VILLAGE INTO OWLS.
...OR MAYBE WE DEPOSED HER FAVORITE MAD PRINCE,
OR HUNG HER LOVER FOR PIRACY,
OR BANISHED THE HETERODYNE BOYS OR POISONED THE WELL OR RAISED THE PRICE OF HERRING—
THAT'S NOT THE POINT.
THE POINT IS THAT THIS WAS JUST THE FIRST.
THEN YOU HAD BETTER BE PREPARED. I'LL GO TO PASS ON YOUR ORDERS. YOU STAY VIGILANT.
WHEN YOU COME BACK, DON'T FORGET TO KNOCK.
NO FEAR OF THAT.
...THAT CAN'T BE AGATHA. I MEAN...GOOD LORD.
AND WOOSTER WOULD NEVER HAVE DARED TO DISOBEY.
...BUT IF SHE IS HERE...
SOMETHING TERRIBLE MUST HAVE HAPPENED TO HIM.
AND IF IT HASN'T—
IT WILL!

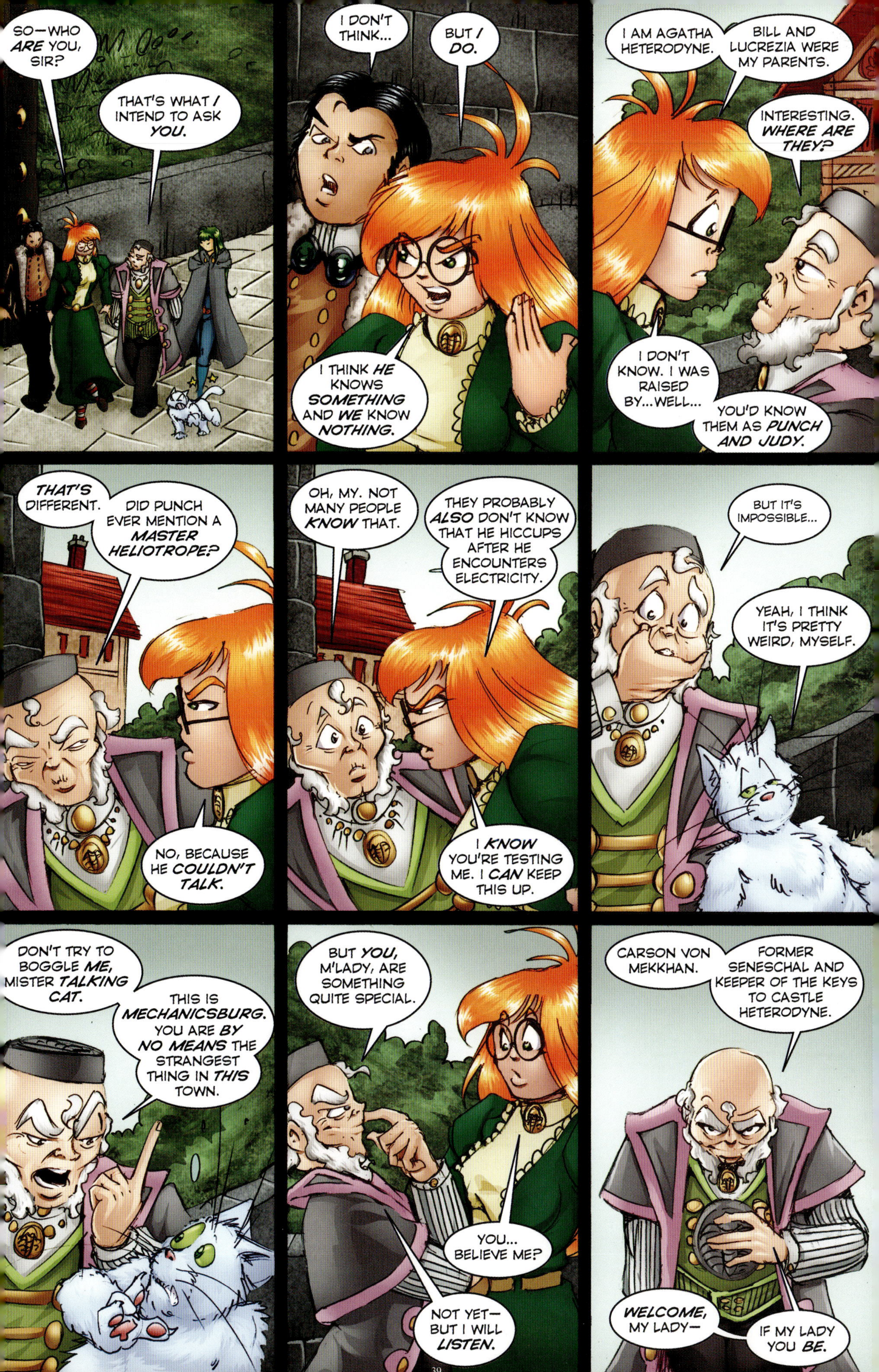
SO—WHO ARE YOU, SIR?
THAT'S WHAT I INTEND TO ASK YOU.
I DON'T THINK...
BUT I DO.
I THINK HE KNOWS SOMETHING AND WE KNOW NOTHING.
I AM AGATHA HETERODYNE.
BILL AND LUCREZIA WERE MY PARENTS.
INTERESTING. WHERE ARE THEY?
I DON'T KNOW. I WAS RAISED BY...WELL...
YOU'D KNOW THEM AS PUNCH AND JUDY.
THAT'S DIFFERENT.
DID PUNCH EVER MENTION A MASTER HELIOTROPE?
NO, BECAUSE HE COULDN'T TALK.
OH, MY. NOT MANY PEOPLE KNOW THAT.
THEY PROBABLY ALSO DON'T KNOW THAT HE HICCUPS AFTER HE ENCOUNTERS ELECTRICITY.
I KNOW YOU'RE TESTING ME. I CAN KEEP THIS UP.
BUT IT'S IMPOSSIBLE...
YEAH, I THINK IT'S PRETTY WEIRD, MYSELF.
DON'T TRY TO BOGGLE ME, MISTER TALKING CAT.
THIS IS MECHANICSBURG. YOU ARE BY NO MEANS THE STRANGEST THING IN THIS TOWN.
BUT YOU, M'LADY, ARE SOMETHING QUITE SPECIAL.
YOU... BELIEVE ME?
NOT YET— BUT I WILL LISTEN.
CARSON VON MEKKHAN.
FORMER SENESCHAL AND KEEPER OF THE KEYS TO CASTLE HETERODYNE.
WELCOME, MY LADY—
IF MY LADY YOU BE.

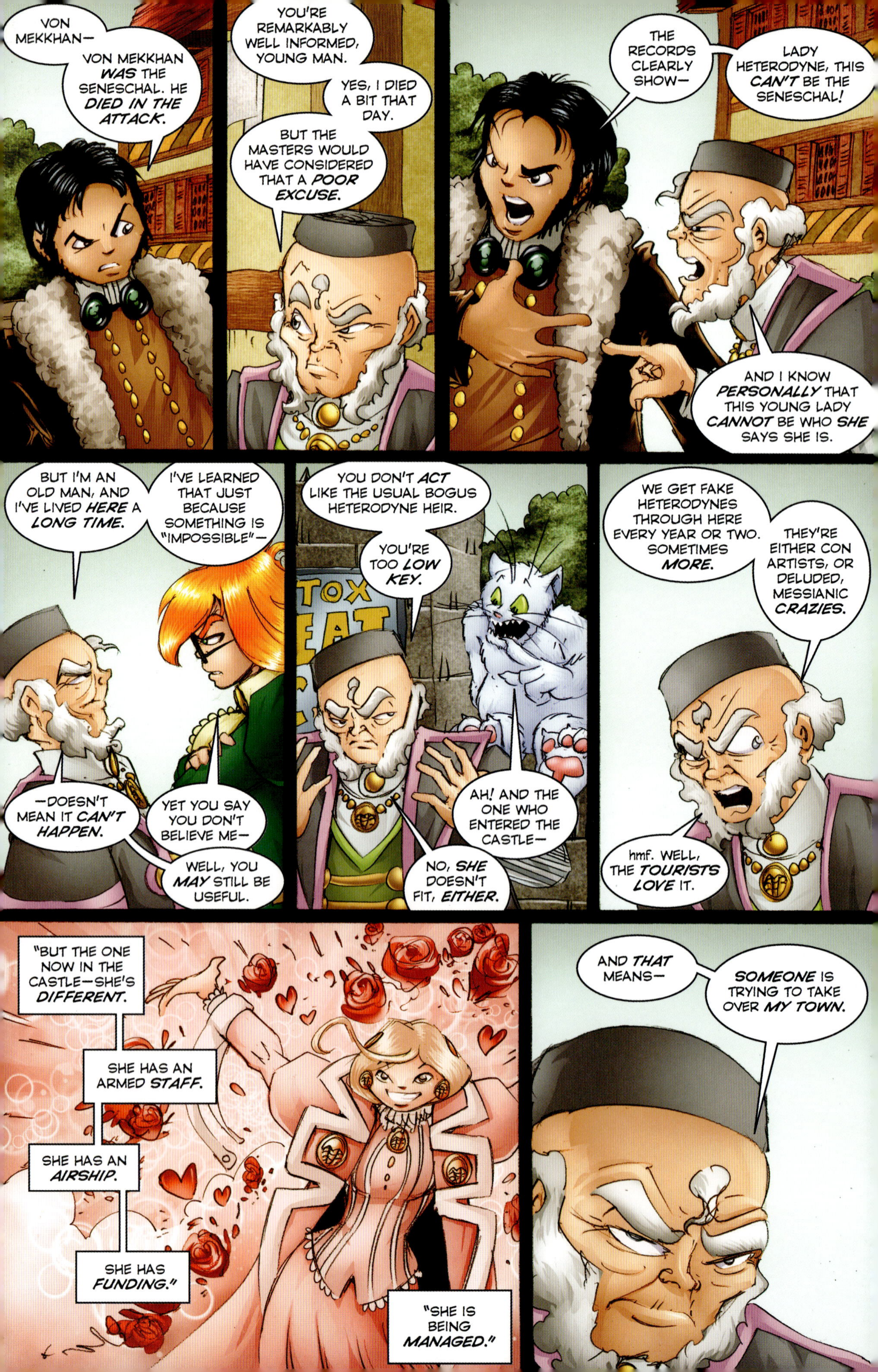
VON MEKKHAN—
VON MEKKHAN WAS THE SENESCHAL. HE DIED IN THE ATTACK.
YOU'RE REMARKABLY WELL INFORMED, YOUNG MAN.
YES, I DIED A BIT THAT DAY.
BUT THE MASTERS WOULD HAVE CONSIDERED THAT A POOR EXCUSE.
THE RECORDS CLEARLY SHOW—
LADY HETERODYNE, THIS CAN'T BE THE SENESCHAL!
AND I KNOW PERSONALLY THAT THIS YOUNG LADY CANNOT BE WHO SHE SAYS SHE IS.
BUT I'M AN OLD MAN, AND I'VE LIVED HERE A LONG TIME.
I'VE LEARNED THAT JUST BECAUSE SOMETHING IS "IMPOSSIBLE"—
—DOESN'T MEAN IT CAN'T HAPPEN.
YET YOU SAY YOU DON'T BELIEVE ME—
WELL, YOU MAY STILL BE USEFUL.
YOU DON'T ACT LIKE THE USUAL BOGUS HETERODYNE HEIR.
YOU'RE TOO LOW KEY.
AH! AND THE ONE WHO ENTERED THE CASTLE—
NO, SHE DOESN'T FIT, EITHER.
WE GET FAKE HETERODYNES THROUGH HERE EVERY YEAR OR TWO. SOMETIMES MORE.
THEY'RE EITHER CON ARTISTS, OR DELUDED, MESSIANIC CRAZIES.
hmf. WELL, THE TOURISTS LOVE IT.
"BUT THE ONE NOW IN THE CASTLE—SHE'S DIFFERENT.
SHE HAS AN ARMED STAFF.
SHE HAS AN AIRSHIP.
SHE HAS FUNDING."
"SHE IS BEING MANAGED."
AND THAT MEANS—
SOMEONE IS TRYING TO TAKE OVER MY TOWN.

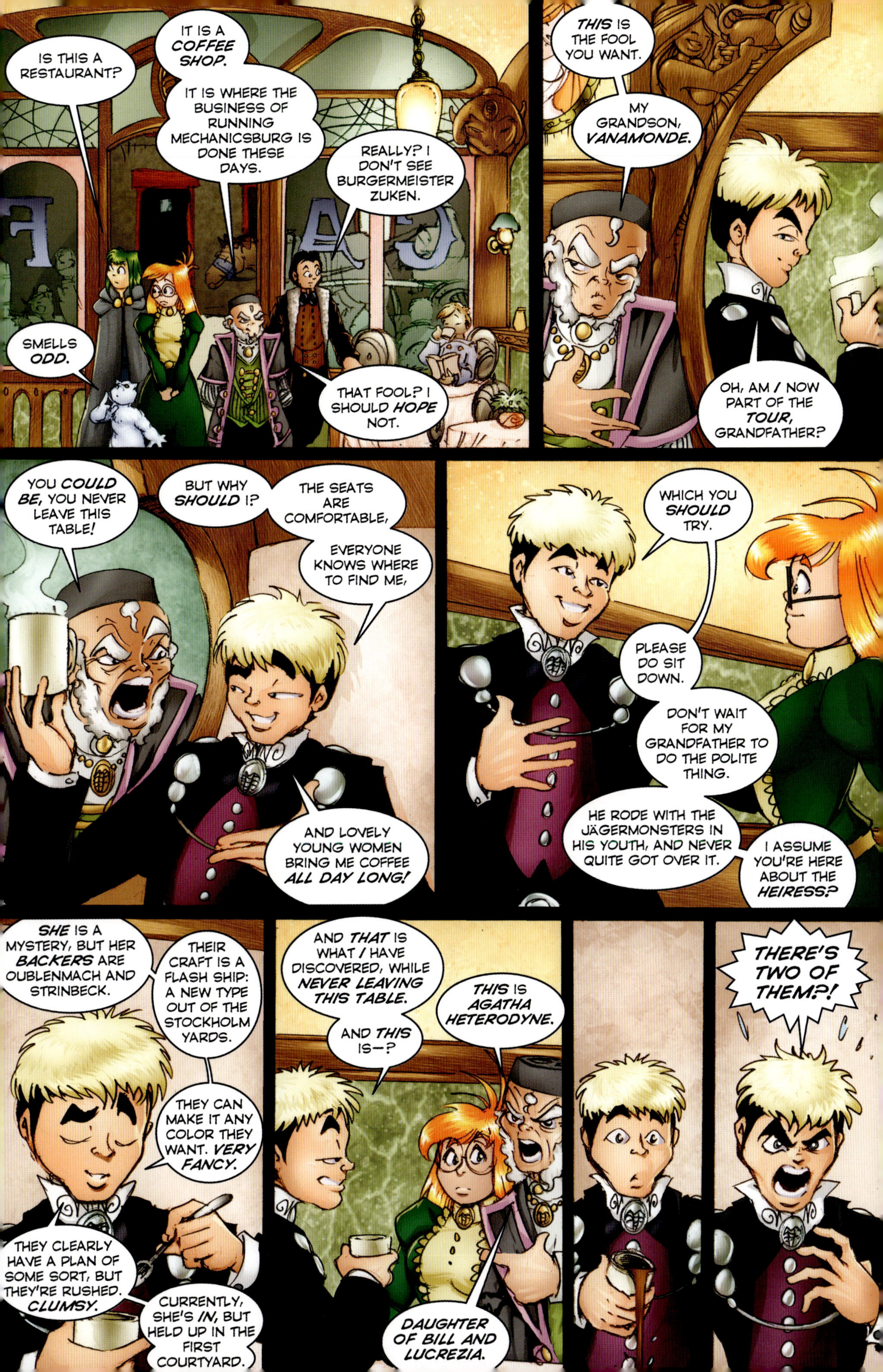
IS THIS A RESTAURANT?
IT IS A *COFFEE SHOP.*
IT IS WHERE THE BUSINESS OF RUNNING MECHANICSBURG IS DONE THESE DAYS.
REALLY? I DON'T SEE BURGERMEISTER ZUKEN.
SMELLS *ODD.*
THAT FOOL? I SHOULD *HOPE* NOT.
THIS IS THE FOOL YOU WANT.
MY GRANDSON, *VANAMONDE.*
OH, AM *I* NOW PART OF THE *TOUR,* GRANDFATHER?
YOU *COULD BE,* YOU NEVER LEAVE THIS TABLE!
BUT WHY *SHOULD* I?
THE SEATS ARE COMFORTABLE,
EVERYONE KNOWS WHERE TO FIND ME,
AND LOVELY YOUNG WOMEN BRING ME COFFEE *ALL DAY LONG!*
WHICH YOU *SHOULD* TRY.
PLEASE DO SIT DOWN.
DON'T WAIT FOR MY GRANDFATHER TO DO THE POLITE THING.
HE RODE WITH THE JÄGERMONSTERS IN HIS YOUTH, AND NEVER QUITE GOT OVER IT.
I ASSUME YOU'RE HERE ABOUT THE *HEIRESS?*
SHE IS A MYSTERY, BUT HER *BACKERS* ARE OUBLENMACH AND STRINBECK.
THEIR CRAFT IS A FLASH SHIP: A NEW TYPE OUT OF THE STOCKHOLM YARDS.
THEY CAN MAKE IT ANY COLOR THEY WANT. *VERY FANCY.*
THEY CLEARLY HAVE A PLAN OF SOME SORT, BUT THEY'RE RUSHED. *CLUMSY.*
CURRENTLY, SHE'S *IN,* BUT HELD UP IN THE FIRST COURTYARD.
AND *THAT* IS WHAT *I* HAVE DISCOVERED, WHILE *NEVER LEAVING THIS TABLE.*
AND *THIS* IS—?
THIS IS *AGATHA HETERODYNE.*
DAUGHTER OF BILL AND LUCREZIA.
THERE'S TWO OF THEM?!

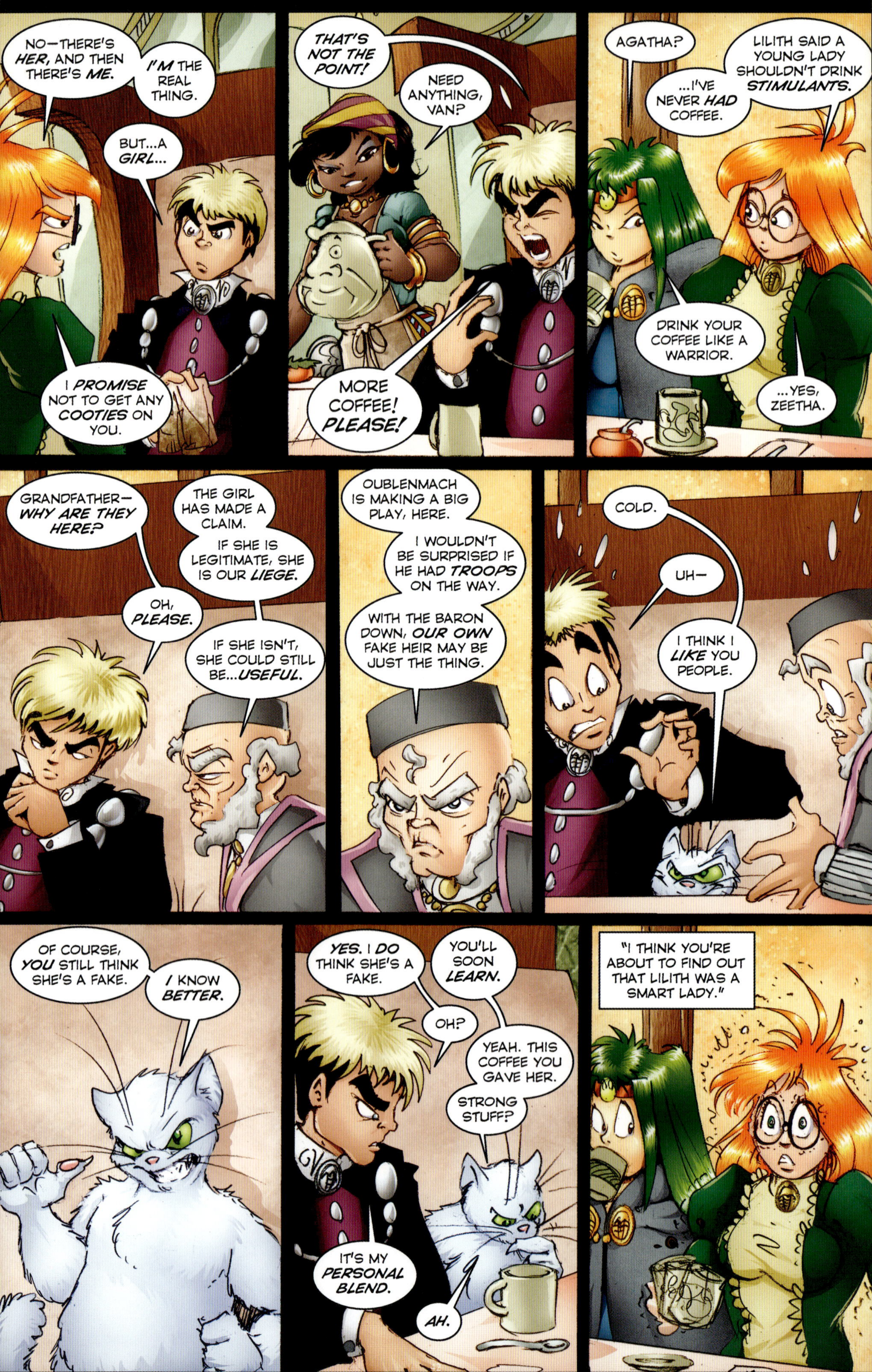
NO—THERE'S HER, AND THEN THERE'S ME.
I'M THE REAL THING.
BUT...A GIRL...
I PROMISE NOT TO GET ANY COOTIES ON YOU.
THAT'S NOT THE POINT!
NEED ANYTHING, VAN?
MORE COFFEE! PLEASE!
AGATHA?
...I'VE NEVER HAD COFFEE.
LILITH SAID A YOUNG LADY SHOULDN'T DRINK STIMULANTS.
DRINK YOUR COFFEE LIKE A WARRIOR.
...YES, ZEETHA.
GRANDFATHER—WHY ARE THEY HERE?
THE GIRL HAS MADE A CLAIM.
IF SHE IS LEGITIMATE, SHE IS OUR LIEGE.
OH, PLEASE.
IF SHE ISN'T, SHE COULD STILL BE...USEFUL.
OUBLENMACH IS MAKING A BIG PLAY, HERE.
I WOULDN'T BE SURPRISED IF HE HAD TROOPS ON THE WAY.
WITH THE BARON DOWN, OUR OWN FAKE HEIR MAY BE JUST THE THING.
COLD.
UH—
I THINK I LIKE YOU PEOPLE.
OF COURSE, YOU STILL THINK SHE'S A FAKE.
I KNOW BETTER.
YES. I DO THINK SHE'S A FAKE.
YOU'LL SOON LEARN.
OH?
YEAH. THIS COFFEE YOU GAVE HER.
STRONG STUFF?
IT'S MY PERSONAL BLEND.
AH.
"I THINK YOU'RE ABOUT TO FIND OUT THAT LILITH WAS A SMART LADY."

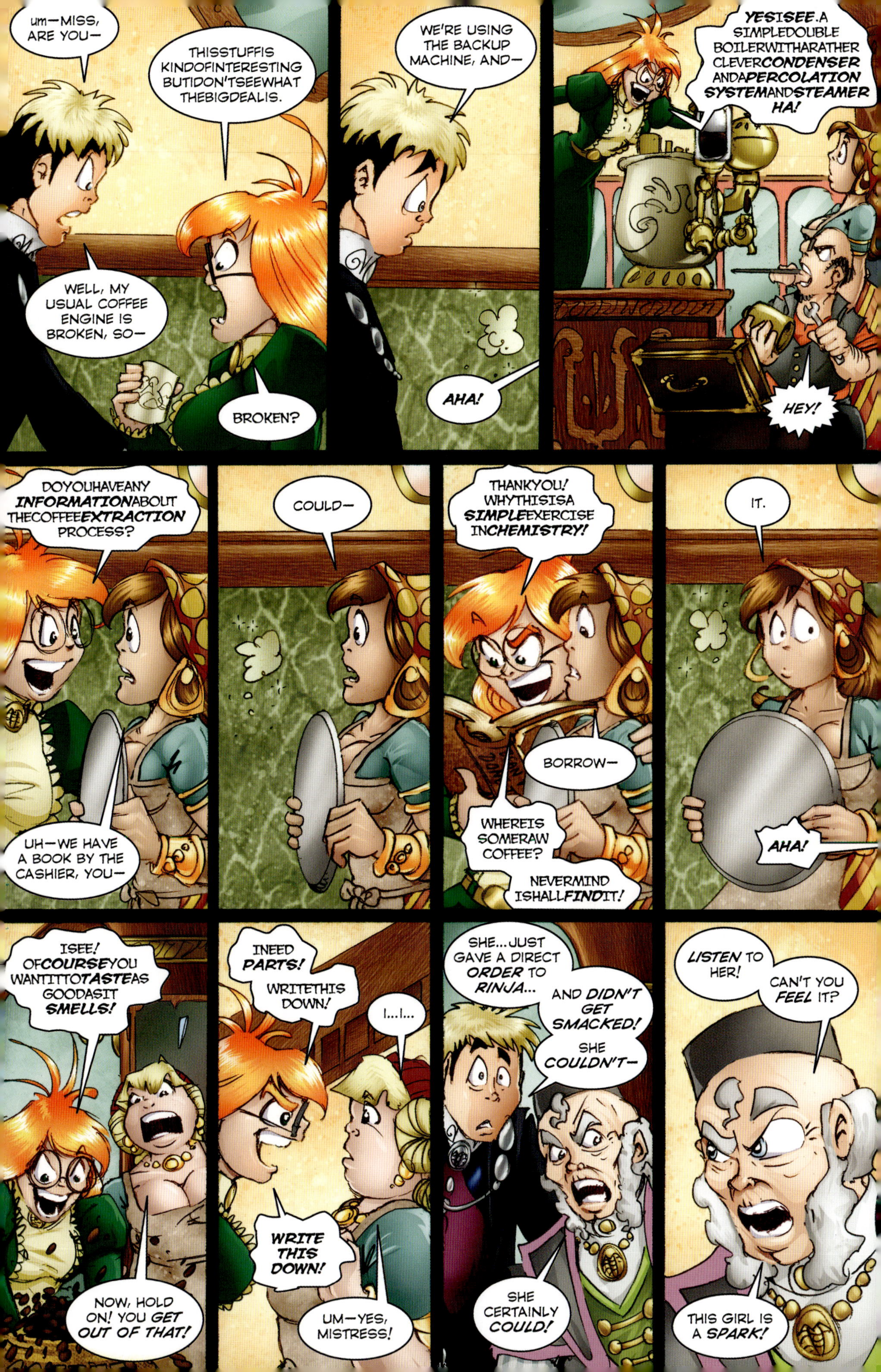
um—MISS, ARE YOU—
THIS STUFF IS KIND OF INTERESTING BUT I DON'T SEE WHAT THE BIG DEAL IS.
WELL, MY USUAL COFFEE ENGINE IS BROKEN, SO—
BROKEN?
WE'RE USING THE BACKUP MACHINE, AND—
AHA!
YES I SEE. A SIMPLE DOUBLE BOILER WITH A RATHER CLEVER **CONDENSER** AND A **PERCOLATION SYSTEM** AND **STEAMER** HA!
HEY!
DO YOU HAVE ANY **INFORMATION** ABOUT THE COFFEE **EXTRACTION** PROCESS?
UH—WE HAVE A BOOK BY THE CASHIER, YOU—
COULD—
THANK YOU! WHY THIS IS A **SIMPLE** EXERCISE IN **CHEMISTRY!**
BORROW—
WHERE IS SOME RAW COFFEE?
NEVER MIND I SHALL **FIND** IT!
IT.
AHA!
I SEE! OF **COURSE** YOU WANT IT TO **TASTE** AS GOOD AS IT **SMELLS!**
NOW, HOLD ON! YOU **GET OUT OF THAT!**
I NEED **PARTS!**
WRITE THIS DOWN!
I...I...
WRITE THIS DOWN!
UM—YES, MISTRESS!
SHE... JUST GAVE A DIRECT **ORDER** TO **RINJA...**
AND **DIDN'T GET SMACKED!**
SHE **COULDN'T—**
SHE CERTAINLY **COULD!**
LISTEN TO HER!
CAN'T YOU **FEEL** IT?
THIS GIRL IS A **SPARK!**

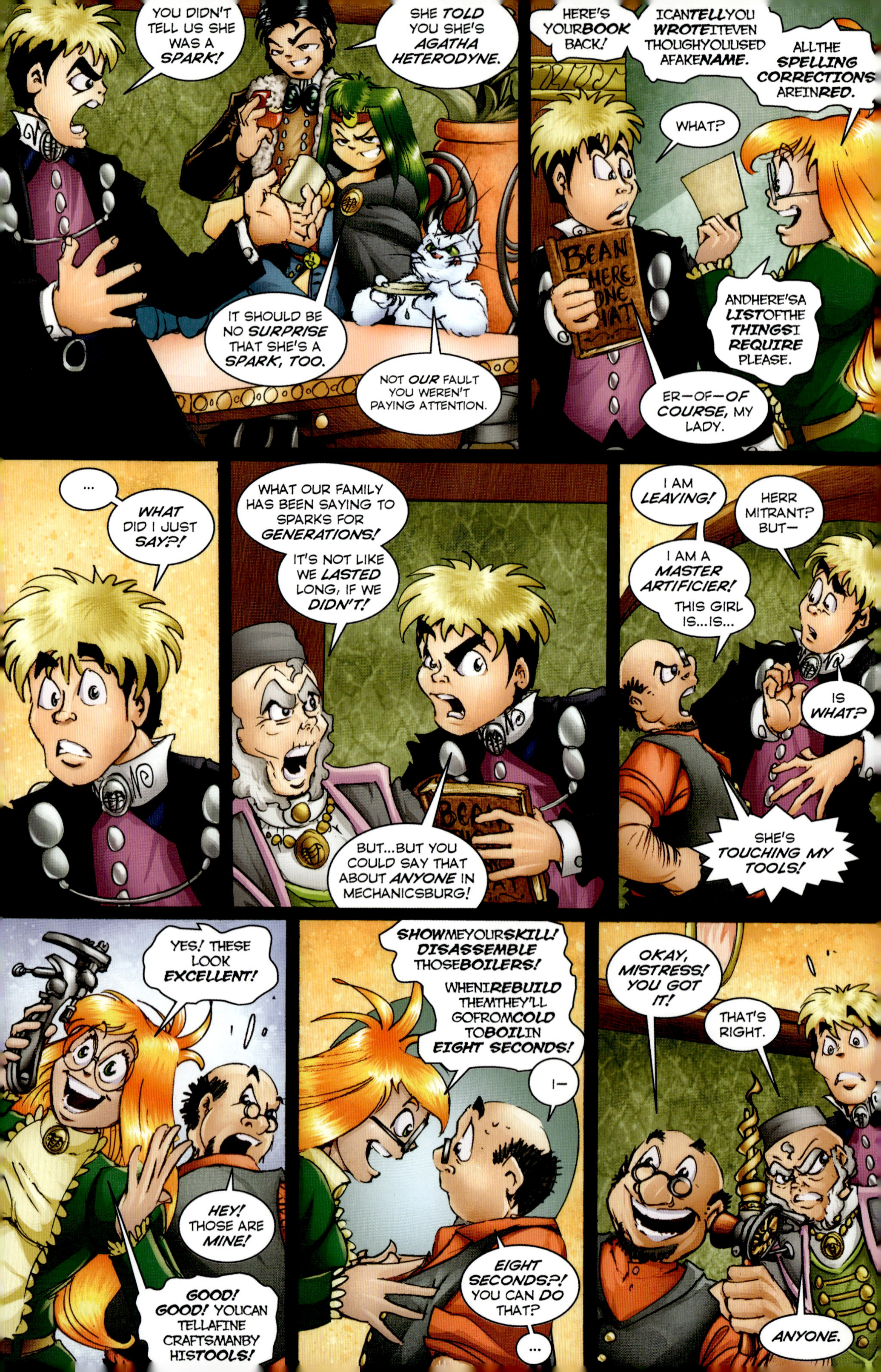

YOU DIDN'T TELL US SHE WAS A SPARK!
SHE TOLD YOU SHE'S AGATHA HETERODYNE.
IT SHOULD BE NO SURPRISE THAT SHE'S A SPARK, TOO.
NOT OUR FAULT YOU WEREN'T PAYING ATTENTION.
HERE'S YOUR BOOK BACK!
I CAN TELL YOU WROTE IT EVEN THOUGH YOU USED A FAKE NAME.
ALL THE SPELLING CORRECTIONS ARE IN RED.
WHAT?
AND HERE'S A LIST OF THE THINGS I REQUIRE PLEASE.
ER—OF—OF COURSE, MY LADY.
...
WHAT DID I JUST SAY?!
WHAT OUR FAMILY HAS BEEN SAYING TO SPARKS FOR GENERATIONS!
IT'S NOT LIKE WE LASTED LONG, IF WE DIDN'T!
BUT...BUT YOU COULD SAY THAT ABOUT ANYONE IN MECHANICSBURG!
I AM LEAVING!
HERR MITRANT? BUT—
I AM A MASTER ARTIFICIER! THIS GIRL IS...IS...
IS WHAT?
SHE'S TOUCHING MY TOOLS!
YES! THESE LOOK EXCELLENT!
HEY! THOSE ARE MINE!
GOOD! GOOD! YOU CAN TELL A FINE CRAFTSMAN BY HIS TOOLS!
SHOW ME YOUR SKILL! DISASSEMBLE THOSE BOILERS!
WHEN I REBUILD THEM THEY'LL GO FROM COLD TO BOIL IN EIGHT SECONDS!
I—
EIGHT SECONDS?! YOU CAN DO THAT?
...
OKAY, MISTRESS! YOU GOT IT!
THAT'S RIGHT.
ANYONE.

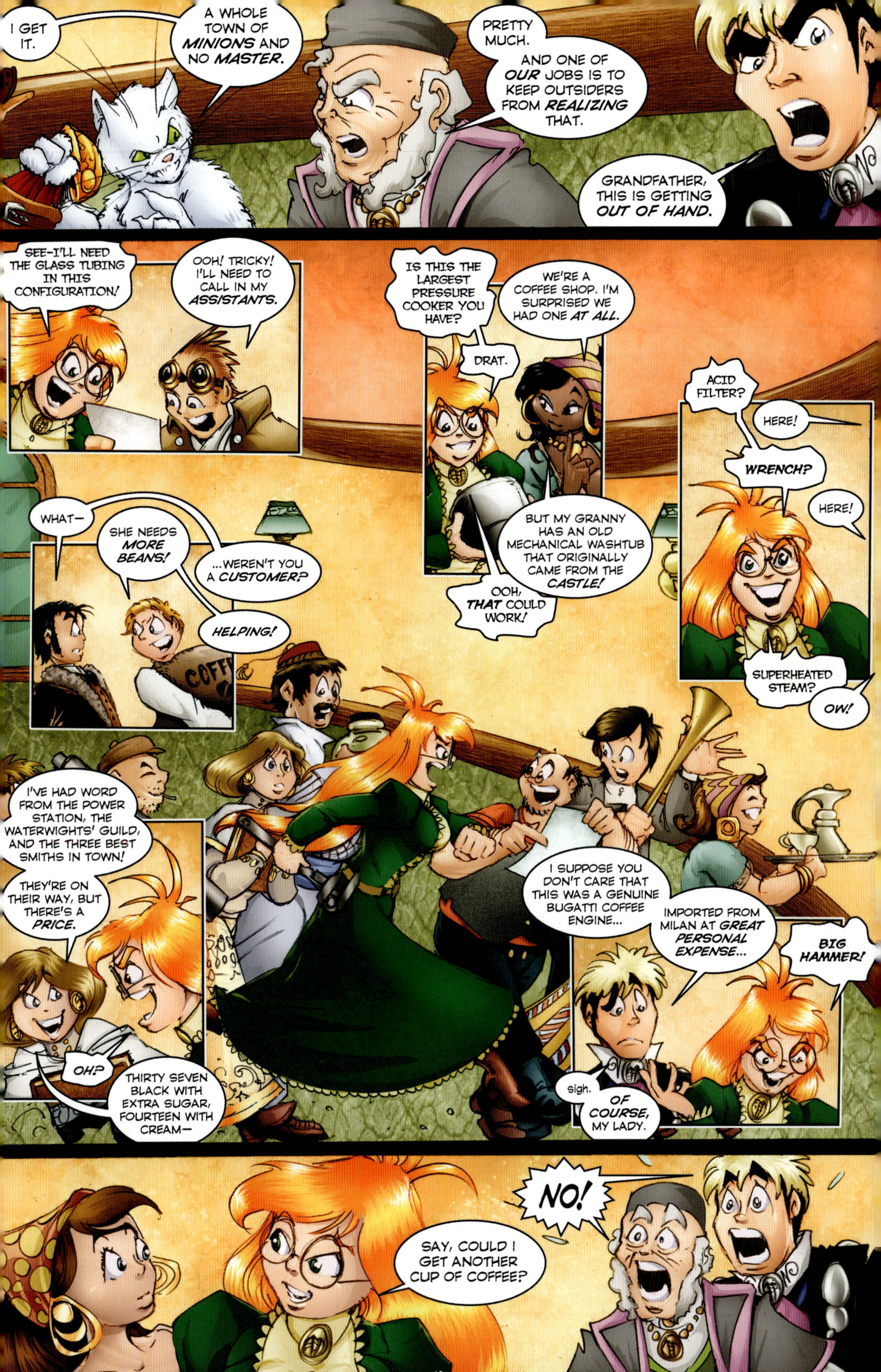
I GET IT.
A WHOLE TOWN OF MINIONS AND NO MASTER.
PRETTY MUCH.
AND ONE OF OUR JOBS IS TO KEEP OUTSIDERS FROM REALIZING THAT.
GRANDFATHER, THIS IS GETTING OUT OF HAND.
SEE–I'LL NEED THE GLASS TUBING IN THIS CONFIGURATION!
OOH! TRICKY! I'LL NEED TO CALL IN MY ASSISTANTS.
IS THIS THE LARGEST PRESSURE COOKER YOU HAVE?
WE'RE A COFFEE SHOP. I'M SURPRISED WE HAD ONE AT ALL.
DRAT.
BUT MY GRANNY HAS AN OLD MECHANICAL WASHTUB THAT ORIGINALLY CAME FROM THE CASTLE!
OOH, THAT COULD WORK!
ACID FILTER?
HERE!
WRENCH?
HERE!
SUPERHEATED STEAM?
OW!
WHAT–
SHE NEEDS MORE BEANS!
...WEREN'T YOU A CUSTOMER?
HELPING!
COFF
I'VE HAD WORD FROM THE POWER STATION, THE WATERWRIGHTS' GUILD, AND THE THREE BEST SMITHS IN TOWN!
THEY'RE ON THEIR WAY, BUT THERE'S A PRICE.
OH?
THIRTY SEVEN BLACK WITH EXTRA SUGAR, FOURTEEN WITH CREAM–
I SUPPOSE YOU DON'T CARE THAT THIS WAS A GENUINE BUGATTI COFFEE ENGINE...
IMPORTED FROM MILAN AT GREAT PERSONAL EXPENSE...
BIG HAMMER!
sigh.
OF COURSE, MY LADY.
SAY, COULD I GET ANOTHER CUP OF COFFEE?
NO!

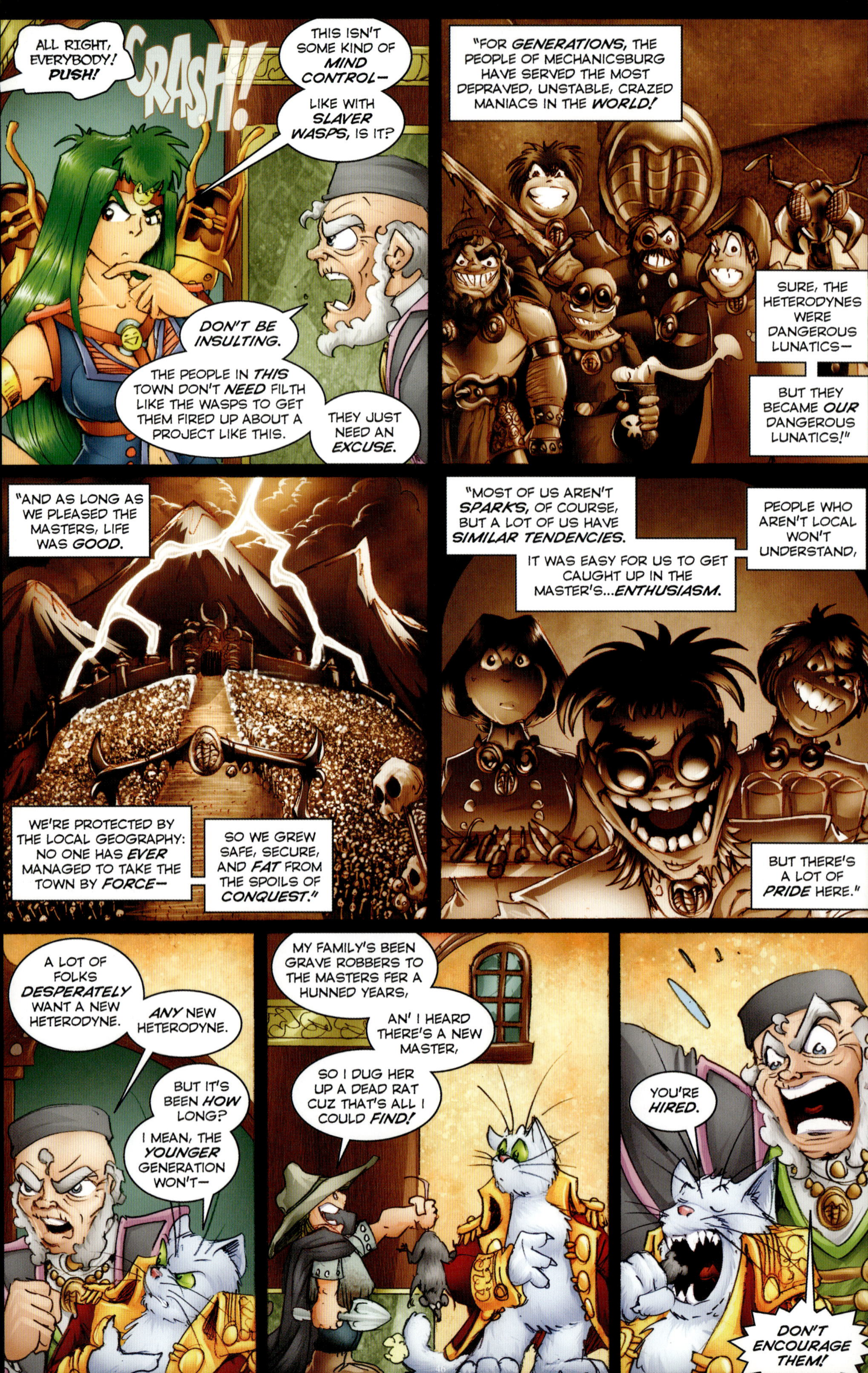
ALL RIGHT, EVERYBODY! PUSH!
CRASH!
THIS ISN'T SOME KIND OF MIND CONTROL—
LIKE WITH SLAVER WASPS, IS IT?
DON'T BE INSULTING.
THE PEOPLE IN THIS TOWN DON'T NEED FILTH LIKE THE WASPS TO GET THEM FIRED UP ABOUT A PROJECT LIKE THIS.
THEY JUST NEED AN EXCUSE.
"FOR GENERATIONS, THE PEOPLE OF MECHANICSBURG HAVE SERVED THE MOST DEPRAVED, UNSTABLE, CRAZED MANIACS IN THE WORLD!
SURE, THE HETERODYNES WERE DANGEROUS LUNATICS—
BUT THEY BECAME OUR DANGEROUS LUNATICS!"
"AND AS LONG AS WE PLEASED THE MASTERS, LIFE WAS GOOD.
WE'RE PROTECTED BY THE LOCAL GEOGRAPHY: NO ONE HAS EVER MANAGED TO TAKE THE TOWN BY FORCE—
SO WE GREW SAFE, SECURE, AND FAT FROM THE SPOILS OF CONQUEST."
"MOST OF US AREN'T SPARKS, OF COURSE, BUT A LOT OF US HAVE SIMILAR TENDENCIES.
IT WAS EASY FOR US TO GET CAUGHT UP IN THE MASTER'S...ENTHUSIASM.
PEOPLE WHO AREN'T LOCAL WON'T UNDERSTAND,
BUT THERE'S A LOT OF PRIDE HERE."
A LOT OF FOLKS DESPERATELY WANT A NEW HETERODYNE.
ANY NEW HETERODYNE.
BUT IT'S BEEN HOW LONG?
I MEAN, THE YOUNGER GENERATION WON'T—
MY FAMILY'S BEEN GRAVE ROBBERS TO THE MASTERS FER A HUNNED YEARS,
AN' I HEARD THERE'S A NEW MASTER,
SO I DUG HER UP A DEAD RAT CUZ THAT'S ALL I COULD FIND!
YOU'RE HIRED.
DON'T ENCOURAGE THEM!

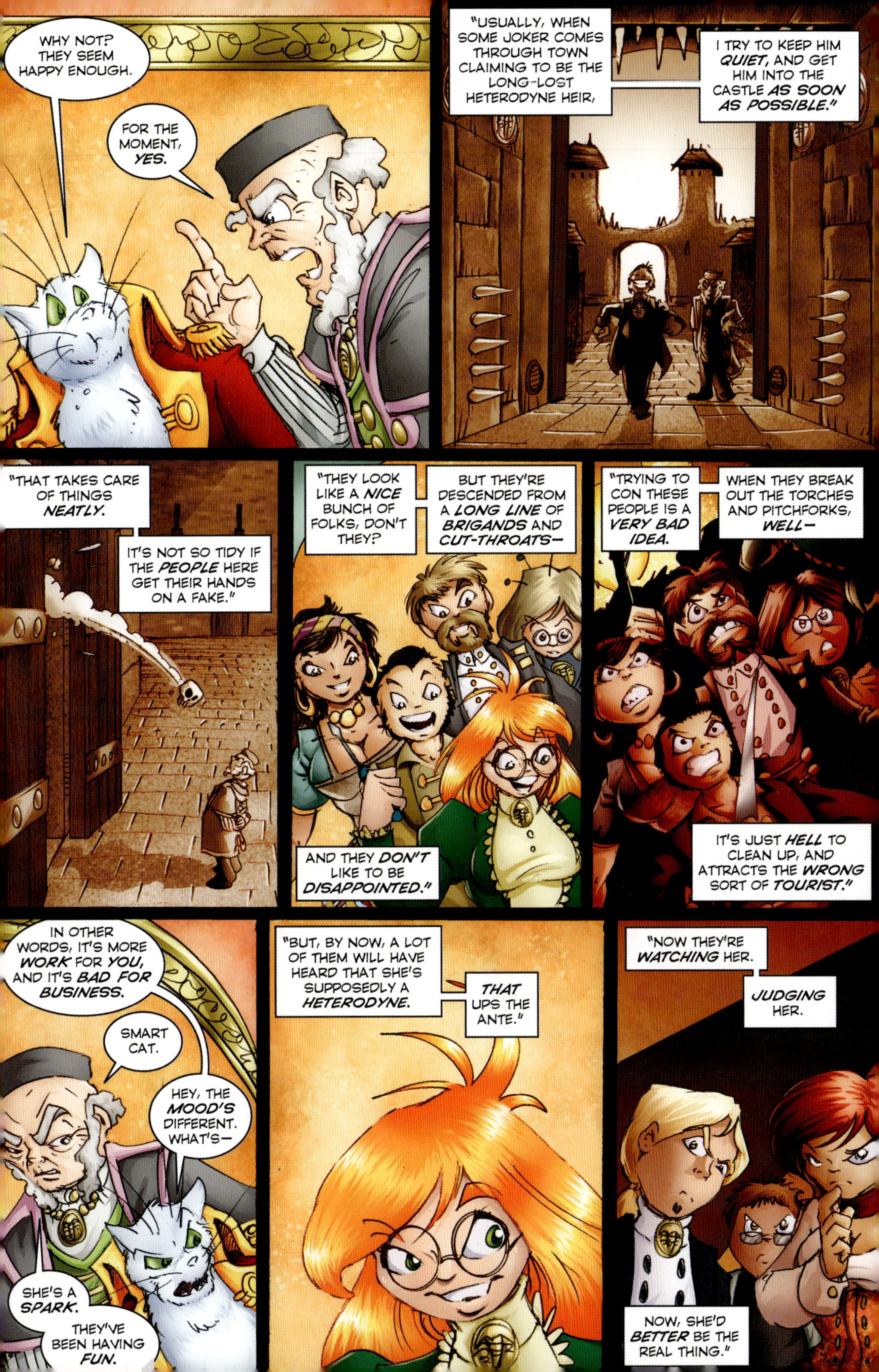
WHY NOT? THEY SEEM HAPPY ENOUGH.
FOR THE MOMENT, *YES.*
"USUALLY, WHEN SOME JOKER COMES THROUGH TOWN CLAIMING TO BE THE LONG-LOST HETERODYNE HEIR,
I TRY TO KEEP HIM *QUIET,* AND GET HIM INTO THE CASTLE *AS SOON AS POSSIBLE."*
"THAT TAKES CARE OF THINGS *NEATLY.*
IT'S NOT SO TIDY IF THE *PEOPLE* HERE GET THEIR HANDS ON A FAKE."
"THEY LOOK LIKE A *NICE* BUNCH OF FOLKS, DON'T THEY?
BUT THEY'RE DESCENDED FROM A *LONG LINE* OF *BRIGANDS* AND *CUT-THROATS—*
AND THEY *DON'T* LIKE TO BE *DISAPPOINTED."*
"TRYING TO CON THESE PEOPLE IS A *VERY BAD IDEA.*
WHEN THEY BREAK OUT THE TORCHES AND PITCHFORKS, *WELL—*
IT'S JUST *HELL* TO CLEAN UP, AND ATTRACTS THE *WRONG* SORT OF *TOURIST."*
IN OTHER WORDS, IT'S MORE *WORK* FOR *YOU,* AND IT'S *BAD FOR BUSINESS.*
SMART CAT.
HEY, THE *MOOD'S* DIFFERENT. WHAT'S—
SHE'S A *SPARK.*
THEY'VE BEEN HAVING *FUN.*
"BUT, BY NOW, A LOT OF THEM WILL HAVE HEARD THAT SHE'S SUPPOSEDLY A *HETERODYNE.*
THAT UPS THE ANTE."
"NOW THEY'RE *WATCHING* HER.
JUDGING HER.
NOW, SHE'D *BETTER* BE THE REAL THING."

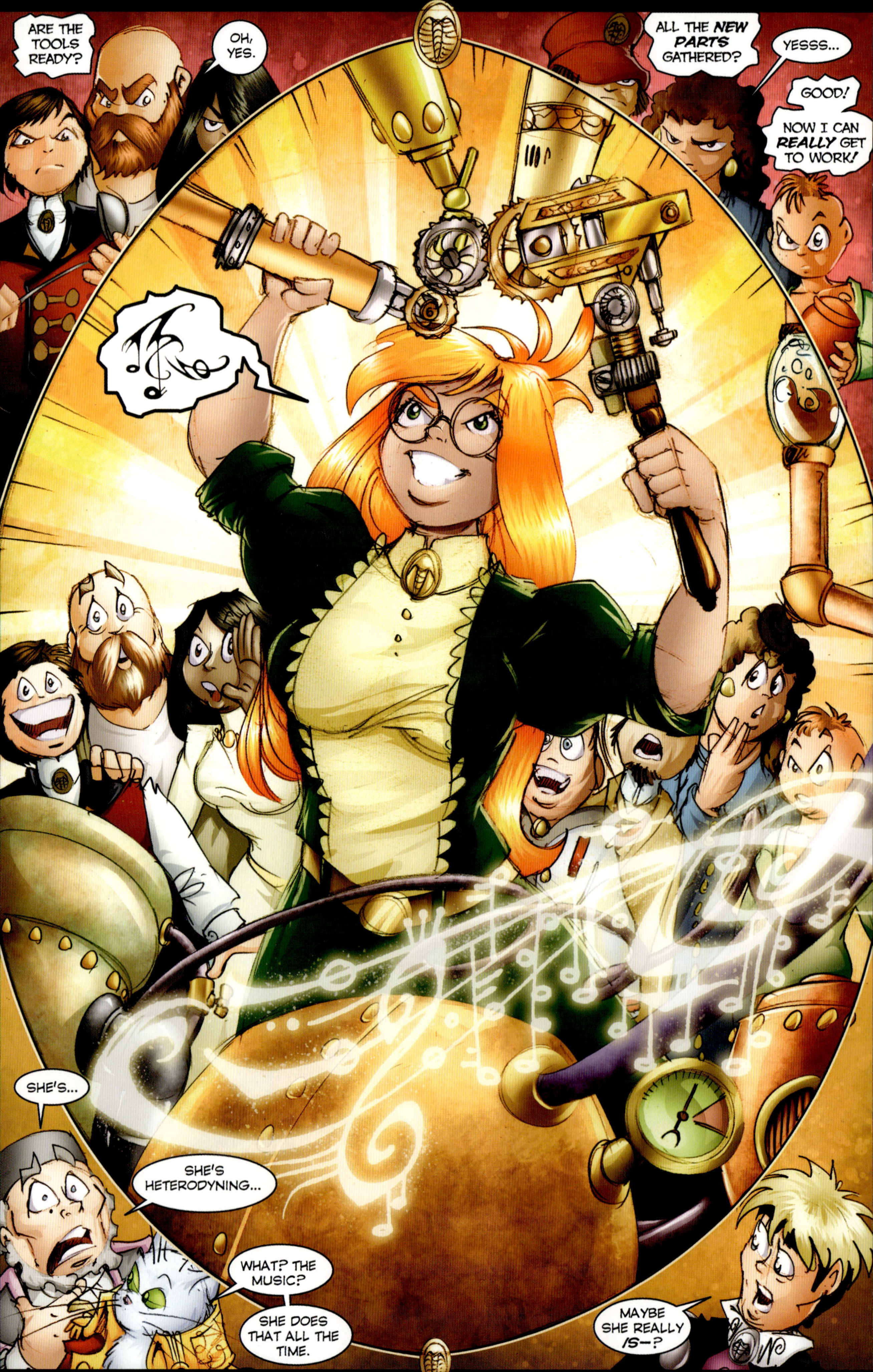

ARE THE TOOLS READY?
OH, YES.
ALL THE NEW PARTS GATHERED?
YESSS...
GOOD!
NOW I CAN REALLY GET TO WORK!
SHE'S...
SHE'S HETERODYNING...
WHAT? THE MUSIC?
SHE DOES THAT ALL THE TIME.
MAYBE SHE REALLY IS—?

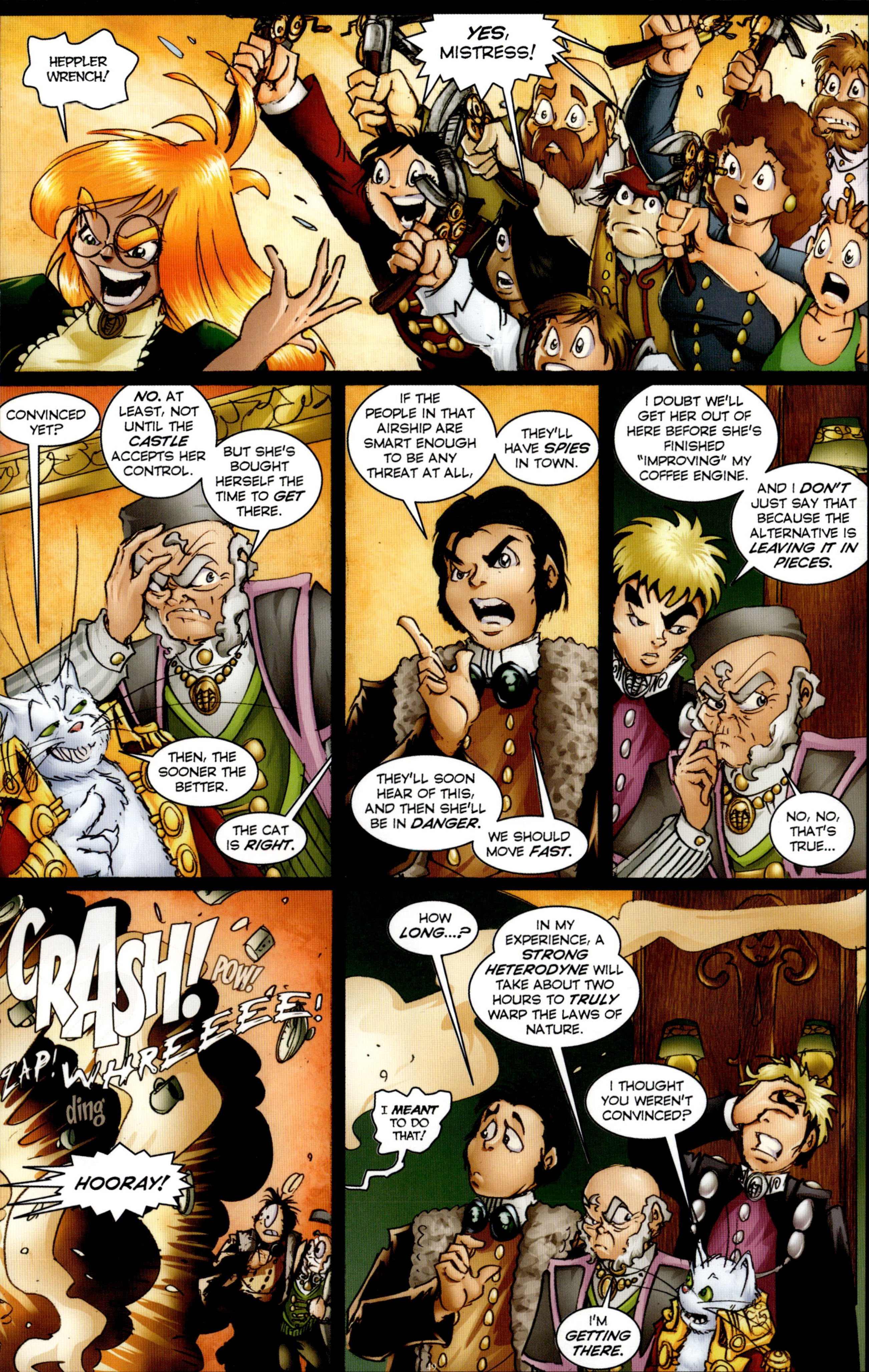
HEPPLER WRENCH!
YES, MISTRESS!
CONVINCED YET?
NO. AT LEAST, NOT UNTIL THE CASTLE ACCEPTS HER CONTROL.
BUT SHE'S BOUGHT HERSELF THE TIME TO GET THERE.
THEN, THE SOONER THE BETTER.
THE CAT IS RIGHT.
IF THE PEOPLE IN THAT AIRSHIP ARE SMART ENOUGH TO BE ANY THREAT AT ALL,
THEY'LL HAVE SPIES IN TOWN.
THEY'LL SOON HEAR OF THIS, AND THEN SHE'LL BE IN DANGER.
WE SHOULD MOVE FAST.
I DOUBT WE'LL GET HER OUT OF HERE BEFORE SHE'S FINISHED "IMPROVING" MY COFFEE ENGINE.
AND I DON'T JUST SAY THAT BECAUSE THE ALTERNATIVE IS LEAVING IT IN PIECES.
NO, NO, THAT'S TRUE...
CRASH!
POW!
WHREEEEEE!
ZAP!
ding
HOORAY!
HOW LONG...?
IN MY EXPERIENCE, A STRONG HETERODYNE WILL TAKE ABOUT TWO HOURS TO TRULY WARP THE LAWS OF NATURE.
I MEANT TO DO THAT!
I THOUGHT YOU WEREN'T CONVINCED?
I'M GETTING THERE.

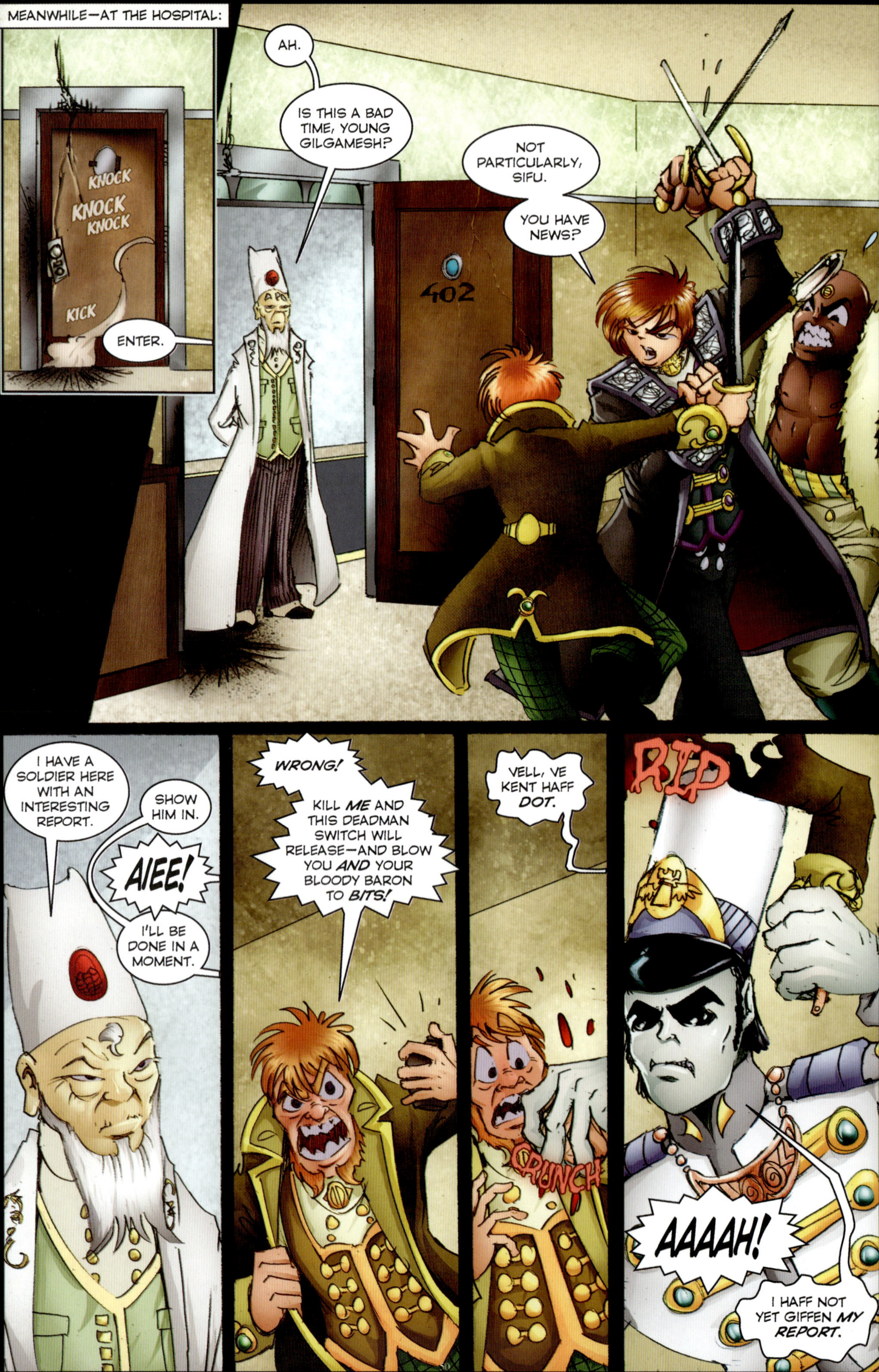

MEANWHILE—AT THE HOSPITAL:
KNOCK
KNOCK
KNOCK
KICK
ENTER.
AH.
IS THIS A BAD TIME, YOUNG GILGAMESH?
NOT PARTICULARLY, SIFU.
YOU HAVE NEWS?
402
I HAVE A SOLDIER HERE WITH AN INTERESTING REPORT.
SHOW HIM IN.
AIEE!
I'LL BE DONE IN A MOMENT.
WRONG!
KILL ME AND THIS DEADMAN SWITCH WILL RELEASE—AND BLOW YOU AND YOUR BLOODY BARON TO BITS!
VELL, VE KENT HAFF DOT.
CRUNCH
RIP
AAAAH!
I HAFF NOT YET GIFFEN MY REPORT.

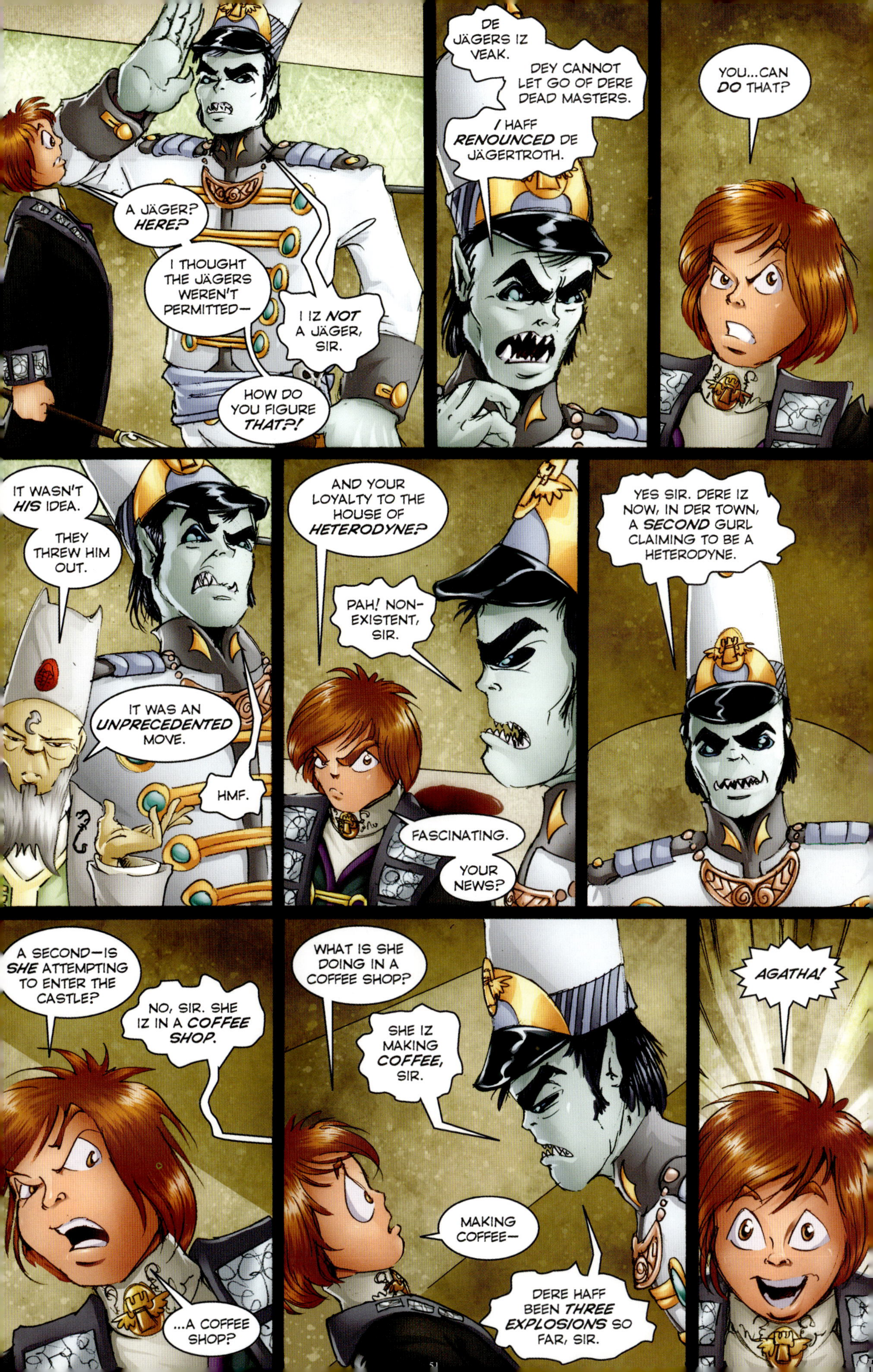
A JÄGER? HERE?
I THOUGHT THE JÄGERS WEREN'T PERMITTED—
I IZ NOT A JÄGER, SIR.
HOW DO YOU FIGURE THAT?!
DE JÄGERS IZ VEAK.
DEY CANNOT LET GO OF DERE DEAD MASTERS.
I HAFF RENOUNCED DE JÄGERTROTH.
YOU...CAN DO THAT?
IT WASN'T HIS IDEA.
THEY THREW HIM OUT.
IT WAS AN UNPRECEDENTED MOVE.
HMF.
AND YOUR LOYALTY TO THE HOUSE OF HETERODYNE?
PAH! NON-EXISTENT, SIR.
FASCINATING.
YOUR NEWS?
YES SIR. DERE IZ NOW, IN DER TOWN, A SECOND GURL CLAIMING TO BE A HETERODYNE.
A SECOND—IS SHE ATTEMPTING TO ENTER THE CASTLE?
NO, SIR. SHE IZ IN A COFFEE SHOP.
...A COFFEE SHOP?
WHAT IS SHE DOING IN A COFFEE SHOP?
SHE IZ MAKING COFFEE, SIR.
MAKING COFFEE—
DERE HAFF BEEN THREE EXPLOSIONS SO FAR, SIR.
AGATHA!

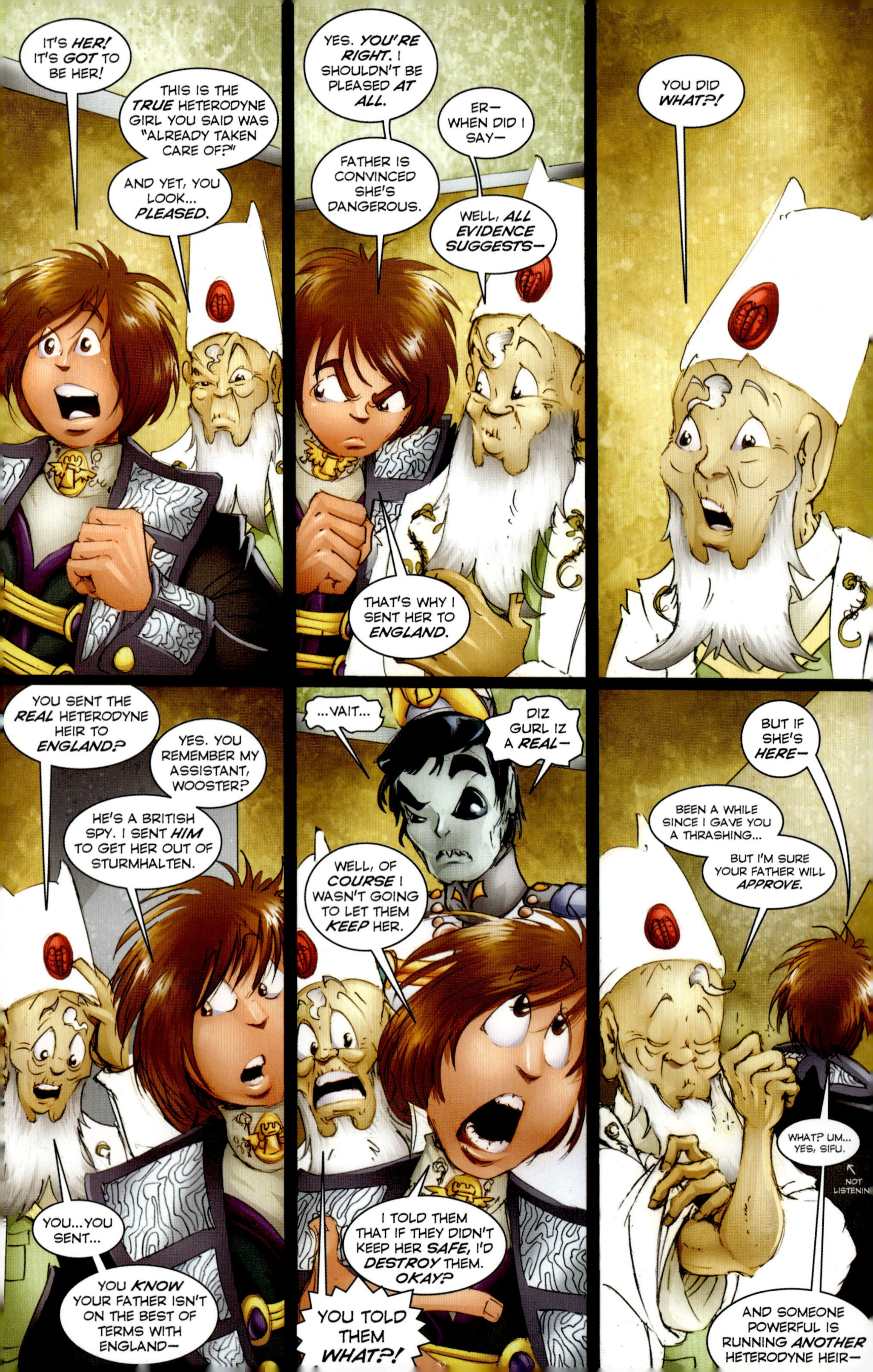
IT'S HER! IT'S GOT TO BE HER!
THIS IS THE TRUE HETERODYNE GIRL YOU SAID WAS "ALREADY TAKEN CARE OF?"
AND YET, YOU LOOK... PLEASED.
YES. YOU'RE RIGHT. I SHOULDN'T BE PLEASED AT ALL.
ER— WHEN DID I SAY—
FATHER IS CONVINCED SHE'S DANGEROUS.
WELL, ALL EVIDENCE SUGGESTS—
THAT'S WHY I SENT HER TO ENGLAND.
YOU DID WHAT?!
YOU SENT THE REAL HETERODYNE HEIR TO ENGLAND?
YES. YOU REMEMBER MY ASSISTANT, WOOSTER?
HE'S A BRITISH SPY. I SENT HIM TO GET HER OUT OF STURMHALTEN.
YOU...YOU SENT...
YOU KNOW YOUR FATHER ISN'T ON THE BEST OF TERMS WITH ENGLAND—
...VAIT...
DIZ GURL IZ A REAL—
WELL, OF COURSE I WASN'T GOING TO LET THEM KEEP HER.
I TOLD THEM THAT IF THEY DIDN'T KEEP HER SAFE, I'D DESTROY THEM. OKAY?
YOU TOLD THEM WHAT?!
BUT IF SHE'S HERE—
BEEN A WHILE SINCE I GAVE YOU A THRASHING...
BUT I'M SURE YOUR FATHER WILL APPROVE.
WHAT? UM... YES, SIFU.
NOT LISTENIN
AND SOMEONE POWERFUL IS RUNNING ANOTHER HETERODYNE HEIR—

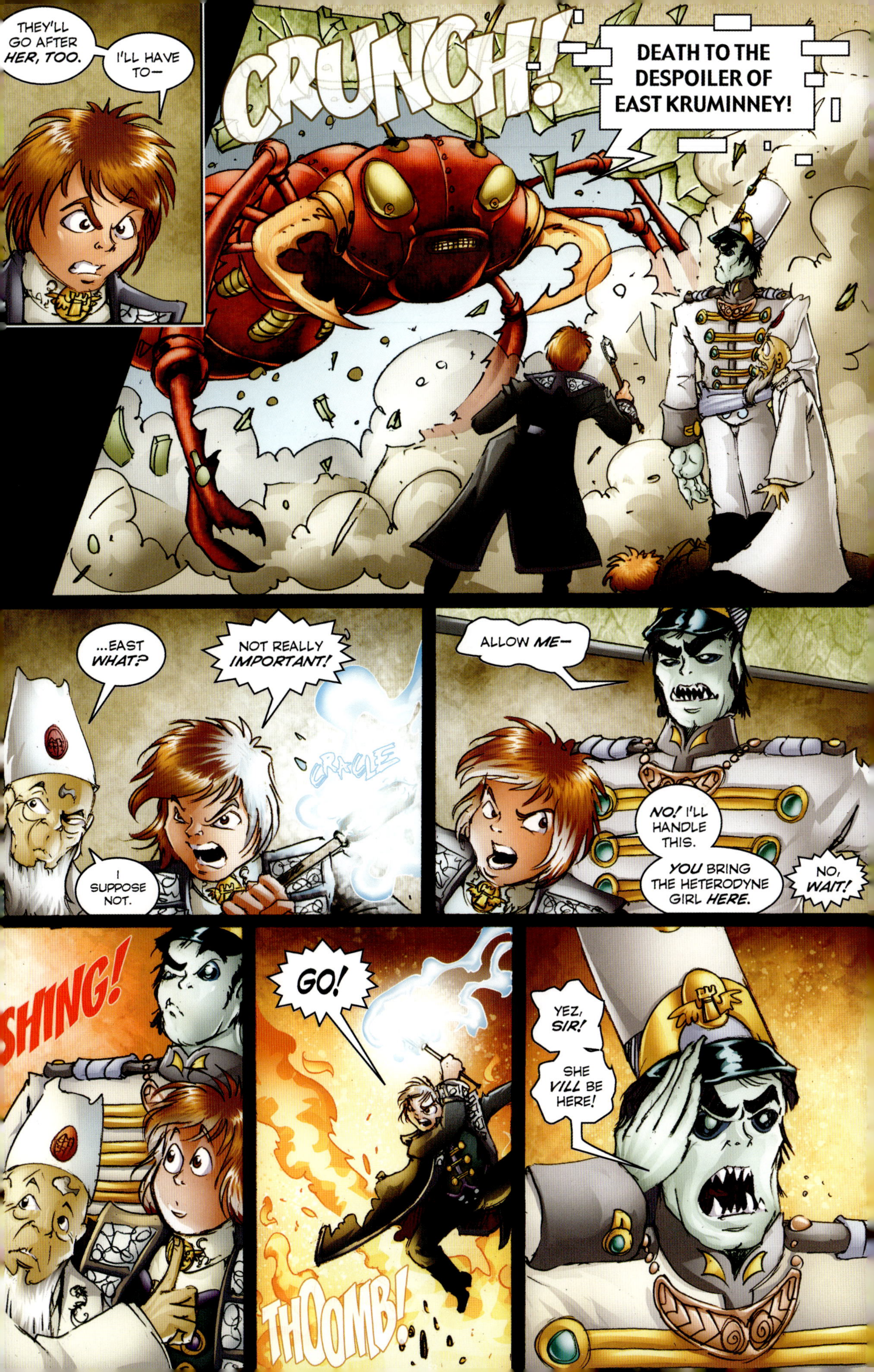
THEY'LL GO AFTER *HER, TOO.*
I'LL HAVE TO—
CRUNCH!
DEATH TO THE DESPOILER OF EAST KRUMINNEY!
...EAST *WHAT?*
NOT REALLY *IMPORTANT!*
I SUPPOSE NOT.
CRACLE
ALLOW *ME*—
NO! I'LL HANDLE THIS.
YOU BRING THE HETERODYNE GIRL *HERE.*
NO, *WAIT!*
SHING!
GO!
THOOMB!
YEZ, *SIR!*
SHE *VILL* BE HERE!

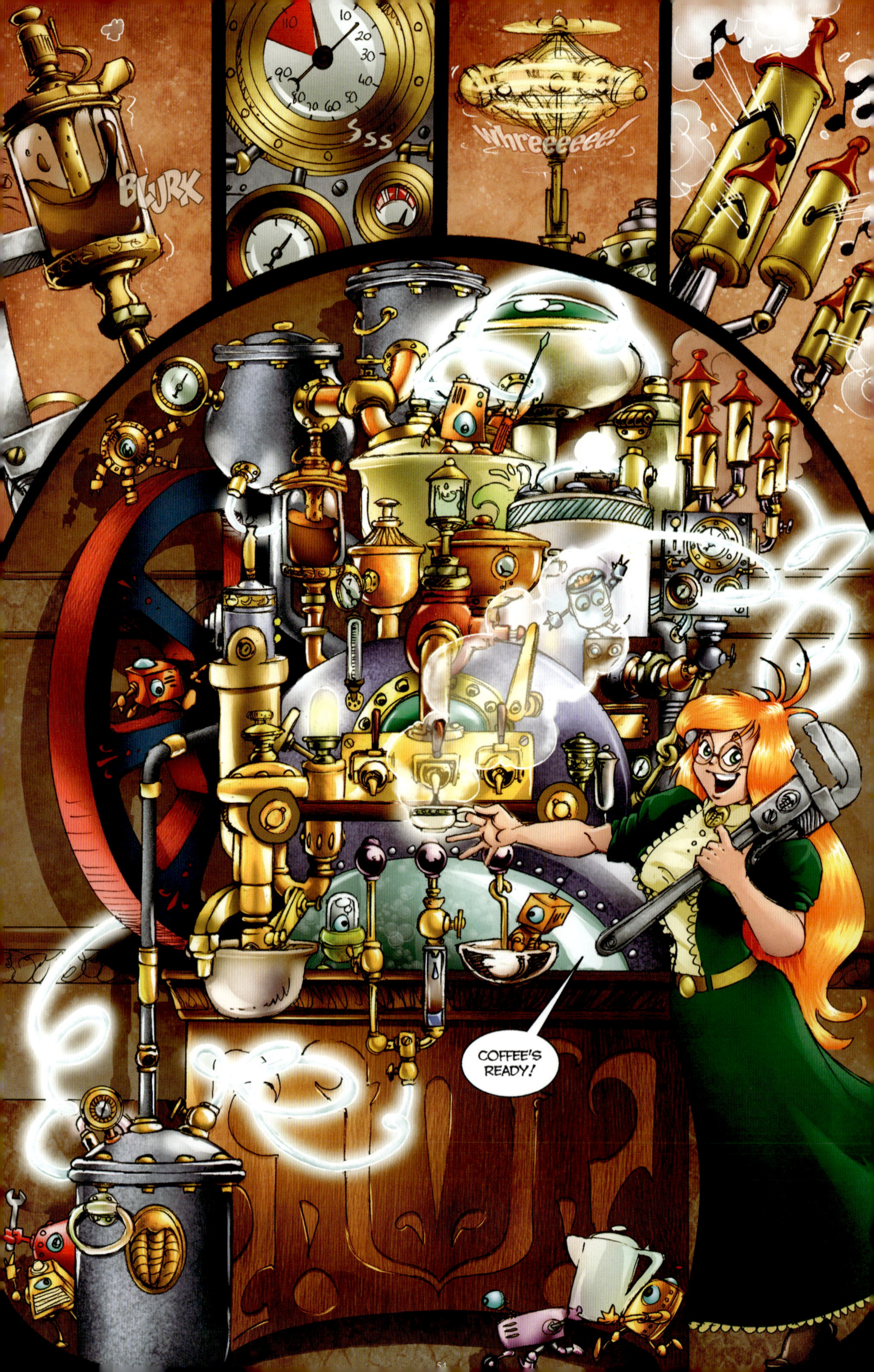
BLURK
Sss
Whreeeeeee!
COFFEE'S READY!

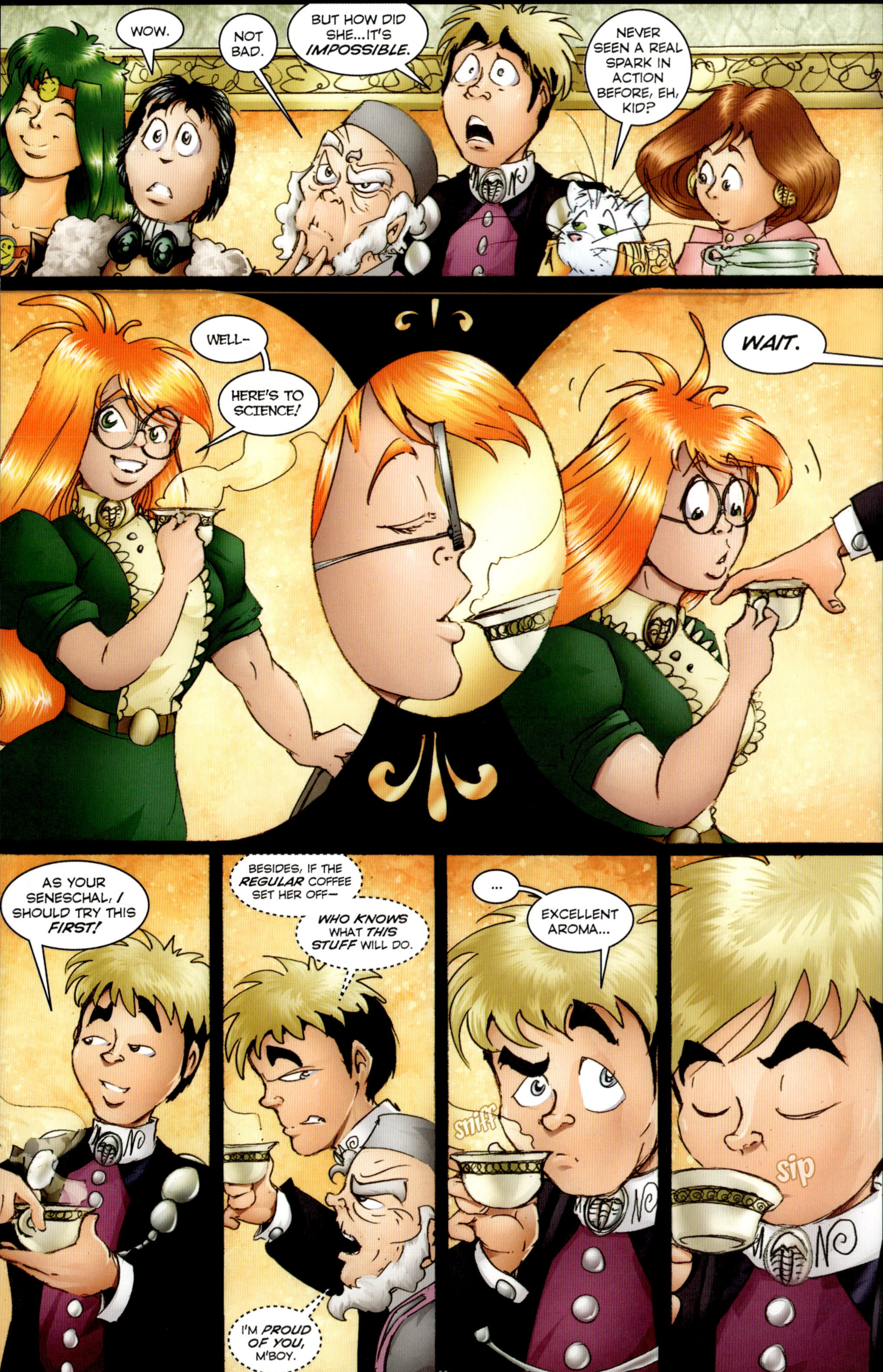
WOW.
NOT BAD.
BUT HOW DID SHE...IT'S *IMPOSSIBLE.*
NEVER SEEN A REAL SPARK IN ACTION BEFORE, EH, KID?
WELL-
HERE'S TO SCIENCE!
WAIT.
AS YOUR SENESCHAL, *I* SHOULD TRY THIS *FIRST!*
BESIDES, IF THE *REGULAR* COFFEE SET HER OFF—
WHO KNOWS WHAT *THIS STUFF* WILL DO.
I'M *PROUD OF YOU,* M'BOY.
...
EXCELLENT AROMA...
sniff
sip

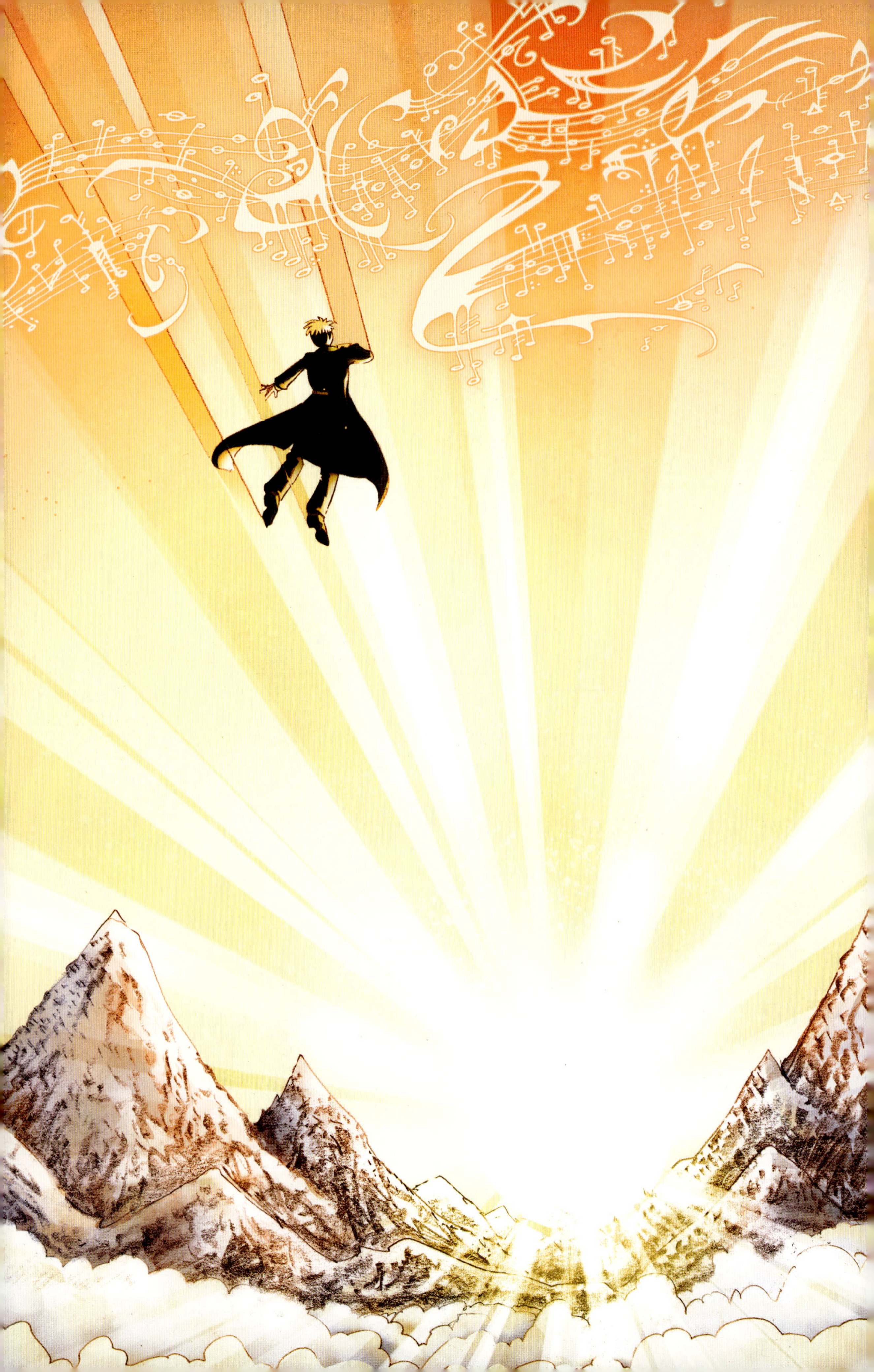

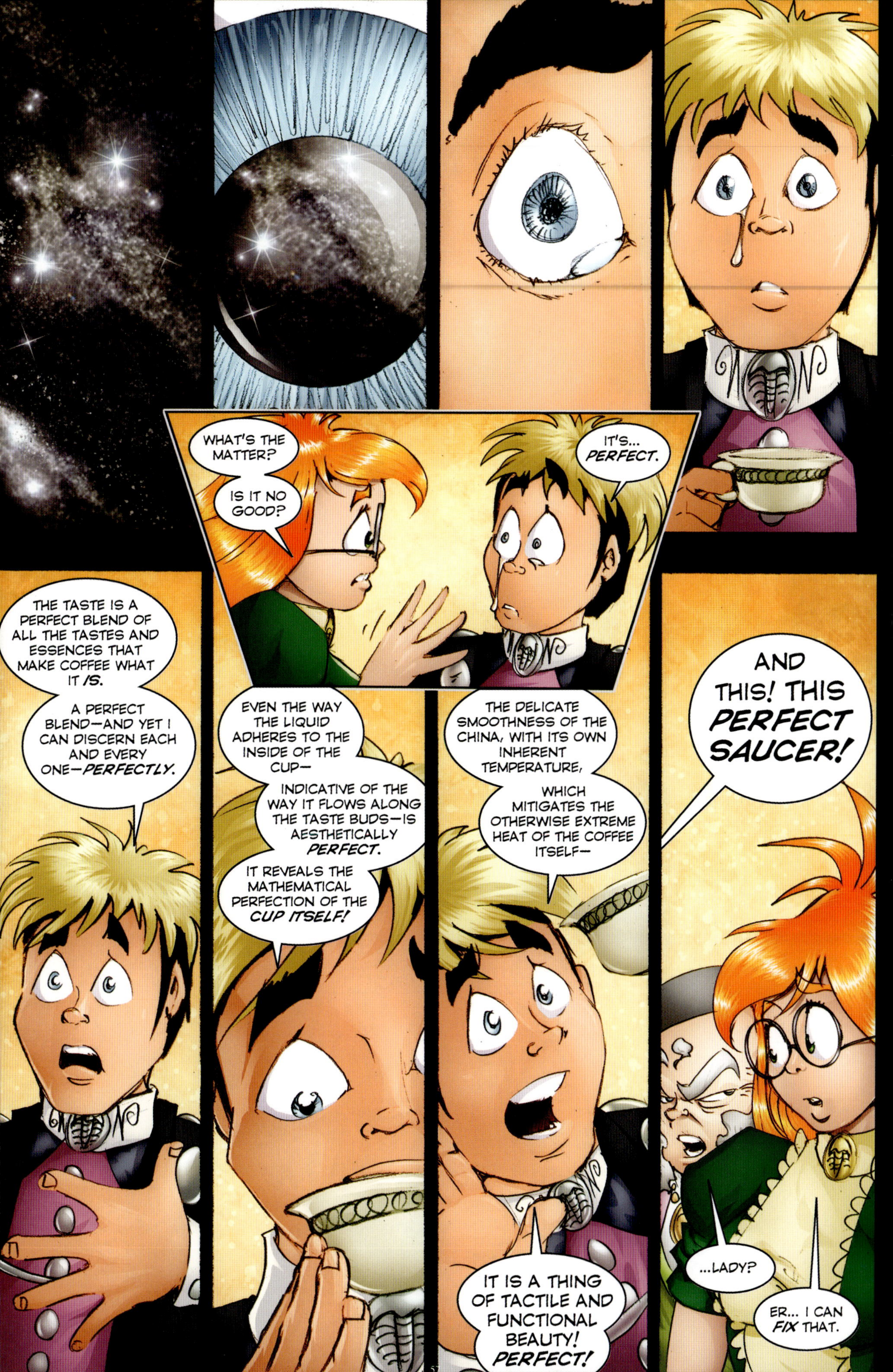
WHAT'S THE MATTER?
IS IT NO GOOD?
IT'S... PERFECT.
THE TASTE IS A PERFECT BLEND OF ALL THE TASTES AND ESSENCES THAT MAKE COFFEE WHAT IT IS.
A PERFECT BLEND—AND YET I CAN DISCERN EACH AND EVERY ONE—PERFECTLY.
EVEN THE WAY THE LIQUID ADHERES TO THE INSIDE OF THE CUP—
INDICATIVE OF THE WAY IT FLOWS ALONG THE TASTE BUDS—IS AESTHETICALLY PERFECT.
IT REVEALS THE MATHEMATICAL PERFECTION OF THE CUP ITSELF!
THE DELICATE SMOOTHNESS OF THE CHINA, WITH ITS OWN INHERENT TEMPERATURE,
WHICH MITIGATES THE OTHERWISE EXTREME HEAT OF THE COFFEE ITSELF—
IT IS A THING OF TACTILE AND FUNCTIONAL BEAUTY! PERFECT!
AND THIS! THIS PERFECT SAUCER!
...LADY?
ER... I CAN FIX THAT.

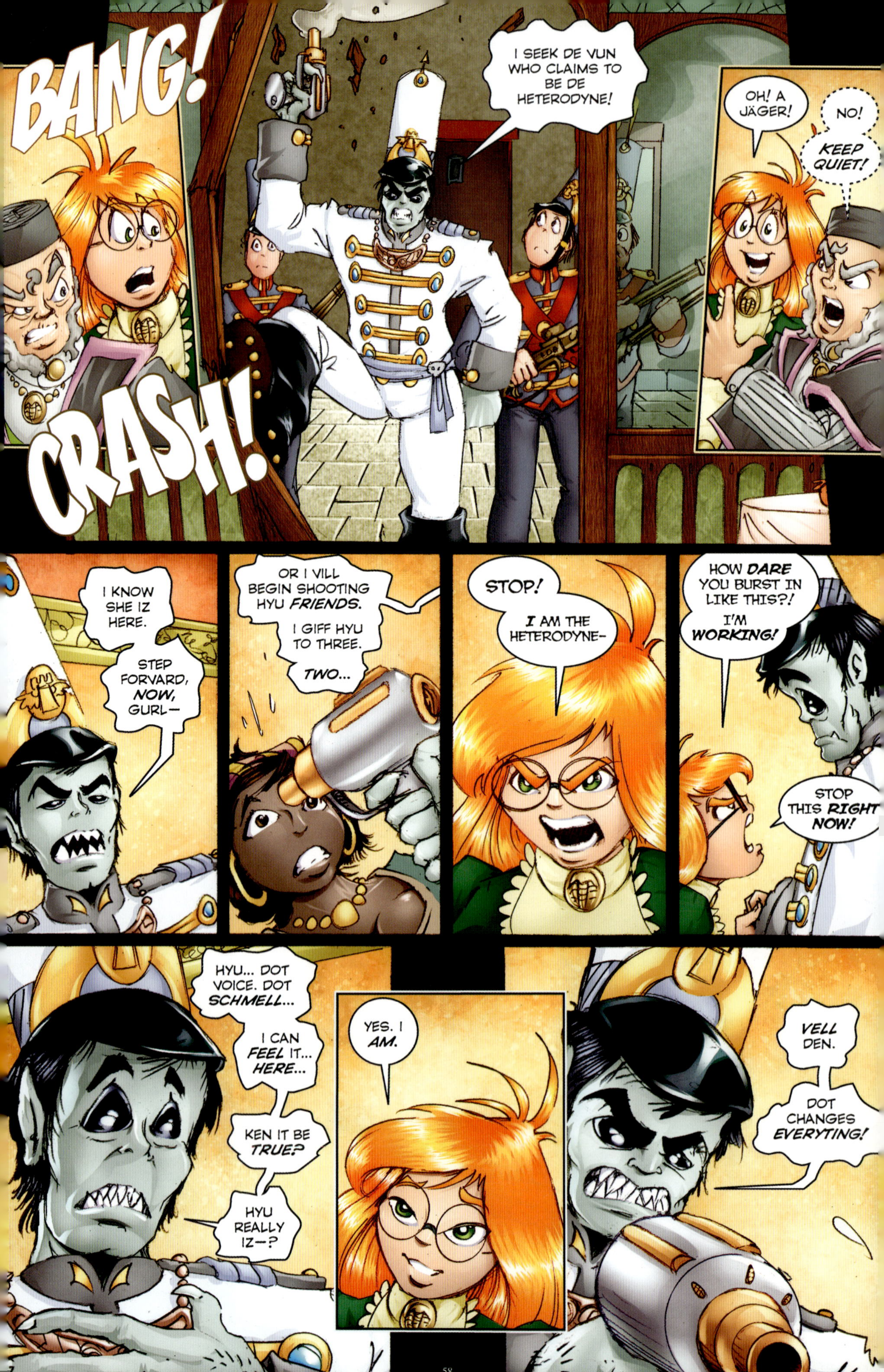
BANG!
I SEEK DE VUN WHO CLAIMS TO BE DE HETERODYNE!
CRASH!
OH! A JÄGER!
NO!
KEEP QUIET!
I KNOW SHE IZ HERE.
STEP FORVARD, NOW, GURL—
OR I VILL BEGIN SHOOTING HYU FRIENDS.
I GIFF HYU TO THREE.
TWO...
STOP!
I AM THE HETERODYNE—
HOW DARE YOU BURST IN LIKE THIS?!
I'M WORKING!
STOP THIS RIGHT NOW!
HYU... DOT VOICE. DOT SCHMELL...
I CAN FEEL IT... HERE...
KEN IT BE TRUE?
HYU REALLY IZ—?
YES. I AM.
VELL DEN.
DOT CHANGES EVERYTING!

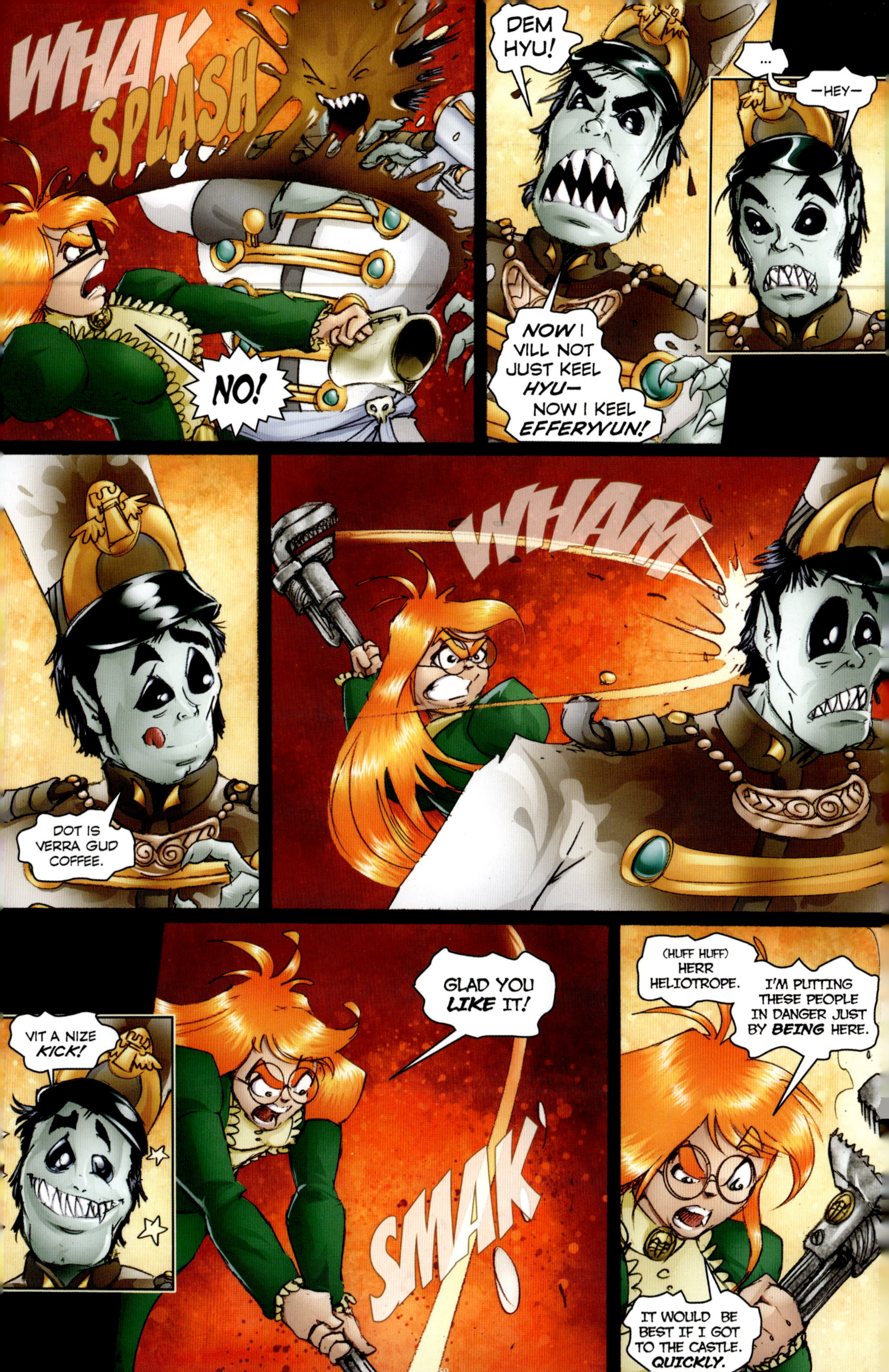
WHAK
SPLASH
NO!
DEM HYU!
NOW I VILL NOT JUST KEEL HYU—
NOW I KEEL EFFERYVUN!
...
—HEY—
DOT IS VERRA GUD COFFEE.
WHAM
VIT A NIZE KICK!
GLAD YOU LIKE IT!
SMAK
(HUFF HUFF) HERR HELIOTROPE.
I'M PUTTING THESE PEOPLE IN DANGER JUST BY BEING HERE.
IT WOULD BE BEST IF I GOT TO THE CASTLE. QUICKLY.

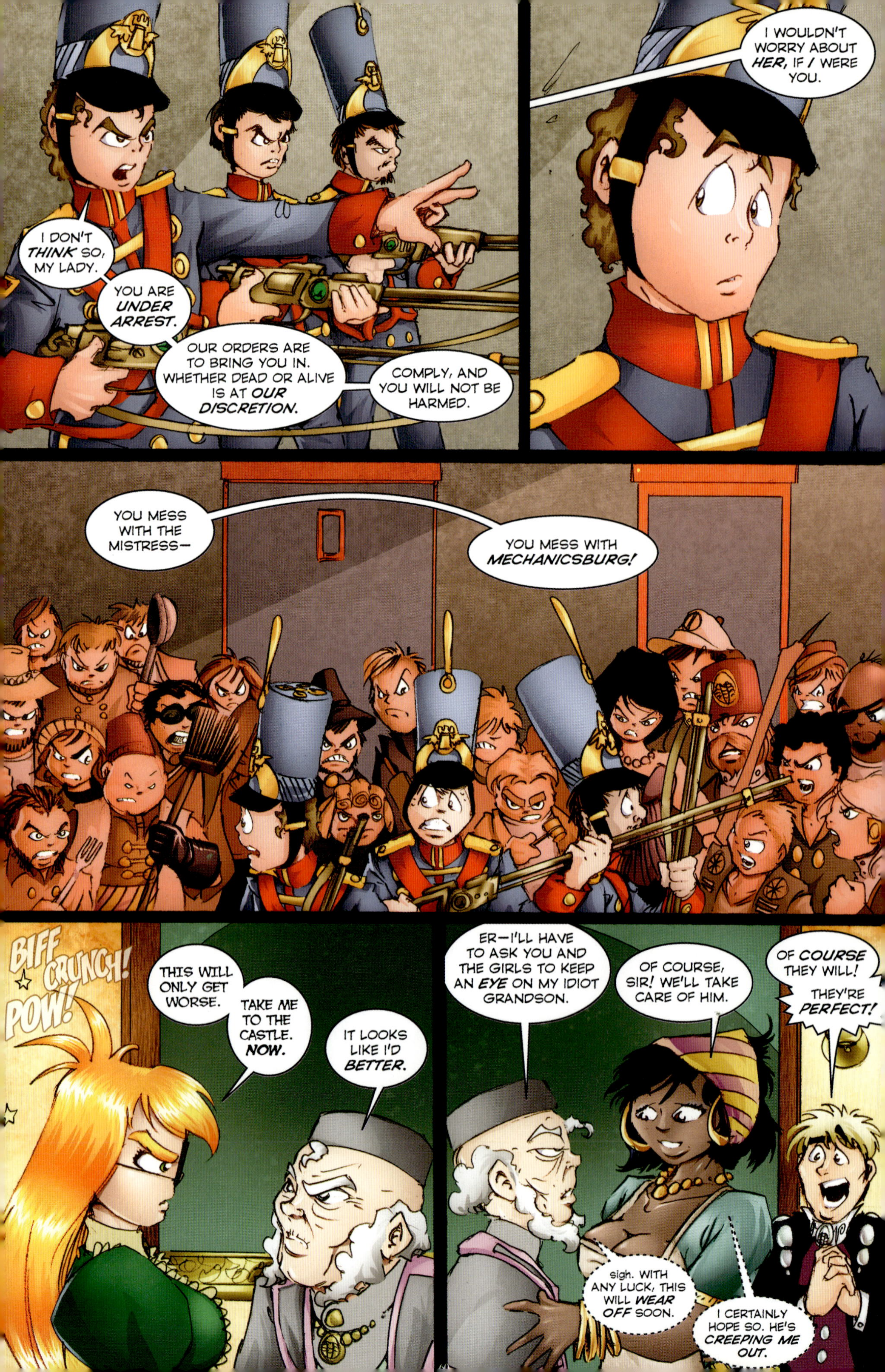
I DON'T THINK SO, MY LADY.
YOU ARE UNDER ARREST.
OUR ORDERS ARE TO BRING YOU IN. WHETHER DEAD OR ALIVE IS AT OUR DISCRETION.
COMPLY, AND YOU WILL NOT BE HARMED.
I WOULDN'T WORRY ABOUT HER, IF I WERE YOU.
YOU MESS WITH THE MISTRESS—
YOU MESS WITH MECHANICSBURG!
BIFF
CRUNCH!
POW!
THIS WILL ONLY GET WORSE.
TAKE ME TO THE CASTLE. NOW.
IT LOOKS LIKE I'D BETTER.
ER—I'LL HAVE TO ASK YOU AND THE GIRLS TO KEEP AN EYE ON MY IDIOT GRANDSON.
OF COURSE, SIR! WE'LL TAKE CARE OF HIM.
OF COURSE THEY WILL!
THEY'RE PERFECT!
sigh. WITH ANY LUCK, THIS WILL WEAR OFF SOON.
I CERTAINLY HOPE SO. HE'S CREEPING ME OUT.

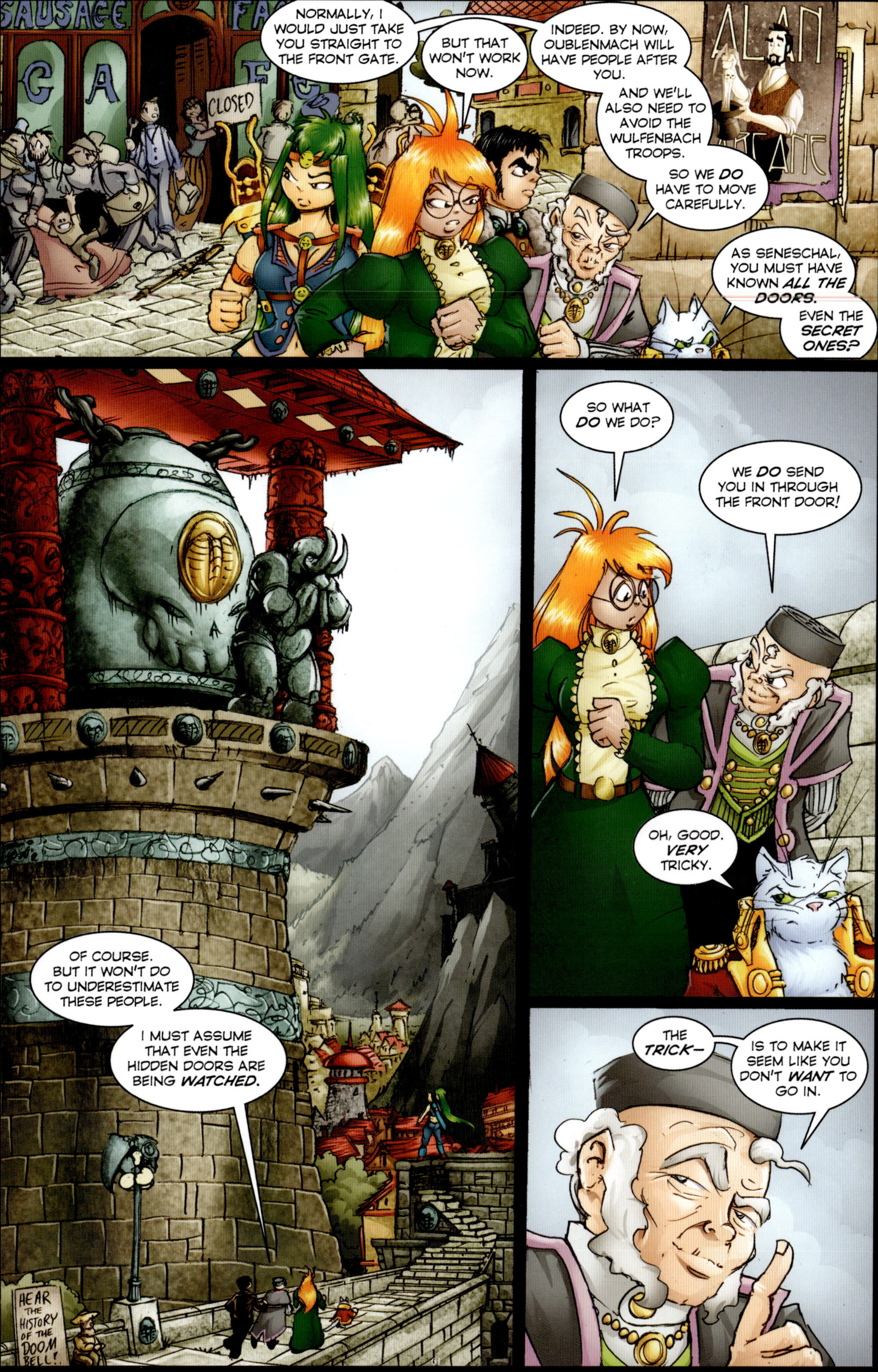
SAUSAGE FA
CLOSED
NORMALLY, I WOULD JUST TAKE YOU STRAIGHT TO THE FRONT GATE.
BUT THAT WON'T WORK NOW.
INDEED. BY NOW, OUBLENMACH WILL HAVE PEOPLE AFTER YOU.
AND WE'LL ALSO NEED TO AVOID THE WULFENBACH TROOPS.
SO WE *DO* HAVE TO MOVE CAREFULLY.
ALAN
AS SENESCHAL, YOU MUST HAVE KNOWN *ALL THE DOORS.*
EVEN THE *SECRET ONES?*
OF COURSE. BUT IT WON'T DO TO UNDERESTIMATE THESE PEOPLE.
I MUST ASSUME THAT EVEN THE HIDDEN DOORS ARE BEING *WATCHED.*
HEAR THE HISTORY OF THE DOOM BELL!
SO WHAT *DO* WE DO?
WE *DO* SEND YOU IN THROUGH THE FRONT DOOR!
OH, GOOD. *VERY* TRICKY.
THE *TRICK*—
IS TO MAKE IT SEEM LIKE YOU DON'T *WANT* TO GO IN.

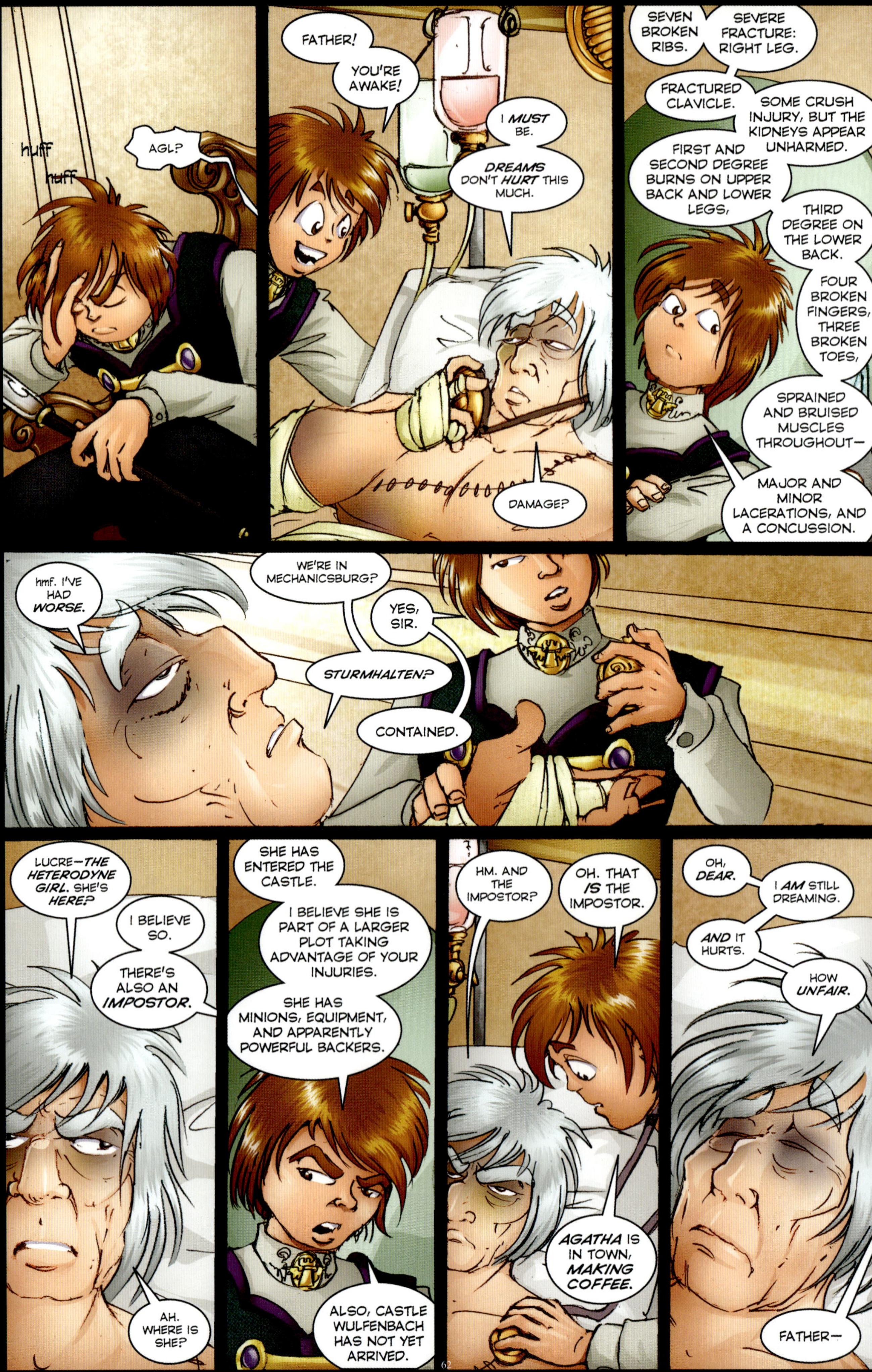

huff
huff
AGL?
FATHER!
YOU'RE AWAKE!
I MUST BE.
DREAMS DON'T HURT THIS MUCH.
DAMAGE?
SEVEN BROKEN RIBS.
SEVERE FRACTURE: RIGHT LEG.
FRACTURED CLAVICLE.
SOME CRUSH INJURY, BUT THE KIDNEYS APPEAR UNHARMED.
FIRST AND SECOND DEGREE BURNS ON UPPER BACK AND LOWER LEGS,
THIRD DEGREE ON THE LOWER BACK.
FOUR BROKEN FINGERS, THREE BROKEN TOES,
SPRAINED AND BRUISED MUSCLES THROUGHOUT—
MAJOR AND MINOR LACERATIONS, AND A CONCUSSION.
hmf. I'VE HAD WORSE.
WE'RE IN MECHANICSBURG?
YES, SIR.
STURMHALTEN?
CONTAINED.
LUCRE—THE HETERODYNE GIRL. SHE'S HERE?
I BELIEVE SO.
THERE'S ALSO AN IMPOSTOR.
AH. WHERE IS SHE?
SHE HAS ENTERED THE CASTLE.
I BELIEVE SHE IS PART OF A LARGER PLOT TAKING ADVANTAGE OF YOUR INJURIES.
SHE HAS MINIONS, EQUIPMENT, AND APPARENTLY POWERFUL BACKERS.
ALSO, CASTLE WULFENBACH HAS NOT YET ARRIVED.
HM. AND THE IMPOSTOR?
OH. THAT IS THE IMPOSTOR.
AGATHA IS IN TOWN, MAKING COFFEE.
OH, DEAR.
I AM STILL DREAMING.
AND IT HURTS.
HOW UNFAIR.
FATHER—

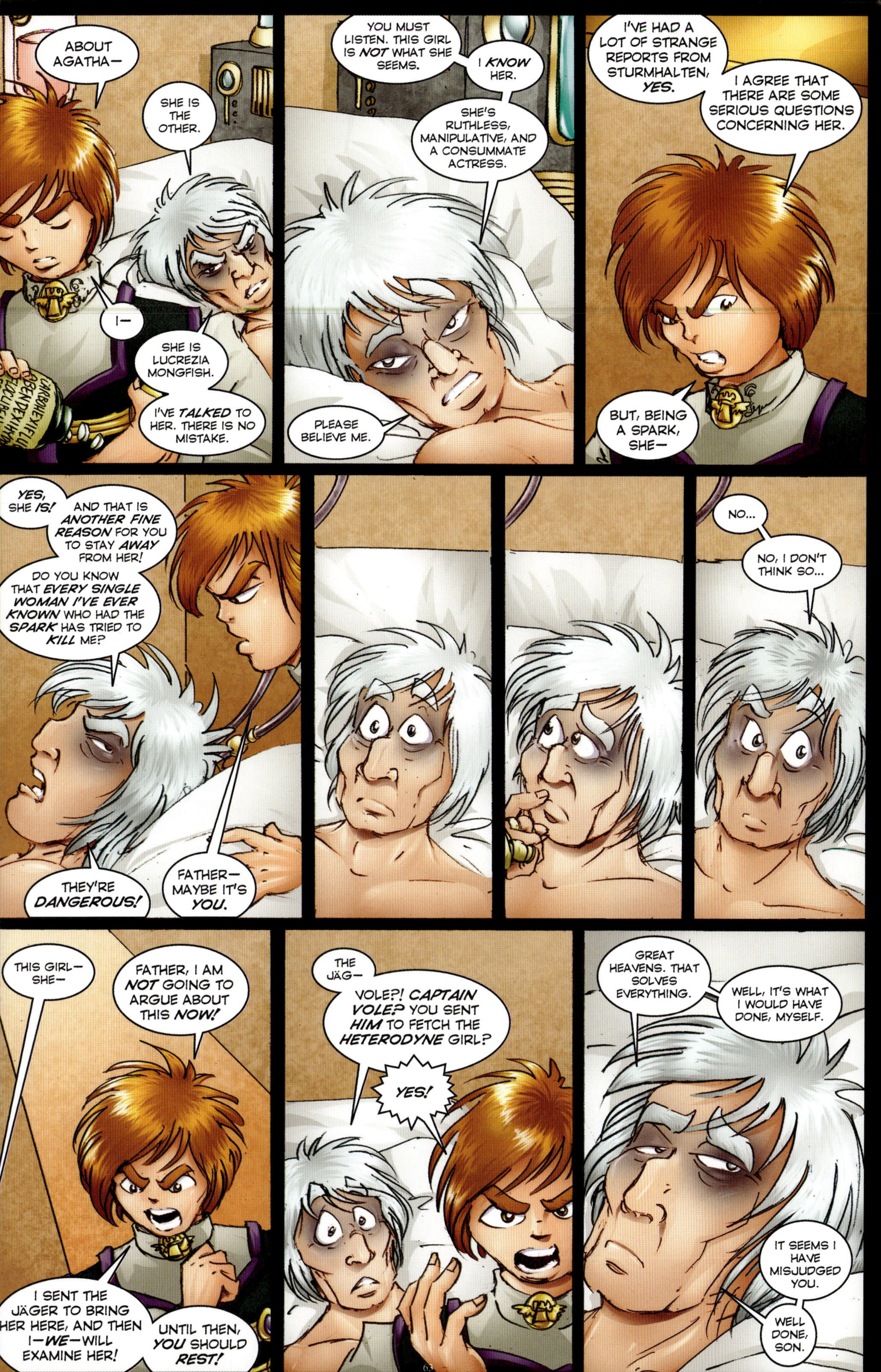
ABOUT AGATHA—
SHE IS THE OTHER.
I—
SHE IS LUCREZIA MONGFISH.
I'VE TALKED TO HER. THERE IS NO MISTAKE.
YOU MUST LISTEN. THIS GIRL IS NOT WHAT SHE SEEMS.
I KNOW HER.
SHE'S RUTHLESS, MANIPULATIVE, AND A CONSUMMATE ACTRESS.
PLEASE BELIEVE ME.
I'VE HAD A LOT OF STRANGE REPORTS FROM STURMHALTEN, YES.
I AGREE THAT THERE ARE SOME SERIOUS QUESTIONS CONCERNING HER.
BUT, BEING A SPARK, SHE—
YES, SHE IS!
AND THAT IS ANOTHER FINE REASON FOR YOU TO STAY AWAY FROM HER!
DO YOU KNOW THAT EVERY SINGLE WOMAN I'VE EVER KNOWN WHO HAD THE SPARK HAS TRIED TO KILL ME?
THEY'RE DANGEROUS!
FATHER— MAYBE IT'S YOU.
NO...
NO, I DON'T THINK SO...
THIS GIRL— SHE—
FATHER, I AM NOT GOING TO ARGUE ABOUT THIS NOW!
I SENT THE JÄGER TO BRING HER HERE, AND THEN I—WE—WILL EXAMINE HER!
UNTIL THEN, YOU SHOULD REST!
THE JÄG—
VOLE?! CAPTAIN VOLE? YOU SENT HIM TO FETCH THE HETERODYNE GIRL?
YES!
GREAT HEAVENS. THAT SOLVES EVERYTHING.
WELL, IT'S WHAT I WOULD HAVE DONE, MYSELF.
IT SEEMS I HAVE MISJUDGED YOU.
WELL DONE, SON.

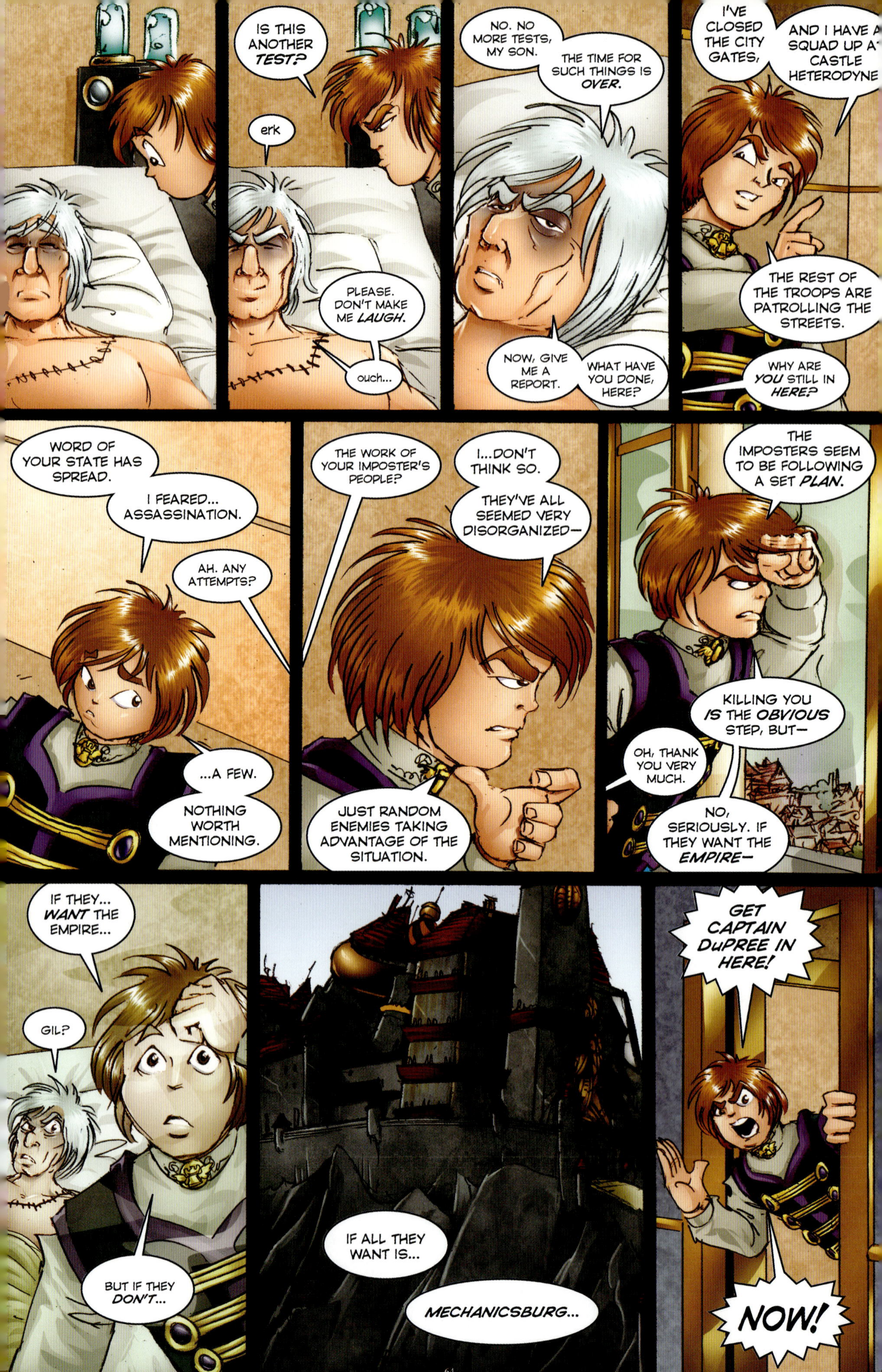
IS THIS ANOTHER TEST?
erk
PLEASE. DON'T MAKE ME LAUGH.
ouch...
NO. NO MORE TESTS, MY SON.
THE TIME FOR SUCH THINGS IS OVER.
NOW, GIVE ME A REPORT.
WHAT HAVE YOU DONE, HERE?
I'VE CLOSED THE CITY GATES,
AND I HAVE A SQUAD UP AT CASTLE HETERODYNE
THE REST OF THE TROOPS ARE PATROLLING THE STREETS.
WHY ARE YOU STILL IN HERE?
WORD OF YOUR STATE HAS SPREAD.
I FEARED... ASSASSINATION.
AH. ANY ATTEMPTS?
...A FEW.
NOTHING WORTH MENTIONING.
THE WORK OF YOUR IMPOSTER'S PEOPLE?
I...DON'T THINK SO.
THEY'VE ALL SEEMED VERY DISORGANIZED—
JUST RANDOM ENEMIES TAKING ADVANTAGE OF THE SITUATION.
THE IMPOSTERS SEEM TO BE FOLLOWING A SET PLAN.
KILLING YOU IS THE OBVIOUS STEP, BUT—
OH, THANK YOU VERY MUCH.
NO, SERIOUSLY. IF THEY WANT THE EMPIRE—
IF THEY... WANT THE EMPIRE...
GIL?
BUT IF THEY DON'T...
IF ALL THEY WANT IS...
MECHANICSBURG...
GET CAPTAIN DuPREE IN HERE!
NOW!

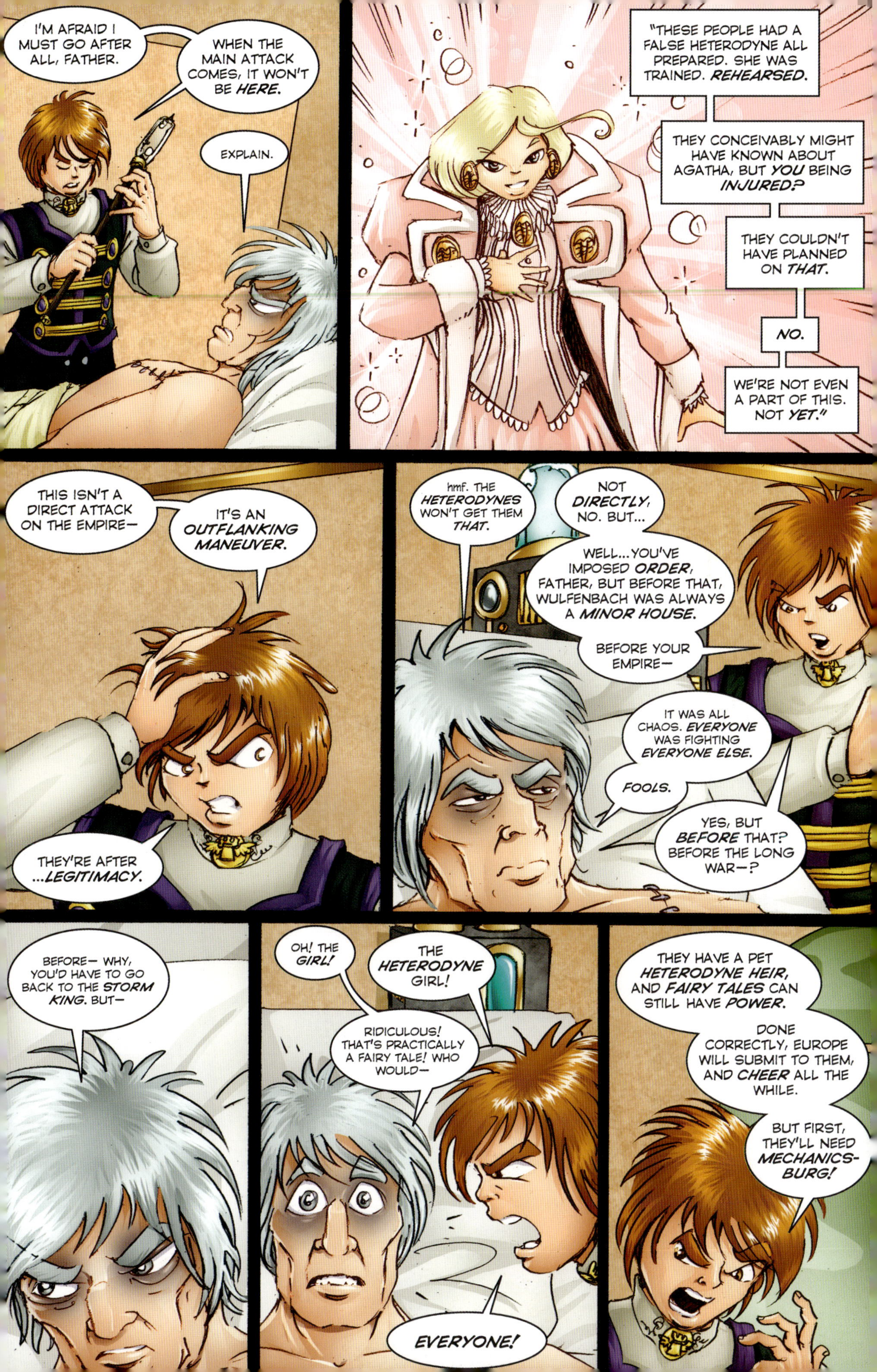
I'M AFRAID I MUST GO AFTER ALL, FATHER.
WHEN THE MAIN ATTACK COMES, IT WON'T BE HERE.
EXPLAIN.
"THESE PEOPLE HAD A FALSE HETERODYNE ALL PREPARED. SHE WAS TRAINED. REHEARSED.
THEY CONCEIVABLY MIGHT HAVE KNOWN ABOUT AGATHA, BUT YOU BEING INJURED?
THEY COULDN'T HAVE PLANNED ON THAT.
NO.
WE'RE NOT EVEN A PART OF THIS. NOT YET."
THIS ISN'T A DIRECT ATTACK ON THE EMPIRE—
IT'S AN OUTFLANKING MANEUVER.
THEY'RE AFTER ...LEGITIMACY.
hmf. THE HETERODYNES WON'T GET THEM THAT.
NOT DIRECTLY, NO. BUT...
WELL...YOU'VE IMPOSED ORDER, FATHER, BUT BEFORE THAT, WULFENBACH WAS ALWAYS A MINOR HOUSE.
BEFORE YOUR EMPIRE—
IT WAS ALL CHAOS. EVERYONE WAS FIGHTING EVERYONE ELSE.
FOOLS.
YES, BUT BEFORE THAT? BEFORE THE LONG WAR—?
BEFORE— WHY, YOU'D HAVE TO GO BACK TO THE STORM KING. BUT—
OH! THE GIRL!
THE HETERODYNE GIRL!
RIDICULOUS! THAT'S PRACTICALLY A FAIRY TALE! WHO WOULD—
EVERYONE!
THEY HAVE A PET HETERODYNE HEIR, AND FAIRY TALES CAN STILL HAVE POWER.
DONE CORRECTLY, EUROPE WILL SUBMIT TO THEM, AND CHEER ALL THE WHILE.
BUT FIRST, THEY'LL NEED MECHANICS-BURG!

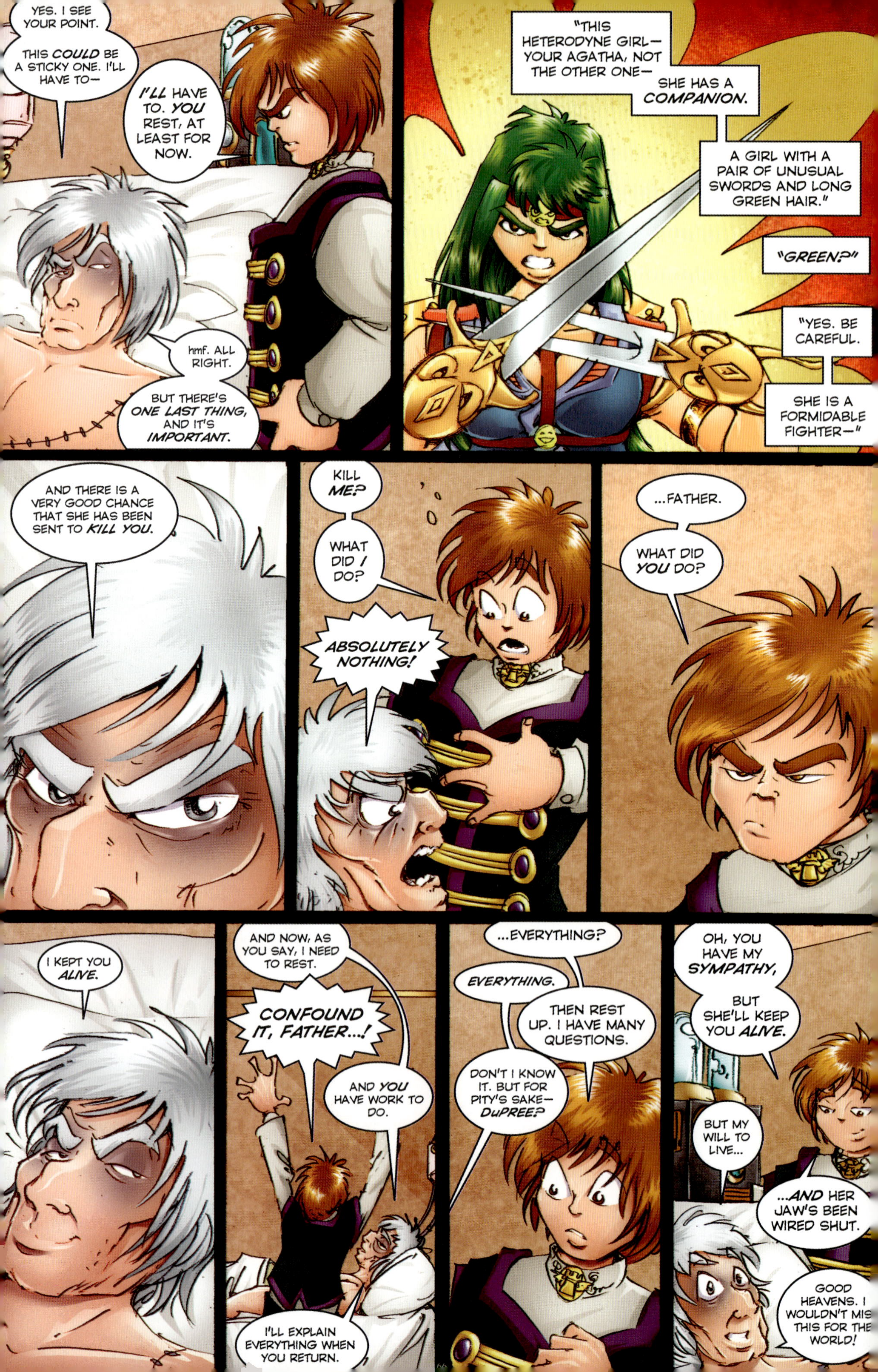
YES. I SEE YOUR POINT.
THIS COULD BE A STICKY ONE. I'LL HAVE TO—
I'LL HAVE TO. YOU REST, AT LEAST FOR NOW.
hmf. ALL RIGHT.
BUT THERE'S ONE LAST THING, AND IT'S IMPORTANT.
"THIS HETERODYNE GIRL— YOUR AGATHA, NOT THE OTHER ONE—
SHE HAS A COMPANION.
A GIRL WITH A PAIR OF UNUSUAL SWORDS AND LONG GREEN HAIR."
"GREEN?"
"YES. BE CAREFUL.
SHE IS A FORMIDABLE FIGHTER—"
AND THERE IS A VERY GOOD CHANCE THAT SHE HAS BEEN SENT TO KILL YOU.
KILL ME?
WHAT DID I DO?
ABSOLUTELY NOTHING!
...FATHER.
WHAT DID YOU DO?
I KEPT YOU ALIVE.
AND NOW, AS YOU SAY, I NEED TO REST.
CONFOUND IT, FATHER...!
AND YOU HAVE WORK TO DO.
I'LL EXPLAIN EVERYTHING WHEN YOU RETURN.
...EVERYTHING?
EVERYTHING.
THEN REST UP. I HAVE MANY QUESTIONS.
DON'T I KNOW IT. BUT FOR PITY'S SAKE— DuPREE?
OH, YOU HAVE MY SYMPATHY,
BUT SHE'LL KEEP YOU ALIVE.
BUT MY WILL TO LIVE...
...AND HER JAW'S BEEN WIRED SHUT.
GOOD HEAVENS. I WOULDN'T MIS THIS FOR THE WORLD!

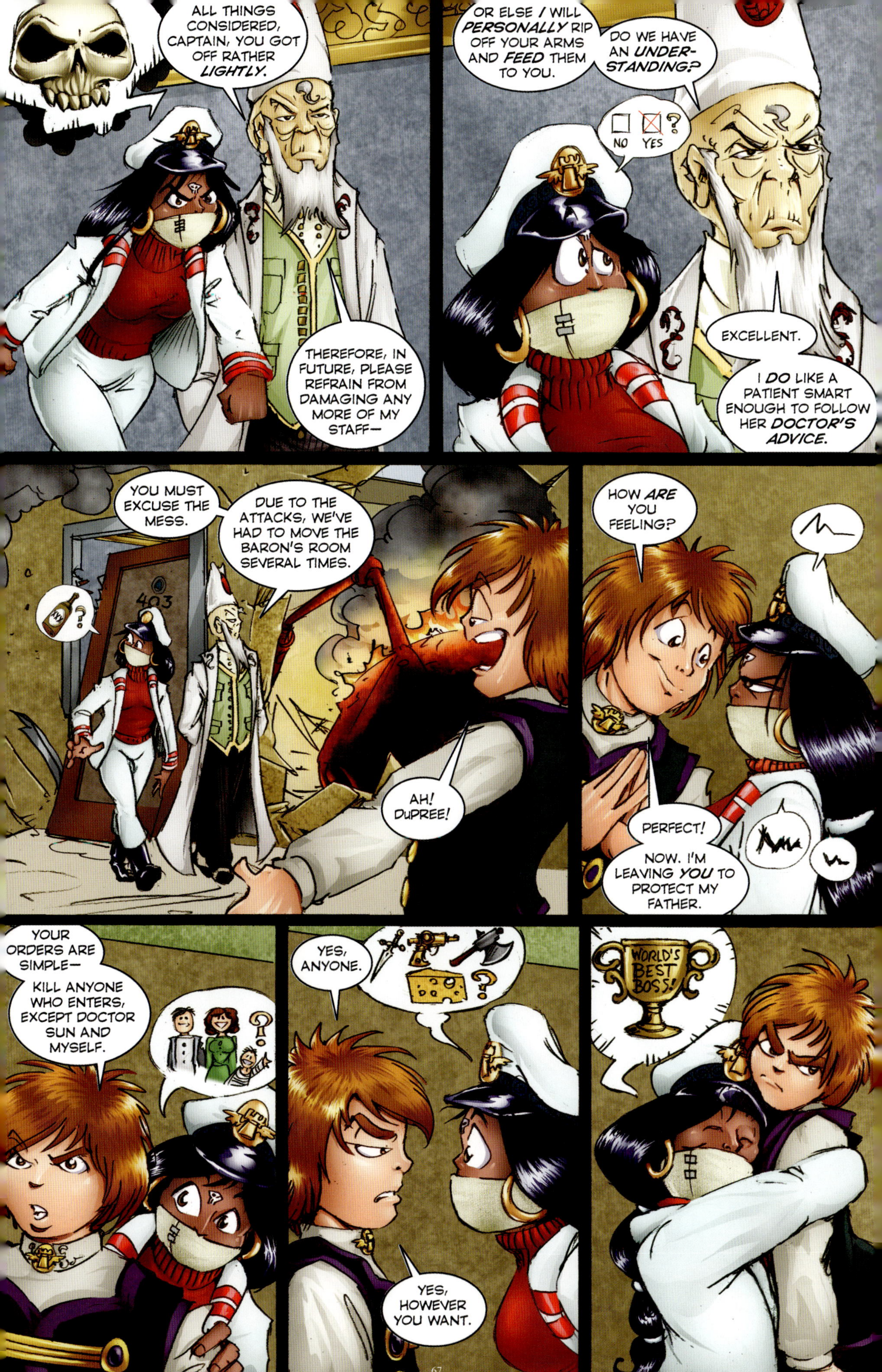
ALL THINGS CONSIDERED, CAPTAIN, YOU GOT OFF RATHER LIGHTLY.
THEREFORE, IN FUTURE, PLEASE REFRAIN FROM DAMAGING ANY MORE OF MY STAFF—
OR ELSE I WILL PERSONALLY RIP OFF YOUR ARMS AND FEED THEM TO YOU.
DO WE HAVE AN UNDER-STANDING?
NO YES ?
EXCELLENT.
I DO LIKE A PATIENT SMART ENOUGH TO FOLLOW HER DOCTOR'S ADVICE.
YOU MUST EXCUSE THE MESS.
DUE TO THE ATTACKS, WE'VE HAD TO MOVE THE BARON'S ROOM SEVERAL TIMES.
403
AH! DuPREE!
HOW ARE YOU FEELING?
PERFECT!
NOW. I'M LEAVING YOU TO PROTECT MY FATHER.
YOUR ORDERS ARE SIMPLE—
KILL ANYONE WHO ENTERS, EXCEPT DOCTOR SUN AND MYSELF.
YES, ANYONE.
YES, HOWEVER YOU WANT.
WORLD'S BEST BOSS!

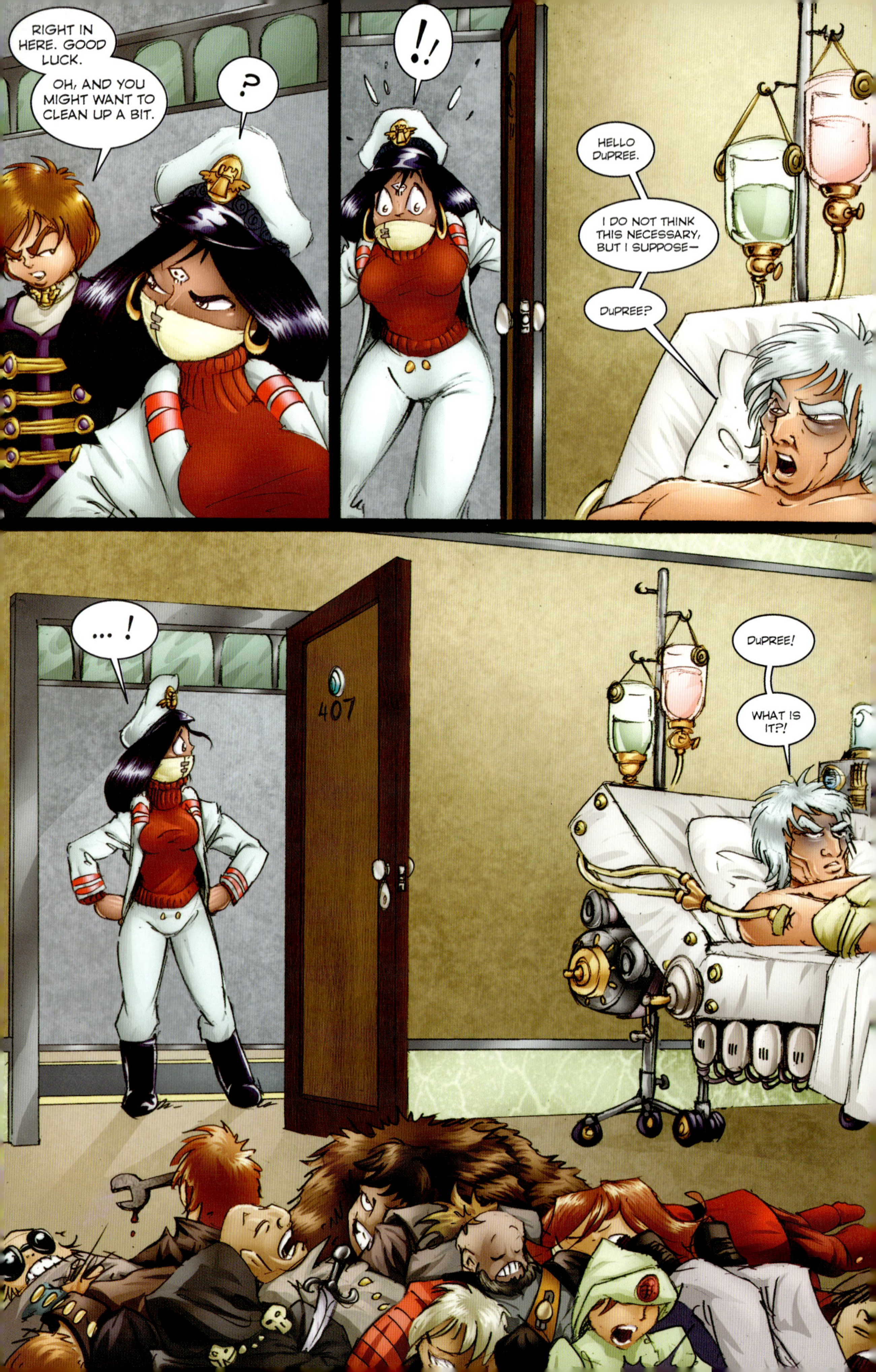
RIGHT IN HERE. GOOD LUCK.
OH, AND YOU MIGHT WANT TO CLEAN UP A BIT.
?
!!
HELLO DUPREE.
I DO NOT THINK THIS NECESSARY, BUT I SUPPOSE—
DUPREE?
... !
407
DUPREE!
WHAT IS IT?!

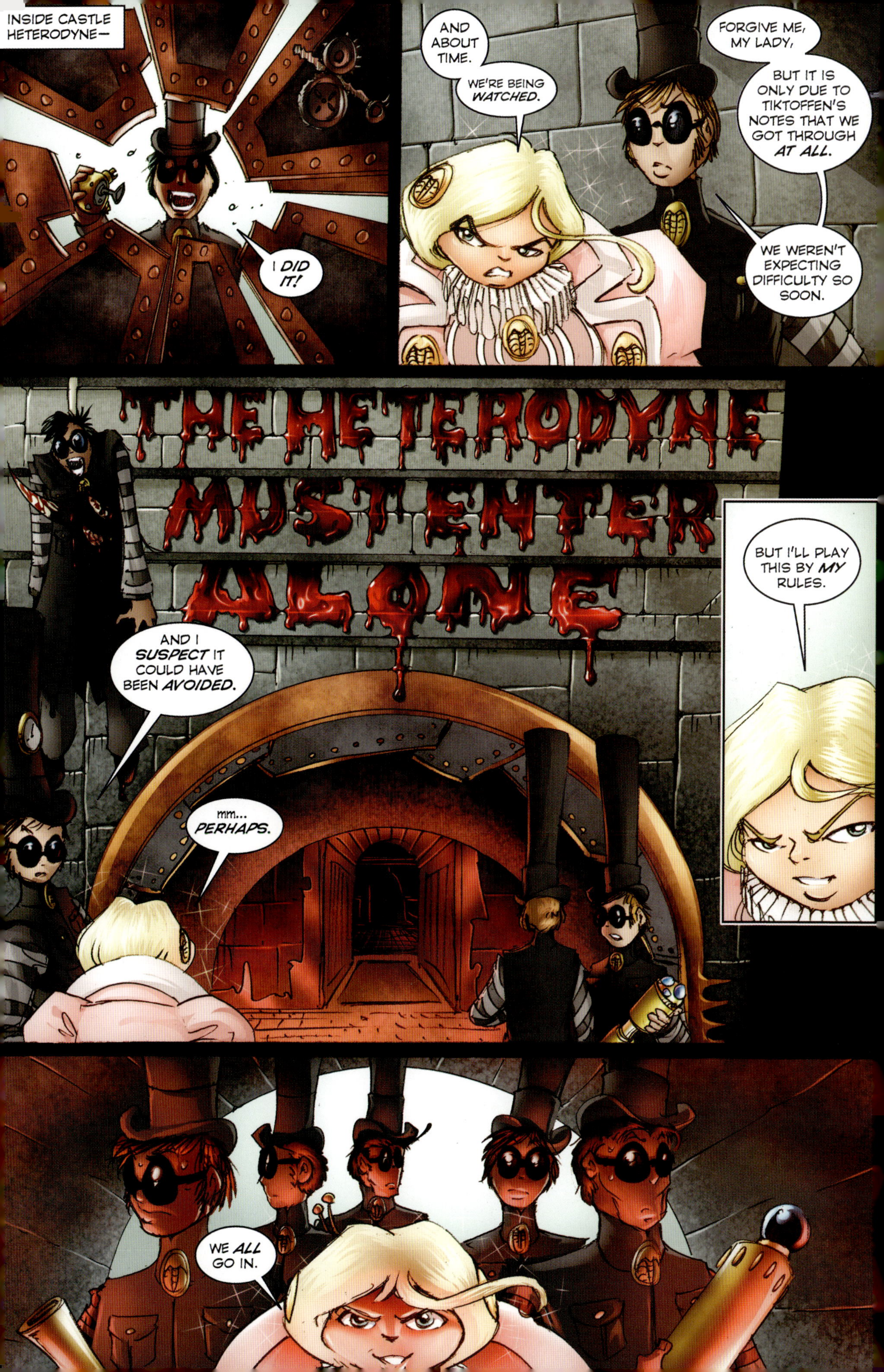
INSIDE CASTLE HETERODYNE—
I DID IT!
AND ABOUT TIME.
WE'RE BEING WATCHED.
FORGIVE ME, MY LADY,
BUT IT IS ONLY DUE TO TIKTOFFEN'S NOTES THAT WE GOT THROUGH AT ALL.
WE WEREN'T EXPECTING DIFFICULTY SO SOON.
THE HETERODYNE MUST ENTER ALONE
AND I SUSPECT IT COULD HAVE BEEN AVOIDED.
mm... PERHAPS.
BUT I'LL PLAY THIS BY MY RULES.
WE ALL GO IN.

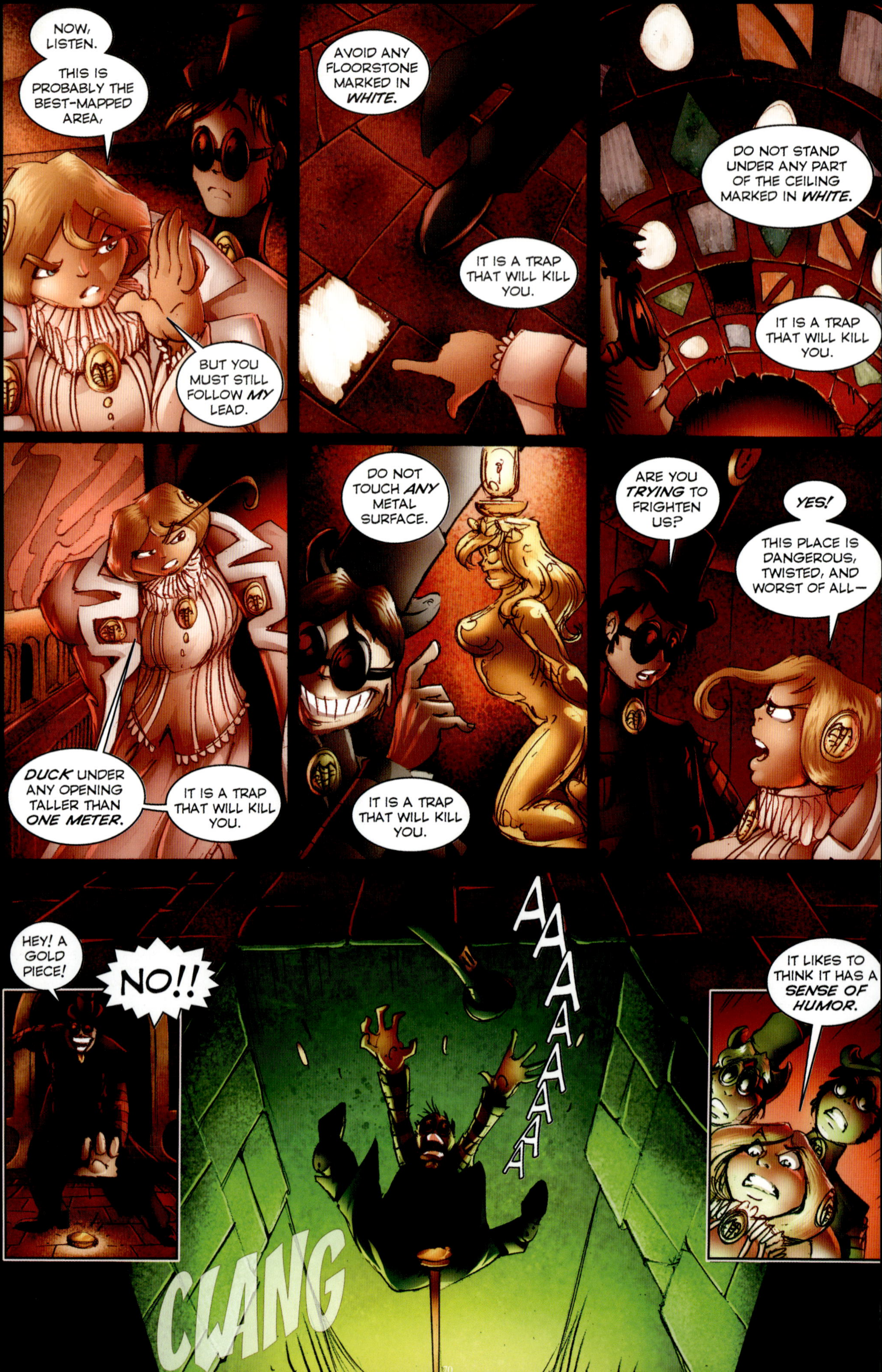
NOW, LISTEN.
THIS IS PROBABLY THE BEST-MAPPED AREA,
BUT YOU MUST STILL FOLLOW *MY* LEAD.
AVOID ANY FLOORSTONE MARKED IN *WHITE*.
IT IS A TRAP THAT WILL KILL YOU.
DO NOT STAND UNDER ANY PART OF THE CEILING MARKED IN *WHITE*.
IT IS A TRAP THAT WILL KILL YOU.
DUCK UNDER ANY OPENING TALLER THAN *ONE METER*.
IT IS A TRAP THAT WILL KILL YOU.
DO NOT TOUCH *ANY* METAL SURFACE.
IT IS A TRAP THAT WILL KILL YOU.
ARE YOU *TRYING* TO FRIGHTEN US?
YES!
THIS PLACE IS DANGEROUS, TWISTED, AND WORST OF ALL—
HEY! A GOLD PIECE!
NO!!
AAAAAAAA
CLANG
IT LIKES TO THINK IT HAS A *SENSE OF HUMOR*.

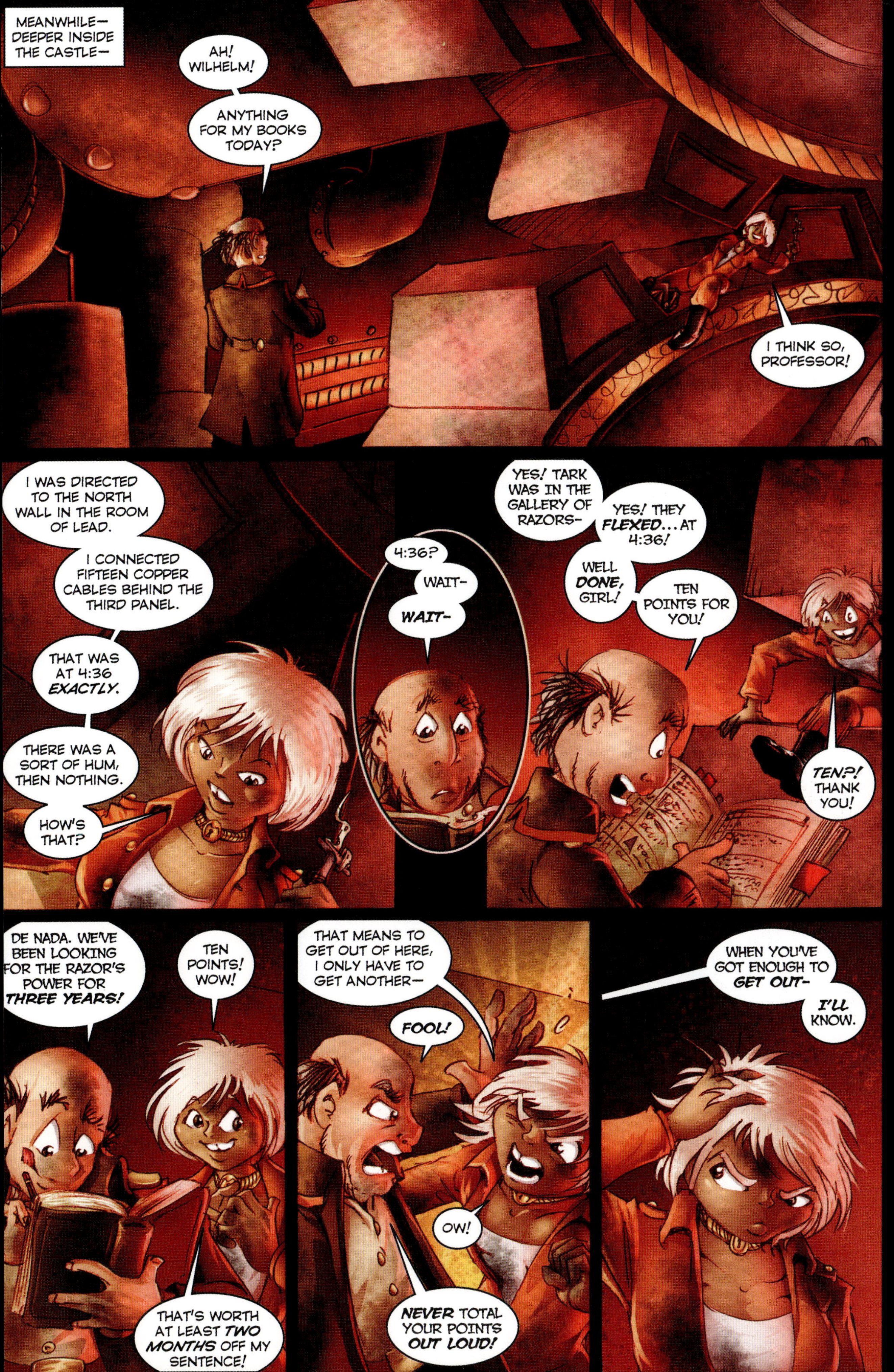
MEANWHILE— DEEPER INSIDE THE CASTLE—
AH! WILHELM!
ANYTHING FOR MY BOOKS TODAY?
I THINK SO, PROFESSOR!
I WAS DIRECTED TO THE NORTH WALL IN THE ROOM OF LEAD.
I CONNECTED FIFTEEN COPPER CABLES BEHIND THE THIRD PANEL.
THAT WAS AT 4:36 EXACTLY.
THERE WAS A SORT OF HUM, THEN NOTHING.
HOW'S THAT?
4:36?
WAIT-
WAIT-
YES! TARK WAS IN THE GALLERY OF RAZORS-
YES! THEY FLEXED... AT 4:36!
WELL DONE, GIRL!
TEN POINTS FOR YOU!
TEN?! THANK YOU!
DE NADA. WE'VE BEEN LOOKING FOR THE RAZOR'S POWER FOR THREE YEARS!
TEN POINTS! WOW!
THAT'S WORTH AT LEAST TWO MONTHS OFF MY SENTENCE!
THAT MEANS TO GET OUT OF HERE, I ONLY HAVE TO GET ANOTHER—
FOOL!
OW!
NEVER TOTAL YOUR POINTS OUT LOUD!
WHEN YOU'VE GOT ENOUGH TO GET OUT-
I'LL KNOW.

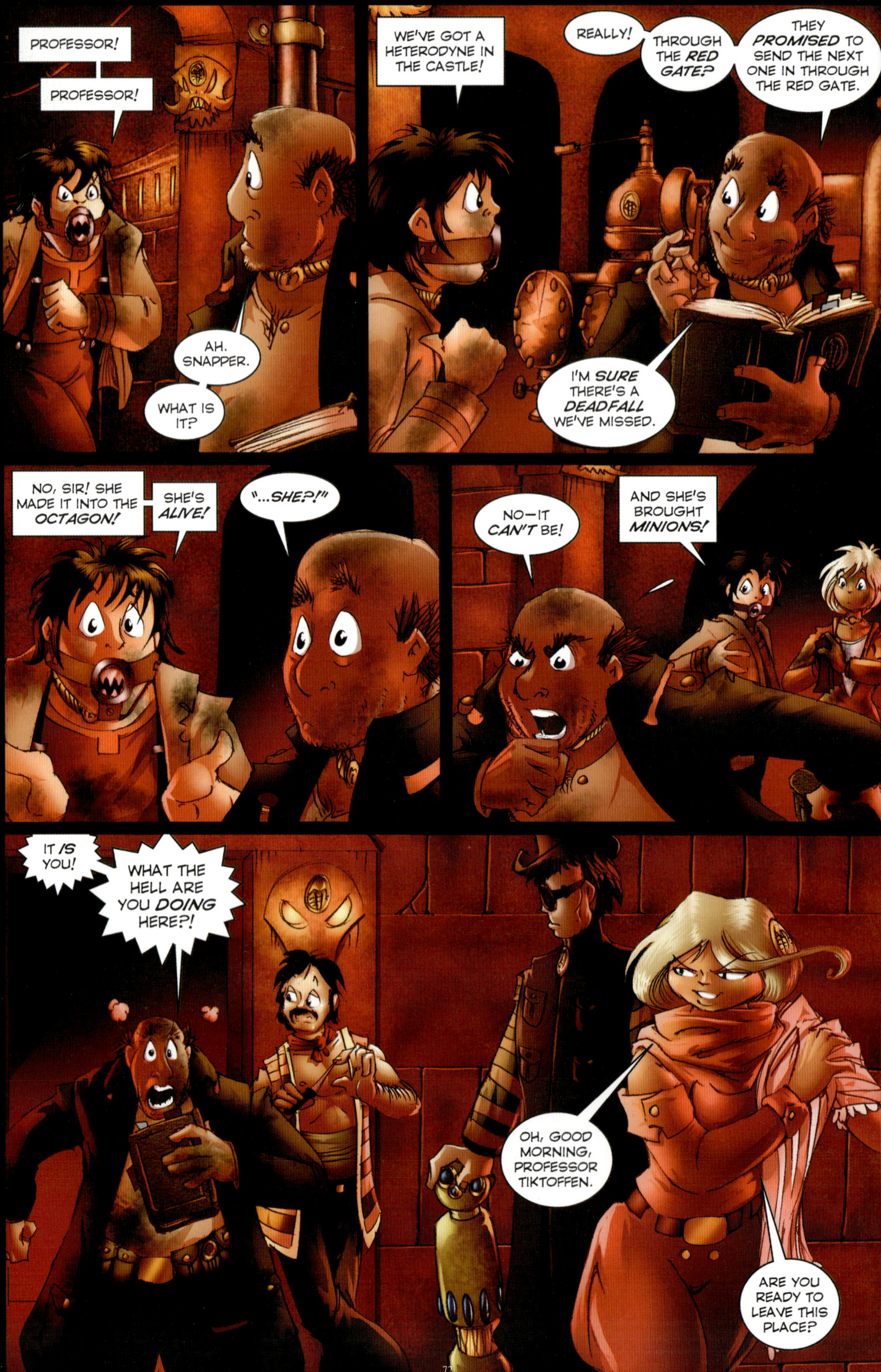
PROFESSOR!
PROFESSOR!
AH. SNAPPER.
WHAT IS IT?
WE'VE GOT A HETERODYNE IN THE CASTLE!
REALLY!
THROUGH THE RED GATE?
THEY PROMISED TO SEND THE NEXT ONE IN THROUGH THE RED GATE.
I'M SURE THERE'S A DEADFALL WE'VE MISSED.
NO, SIR! SHE MADE IT INTO THE OCTAGON!
SHE'S ALIVE!
"...SHE?!"
NO—IT CAN'T BE!
AND SHE'S BROUGHT MINIONS!
IT IS YOU!
WHAT THE HELL ARE YOU DOING HERE?!
OH, GOOD MORNING, PROFESSOR TIKTOFFEN.
ARE YOU READY TO LEAVE THIS PLACE?

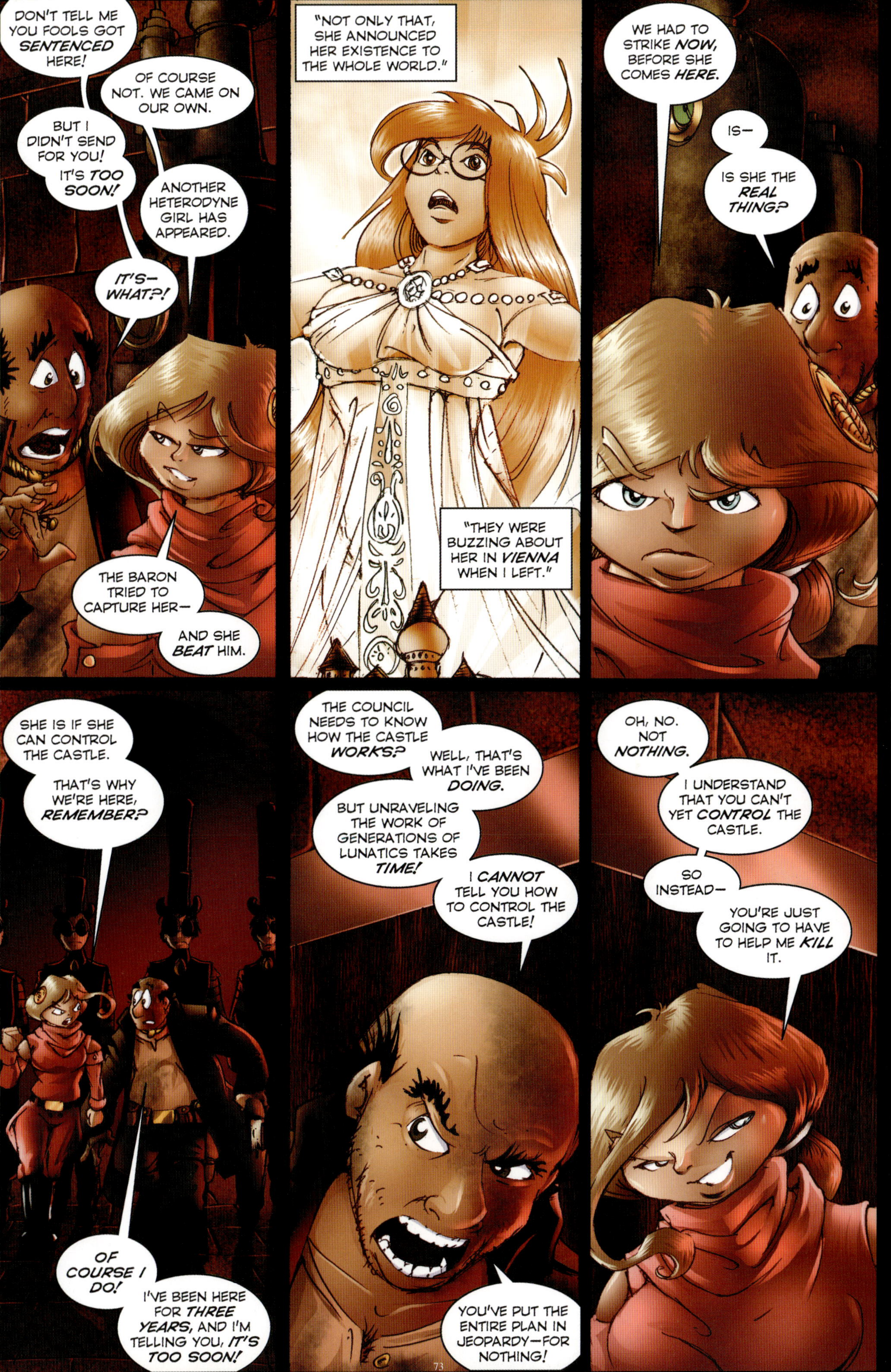
DON'T TELL ME YOU FOOLS GOT SENTENCED HERE!
OF COURSE NOT. WE CAME ON OUR OWN.
BUT I DIDN'T SEND FOR YOU!
IT'S TOO SOON!
ANOTHER HETERODYNE GIRL HAS APPEARED.
IT'S— WHAT?!
THE BARON TRIED TO CAPTURE HER—
AND SHE BEAT HIM.
"NOT ONLY THAT, SHE ANNOUNCED HER EXISTENCE TO THE WHOLE WORLD."
"THEY WERE BUZZING ABOUT HER IN VIENNA WHEN I LEFT."
WE HAD TO STRIKE NOW, BEFORE SHE COMES HERE.
IS—
IS SHE THE REAL THING?
SHE IS IF SHE CAN CONTROL THE CASTLE.
THAT'S WHY WE'RE HERE, REMEMBER?
OF COURSE I DO!
I'VE BEEN HERE FOR THREE YEARS, AND I'M TELLING YOU, IT'S TOO SOON!
THE COUNCIL NEEDS TO KNOW HOW THE CASTLE WORKS?
WELL, THAT'S WHAT I'VE BEEN DOING.
BUT UNRAVELING THE WORK OF GENERATIONS OF LUNATICS TAKES TIME!
I CANNOT TELL YOU HOW TO CONTROL THE CASTLE!
YOU'VE PUT THE ENTIRE PLAN IN JEOPARDY—FOR NOTHING!
OH, NO. NOT NOTHING.
I UNDERSTAND THAT YOU CAN'T YET CONTROL THE CASTLE.
SO INSTEAD—
YOU'RE JUST GOING TO HAVE TO HELP ME KILL IT.

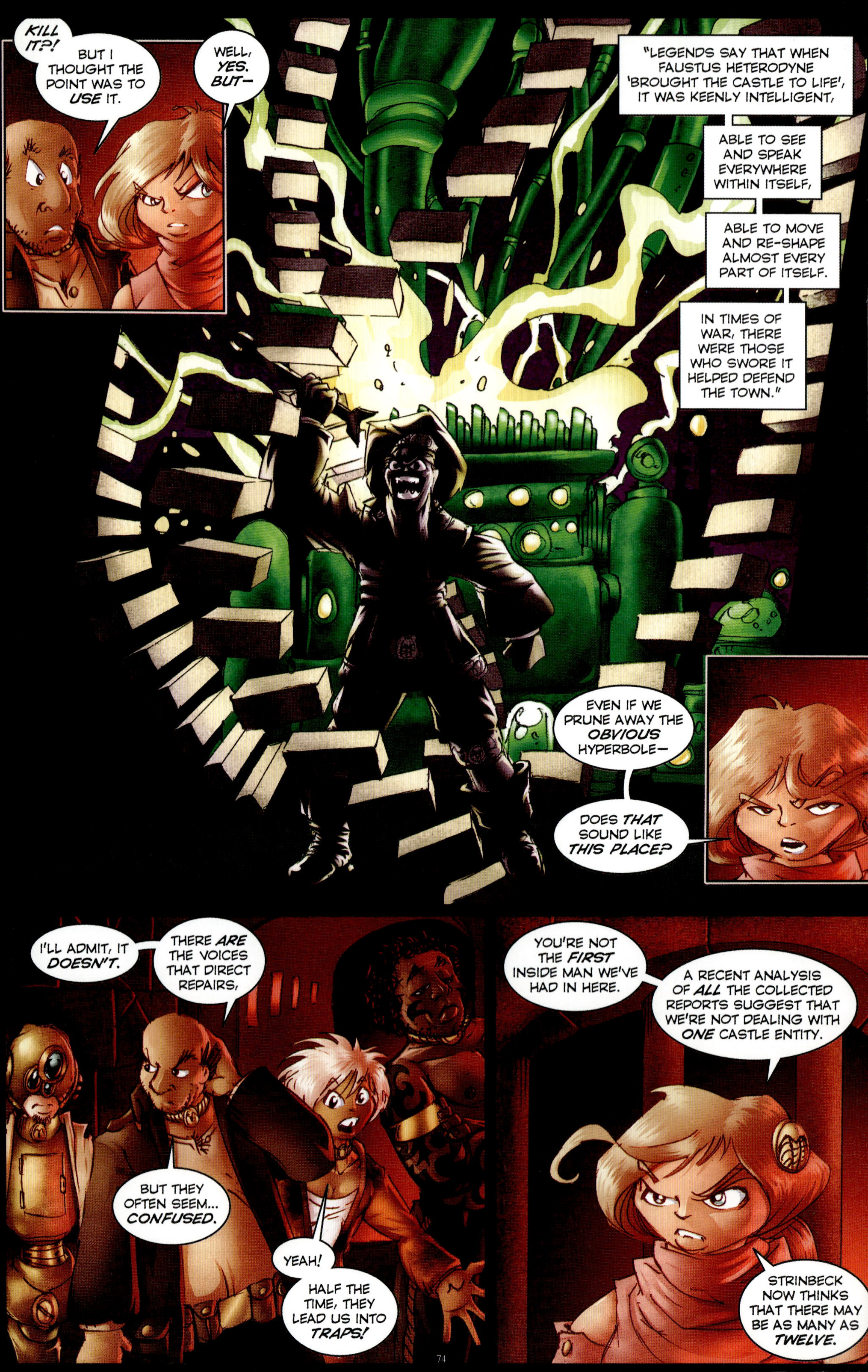
KILL IT?!
BUT I THOUGHT THE POINT WAS TO USE IT.
WELL, YES. BUT—
"LEGENDS SAY THAT WHEN FAUSTUS HETERODYNE 'BROUGHT THE CASTLE TO LIFE', IT WAS KEENLY INTELLIGENT,
ABLE TO SEE AND SPEAK EVERYWHERE WITHIN ITSELF,
ABLE TO MOVE AND RE-SHAPE ALMOST EVERY PART OF ITSELF.
IN TIMES OF WAR, THERE WERE THOSE WHO SWORE IT HELPED DEFEND THE TOWN."
EVEN IF WE PRUNE AWAY THE OBVIOUS HYPERBOLE—
DOES THAT SOUND LIKE THIS PLACE?
I'LL ADMIT, IT DOESN'T.
THERE ARE THE VOICES THAT DIRECT REPAIRS,
BUT THEY OFTEN SEEM... CONFUSED.
YEAH!
HALF THE TIME, THEY LEAD US INTO TRAPS!
YOU'RE NOT THE FIRST INSIDE MAN WE'VE HAD IN HERE.
A RECENT ANALYSIS OF ALL THE COLLECTED REPORTS SUGGEST THAT WE'RE NOT DEALING WITH ONE CASTLE ENTITY.
STRINBECK NOW THINKS THAT THERE MAY BE AS MANY AS TWELVE.

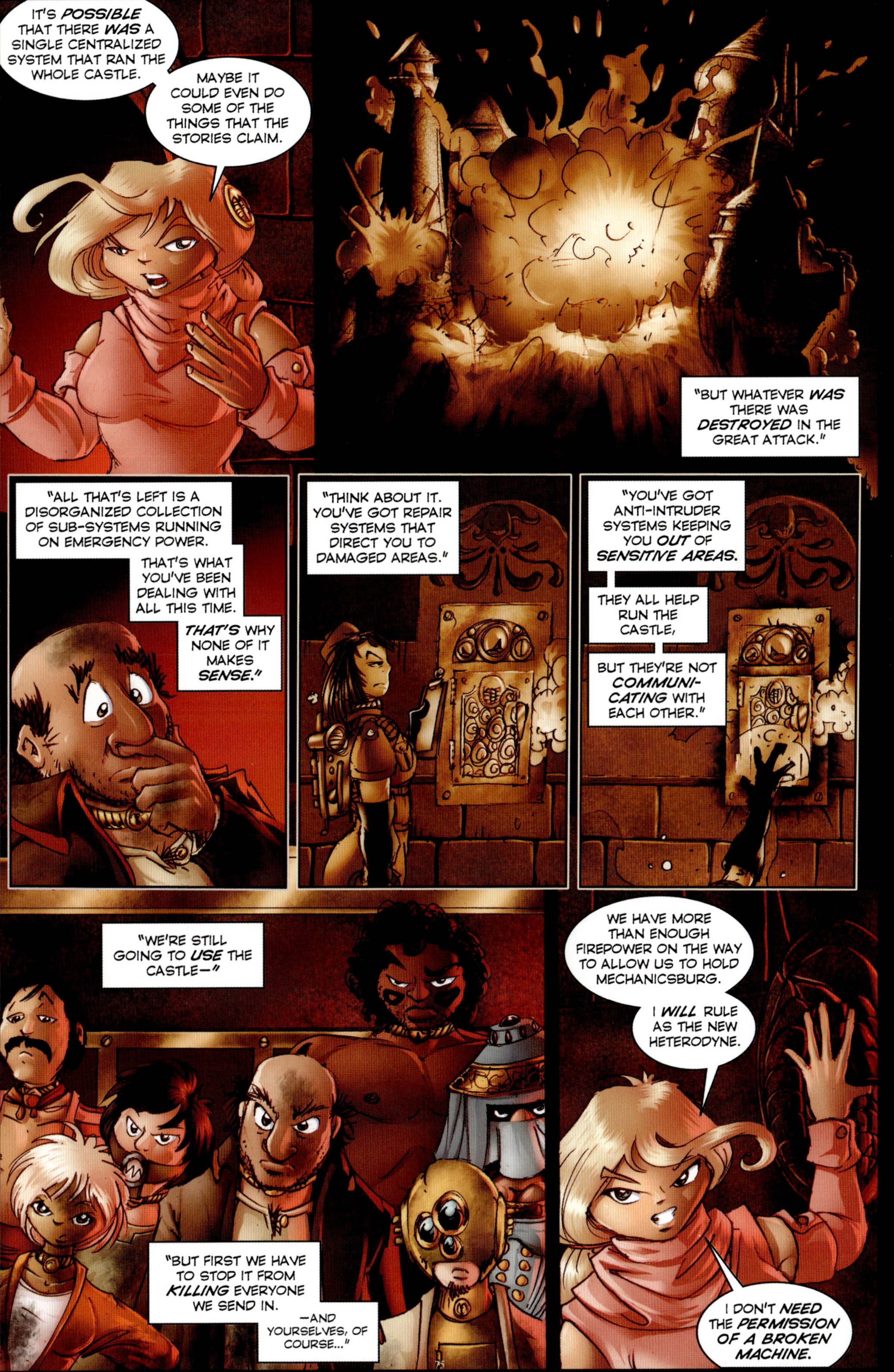
IT'S POSSIBLE THAT THERE WAS A SINGLE CENTRALIZED SYSTEM THAT RAN THE WHOLE CASTLE.
MAYBE IT COULD EVEN DO SOME OF THE THINGS THAT THE STORIES CLAIM.
"BUT WHATEVER WAS THERE WAS DESTROYED IN THE GREAT ATTACK."
"ALL THAT'S LEFT IS A DISORGANIZED COLLECTION OF SUB-SYSTEMS RUNNING ON EMERGENCY POWER.
THAT'S WHAT YOU'VE BEEN DEALING WITH ALL THIS TIME.
THAT'S WHY NONE OF IT MAKES SENSE."
"THINK ABOUT IT. YOU'VE GOT REPAIR SYSTEMS THAT DIRECT YOU TO DAMAGED AREAS."
"YOU'VE GOT ANTI-INTRUDER SYSTEMS KEEPING YOU OUT OF SENSITIVE AREAS.
THEY ALL HELP RUN THE CASTLE,
BUT THEY'RE NOT COMMUNI-CATING WITH EACH OTHER."
"WE'RE STILL GOING TO USE THE CASTLE—"
"BUT FIRST WE HAVE TO STOP IT FROM KILLING EVERYONE WE SEND IN.
—AND YOURSELVES, OF COURSE..."
WE HAVE MORE THAN ENOUGH FIREPOWER ON THE WAY TO ALLOW US TO HOLD MECHANICSBURG.
I WILL RULE AS THE NEW HETERODYNE.
I DON'T NEED THE PERMISSION OF A BROKEN MACHINE.

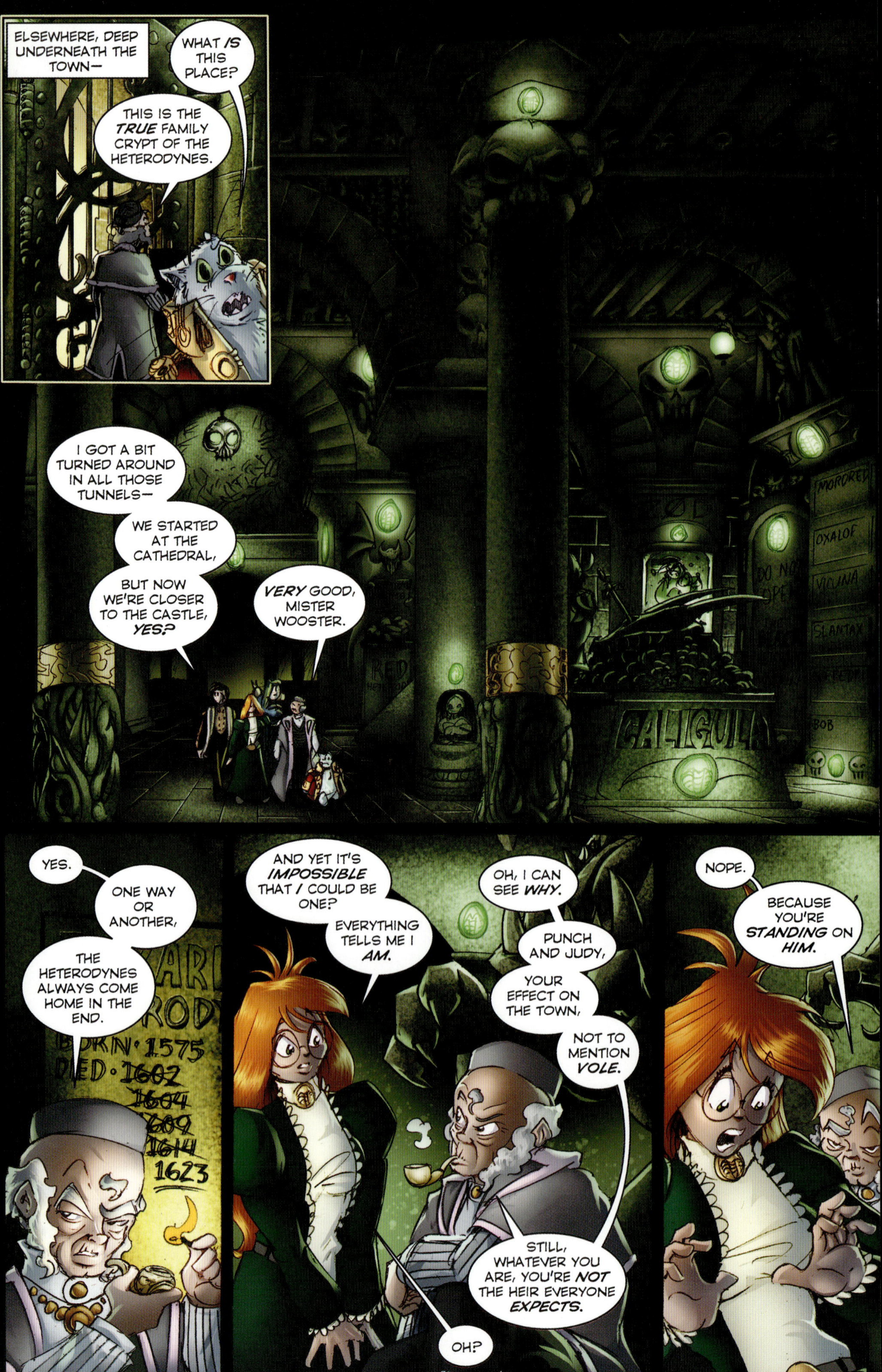

ELSEWHERE, DEEP UNDERNEATH THE TOWN—
WHAT *IS* THIS PLACE?
THIS IS THE *TRUE* FAMILY CRYPT OF THE HETERODYNES.
I GOT A BIT TURNED AROUND IN ALL THOSE TUNNELS—
WE STARTED AT THE CATHEDRAL,
BUT NOW WE'RE CLOSER TO THE CASTLE, *YES?*
VERY GOOD, MISTER WOOSTER.
OXALOF
SLANTAX
CALIGULA
BOB
YES.
ONE WAY OR ANOTHER,
THE HETERODYNES ALWAYS COME HOME IN THE END.
BORN·1575
DIED·1602
1604
1609
1614
1623
AND YET IT'S *IMPOSSIBLE* THAT *I* COULD BE ONE?
EVERYTHING TELLS ME I *AM.*
OH, I CAN SEE *WHY.*
PUNCH AND JUDY,
YOUR EFFECT ON THE TOWN,
NOT TO MENTION *VOLE.*
STILL, WHATEVER YOU ARE, YOU'RE *NOT* THE HEIR EVERYONE *EXPECTS.*
OH?
NOPE.
BECAUSE YOU'RE *STANDING* ON *HIM.*

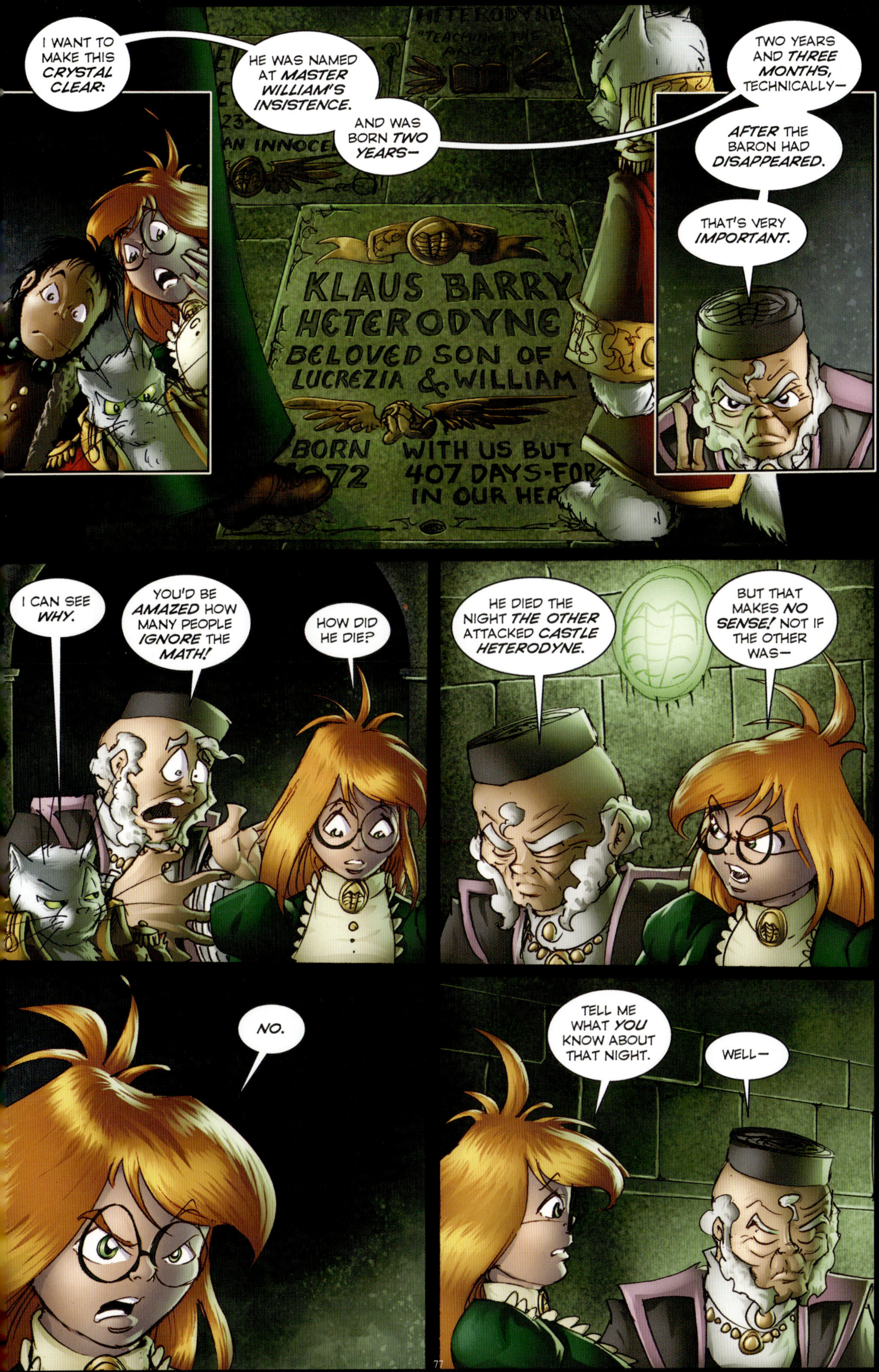

I WANT TO MAKE THIS *CRYSTAL CLEAR:*
HE WAS NAMED AT *MASTER WILLIAM'S INSISTENCE.*
AND WAS BORN *TWO YEARS—*
TWO YEARS AND *THREE MONTHS,* TECHNICALLY—
AFTER THE BARON HAD *DISAPPEARED.*
THAT'S VERY *IMPORTANT.*
KLAUS BARRY
HETERODYNE
BELOVED SON OF
LUCREZIA & WILLIAM
WITH US BUT
I CAN SEE *WHY.*
YOU'D BE *AMAZED* HOW MANY PEOPLE *IGNORE* THE *MATH!*
HOW DID HE DIE?
HE DIED THE NIGHT *THE OTHER* ATTACKED *CASTLE HETERODYNE.*
BUT THAT MAKES *NO SENSE!* NOT IF THE OTHER WAS—
NO.
TELL ME WHAT *YOU* KNOW ABOUT THAT NIGHT.
WELL—

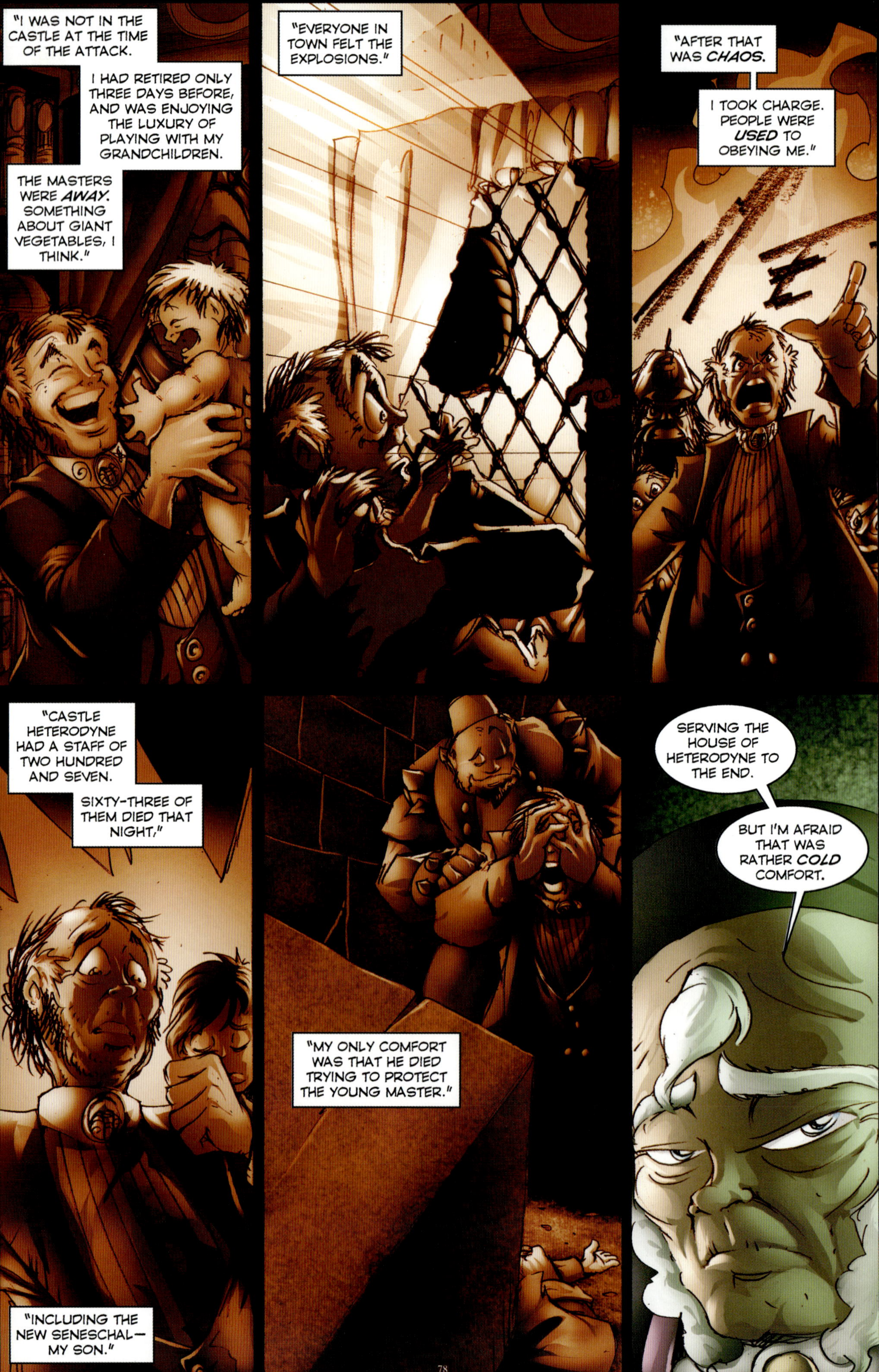
"I WAS NOT IN THE CASTLE AT THE TIME OF THE ATTACK.
I HAD RETIRED ONLY THREE DAYS BEFORE, AND WAS ENJOYING THE LUXURY OF PLAYING WITH MY GRANDCHILDREN.
THE MASTERS WERE AWAY. SOMETHING ABOUT GIANT VEGETABLES, I THINK."
"EVERYONE IN TOWN FELT THE EXPLOSIONS."
"AFTER THAT WAS CHAOS.
I TOOK CHARGE. PEOPLE WERE USED TO OBEYING ME."
"CASTLE HETERODYNE HAD A STAFF OF TWO HUNDRED AND SEVEN.
SIXTY-THREE OF THEM DIED THAT NIGHT,"
"INCLUDING THE NEW SENESCHAL— MY SON."
"MY ONLY COMFORT WAS THAT HE DIED TRYING TO PROTECT THE YOUNG MASTER."
SERVING THE HOUSE OF HETERODYNE TO THE END.
BUT I'M AFRAID THAT WAS RATHER COLD COMFORT.

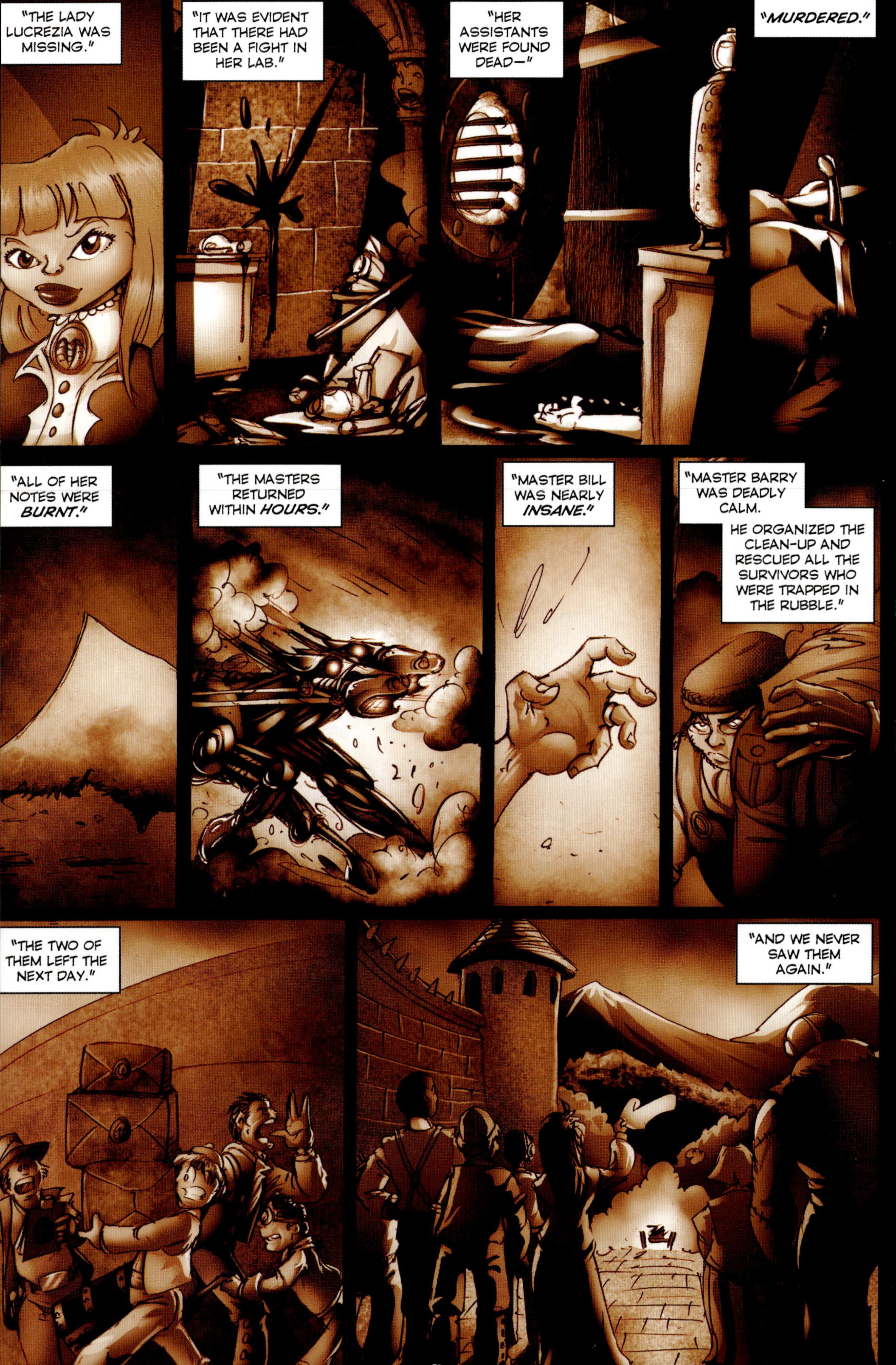
"THE LADY LUCREZIA WAS MISSING."
"IT WAS EVIDENT THAT THERE HAD BEEN A FIGHT IN HER LAB."
"HER ASSISTANTS WERE FOUND DEAD—"
"MURDERED."
"ALL OF HER NOTES WERE BURNT."
"THE MASTERS RETURNED WITHIN HOURS."
"MASTER BILL WAS NEARLY INSANE."
"MASTER BARRY WAS DEADLY CALM.
HE ORGANIZED THE CLEAN-UP AND RESCUED ALL THE SURVIVORS WHO WERE TRAPPED IN THE RUBBLE."
"THE TWO OF THEM LEFT THE NEXT DAY."
"AND WE NEVER SAW THEM AGAIN."

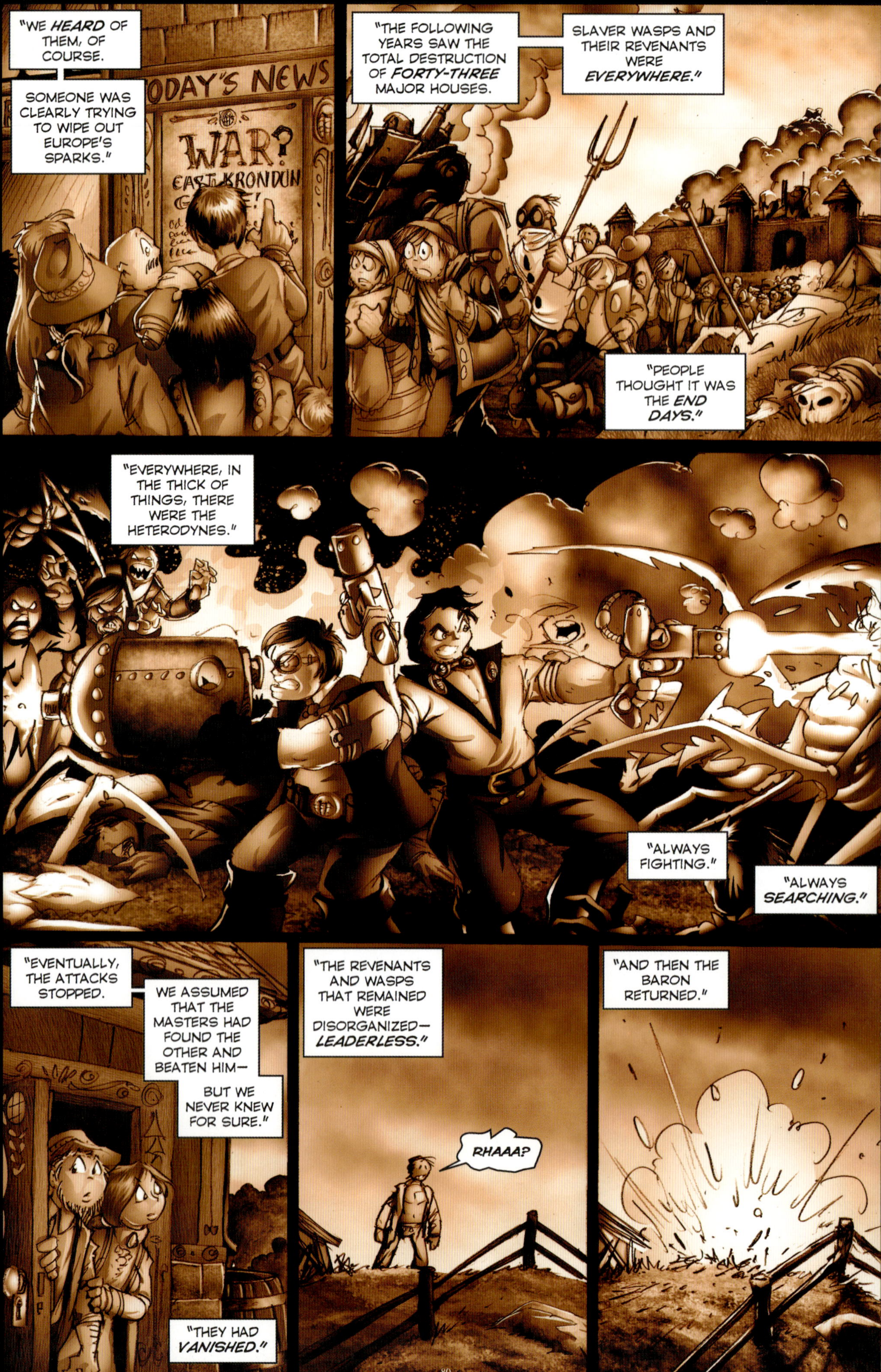
"WE *HEARD* OF THEM, OF COURSE.
SOMEONE WAS CLEARLY TRYING TO WIPE OUT EUROPE'S SPARKS."
ODAY'S NEWS
WAR?
EAST KRONDUN
"THE FOLLOWING YEARS SAW THE TOTAL DESTRUCTION OF *FORTY-THREE* MAJOR HOUSES.
SLAVER WASPS AND THEIR REVENANTS WERE *EVERYWHERE.*"
"PEOPLE THOUGHT IT WAS THE *END DAYS.*"
"EVERYWHERE, IN THE THICK OF THINGS, THERE WERE THE HETERODYNES."
"ALWAYS FIGHTING."
"ALWAYS *SEARCHING.*"
"EVENTUALLY, THE ATTACKS STOPPED.
WE ASSUMED THAT THE MASTERS HAD FOUND THE OTHER AND BEATEN HIM—
BUT WE NEVER KNEW FOR SURE."
"THEY HAD *VANISHED.*"
"THE REVENANTS AND WASPS THAT REMAINED WERE DISORGANIZED— *LEADERLESS.*"
RHAAA?
"AND THEN THE BARON RETURNED."

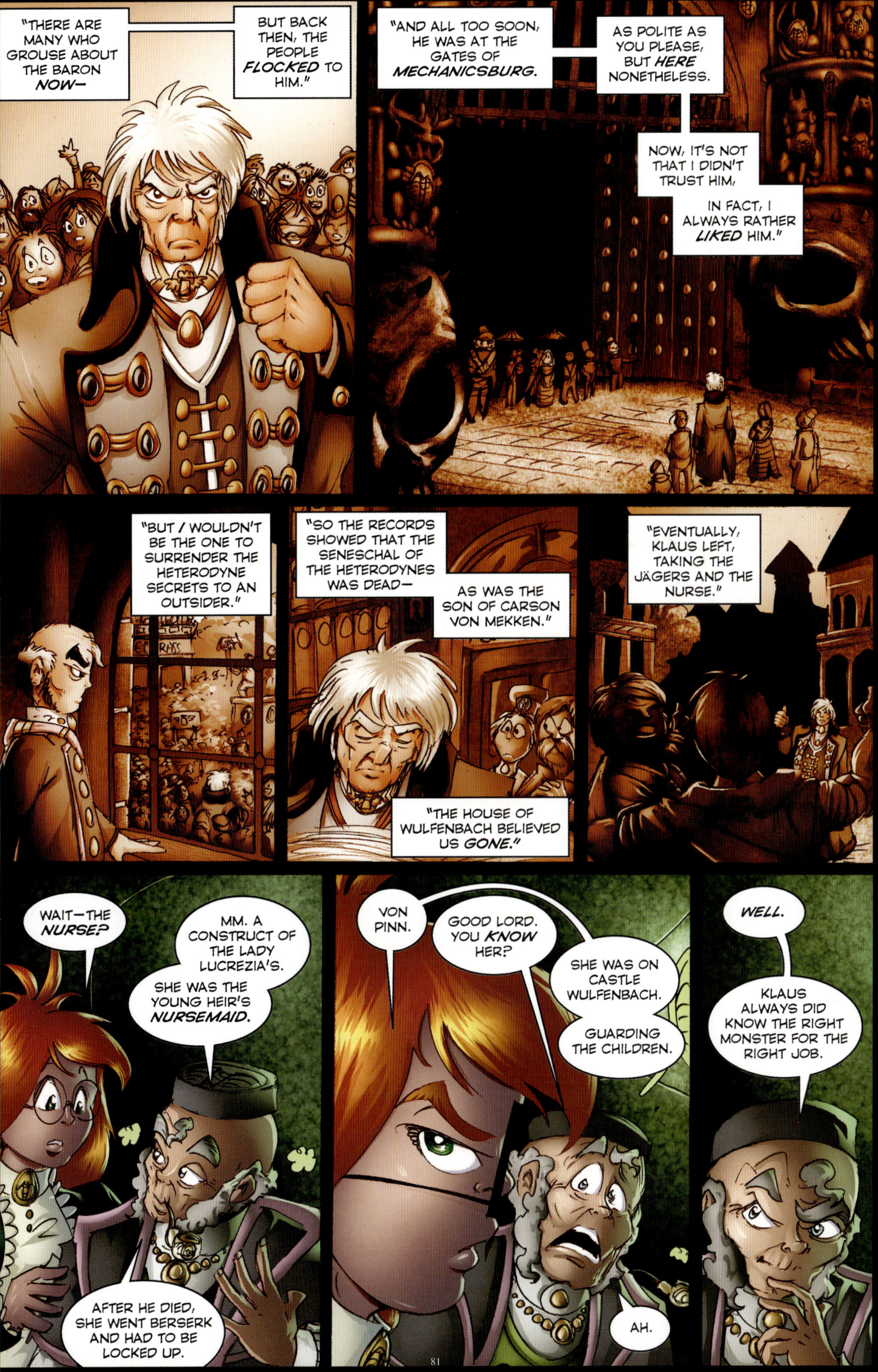
"THERE ARE MANY WHO GROUSE ABOUT THE BARON NOW—
BUT BACK THEN, THE PEOPLE FLOCKED TO HIM."
"AND ALL TOO SOON, HE WAS AT THE GATES OF MECHANICSBURG.
AS POLITE AS YOU PLEASE, BUT HERE NONETHELESS.
NOW, IT'S NOT THAT I DIDN'T TRUST HIM,
IN FACT, I ALWAYS RATHER LIKED HIM."
"BUT I WOULDN'T BE THE ONE TO SURRENDER THE HETERODYNE SECRETS TO AN OUTSIDER."
"SO THE RECORDS SHOWED THAT THE SENESCHAL OF THE HETERODYNES WAS DEAD—
AS WAS THE SON OF CARSON VON MEKKEN."
"THE HOUSE OF WULFENBACH BELIEVED US GONE."
"EVENTUALLY, KLAUS LEFT, TAKING THE JÄGERS AND THE NURSE."
WAIT—THE NURSE?
MM. A CONSTRUCT OF THE LADY LUCREZIA'S.
SHE WAS THE YOUNG HEIR'S NURSEMAID.
AFTER HE DIED, SHE WENT BERSERK AND HAD TO BE LOCKED UP.
VON PINN.
GOOD LORD. YOU KNOW HER?
SHE WAS ON CASTLE WULFENBACH.
GUARDING THE CHILDREN.
AH.
WELL.
KLAUS ALWAYS DID KNOW THE RIGHT MONSTER FOR THE RIGHT JOB.

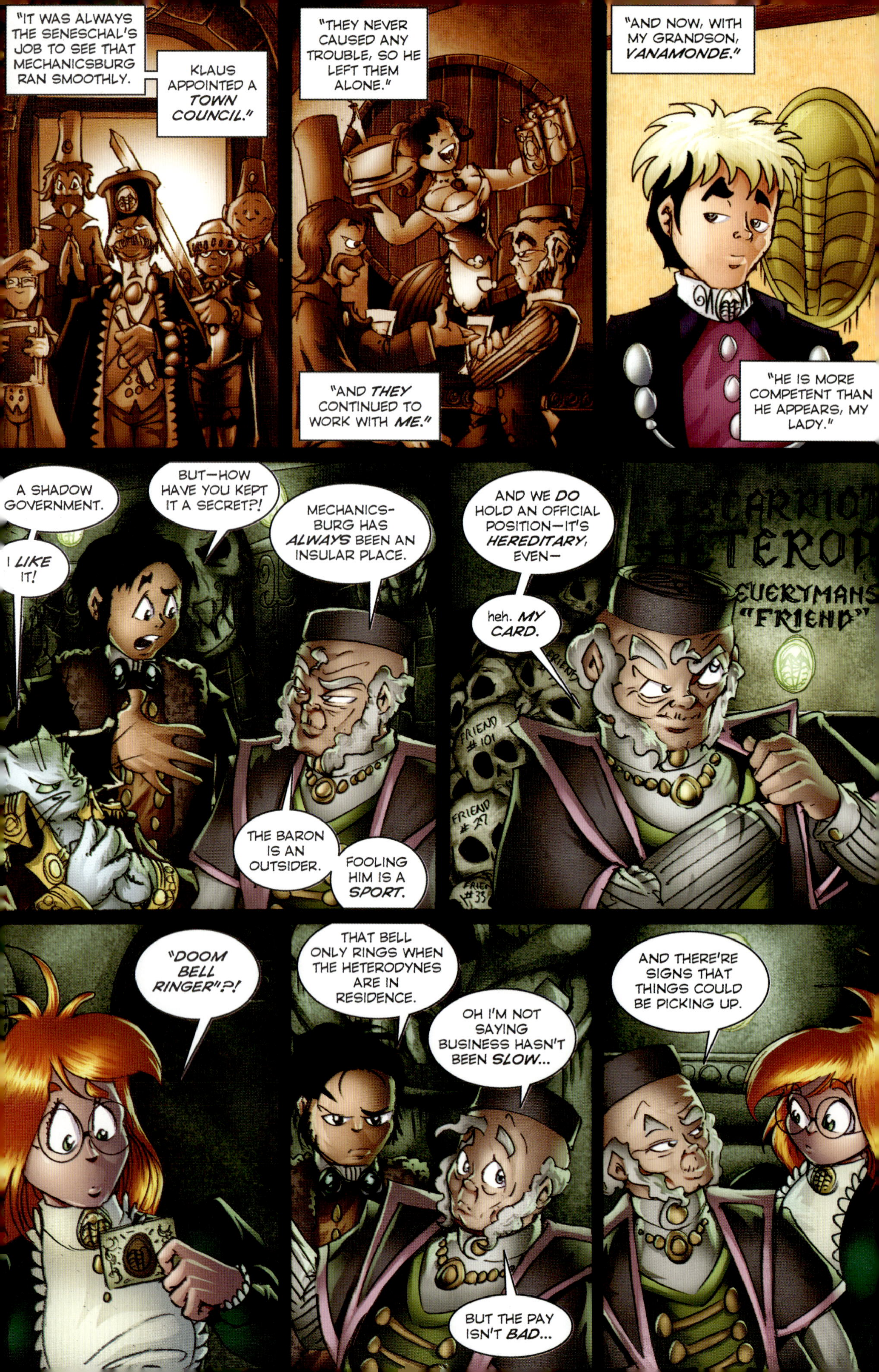
"IT WAS ALWAYS THE SENESCHAL'S JOB TO SEE THAT MECHANICSBURG RAN SMOOTHLY.
KLAUS APPOINTED A *TOWN COUNCIL."*
"THEY NEVER CAUSED ANY TROUBLE, SO HE LEFT THEM ALONE."
"AND *THEY* CONTINUED TO WORK WITH *ME."*
"AND NOW, WITH MY GRANDSON, *VANAMONDE."*
"HE IS MORE COMPETENT THAN HE APPEARS, MY LADY."
A SHADOW GOVERNMENT.
I *LIKE* IT!
BUT—HOW HAVE YOU KEPT IT A SECRET?!
MECHANICS-BURG HAS *ALWAYS* BEEN AN INSULAR PLACE.
THE BARON IS AN OUTSIDER.
FOOLING HIM IS A *SPORT.*
AND WE *DO* HOLD AN OFFICIAL POSITION—IT'S *HEREDITARY,* EVEN—
heh. *MY CARD.*
EVERYMANS "FRIEND"
FRIEND #101
FRIEND #27
"DOOM BELL RINGER"?!
THAT BELL ONLY RINGS WHEN THE HETERODYNES ARE IN RESIDENCE.
OH I'M NOT SAYING BUSINESS HASN'T BEEN *SLOW...*
BUT THE PAY ISN'T *BAD...*
AND THERE'RE SIGNS THAT THINGS COULD BE PICKING UP.

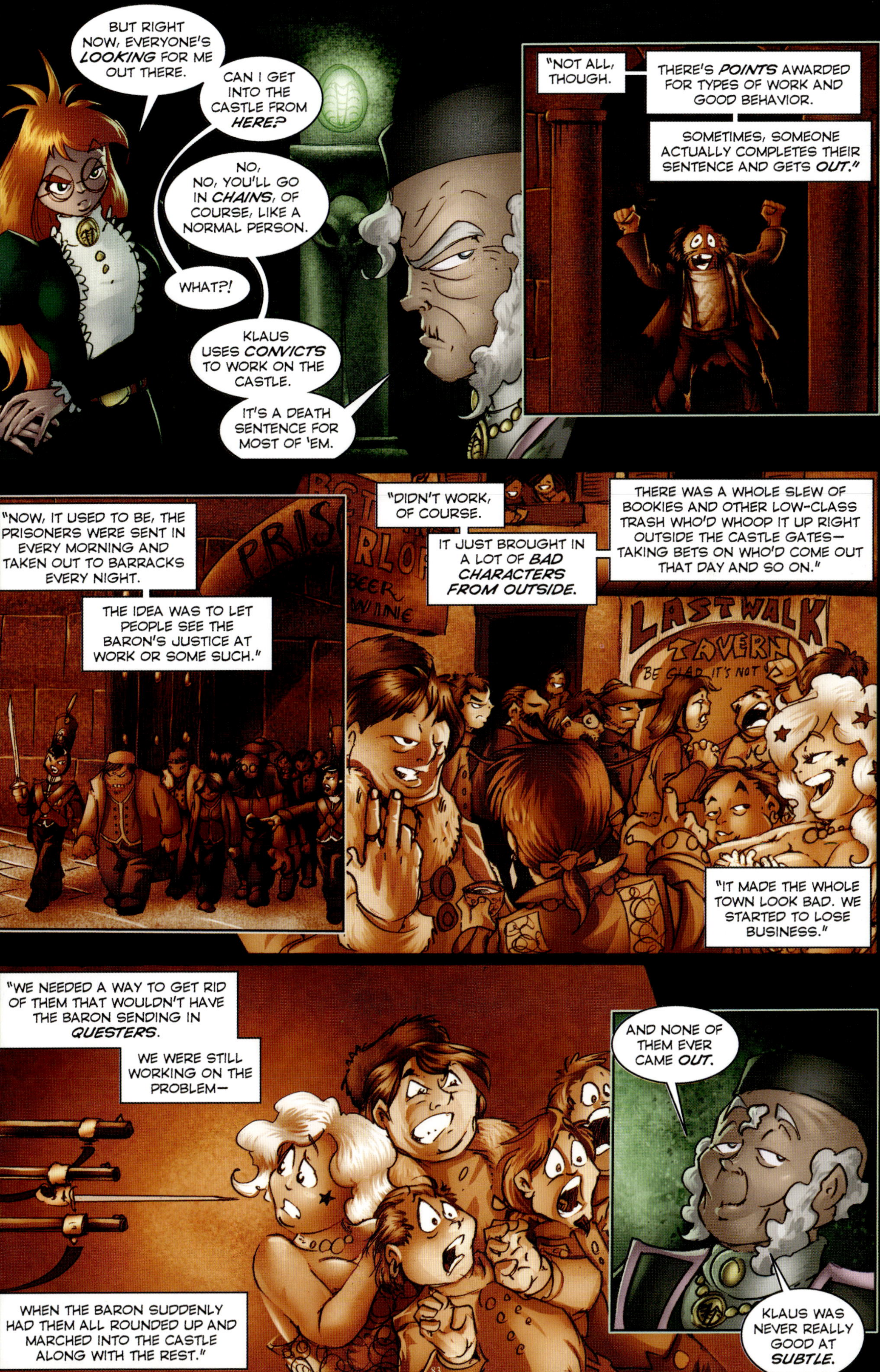

BUT RIGHT NOW, EVERYONE'S LOOKING FOR ME OUT THERE.
CAN I GET INTO THE CASTLE FROM HERE?
NO, NO, YOU'LL GO IN CHAINS, OF COURSE, LIKE A NORMAL PERSON.
WHAT?!
KLAUS USES CONVICTS TO WORK ON THE CASTLE.
IT'S A DEATH SENTENCE FOR MOST OF 'EM.
"NOT ALL, THOUGH.
THERE'S POINTS AWARDED FOR TYPES OF WORK AND GOOD BEHAVIOR.
SOMETIMES, SOMEONE ACTUALLY COMPLETES THEIR SENTENCE AND GETS OUT."
"NOW, IT USED TO BE, THE PRISONERS WERE SENT IN EVERY MORNING AND TAKEN OUT TO BARRACKS EVERY NIGHT.
THE IDEA WAS TO LET PEOPLE SEE THE BARON'S JUSTICE AT WORK OR SOME SUCH."
"DIDN'T WORK, OF COURSE.
IT JUST BROUGHT IN A LOT OF BAD CHARACTERS FROM OUTSIDE.
THERE WAS A WHOLE SLEW OF BOOKIES AND OTHER LOW-CLASS TRASH WHO'D WHOOP IT UP RIGHT OUTSIDE THE CASTLE GATES—TAKING BETS ON WHO'D COME OUT THAT DAY AND SO ON."
BEER
WINE
LAST WALK TAVERN
"BE GLAD IT'S NOT
"IT MADE THE WHOLE TOWN LOOK BAD. WE STARTED TO LOSE BUSINESS."
"WE NEEDED A WAY TO GET RID OF THEM THAT WOULDN'T HAVE THE BARON SENDING IN QUESTERS.
WE WERE STILL WORKING ON THE PROBLEM—
WHEN THE BARON SUDDENLY HAD THEM ALL ROUNDED UP AND MARCHED INTO THE CASTLE ALONG WITH THE REST."
AND NONE OF THEM EVER CAME OUT.
KLAUS WAS NEVER REALLY GOOD AT SUBTLE.

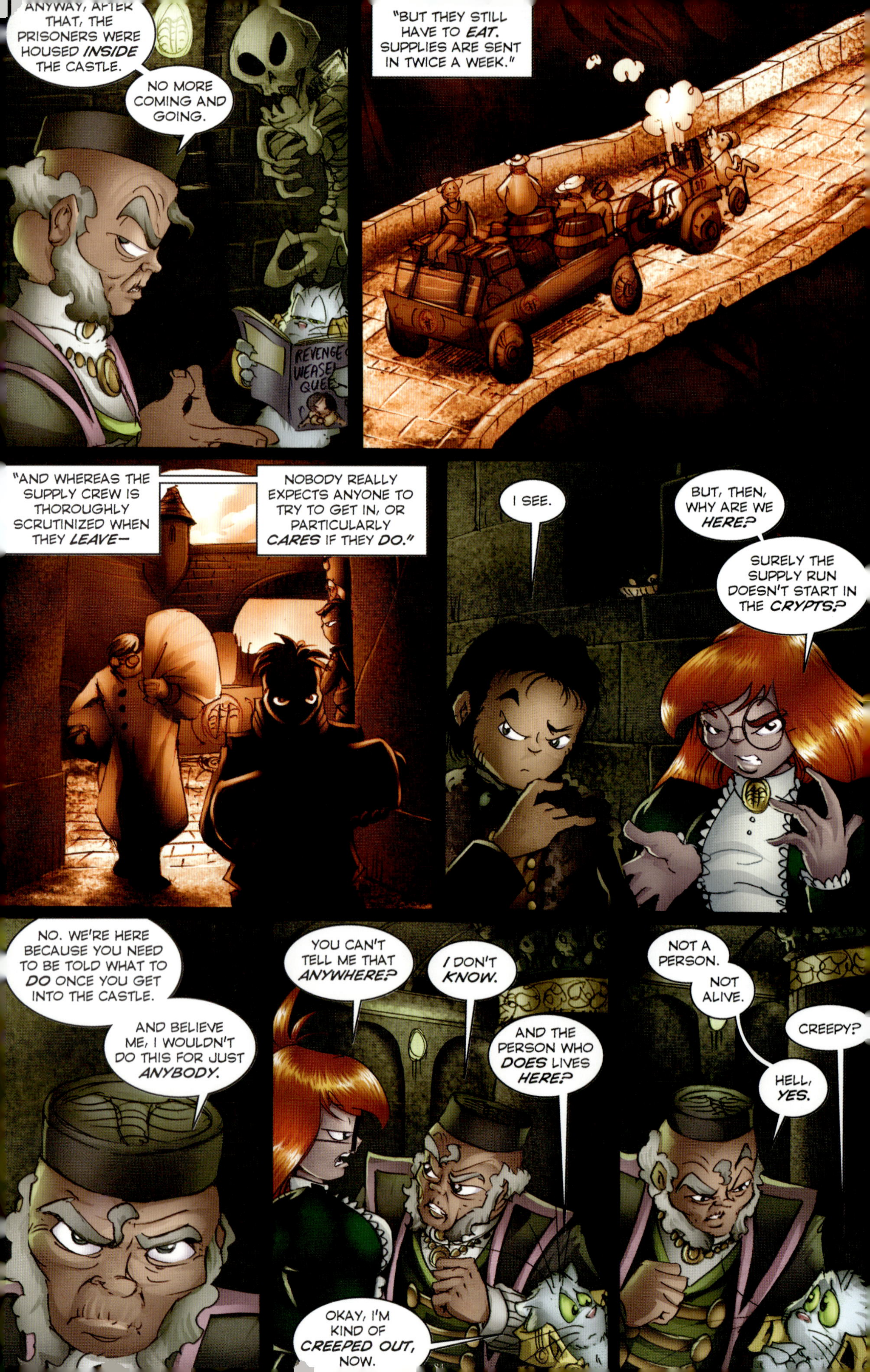
ANYWAY, AFTER THAT, THE PRISONERS WERE HOUSED *INSIDE* THE CASTLE.
NO MORE COMING AND GOING.
REVENGE WEASEL QUEE
"BUT THEY STILL HAVE TO *EAT*. SUPPLIES ARE SENT IN TWICE A WEEK."
"AND WHEREAS THE SUPPLY CREW IS THOROUGHLY SCRUTINIZED WHEN THEY *LEAVE*—
NOBODY REALLY EXPECTS ANYONE TO TRY TO GET IN, OR PARTICULARLY *CARES* IF THEY *DO*."
I SEE.
BUT, THEN, WHY ARE WE *HERE?*
SURELY THE SUPPLY RUN DOESN'T START IN THE *CRYPTS?*
NO. WE'RE HERE BECAUSE YOU NEED TO BE TOLD WHAT TO *DO* ONCE YOU GET INTO THE CASTLE.
AND BELIEVE ME, I WOULDN'T DO THIS FOR JUST *ANYBODY*.
YOU CAN'T TELL ME THAT *ANYWHERE?*
I DON'T KNOW.
AND THE PERSON WHO *DOES* LIVES *HERE?*
OKAY, I'M KIND OF *CREEPED OUT*, NOW.
NOT A PERSON.
NOT ALIVE.
CREEPY?
HELL, *YES*.

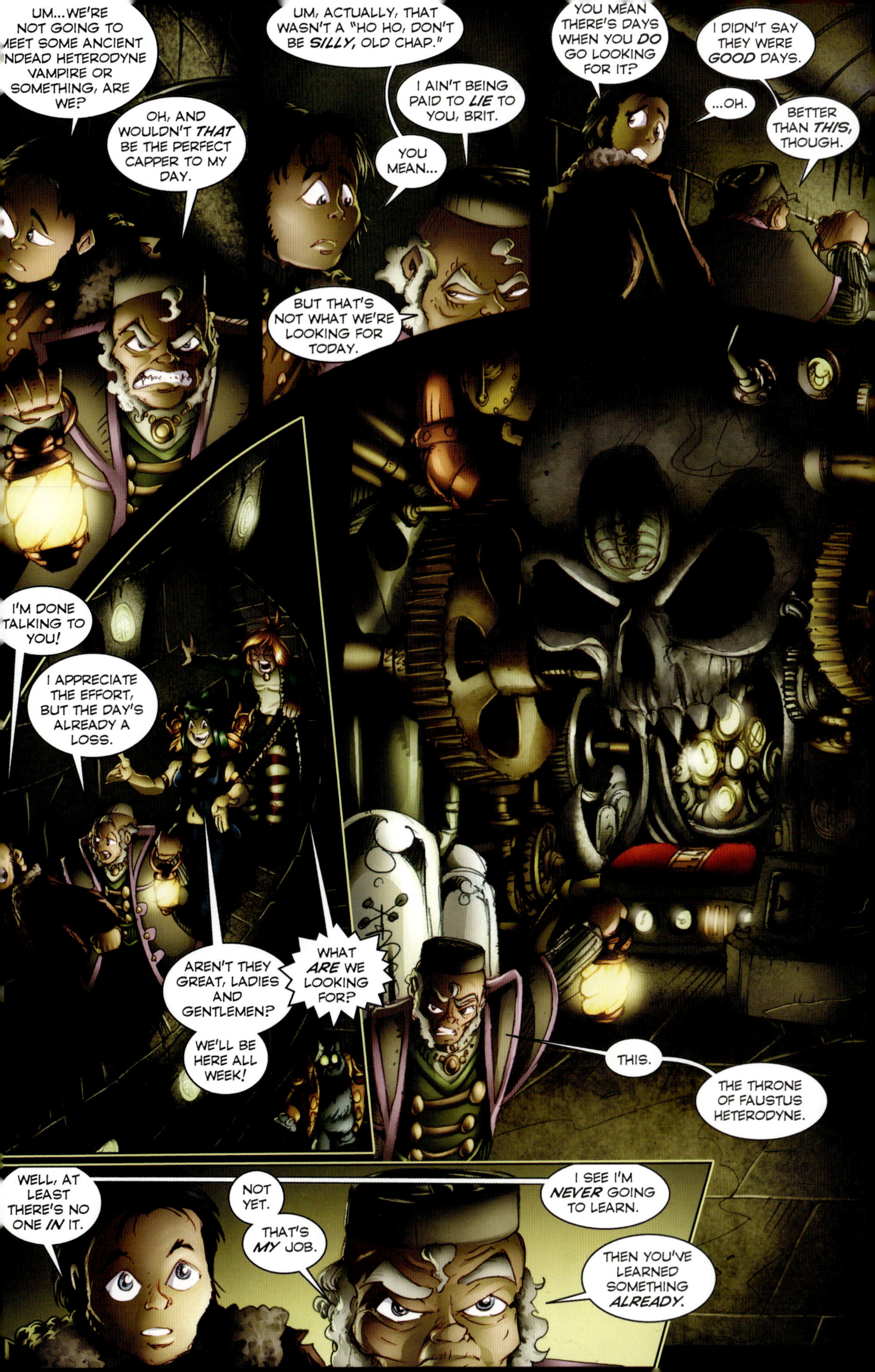
UM...WE'RE NOT GOING TO MEET SOME ANCIENT UNDEAD HETERODYNE VAMPIRE OR SOMETHING, ARE WE?
OH, AND WOULDN'T *THAT* BE THE PERFECT CAPPER TO MY DAY.
UM, ACTUALLY, THAT WASN'T A "HO HO, DON'T BE *SILLY,* OLD CHAP."
I AIN'T BEING PAID TO *LIE* TO YOU, BRIT.
YOU MEAN...
BUT THAT'S NOT WHAT WE'RE LOOKING FOR TODAY.
YOU MEAN THERE'S DAYS WHEN YOU *DO* GO LOOKING FOR IT?
I DIDN'T SAY THEY WERE *GOOD* DAYS.
...OH.
BETTER THAN *THIS,* THOUGH.
I'M DONE TALKING TO YOU!
I APPRECIATE THE EFFORT, BUT THE DAY'S ALREADY A LOSS.
AREN'T THEY GREAT, LADIES AND GENTLEMEN?
WE'LL BE HERE ALL WEEK!
WHAT *ARE* WE LOOKING FOR?
THIS.
THE THRONE OF FAUSTUS HETERODYNE.
WELL, AT LEAST THERE'S NO ONE *IN* IT.
NOT YET.
THAT'S *MY* JOB.
I SEE I'M *NEVER* GOING TO LEARN.
THEN YOU'VE LEARNED SOMETHING *ALREADY.*

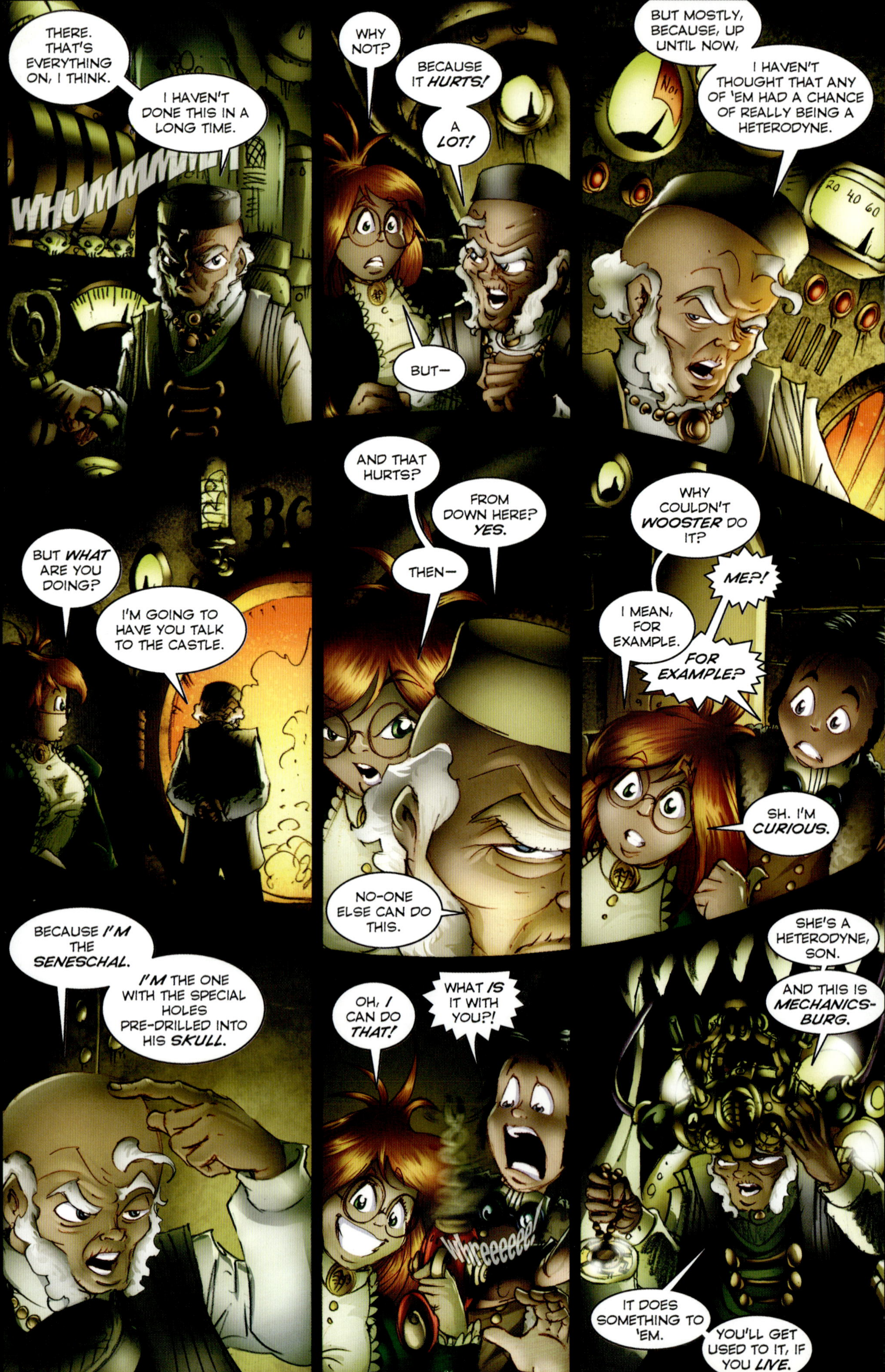
THERE. THAT'S EVERYTHING ON, I THINK.
I HAVEN'T DONE THIS IN A LONG TIME.
WHUMMMMM
WHY NOT?
BECAUSE IT HURTS!
A LOT!
BUT—
BUT MOSTLY, BECAUSE, UP UNTIL NOW,
I HAVEN'T THOUGHT THAT ANY OF 'EM HAD A CHANCE OF REALLY BEING A HETERODYNE.
BUT WHAT ARE YOU DOING?
I'M GOING TO HAVE YOU TALK TO THE CASTLE.
AND THAT HURTS?
FROM DOWN HERE? YES.
THEN—
NO-ONE ELSE CAN DO THIS.
WHY COULDN'T WOOSTER DO IT?
ME?!
I MEAN, FOR EXAMPLE.
FOR EXAMPLE?
SH. I'M CURIOUS.
BECAUSE I'M THE SENESCHAL.
I'M THE ONE WITH THE SPECIAL HOLES PRE-DRILLED INTO HIS SKULL.
OH, I CAN DO THAT!
WHAT IS IT WITH YOU?!
SHE'S A HETERODYNE, SON.
AND THIS IS MECHANICSBURG.
IT DOES SOMETHING TO 'EM.
YOU'LL GET USED TO IT, IF YOU LIVE.

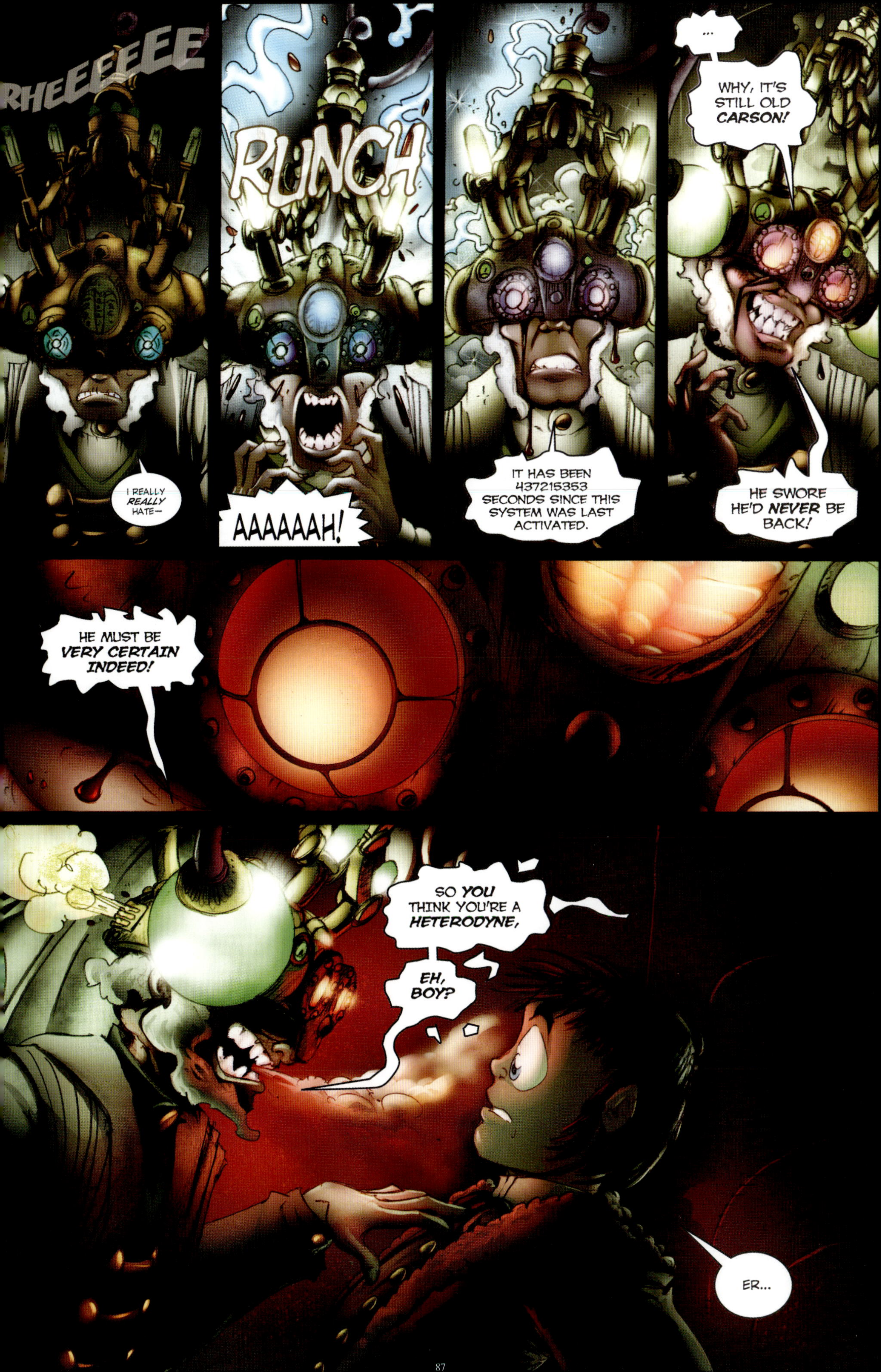
RHEEEEEE
I REALLY REALLY HATE—
RUNCH
AAAAAAH!
IT HAS BEEN 437215353 SECONDS SINCE THIS SYSTEM WAS LAST ACTIVATED.
...
WHY, IT'S STILL OLD CARSON!
HE SWORE HE'D NEVER BE BACK!
HE MUST BE VERY CERTAIN INDEED!
SO YOU THINK YOU'RE A HETERODYNE,
EH, BOY?
ER...

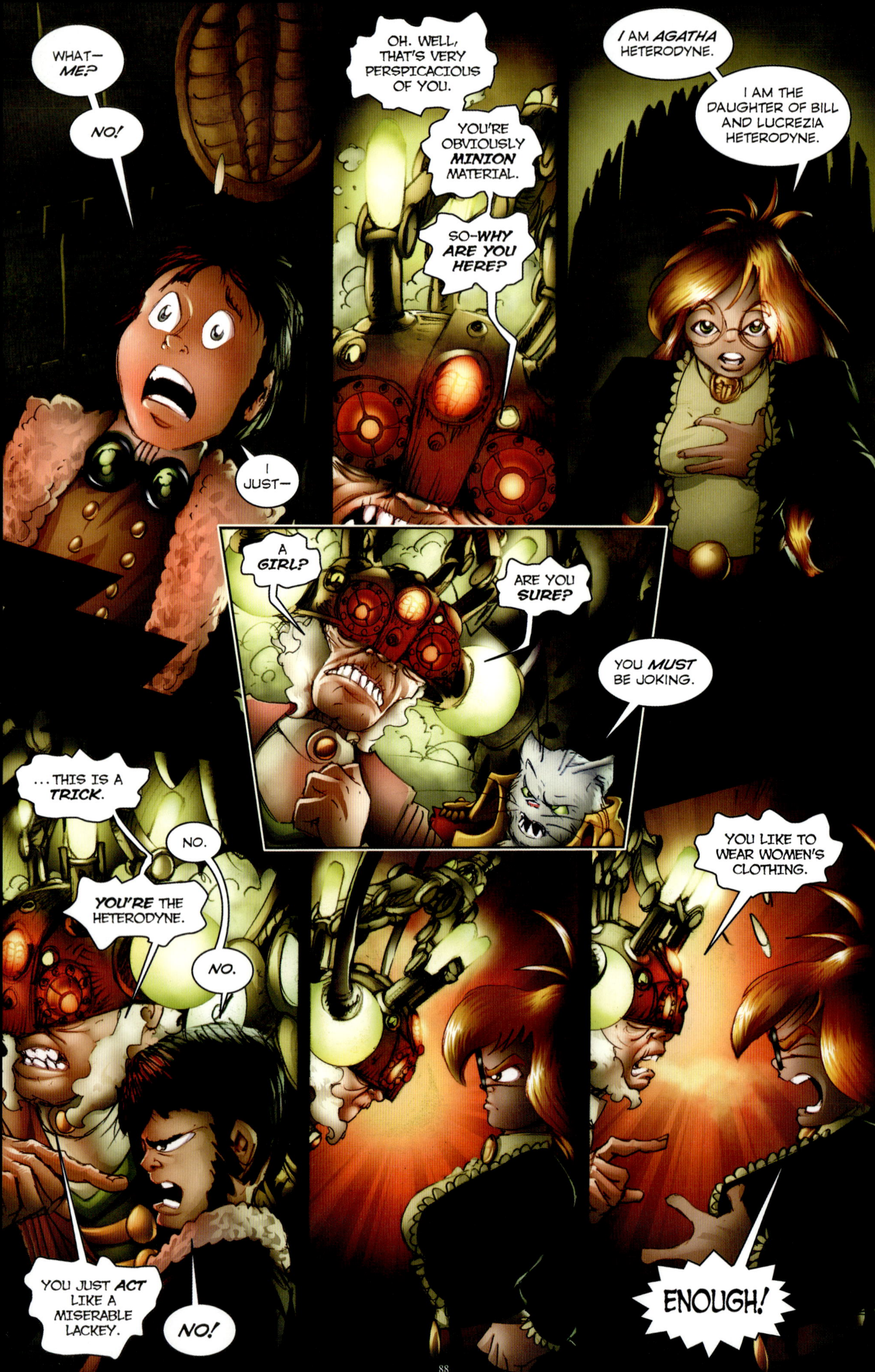
WHAT—
ME?
NO!
I JUST—
OH. WELL, THAT'S VERY PERSPICACIOUS OF YOU.
YOU'RE OBVIOUSLY ***MINION*** MATERIAL.
SO—***WHY ARE YOU HERE?***
I AM ***AGATHA*** HETERODYNE.
I AM THE DAUGHTER OF BILL AND LUCREZIA HETERODYNE.
A ***GIRL?***
ARE YOU ***SURE?***
YOU ***MUST*** BE JOKING.
...THIS IS A ***TRICK.***
NO.
YOU'RE THE HETERODYNE.
NO.
YOU JUST ***ACT*** LIKE A MISERABLE LACKEY.
NO!
YOU LIKE TO WEAR WOMEN'S CLOTHING.
ENOUGH!

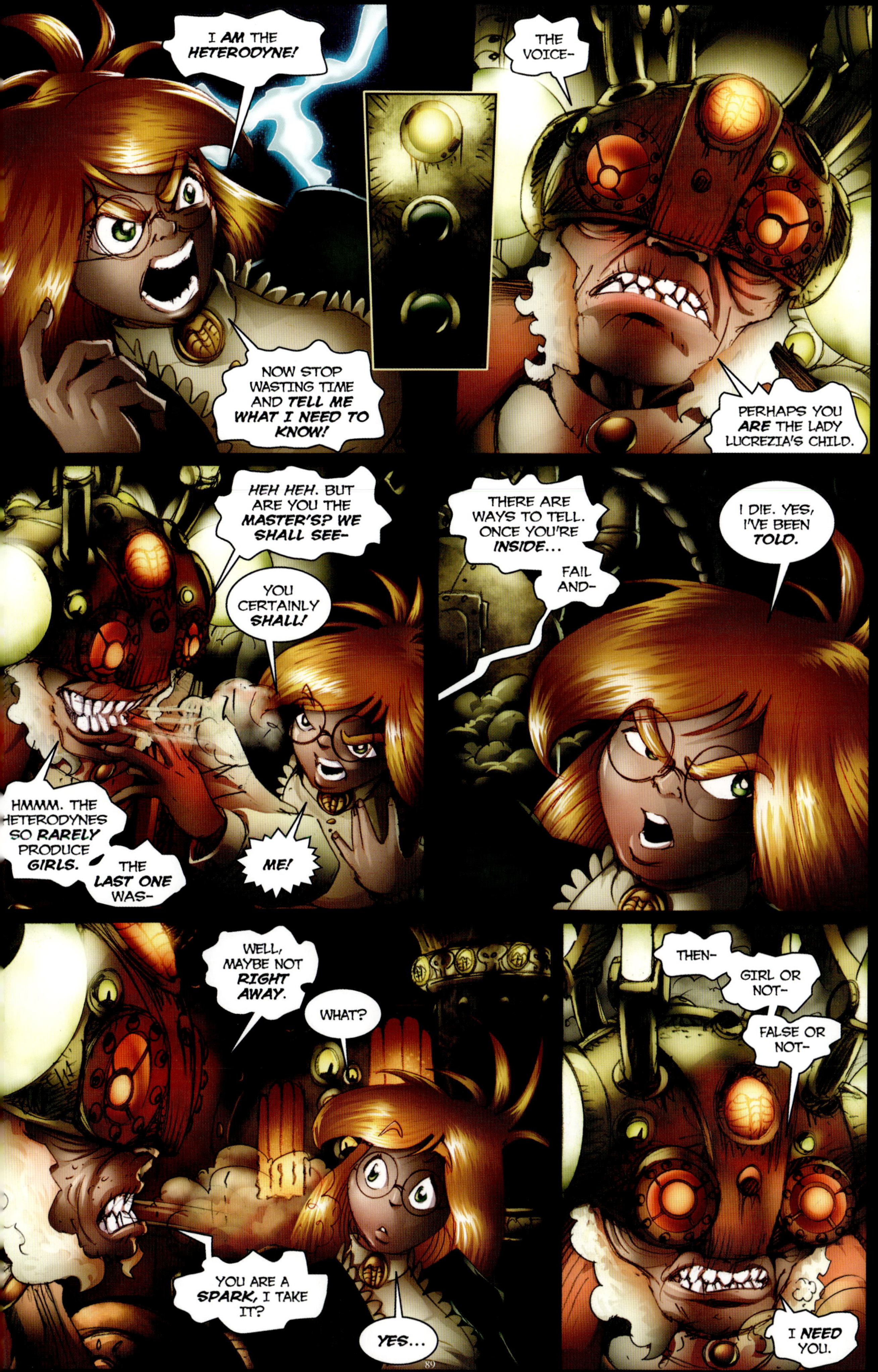
I AM THE HETERODYNE!
NOW STOP WASTING TIME AND TELL ME WHAT I NEED TO KNOW!
THE VOICE-
PERHAPS YOU ARE THE LADY LUCREZIA'S CHILD.
HEH HEH. BUT ARE YOU THE MASTER'S? WE SHALL SEE-
YOU CERTAINLY SHALL!
HMMM. THE HETERODYNES SO RARELY PRODUCE GIRLS.
THE LAST ONE WAS-
ME!
THERE ARE WAYS TO TELL. ONCE YOU'RE INSIDE...
FAIL AND-
I DIE. YES, I'VE BEEN TOLD.
WELL, MAYBE NOT RIGHT AWAY.
WHAT?
YOU ARE A SPARK, I TAKE IT?
YES...
THEN-
GIRL OR NOT-
FALSE OR NOT-
I NEED YOU.

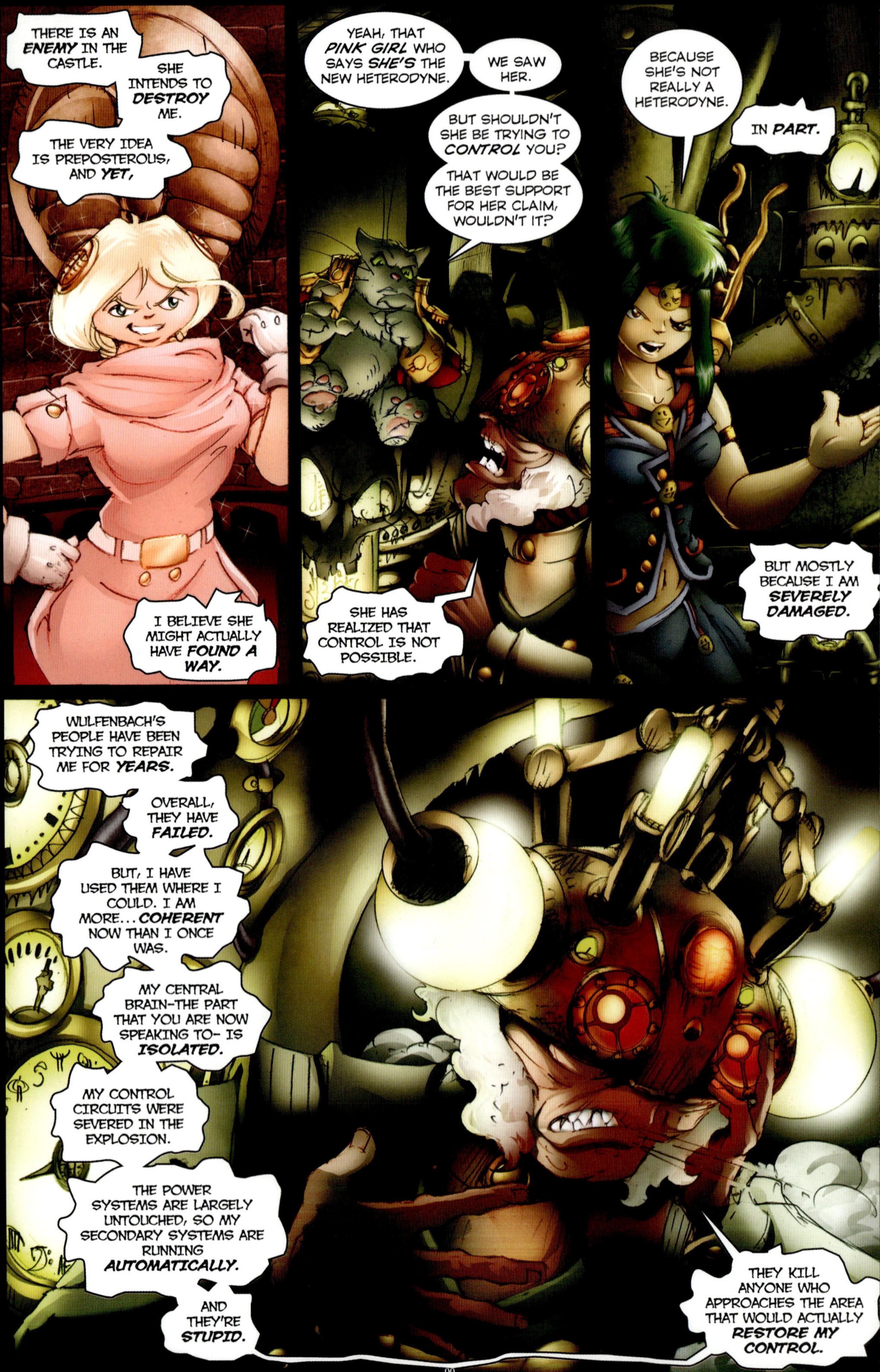
THERE IS AN ENEMY IN THE CASTLE.
SHE INTENDS TO DESTROY ME.
THE VERY IDEA IS PREPOSTEROUS, AND YET,
I BELIEVE SHE MIGHT ACTUALLY HAVE FOUND A WAY.
YEAH, THAT PINK GIRL WHO SAYS SHE'S THE NEW HETERODYNE.
WE SAW HER.
BUT SHOULDN'T SHE BE TRYING TO CONTROL YOU?
THAT WOULD BE THE BEST SUPPORT FOR HER CLAIM, WOULDN'T IT?
SHE HAS REALIZED THAT CONTROL IS NOT POSSIBLE.
BECAUSE SHE'S NOT REALLY A HETERODYNE.
IN PART.
BUT MOSTLY BECAUSE I AM SEVERELY DAMAGED.
WULFENBACH'S PEOPLE HAVE BEEN TRYING TO REPAIR ME FOR YEARS.
OVERALL, THEY HAVE FAILED.
BUT, I HAVE USED THEM WHERE I COULD. I AM MORE... COHERENT NOW THAN I ONCE WAS.
MY CENTRAL BRAIN–THE PART THAT YOU ARE NOW SPEAKING TO– IS ISOLATED.
MY CONTROL CIRCUITS WERE SEVERED IN THE EXPLOSION.
THE POWER SYSTEMS ARE LARGELY UNTOUCHED, SO MY SECONDARY SYSTEMS ARE RUNNING AUTOMATICALLY.
AND THEY'RE STUPID.
THEY KILL ANYONE WHO APPROACHES THE AREA THAT WOULD ACTUALLY RESTORE MY CONTROL.

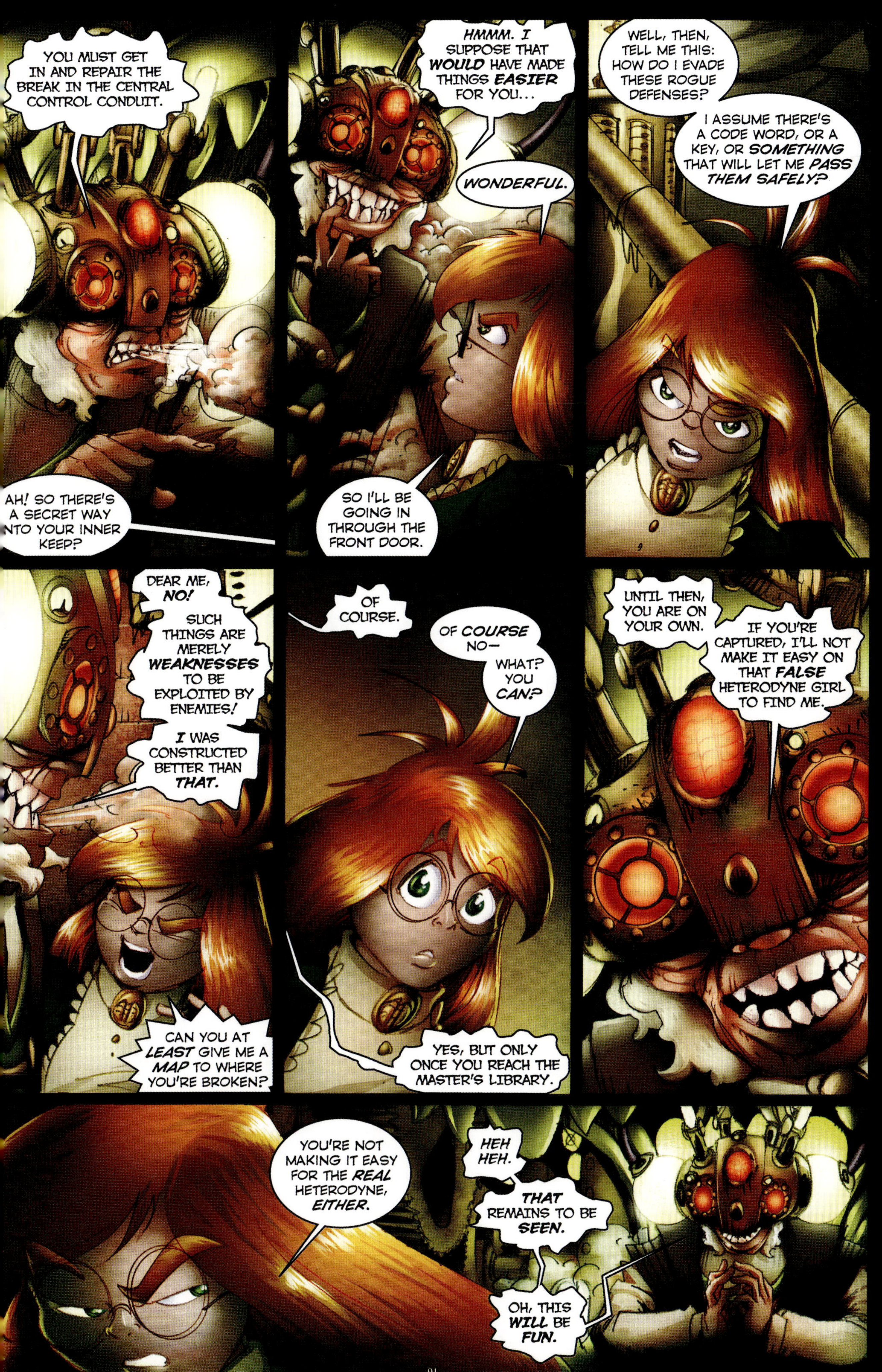
YOU MUST GET IN AND REPAIR THE BREAK IN THE CENTRAL CONTROL CONDUIT.
AH! SO THERE'S A SECRET WAY NTO YOUR INNER KEEP?
HMMM. I SUPPOSE THAT WOULD HAVE MADE THINGS EASIER FOR YOU...
WONDERFUL.
SO I'LL BE GOING IN THROUGH THE FRONT DOOR.
WELL, THEN, TELL ME THIS: HOW DO I EVADE THESE ROGUE DEFENSES?
I ASSUME THERE'S A CODE WORD, OR A KEY, OR SOMETHING THAT WILL LET ME PASS THEM SAFELY?
DEAR ME, NO!
SUCH THINGS ARE MERELY WEAKNESSES TO BE EXPLOITED BY ENEMIES!
I WAS CONSTRUCTED BETTER THAN THAT.
CAN YOU AT LEAST GIVE ME A MAP TO WHERE YOU'RE BROKEN?
OF COURSE.
OF COURSE NO—
WHAT? YOU CAN?
YES, BUT ONLY ONCE YOU REACH THE MASTER'S LIBRARY.
UNTIL THEN, YOU ARE ON YOUR OWN.
IF YOU'RE CAPTURED, I'LL NOT MAKE IT EASY ON THAT FALSE HETERODYNE GIRL TO FIND ME.
YOU'RE NOT MAKING IT EASY FOR THE REAL HETERODYNE, EITHER.
HEH HEH.
THAT REMAINS TO BE SEEN.
OH, THIS WILL BE FUN.

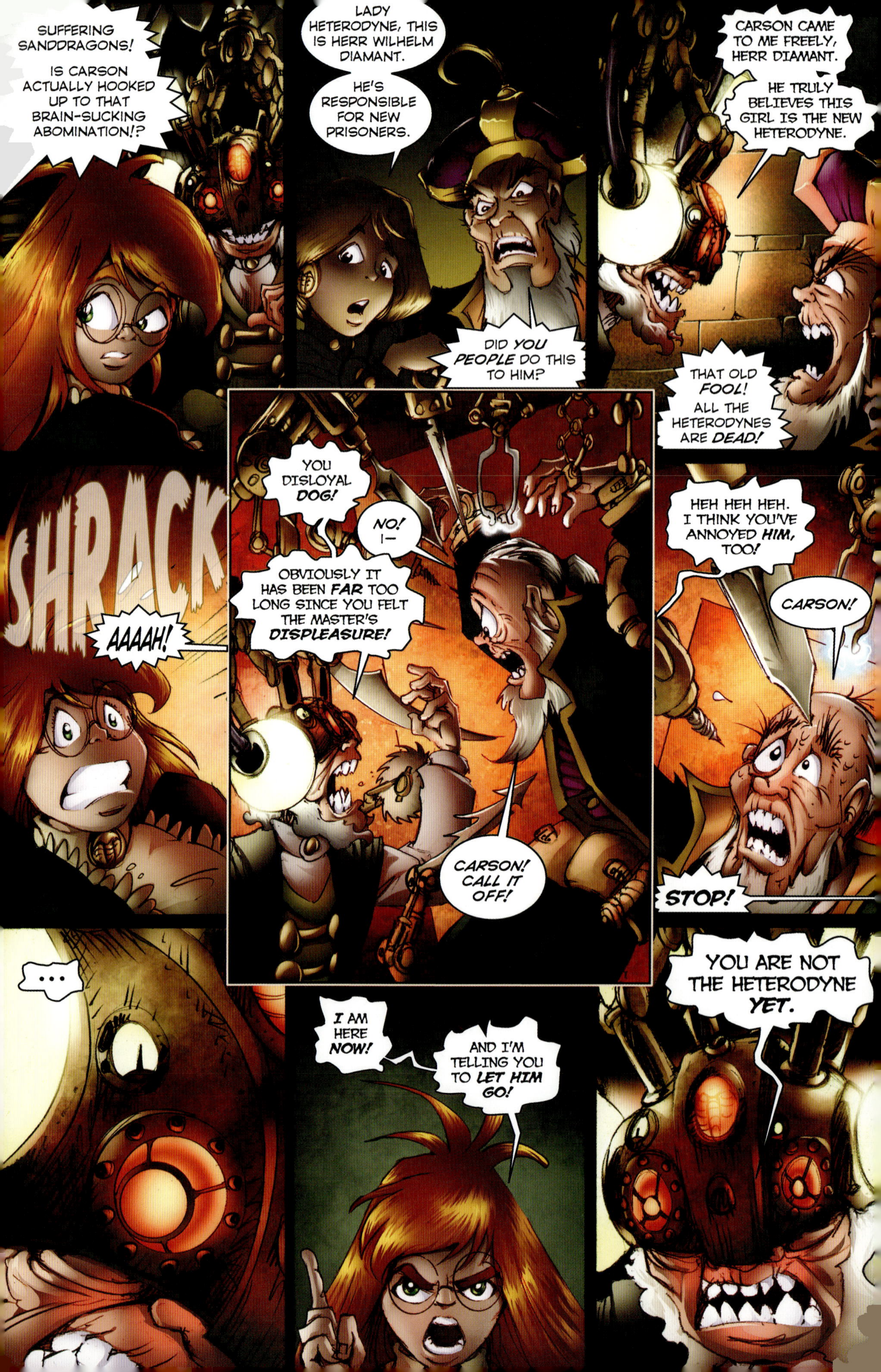
SUFFERING SANDDRAGONS!
IS CARSON ACTUALLY HOOKED UP TO THAT BRAIN-SUCKING ABOMINATION!?
LADY HETERODYNE, THIS IS HERR WILHELM DIAMANT.
HE'S RESPONSIBLE FOR NEW PRISONERS.
DID YOU PEOPLE DO THIS TO HIM?
CARSON CAME TO ME FREELY, HERR DIAMANT.
HE TRULY BELIEVES THIS GIRL IS THE NEW HETERODYNE.
THAT OLD FOOL! ALL THE HETERODYNES ARE DEAD!
SHRACK
AAAAH!
YOU DISLOYAL DOG!
NO! I—
OBVIOUSLY IT HAS BEEN FAR TOO LONG SINCE YOU FELT THE MASTER'S DISPLEASURE!
CARSON! CALL IT OFF!
HEH HEH HEH. I THINK YOU'VE ANNOYED HIM, TOO!
CARSON!
STOP!
...
I AM HERE NOW!
AND I'M TELLING YOU TO LET HIM GO!
YOU ARE NOT THE HETERODYNE YET.

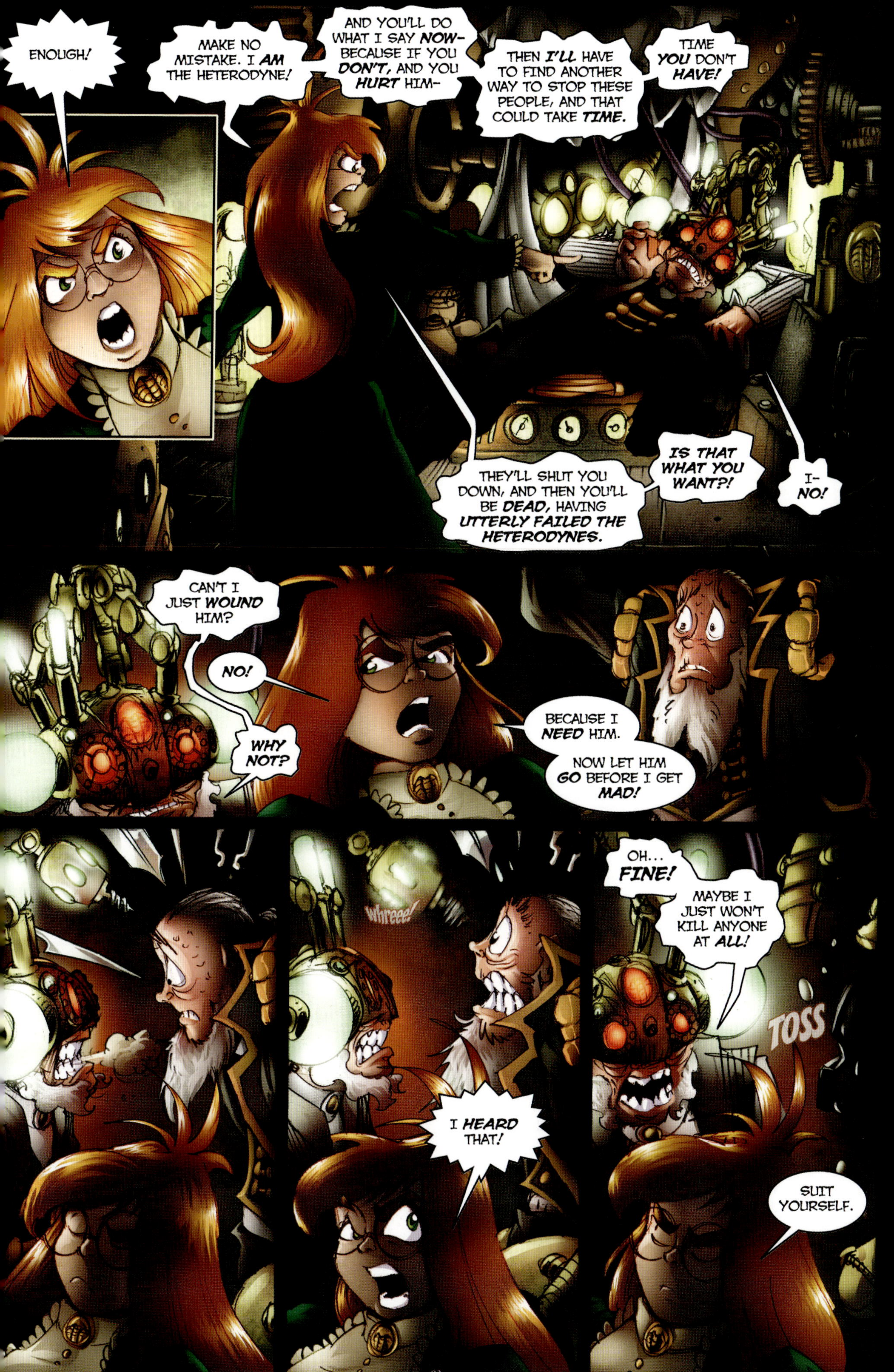
ENOUGH!
MAKE NO MISTAKE. I AM THE HETERODYNE!
AND YOU'LL DO WHAT I SAY NOW- BECAUSE IF YOU DON'T, AND YOU HURT HIM-
THEN I'LL HAVE TO FIND ANOTHER WAY TO STOP THESE PEOPLE, AND THAT COULD TAKE TIME.
TIME YOU DON'T HAVE!
THEY'LL SHUT YOU DOWN, AND THEN YOU'LL BE DEAD, HAVING UTTERLY FAILED THE HETERODYNES.
IS THAT WHAT YOU WANT?!
I- NO!
CAN'T I JUST WOUND HIM?
NO!
WHY NOT?
BECAUSE I NEED HIM.
NOW LET HIM GO BEFORE I GET MAD!
whreee!
I HEARD THAT!
OH... FINE!
MAYBE I JUST WON'T KILL ANYONE AT ALL!
TOSS
SUIT YOURSELF.

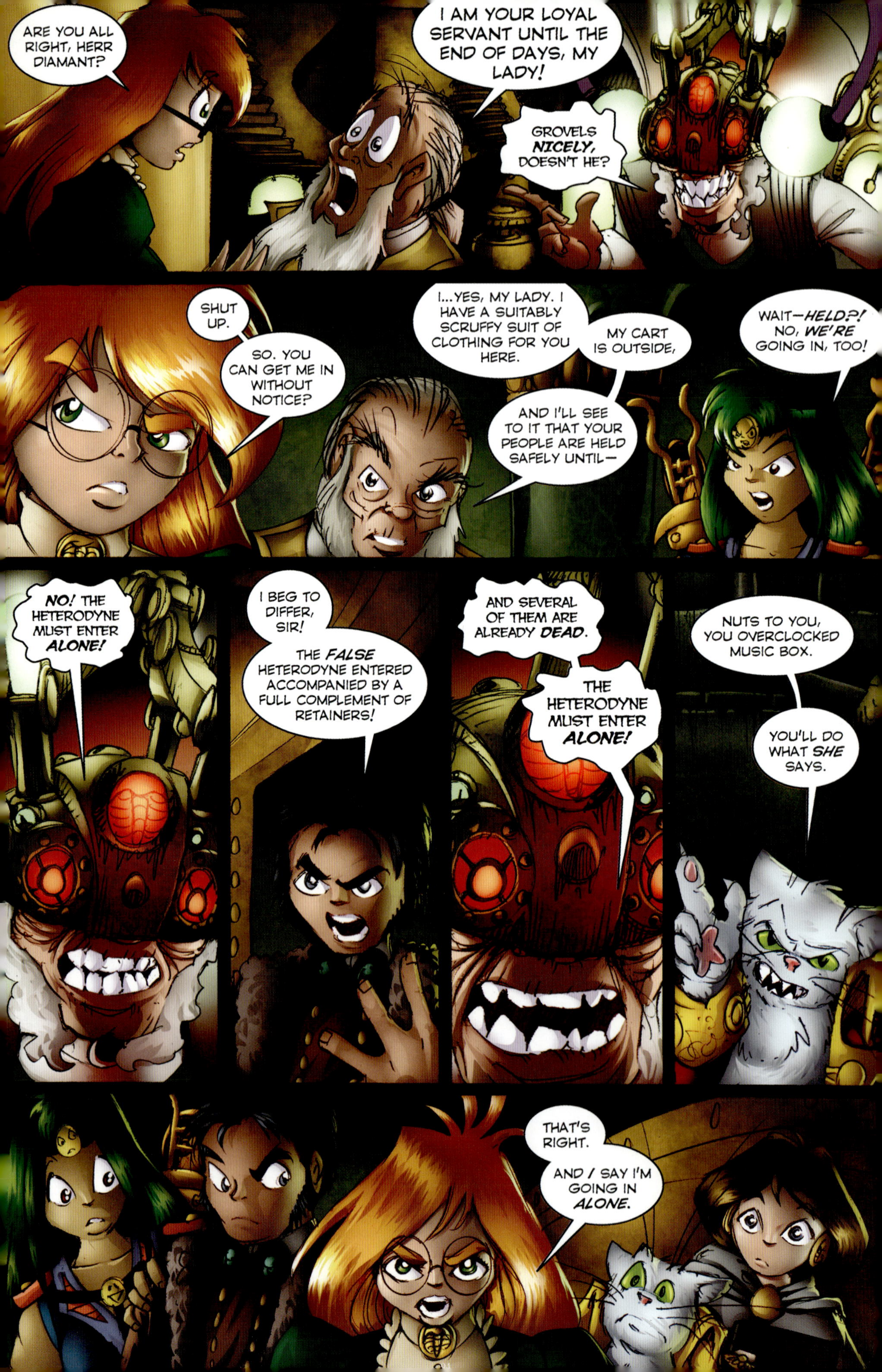
ARE YOU ALL RIGHT, HERR DIAMANT?
I AM YOUR LOYAL SERVANT UNTIL THE END OF DAYS, MY LADY!
GROVELS NICELY, DOESN'T HE?
SHUT UP.
SO. YOU CAN GET ME IN WITHOUT NOTICE?
I...YES, MY LADY. I HAVE A SUITABLY SCRUFFY SUIT OF CLOTHING FOR YOU HERE.
MY CART IS OUTSIDE,
AND I'LL SEE TO IT THAT YOUR PEOPLE ARE HELD SAFELY UNTIL—
WAIT—HELD?! NO, WE'RE GOING IN, TOO!
NO! THE HETERODYNE MUST ENTER ALONE!
I BEG TO DIFFER, SIR!
THE FALSE HETERODYNE ENTERED ACCOMPANIED BY A FULL COMPLEMENT OF RETAINERS!
AND SEVERAL OF THEM ARE ALREADY DEAD.
THE HETERODYNE MUST ENTER ALONE!
NUTS TO YOU, YOU OVERCLOCKED MUSIC BOX.
YOU'LL DO WHAT SHE SAYS.
THAT'S RIGHT.
AND I SAY I'M GOING IN ALONE.

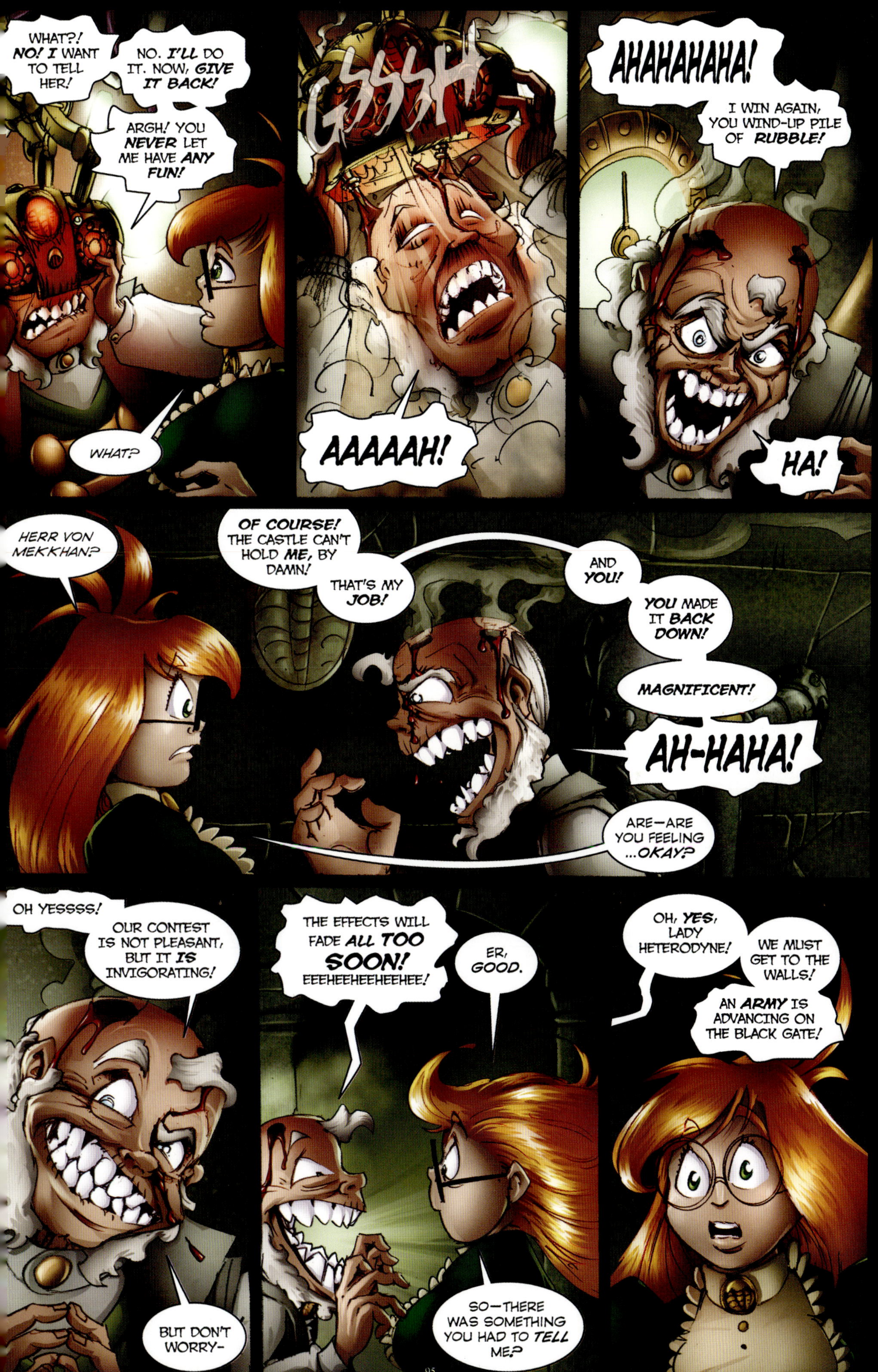
WHAT?! NO! I WANT TO TELL HER!
NO. I'LL DO IT. NOW, GIVE IT BACK!
ARGH! YOU NEVER LET ME HAVE ANY FUN!
WHAT?
GSSSH
AAAAAH!
AHAHAHAHA!
I WIN AGAIN, YOU WIND-UP PILE OF RUBBLE!
HA!
HERR VON MEKKHAN?
OF COURSE! THE CASTLE CAN'T HOLD ME, BY DAMN!
THAT'S MY JOB!
AND YOU!
YOU MADE IT BACK DOWN!
MAGNIFICENT!
AH-HAHA!
ARE—ARE YOU FEELING ...OKAY?
OH YESSSS!
OUR CONTEST IS NOT PLEASANT, BUT IT IS INVIGORATING!
BUT DON'T WORRY-
THE EFFECTS WILL FADE ALL TOO SOON! EEEHEEHEEHEEHEE!
ER, GOOD.
SO—THERE WAS SOMETHING YOU HAD TO TELL ME?
OH, YES, LADY HETERODYNE!
WE MUST GET TO THE WALLS!
AN ARMY IS ADVANCING ON THE BLACK GATE!

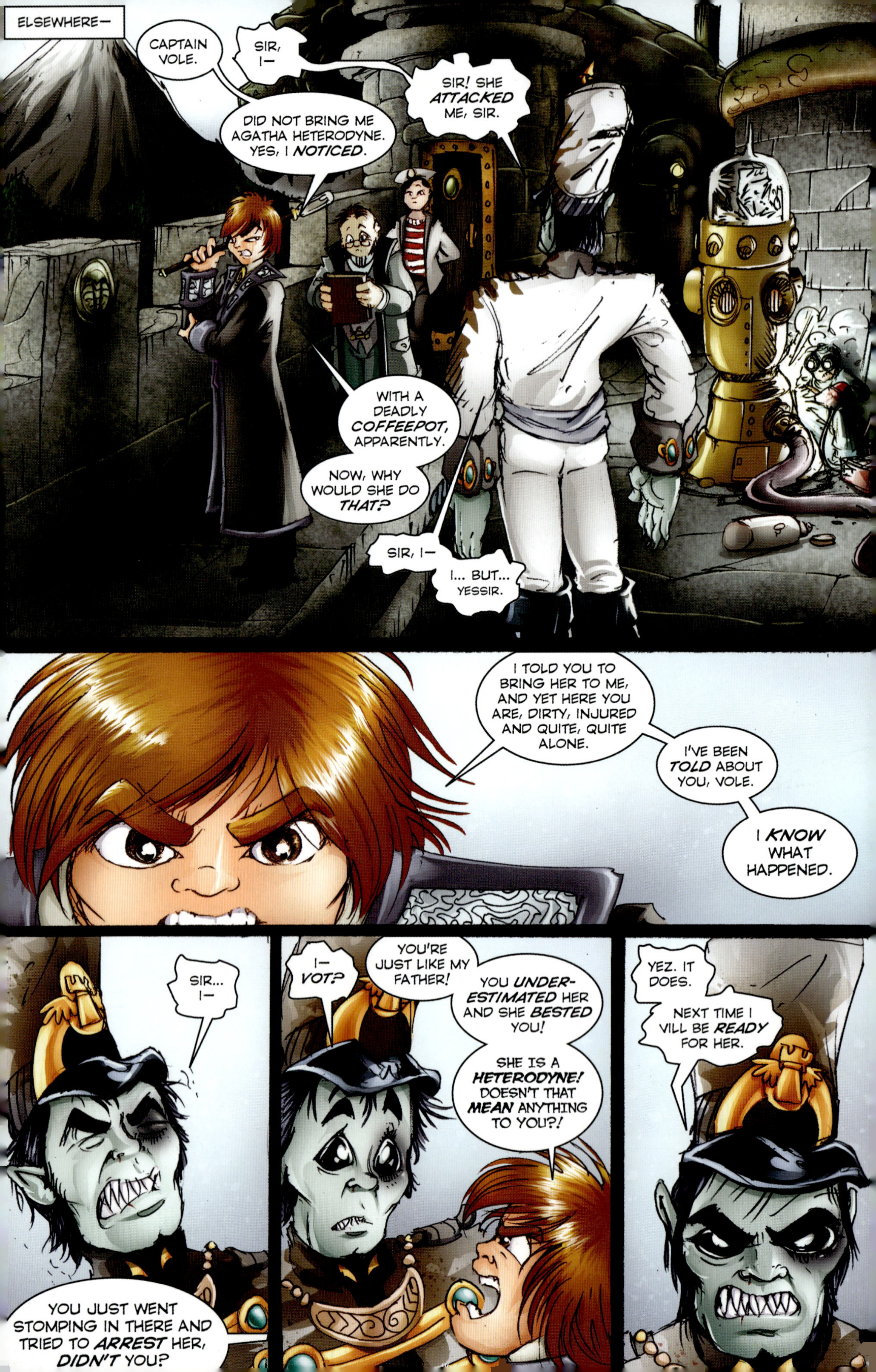
ELSEWHERE—
CAPTAIN VOLE.
SIR, I—
SIR! SHE ATTACKED ME, SIR.
DID NOT BRING ME AGATHA HETERODYNE. YES, I NOTICED.
WITH A DEADLY COFFEEPOT, APPARENTLY.
NOW, WHY WOULD SHE DO THAT?
SIR, I—
I... BUT... YESSIR.
I TOLD YOU TO BRING HER TO ME, AND YET HERE YOU ARE, DIRTY, INJURED AND QUITE, QUITE ALONE.
I'VE BEEN TOLD ABOUT YOU, VOLE.
I KNOW WHAT HAPPENED.
SIR... I—
YOU JUST WENT STOMPING IN THERE AND TRIED TO ARREST HER, DIDN'T YOU?
I— VOT?
YOU'RE JUST LIKE MY FATHER!
YOU UNDER-ESTIMATED HER AND SHE BESTED YOU!
SHE IS A HETERODYNE! DOESN'T THAT MEAN ANYTHING TO YOU?!
YEZ. IT DOES.
NEXT TIME I VILL BE READY FOR HER.

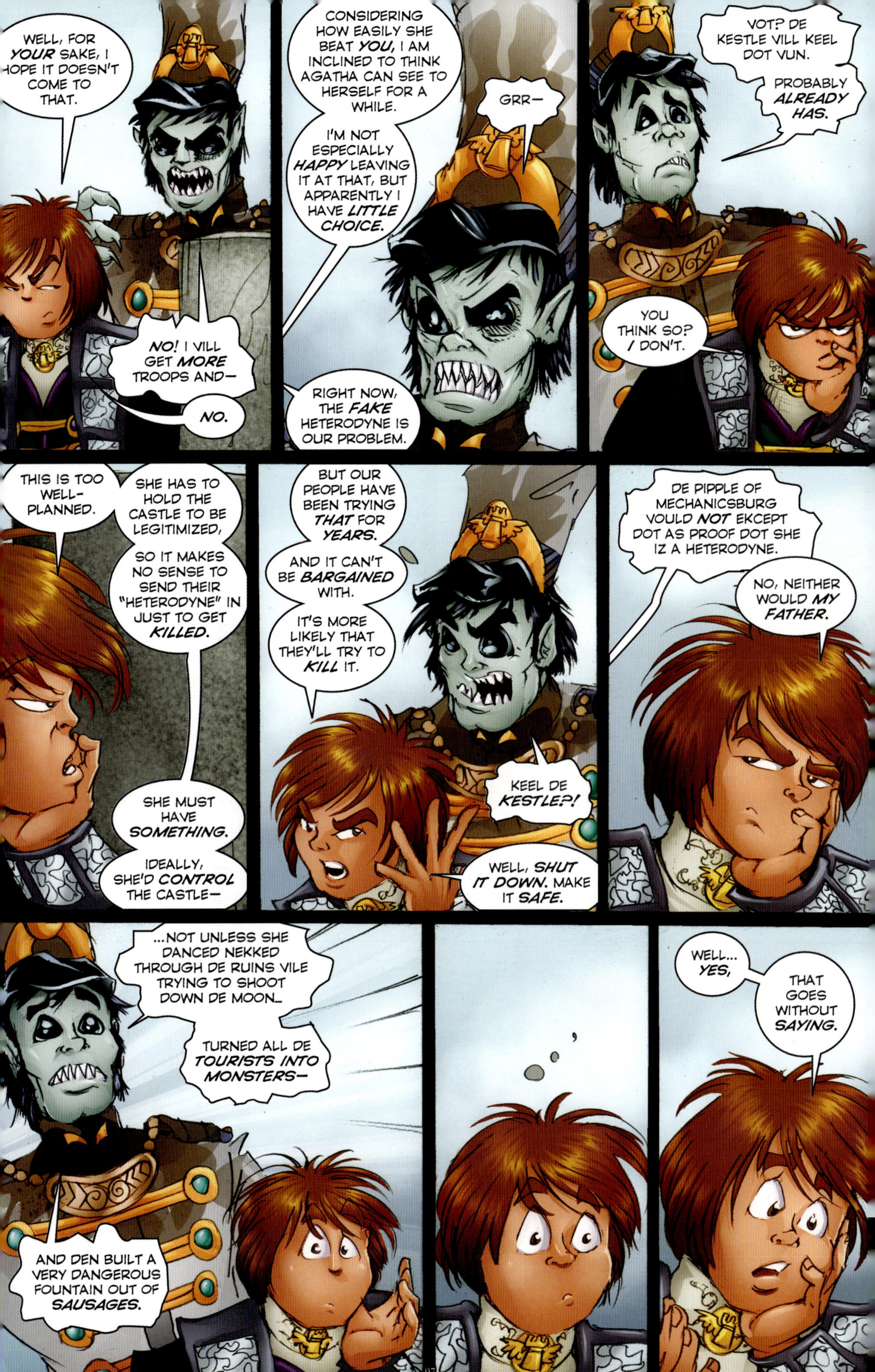

WELL, FOR *YOUR* SAKE, I HOPE IT DOESN'T COME TO THAT.
NO! I VILL GET *MORE* TROOPS AND—
NO.
CONSIDERING HOW EASILY SHE BEAT *YOU,* I AM INCLINED TO THINK AGATHA CAN SEE TO HERSELF FOR A WHILE.
GRR—
I'M NOT ESPECIALLY *HAPPY* LEAVING IT AT THAT, BUT APPARENTLY I HAVE *LITTLE CHOICE.*
RIGHT NOW, THE *FAKE* HETERODYNE IS OUR PROBLEM.
VOT? DE KESTLE VILL KEEL DOT VUN.
PROBABLY *ALREADY HAS.*
YOU THINK SO? *I* DON'T.
THIS IS TOO WELL-PLANNED.
SHE HAS TO HOLD THE CASTLE TO BE LEGITIMIZED,
SO IT MAKES NO SENSE TO SEND THEIR "HETERODYNE" IN JUST TO GET *KILLED.*
SHE MUST HAVE *SOMETHING.*
IDEALLY, SHE'D *CONTROL* THE CASTLE—
BUT OUR PEOPLE HAVE BEEN TRYING *THAT* FOR *YEARS.*
AND IT CAN'T BE *BARGAINED* WITH.
IT'S MORE LIKELY THAT THEY'LL TRY TO *KILL* IT.
KEEL DE *KESTLE?!*
WELL, *SHUT IT DOWN.* MAKE IT *SAFE.*
DE PIPPLE OF MECHANICSBURG VOULD *NOT* EKCEPT DOT AS PROOF DOT SHE IZ A HETERODYNE.
NO, NEITHER WOULD *MY FATHER.*
...NOT UNLESS SHE DANCED NEKKED THROUGH DE RUINS VILE TRYING TO SHOOT DOWN DE MOON...
TURNED ALL DE *TOURISTS INTO MONSTERS—*
AND DEN BUILT A VERY DANGEROUS FOUNTAIN OUT OF *SAUSAGES.*
WELL... *YES,*
THAT GOES WITHOUT *SAYING.*

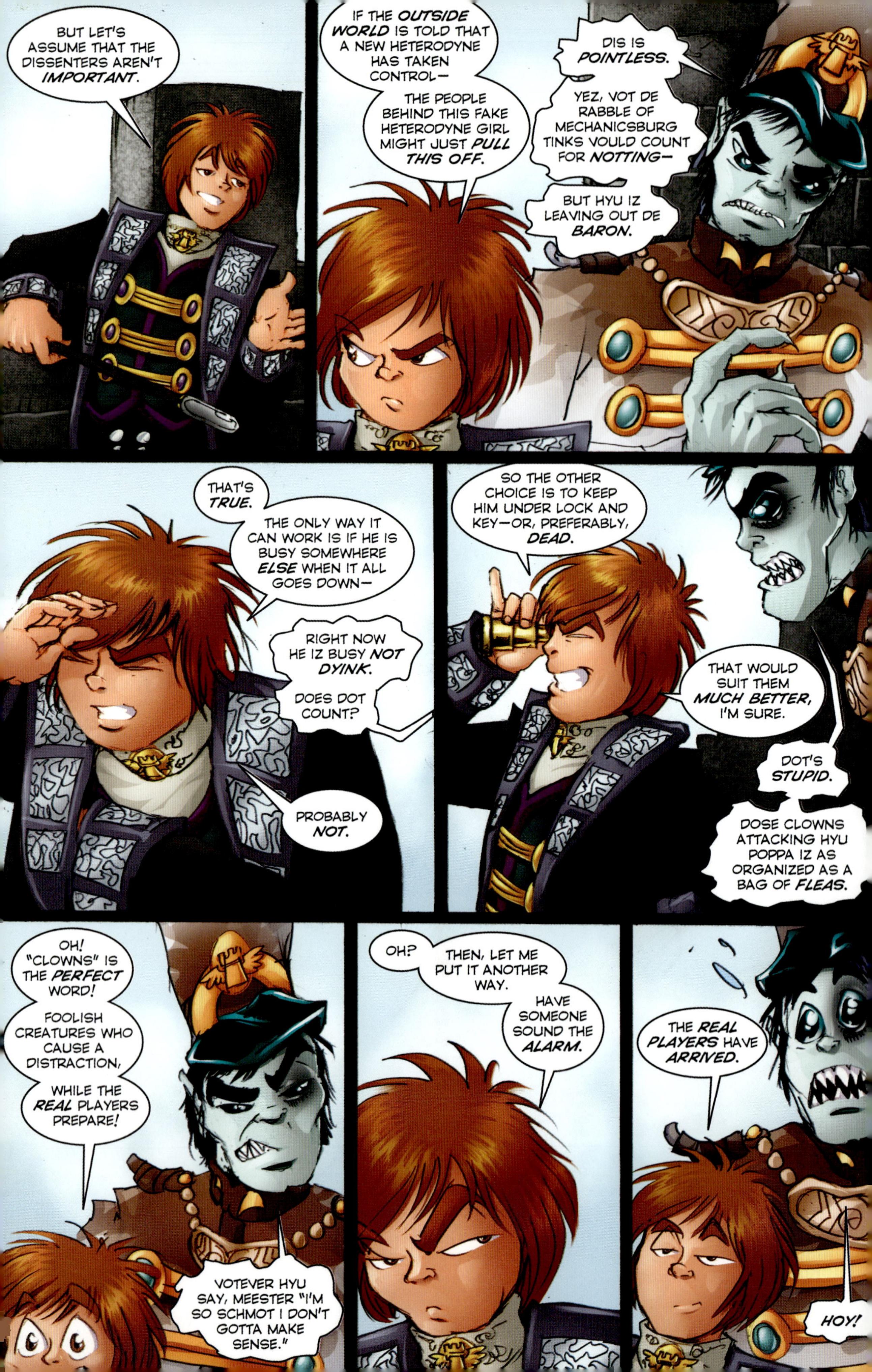
BUT LET'S ASSUME THAT THE DISSENTERS AREN'T *IMPORTANT*.
IF THE *OUTSIDE WORLD* IS TOLD THAT A NEW HETERODYNE HAS TAKEN CONTROL—
THE PEOPLE BEHIND THIS FAKE HETERODYNE GIRL MIGHT JUST *PULL THIS OFF*.
DIS IS *POINTLESS*.
YEZ, VOT DE RABBLE OF MECHANICSBURG TINKS VOULD COUNT FOR *NOTTING*—
BUT HYU IZ LEAVING OUT DE *BARON*.
THAT'S *TRUE*.
THE ONLY WAY IT CAN WORK IS IF HE IS BUSY SOMEWHERE *ELSE* WHEN IT ALL GOES DOWN—
RIGHT NOW HE IZ BUSY *NOT DYINK*.
DOES DOT COUNT?
PROBABLY *NOT*.
SO THE OTHER CHOICE IS TO KEEP HIM UNDER LOCK AND KEY—OR, PREFERABLY, *DEAD*.
THAT WOULD SUIT THEM *MUCH BETTER*, I'M SURE.
DOT'S *STUPID*.
DOSE CLOWNS ATTACKING HYU POPPA IZ AS ORGANIZED AS A BAG OF *FLEAS*.
OH! "CLOWNS" IS THE *PERFECT* WORD!
FOOLISH CREATURES WHO CAUSE A DISTRACTION,
WHILE THE *REAL* PLAYERS PREPARE!
VOTEVER HYU SAY, MEESTER "I'M SO SCHMOT I DON'T GOTTA MAKE SENSE."
OH?
THEN, LET ME PUT IT ANOTHER WAY.
HAVE SOMEONE SOUND THE *ALARM*.
THE *REAL PLAYERS* HAVE *ARRIVED*.
HOY!

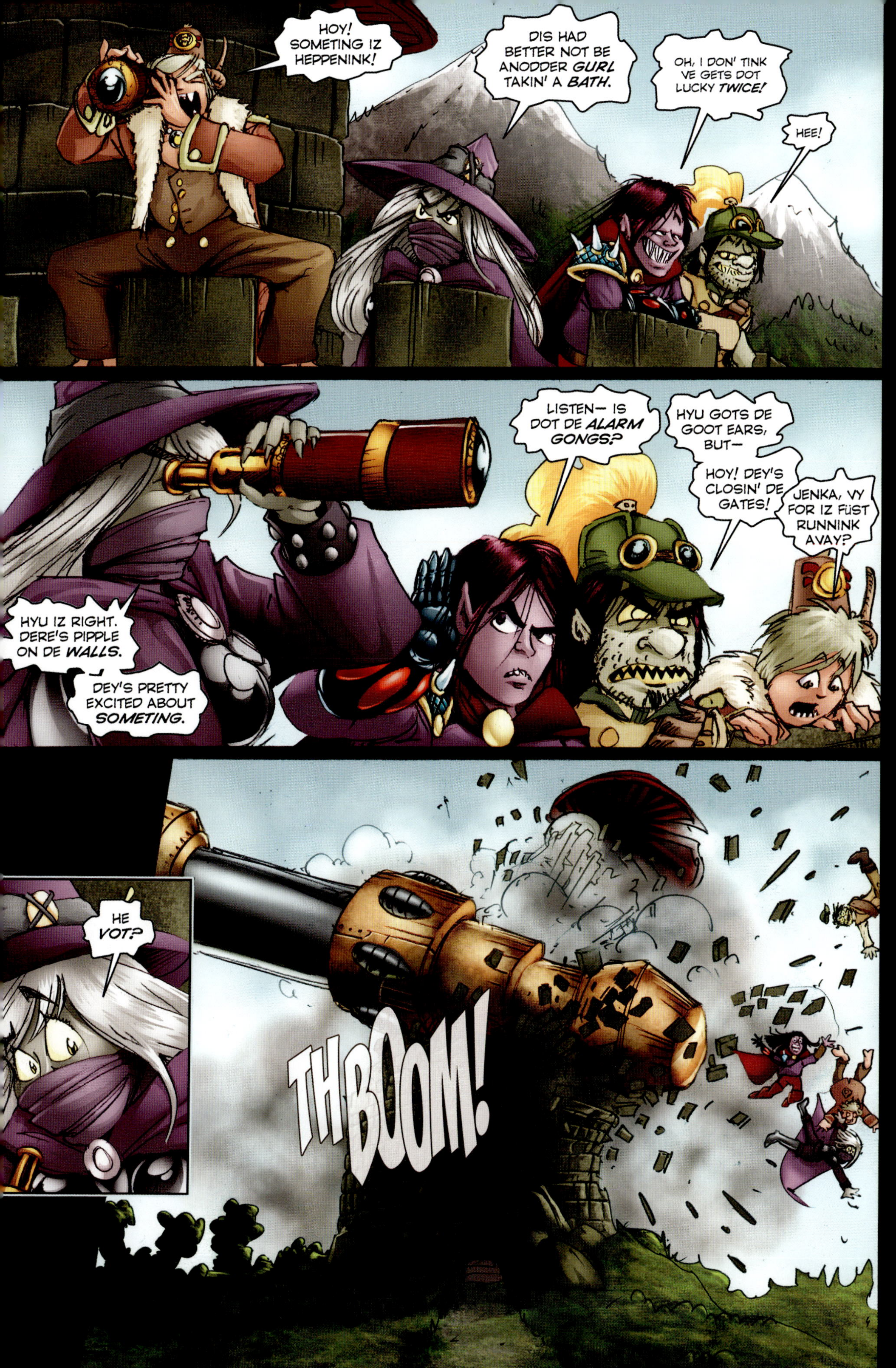
HOY! SOMETING IZ HEPPENINK!
DIS HAD BETTER NOT BE ANODDER GURL TAKIN' A BATH.
OH, I DON' TINK VE GETS DOT LUCKY TWICE!
HEE!
HYU IZ RIGHT. DERE'S PIPPLE ON DE WALLS.
DEY'S PRETTY EXCITED ABOUT SOMETING.
LISTEN— IS DOT DE ALARM GONGS?
HYU GOTS DE GOOT EARS, BUT—
HOY! DEY'S CLOSIN' DE GATES!
JENKA, VY FOR IZ FÜST RUNNINK AVAY?
HE VOT?
THBOOM!

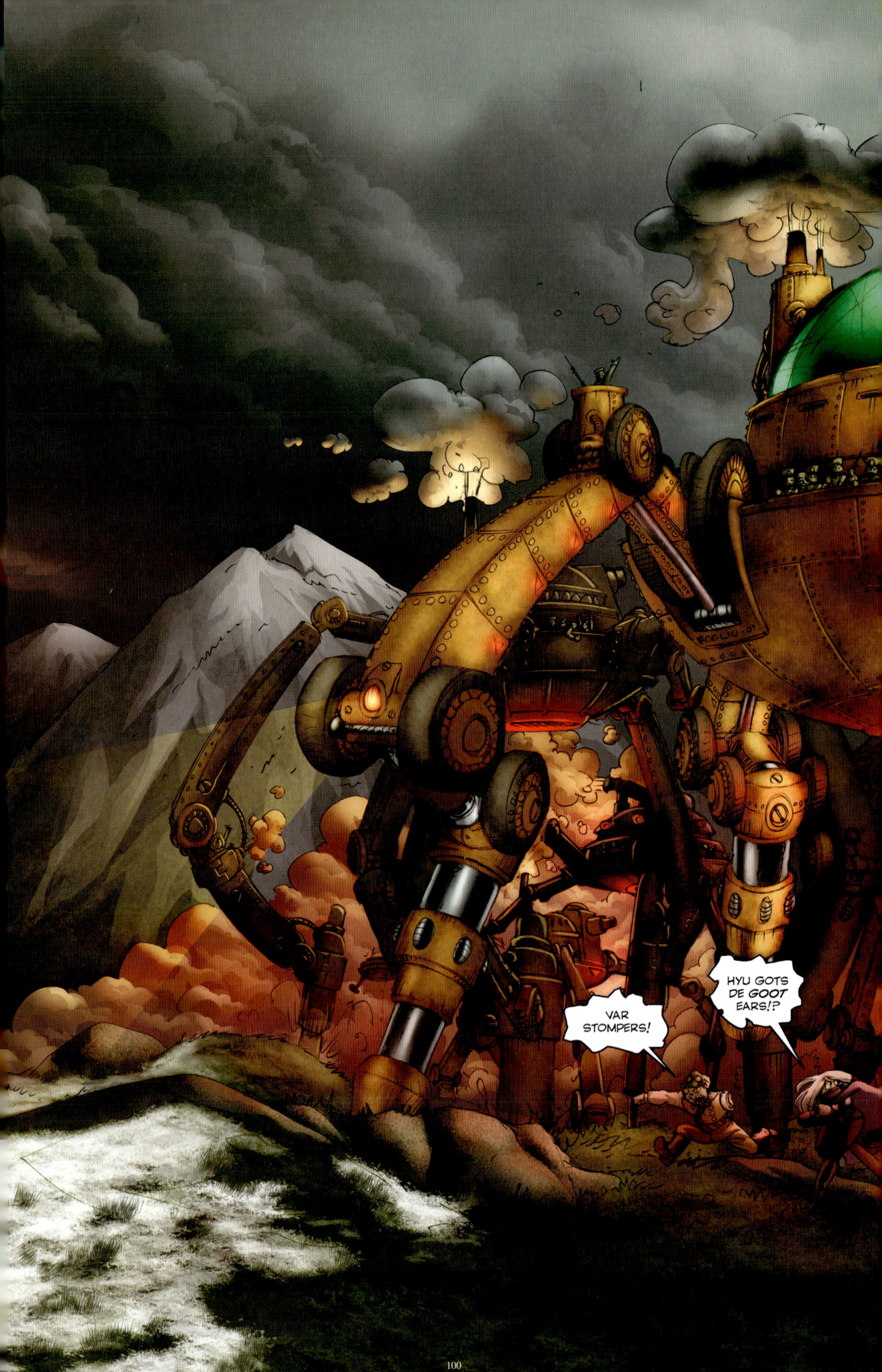
VAR STOMPERS!
HYU GOTS DE GOOT EARS!?

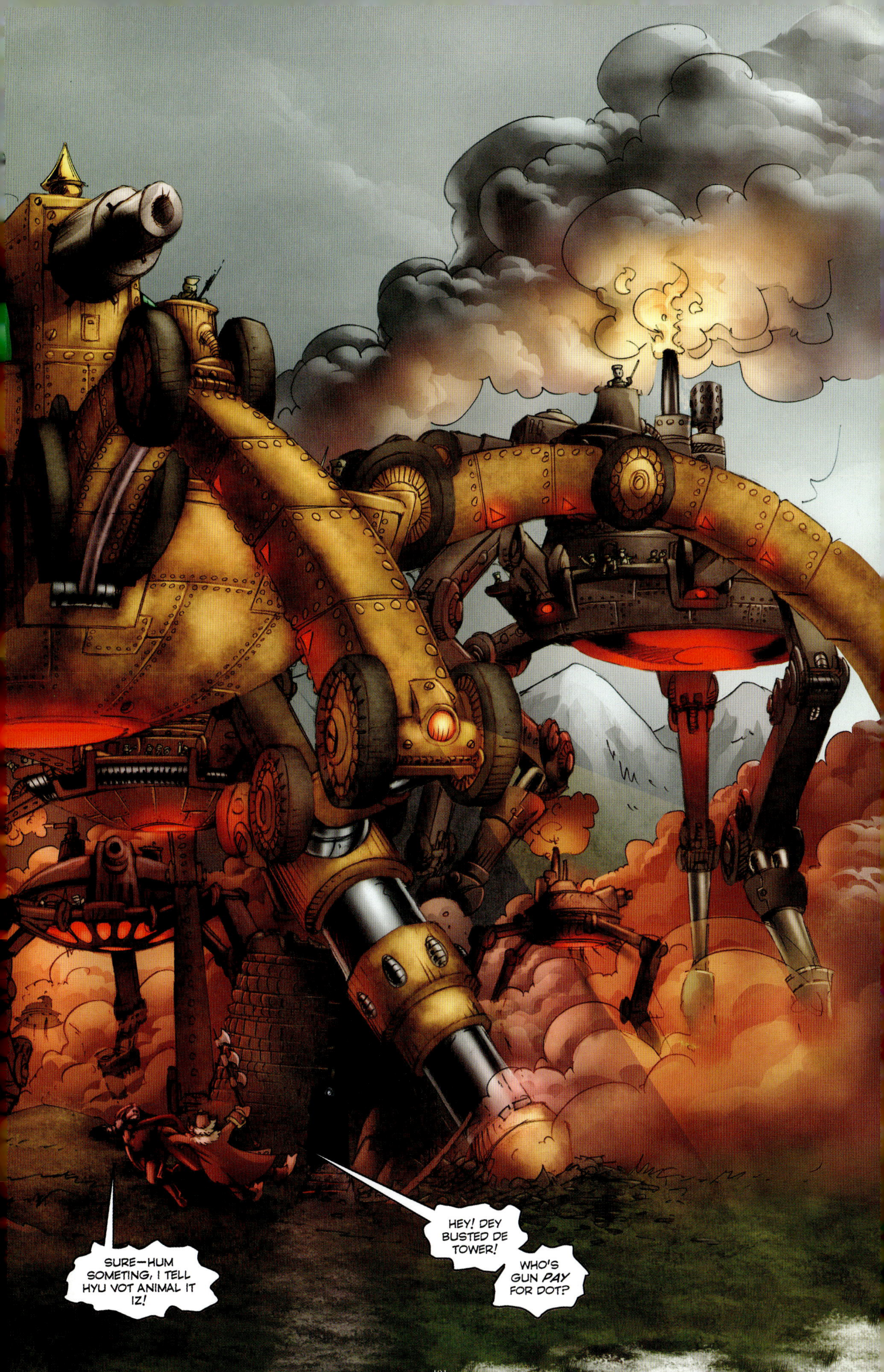
SURE—HUM SOMETING, I TELL HYU VOT ANIMAL IT IZ!
HEY! DEY BUSTED DE TOWER!
WHO'S GUN PAY FOR DOT?

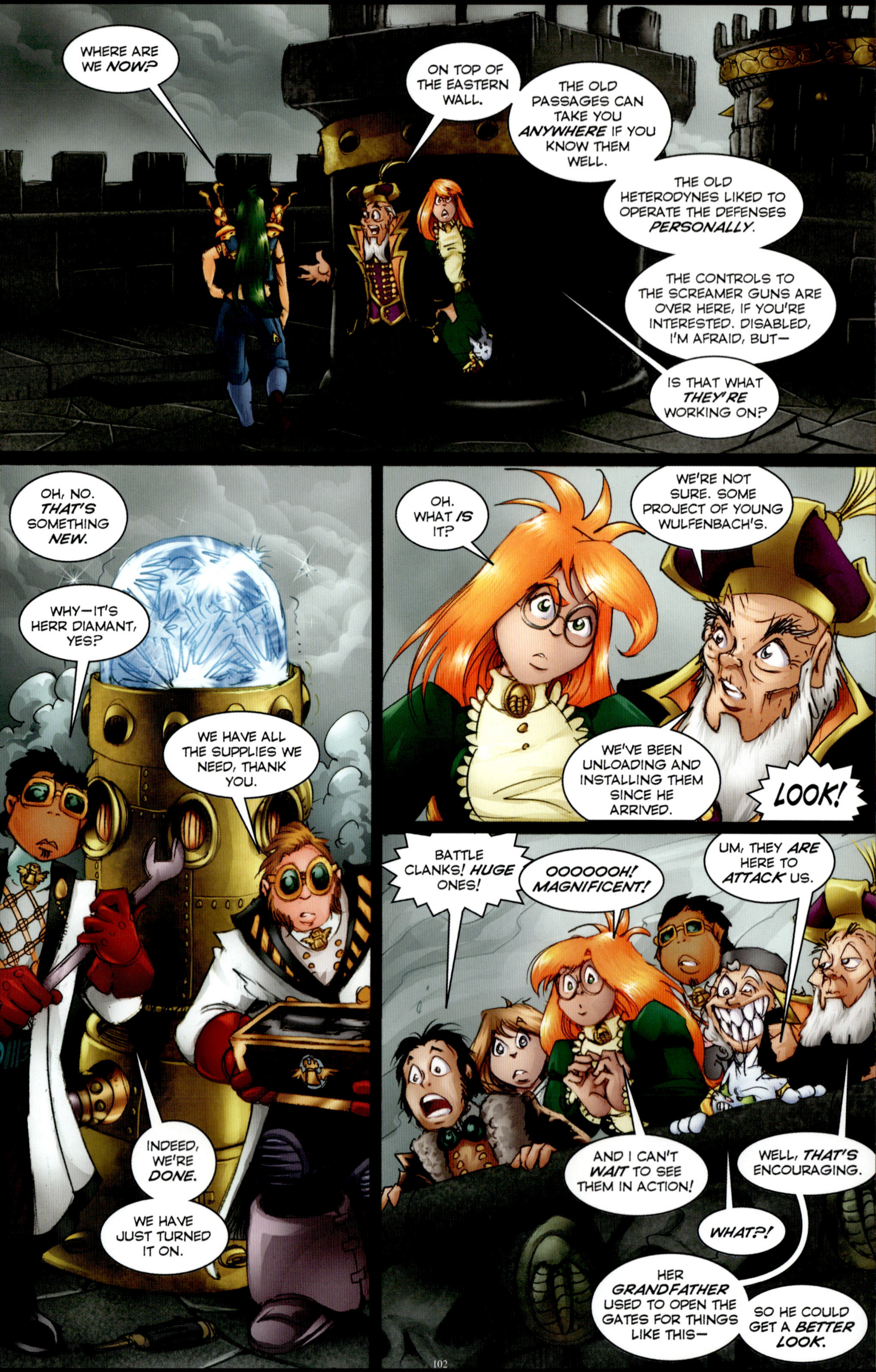
WHERE ARE WE NOW?
ON TOP OF THE EASTERN WALL.
THE OLD PASSAGES CAN TAKE YOU ANYWHERE IF YOU KNOW THEM WELL.
THE OLD HETERODYNES LIKED TO OPERATE THE DEFENSES PERSONALLY.
THE CONTROLS TO THE SCREAMER GUNS ARE OVER HERE, IF YOU'RE INTERESTED. DISABLED, I'M AFRAID, BUT—
IS THAT WHAT THEY'RE WORKING ON?
OH, NO. THAT'S SOMETHING NEW.
WHY—IT'S HERR DIAMANT, YES?
WE HAVE ALL THE SUPPLIES WE NEED, THANK YOU.
INDEED, WE'RE DONE.
WE HAVE JUST TURNED IT ON.
OH. WHAT IS IT?
WE'RE NOT SURE. SOME PROJECT OF YOUNG WULFENBACH'S.
WE'VE BEEN UNLOADING AND INSTALLING THEM SINCE HE ARRIVED.
LOOK!
BATTLE CLANKS! HUGE ONES!
OOOOOOH! MAGNIFICENT!
UM, THEY ARE HERE TO ATTACK US.
AND I CAN'T WAIT TO SEE THEM IN ACTION!
WELL, THAT'S ENCOURAGING.
WHAT?!
HER GRANDFATHER USED TO OPEN THE GATES FOR THINGS LIKE THIS—
SO HE COULD GET A BETTER LOOK.

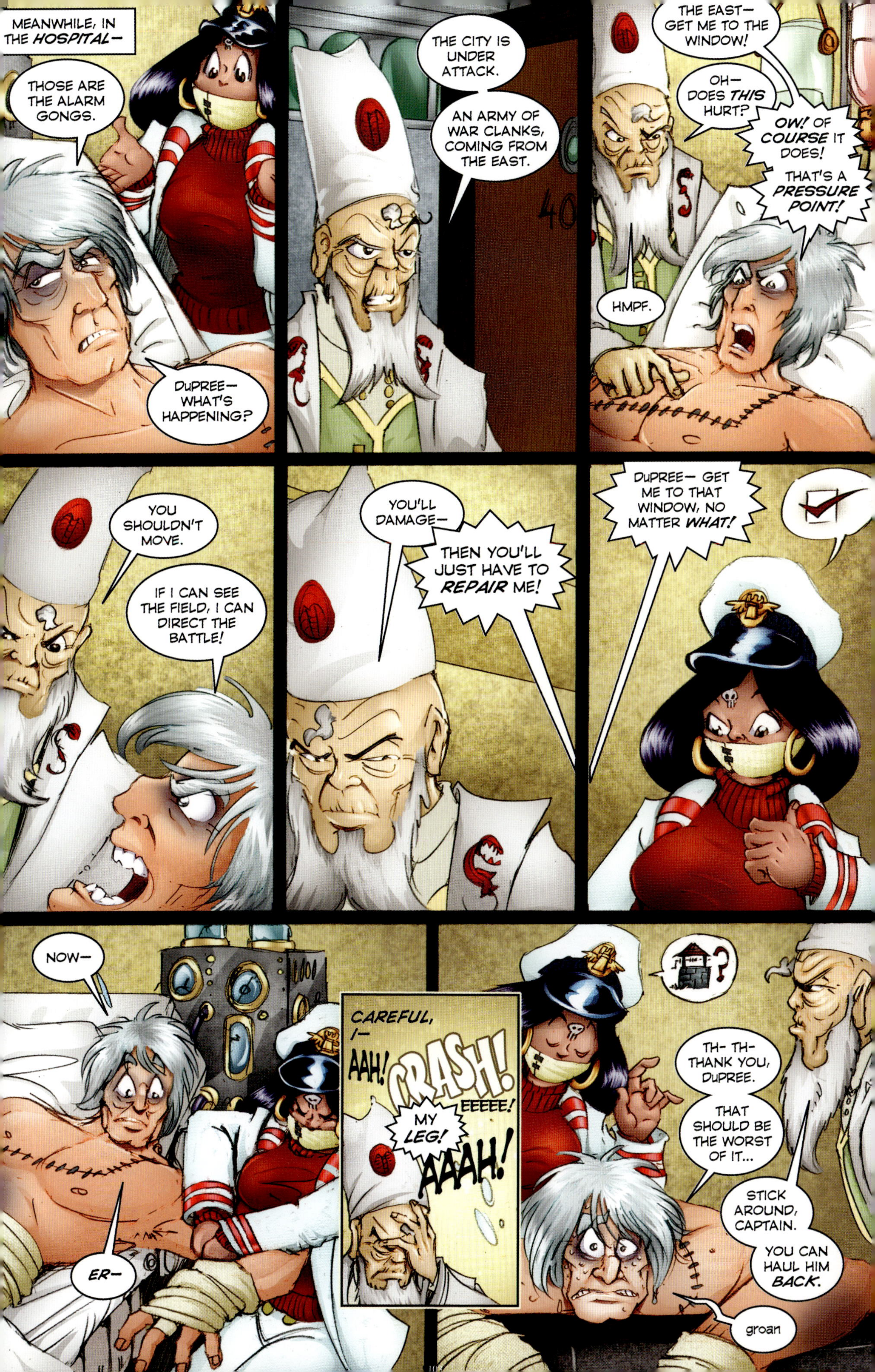
MEANWHILE, IN THE *HOSPITAL*—
THOSE ARE THE ALARM GONGS.
DuPREE— WHAT'S HAPPENING?
THE CITY IS UNDER ATTACK.
AN ARMY OF WAR CLANKS, COMING FROM THE EAST.
THE EAST— GET ME TO THE WINDOW!
OH— DOES *THIS* HURT?
OW! OF *COURSE* IT DOES!
THAT'S A *PRESSURE POINT!*
HMPF.
YOU SHOULDN'T MOVE.
IF I CAN SEE THE FIELD, I CAN DIRECT THE BATTLE!
YOU'LL DAMAGE—
THEN YOU'LL JUST HAVE TO *REPAIR* ME!
DuPREE— GET ME TO THAT WINDOW, NO MATTER *WHAT!*
NOW—
ER—
CAREFUL, I—
AAH!
CRASH!
EEEEE!
MY *LEG!*
AAAH!
TH- TH- THANK YOU, DuPREE.
THAT SHOULD BE THE WORST OF IT...
STICK AROUND, CAPTAIN.
YOU CAN HAUL HIM *BACK*.
groan

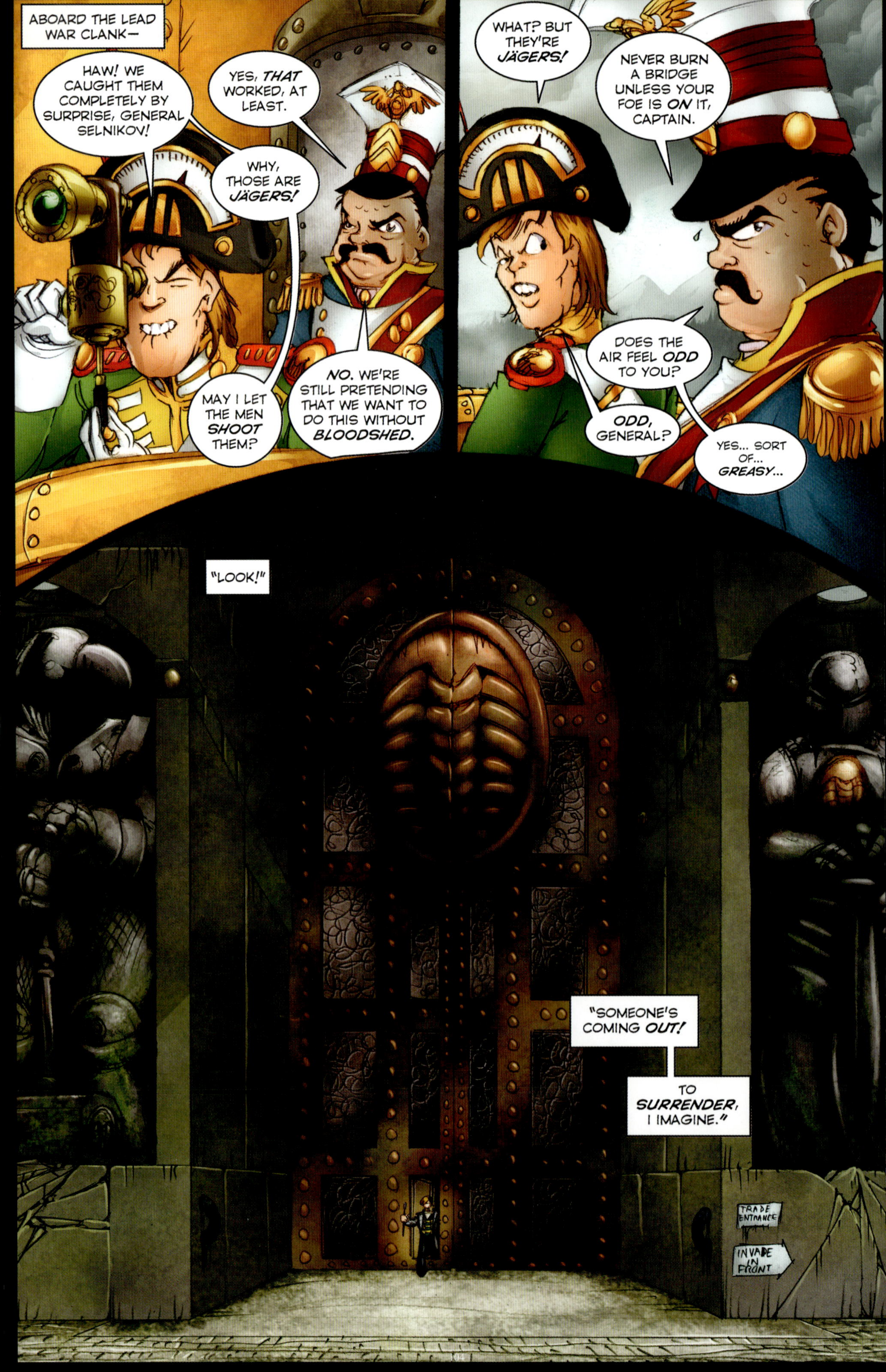
ABOARD THE LEAD WAR CLANK—
HAW! WE CAUGHT THEM COMPLETELY BY SURPRISE, GENERAL SELNIKOV!
YES, THAT WORKED, AT LEAST.
WHY, THOSE ARE JÄGERS!
MAY I LET THE MEN SHOOT THEM?
NO. WE'RE STILL PRETENDING THAT WE WANT TO DO THIS WITHOUT BLOODSHED.
WHAT? BUT THEY'RE JÄGERS!
NEVER BURN A BRIDGE UNLESS YOUR FOE IS ON IT, CAPTAIN.
DOES THE AIR FEEL ODD TO YOU?
ODD, GENERAL?
YES... SORT OF... GREASY...
"LOOK!"
"SOMEONE'S COMING OUT!
TO SURRENDER, I IMAGINE."
TRADE ENTRANCE
INVADE IN FRONT

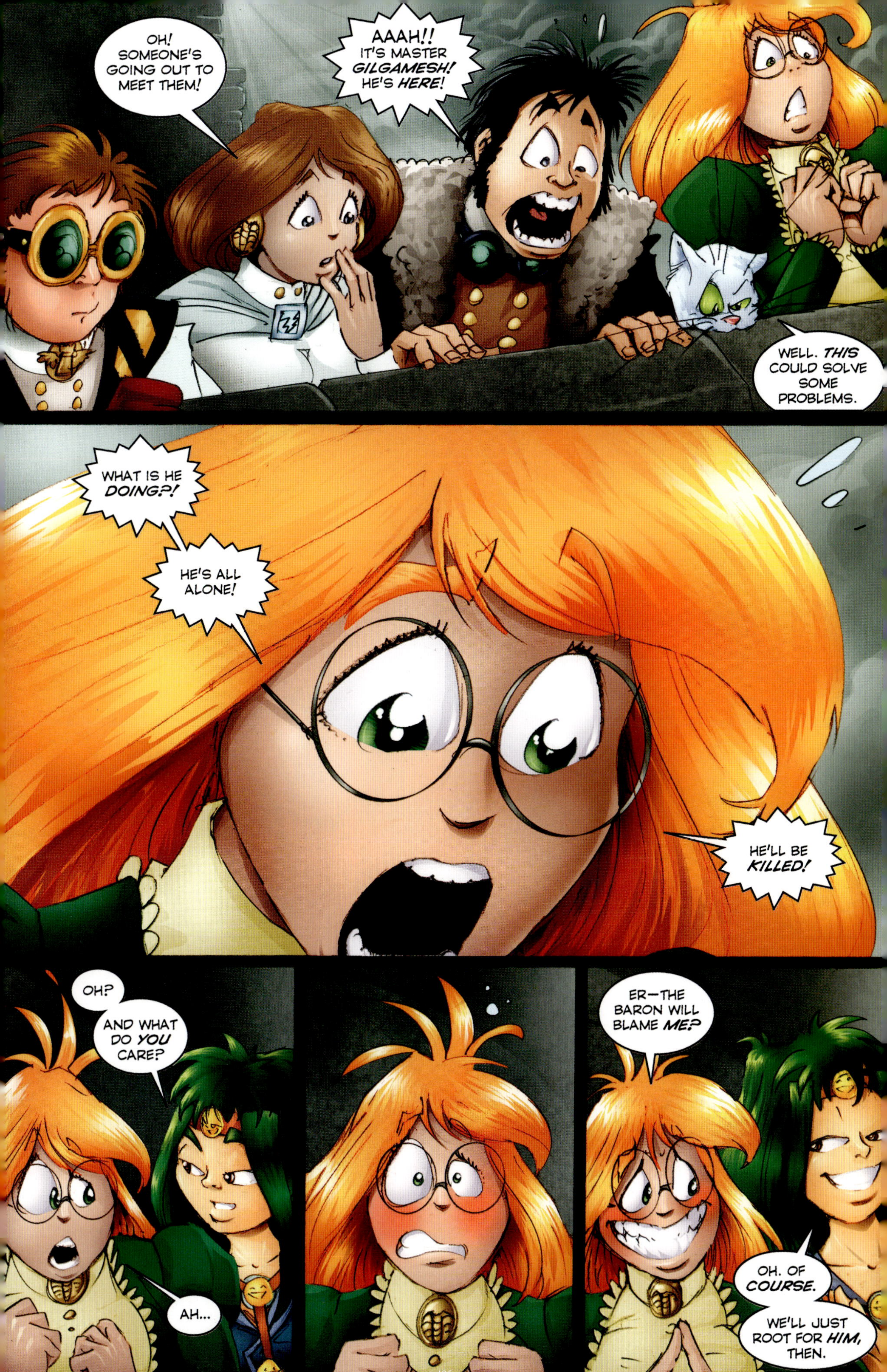
OH! SOMEONE'S GOING OUT TO MEET THEM!
AAAH!! IT'S MASTER *GILGAMESH!* HE'S *HERE!*
WELL. *THIS* COULD SOLVE SOME PROBLEMS.
WHAT IS HE *DOING?!*
HE'S ALL ALONE!
HE'LL BE *KILLED!*
OH?
AND WHAT DO *YOU* CARE?
AH...
ER—THE BARON WILL BLAME *ME?*
OH. OF *COURSE.*
WE'LL JUST ROOT FOR *HIM,* THEN.

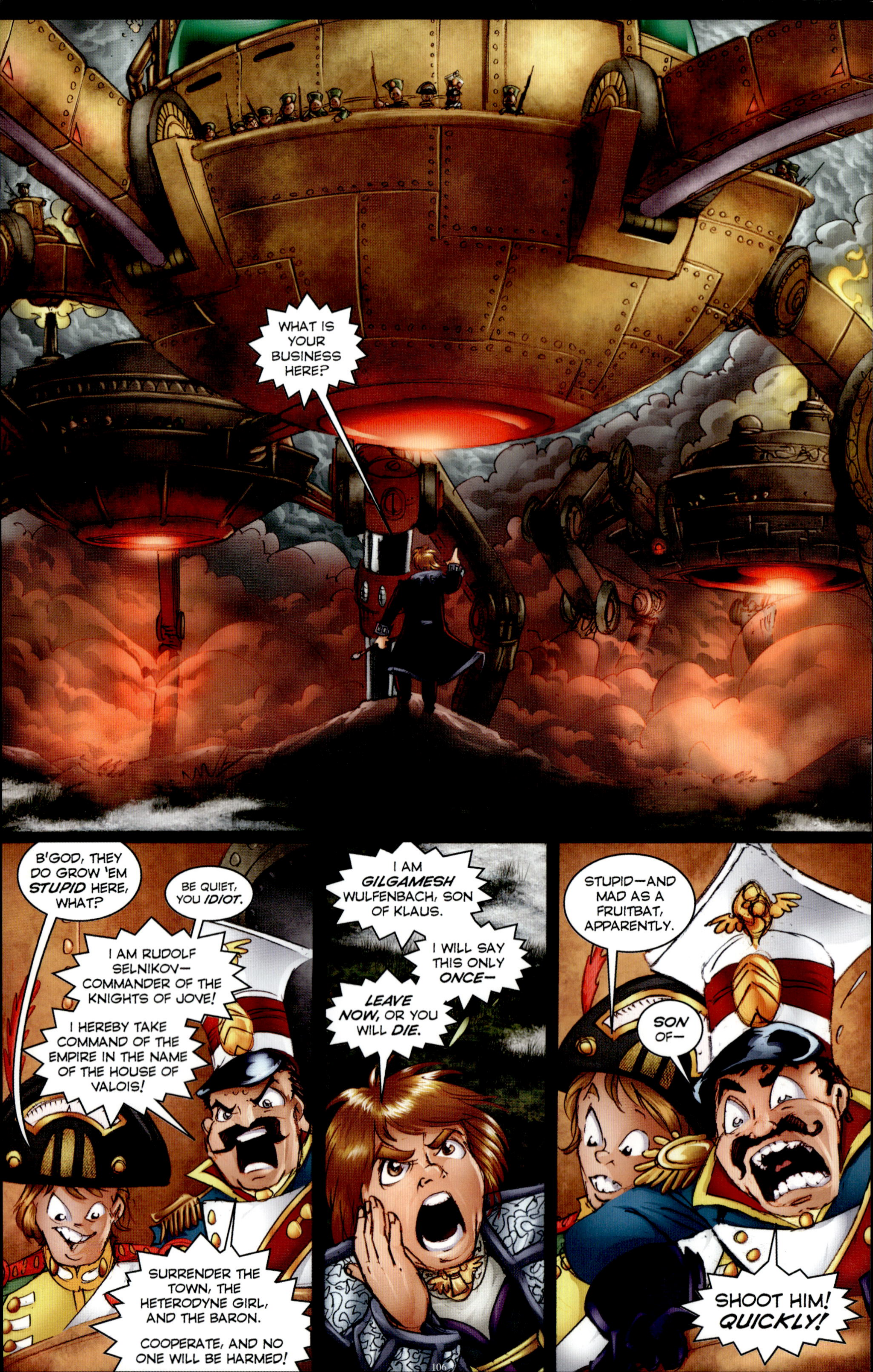
WHAT IS YOUR BUSINESS HERE?
B'GOD, THEY DO GROW 'EM **STUPID** HERE, WHAT?
BE QUIET, YOU *IDIOT*.
I AM RUDOLF SELNIKOV—COMMANDER OF THE KNIGHTS OF JOVE!
I HEREBY TAKE COMMAND OF THE EMPIRE IN THE NAME OF THE HOUSE OF VALOIS!
SURRENDER THE TOWN, THE HETERODYNE GIRL, AND THE BARON.
COOPERATE, AND NO ONE WILL BE HARMED!
I AM **GILGAMESH** WULFENBACH, SON OF KLAUS.
I WILL SAY THIS ONLY **ONCE—**
LEAVE NOW, OR YOU WILL **DIE**.
STUPID—AND MAD AS A FRUITBAT, APPARENTLY.
SON OF—
SHOOT HIM! **QUICKLY!**

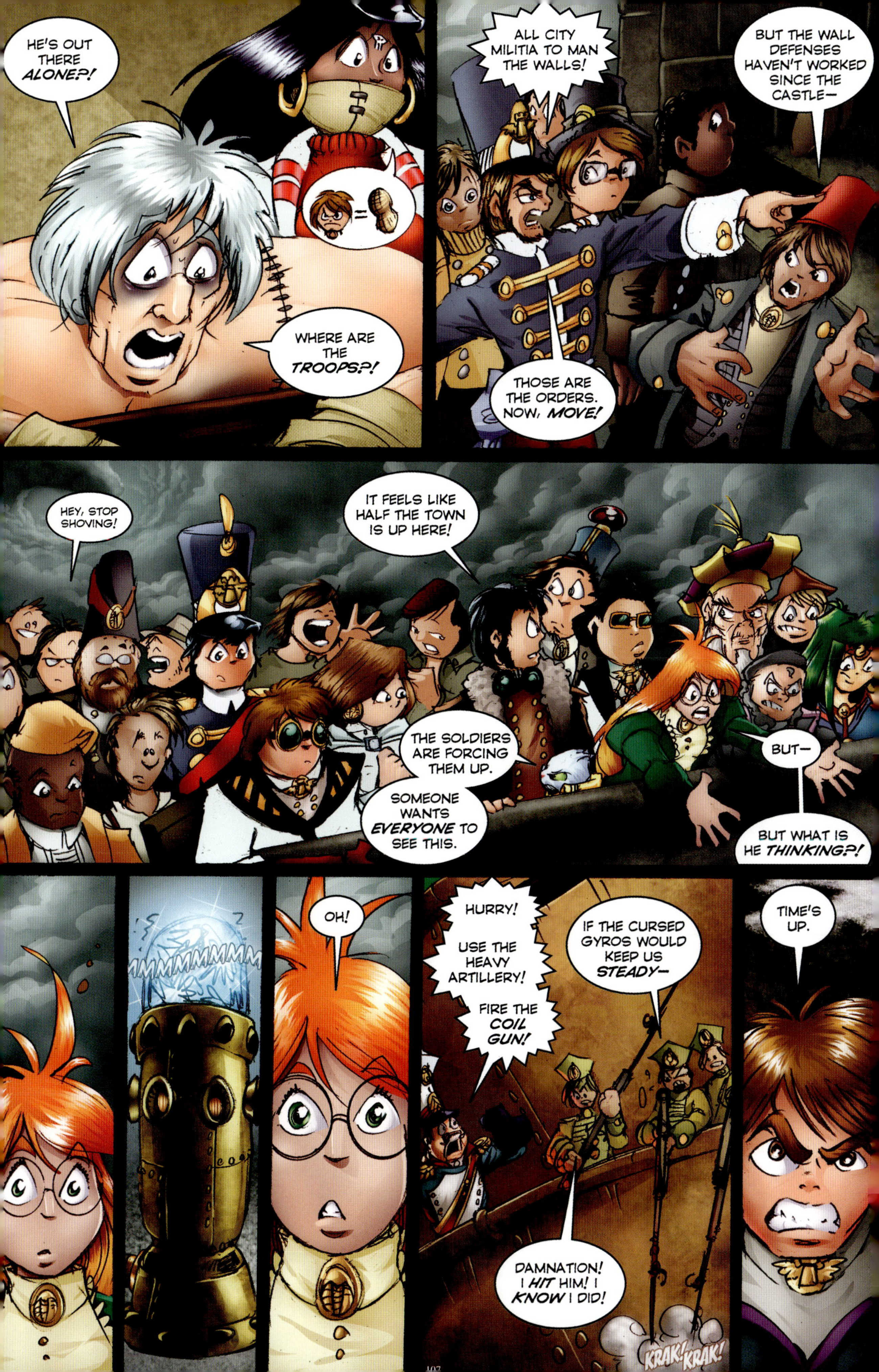
HE'S OUT THERE *ALONE?!*
WHERE ARE THE *TROOPS?!*
ALL CITY MILITIA TO MAN THE WALLS!
BUT THE WALL DEFENSES HAVEN'T WORKED SINCE THE CASTLE—
THOSE ARE THE ORDERS. NOW, *MOVE!*
HEY, STOP SHOVING!
IT FEELS LIKE HALF THE TOWN IS UP HERE!
THE SOLDIERS ARE FORCING THEM UP.
SOMEONE WANTS *EVERYONE* TO SEE THIS.
BUT—
BUT WHAT IS HE *THINKING?!*
OH!
HURRY!
USE THE HEAVY ARTILLERY!
FIRE THE *COIL GUN!*
IF THE CURSED GYROS WOULD KEEP US *STEADY—*
DAMNATION! I *HIT* HIM! I *KNOW* I DID!
KRAK! KRAK!
TIME'S UP.

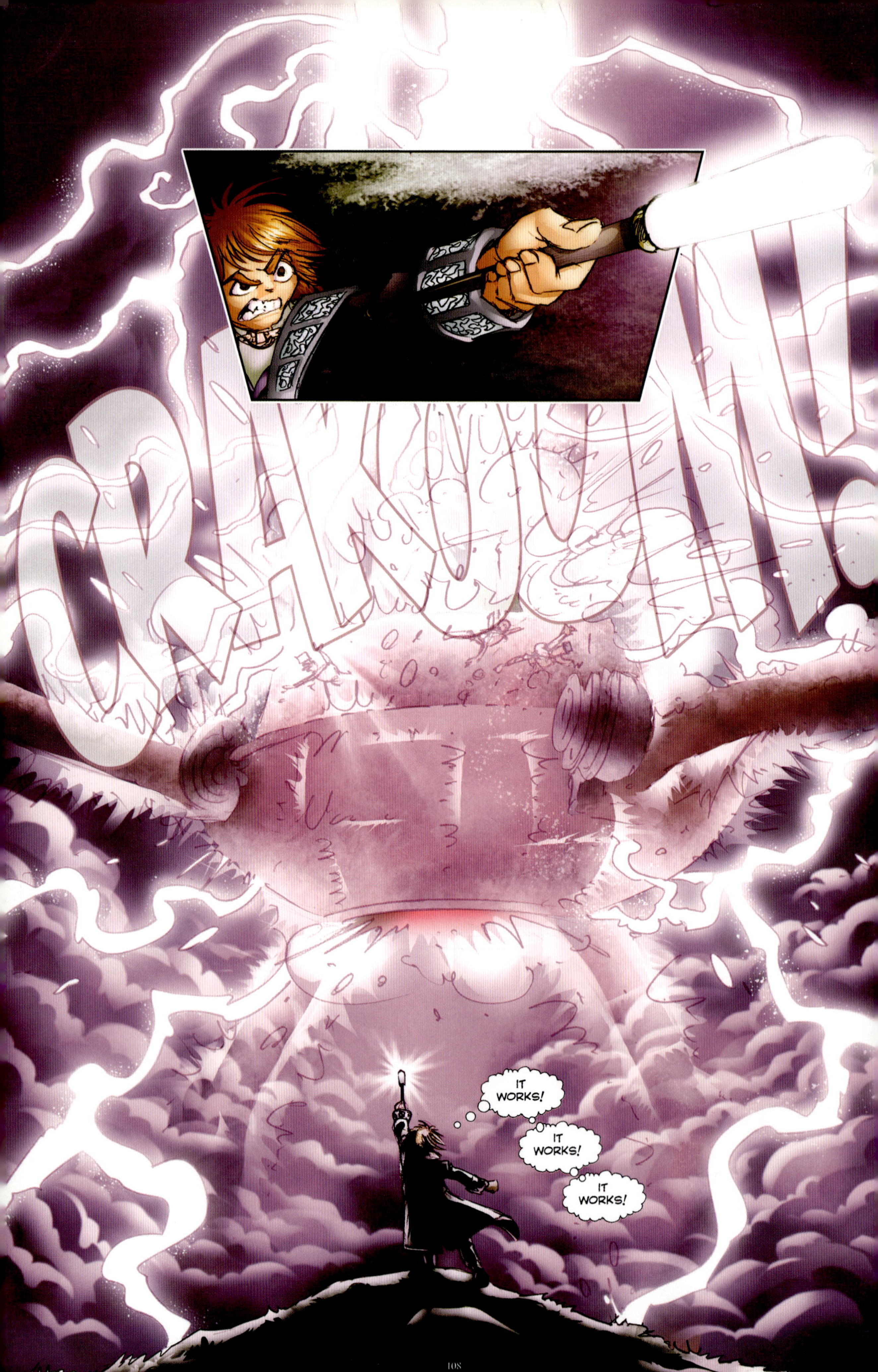
IT WORKS!
IT WORKS!
IT WORKS!

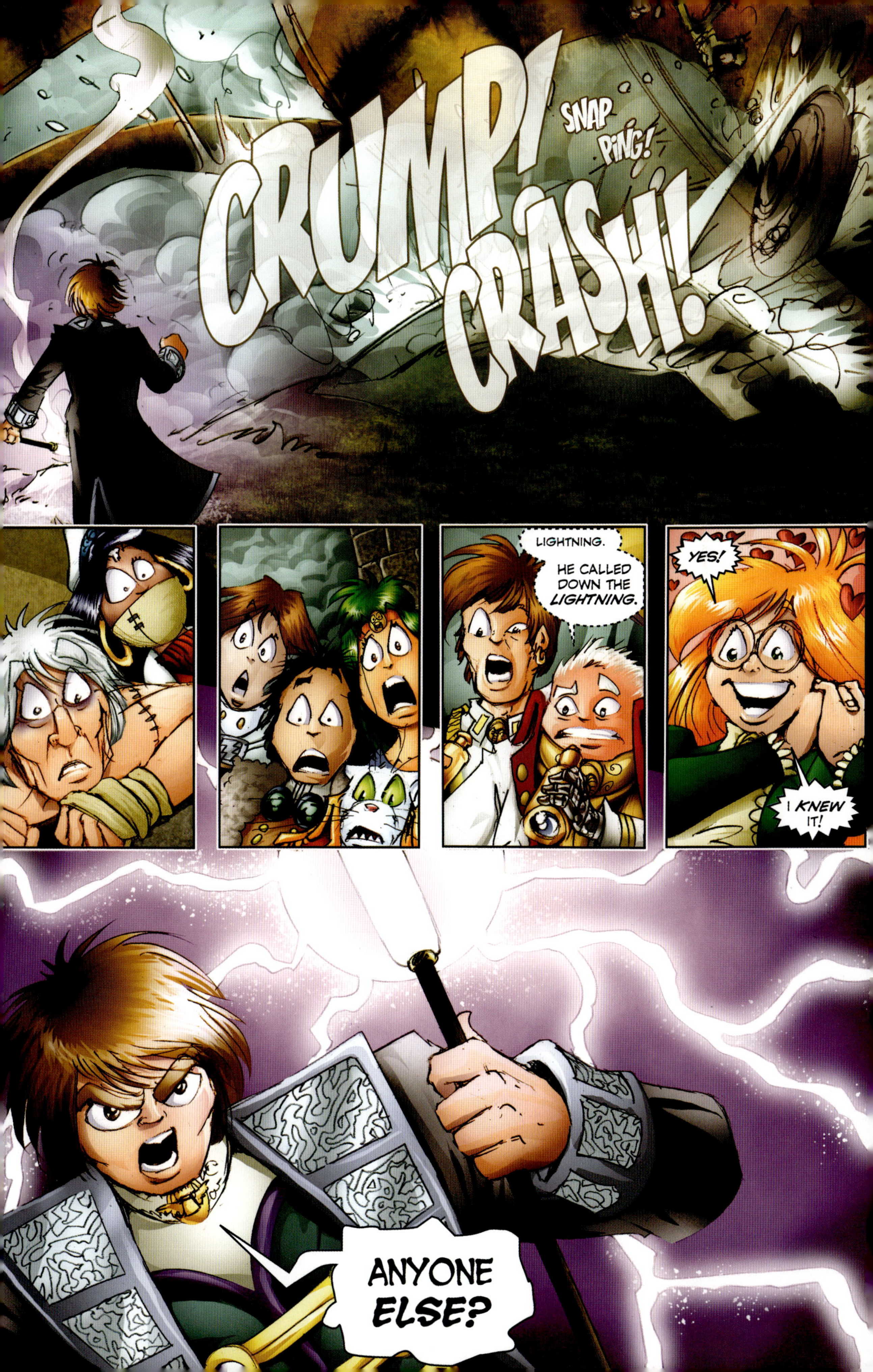

CRUMP!
SNAP
PING!
CRASH!
LIGHTNING.
HE CALLED DOWN THE *LIGHTNING.*
YES!
I *KNEW* IT!
ANYONE *ELSE?*

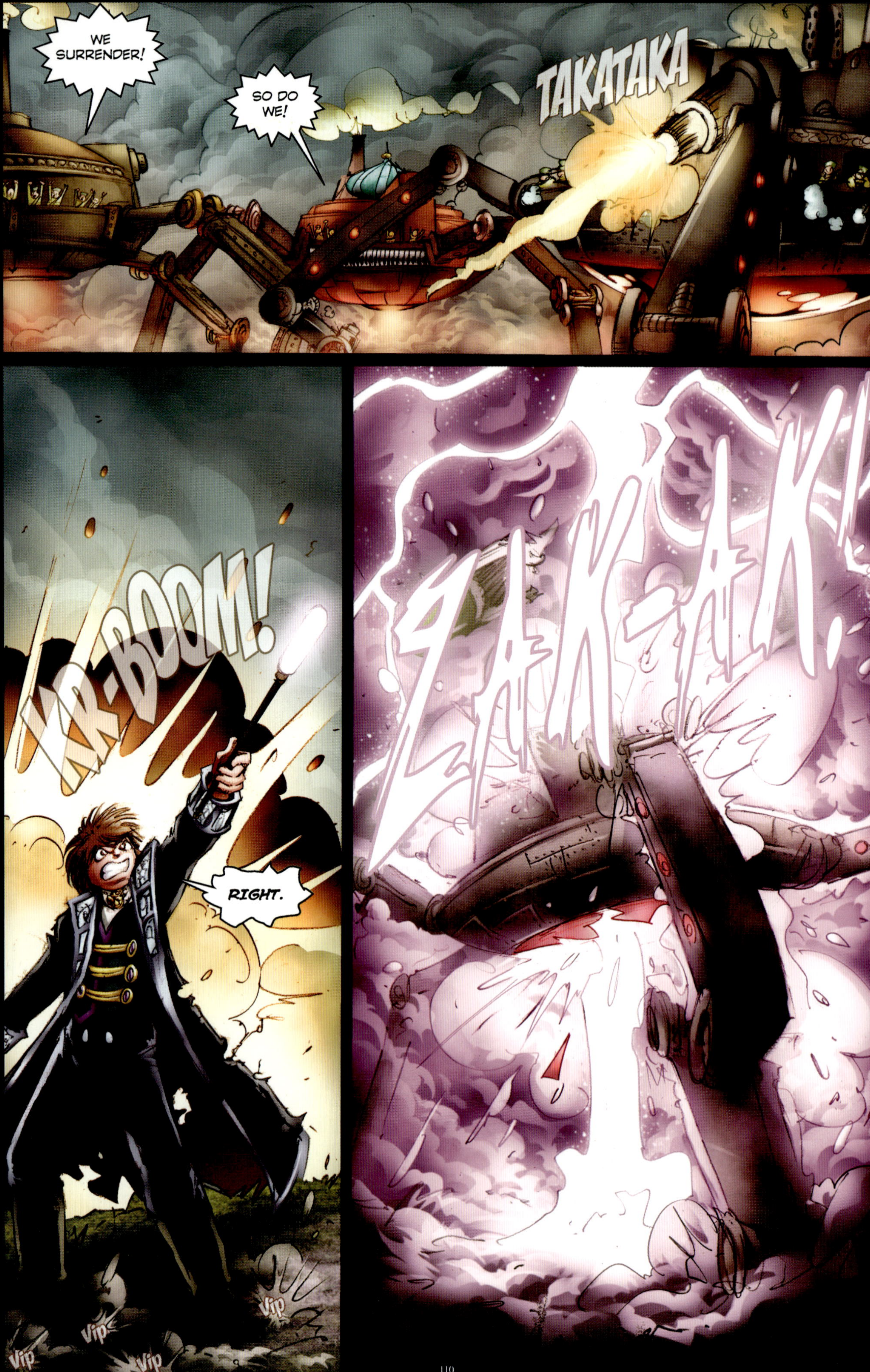
WE SURRENDER!
SO DO WE!
TAKATAKA
KR-BOOM!
RIGHT.
ZAK-AK!
Vip
Vip
Vip
Vip

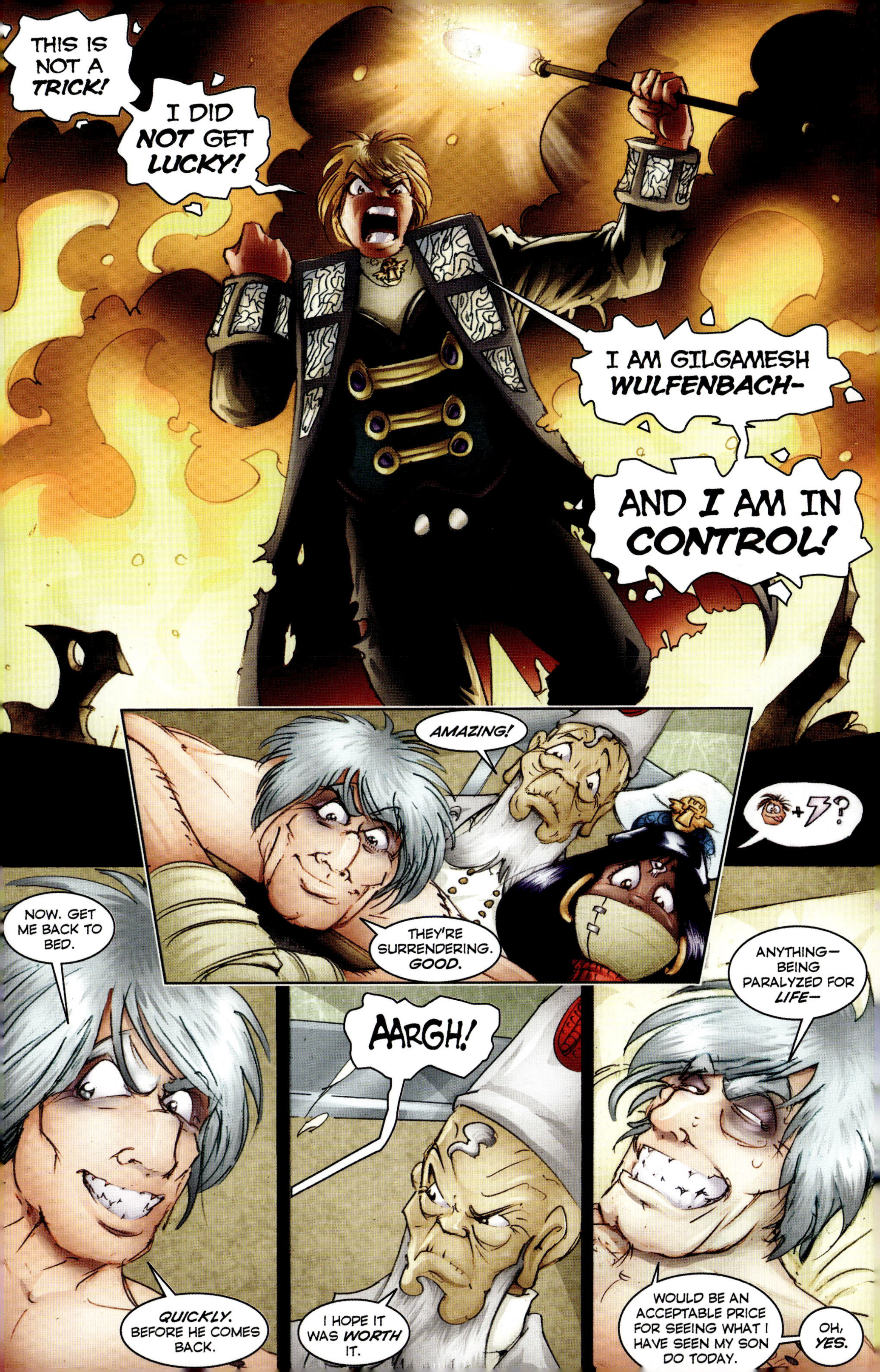
THIS IS NOT A TRICK!
I DID NOT GET LUCKY!
I AM GILGAMESH WULFENBACH-
AND I AM IN CONTROL!
AMAZING!
?
THEY'RE SURRENDERING. GOOD.
NOW. GET ME BACK TO BED.
QUICKLY. BEFORE HE COMES BACK.
AARGH!
I HOPE IT WAS WORTH IT.
ANYTHING— BEING PARALYZED FOR LIFE—
WOULD BE AN ACCEPTABLE PRICE FOR SEEING WHAT I HAVE SEEN MY SON DO TODAY.
OH, YES.

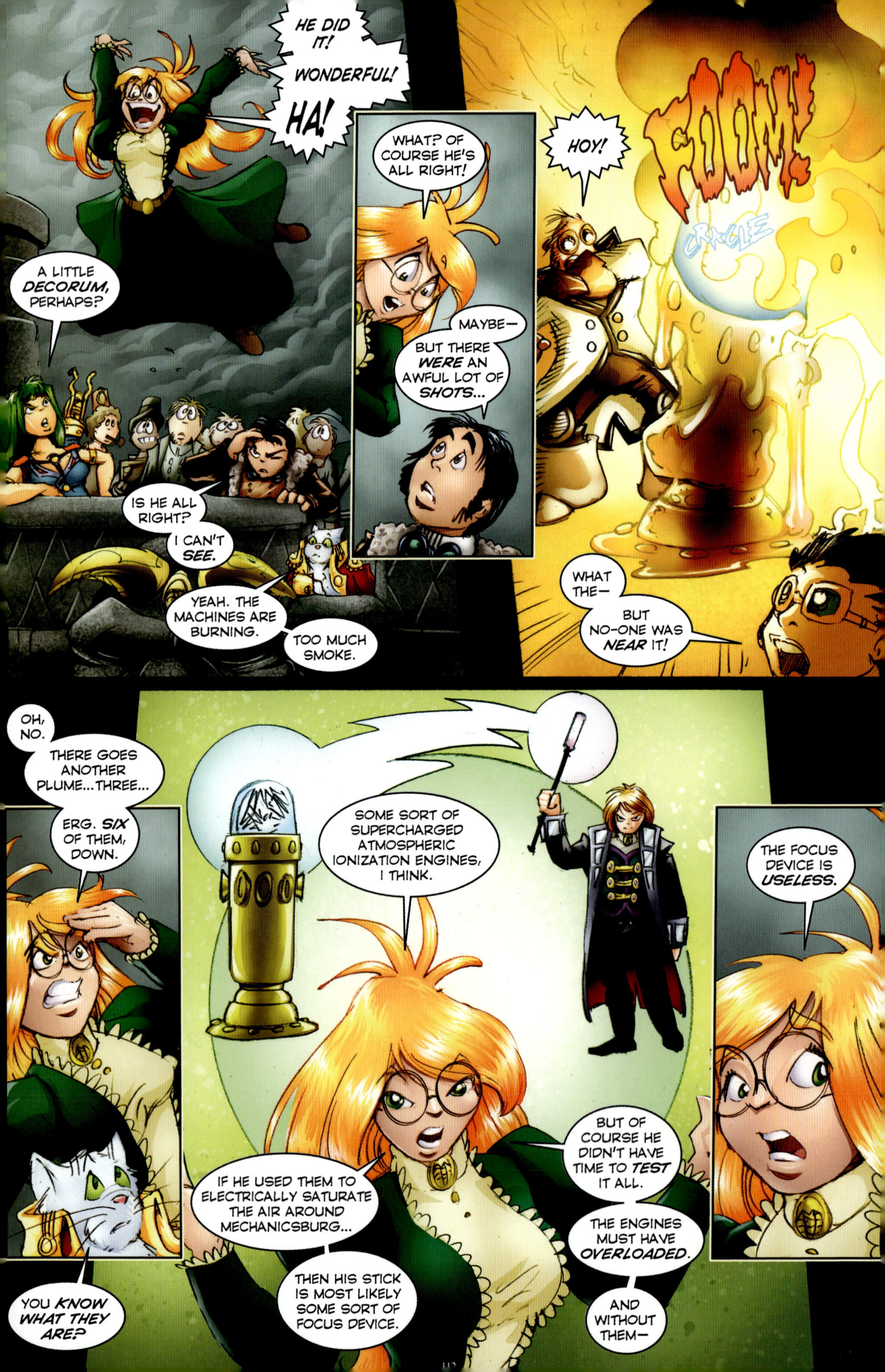
HE DID IT!
WONDERFUL!
HA!
A LITTLE DECORUM, PERHAPS?
IS HE ALL RIGHT?
I CAN'T SEE.
YEAH. THE MACHINES ARE BURNING.
TOO MUCH SMOKE.
WHAT? OF COURSE HE'S ALL RIGHT!
MAYBE—
BUT THERE WERE AN AWFUL LOT OF SHOTS...
HOY!
FOOM!
CRACKLE
WHAT THE—
BUT NO-ONE WAS NEAR IT!
OH, NO.
THERE GOES ANOTHER PLUME...THREE...
ERG. SIX OF THEM, DOWN.
YOU KNOW WHAT THEY ARE?
SOME SORT OF SUPERCHARGED ATMOSPHERIC IONIZATION ENGINES, I THINK.
IF HE USED THEM TO ELECTRICALLY SATURATE THE AIR AROUND MECHANICSBURG...
THEN HIS STICK IS MOST LIKELY SOME SORT OF FOCUS DEVICE.
BUT OF COURSE HE DIDN'T HAVE TIME TO TEST IT ALL.
THE ENGINES MUST HAVE OVERLOADED.
AND WITHOUT THEM—
THE FOCUS DEVICE IS USELESS.

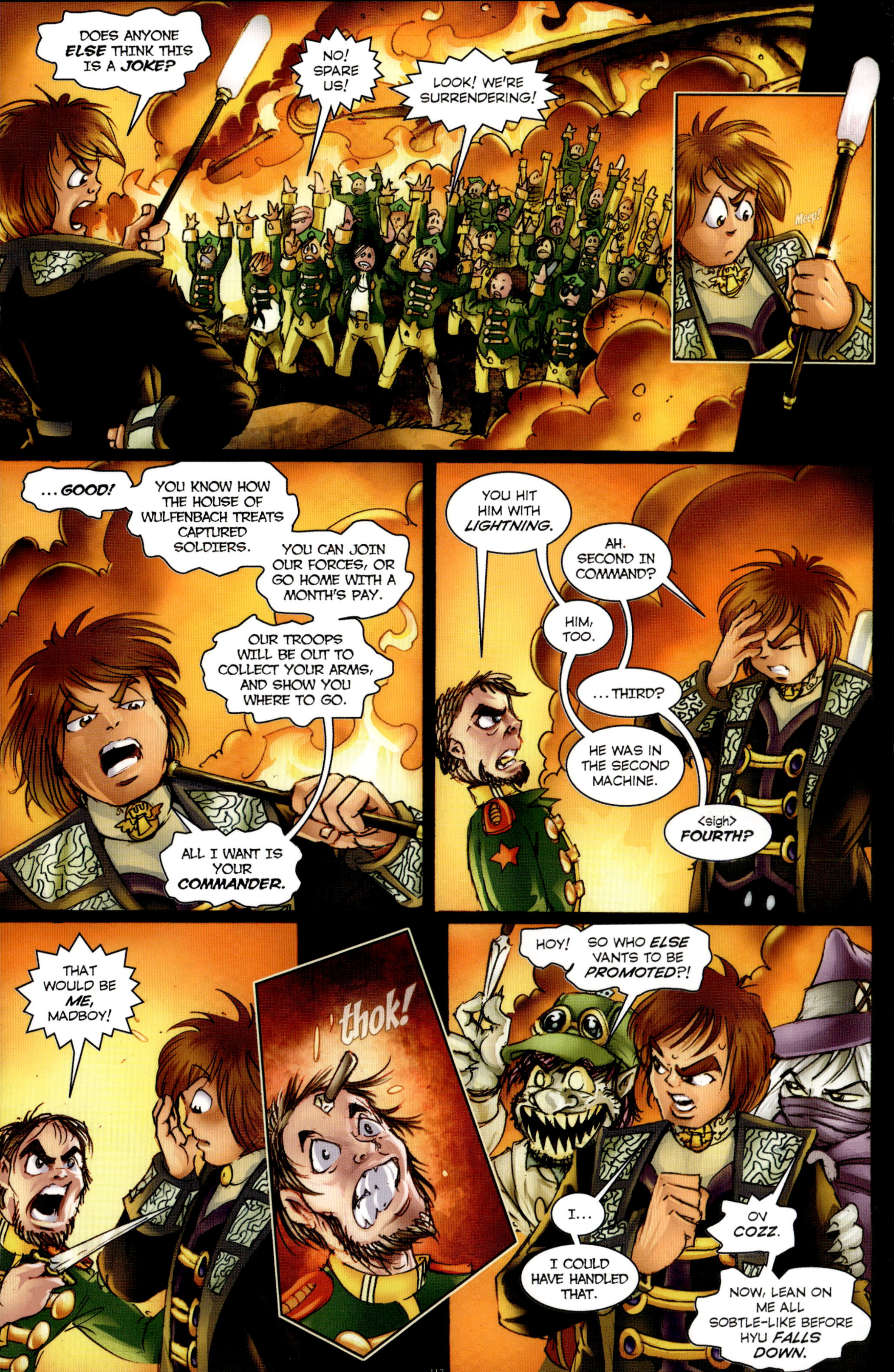
DOES ANYONE ELSE THINK THIS IS A JOKE?
NO! SPARE US!
LOOK! WE'RE SURRENDERING!
Meep!
...GOOD!
YOU KNOW HOW THE HOUSE OF WULFENBACH TREATS CAPTURED SOLDIERS.
YOU CAN JOIN OUR FORCES, OR GO HOME WITH A MONTH'S PAY.
OUR TROOPS WILL BE OUT TO COLLECT YOUR ARMS, AND SHOW YOU WHERE TO GO.
ALL I WANT IS YOUR COMMANDER.
YOU HIT HIM WITH LIGHTNING.
AH. SECOND IN COMMAND?
HIM, TOO.
...THIRD?
HE WAS IN THE SECOND MACHINE.
<sigh> FOURTH?
THAT WOULD BE ME, MADBOY!
thok!
HOY!
SO WHO ELSE VANTS TO BE PROMOTED?!
I...
I COULD HAVE HANDLED THAT.
OV COZZ.
NOW, LEAN ON ME ALL SOBTLE-LIKE BEFORE HYU FALLS DOWN.

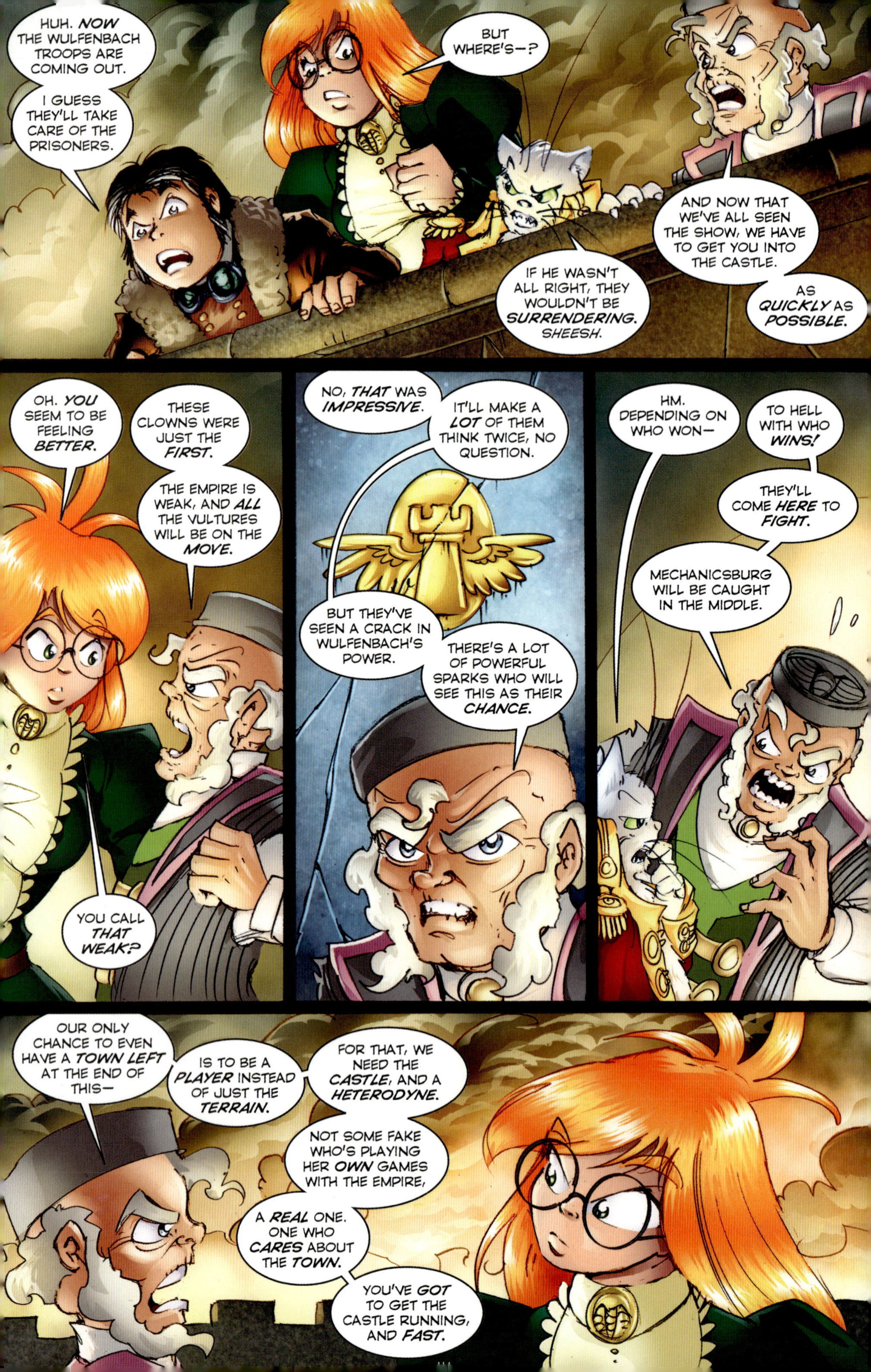
HUH. NOW THE WULFENBACH TROOPS ARE COMING OUT.
I GUESS THEY'LL TAKE CARE OF THE PRISONERS.
BUT WHERE'S—?
IF HE WASN'T ALL RIGHT, THEY WOULDN'T BE SURRENDERING. SHEESH.
AND NOW THAT WE'VE ALL SEEN THE SHOW, WE HAVE TO GET YOU INTO THE CASTLE.
AS QUICKLY AS POSSIBLE.
OH. YOU SEEM TO BE FEELING BETTER.
THESE CLOWNS WERE JUST THE FIRST.
THE EMPIRE IS WEAK, AND ALL THE VULTURES WILL BE ON THE MOVE.
YOU CALL THAT WEAK?
NO, THAT WAS IMPRESSIVE.
IT'LL MAKE A LOT OF THEM THINK TWICE, NO QUESTION.
BUT THEY'VE SEEN A CRACK IN WULFENBACH'S POWER.
THERE'S A LOT OF POWERFUL SPARKS WHO WILL SEE THIS AS THEIR CHANCE.
HM. DEPENDING ON WHO WON—
TO HELL WITH WHO WINS!
THEY'LL COME HERE TO FIGHT.
MECHANICSBURG WILL BE CAUGHT IN THE MIDDLE.
OUR ONLY CHANCE TO EVEN HAVE A TOWN LEFT AT THE END OF THIS—
IS TO BE A PLAYER INSTEAD OF JUST THE TERRAIN.
FOR THAT, WE NEED THE CASTLE, AND A HETERODYNE.
NOT SOME FAKE WHO'S PLAYING HER OWN GAMES WITH THE EMPIRE,
A REAL ONE. ONE WHO CARES ABOUT THE TOWN.
YOU'VE GOT TO GET THE CASTLE RUNNING, AND FAST.

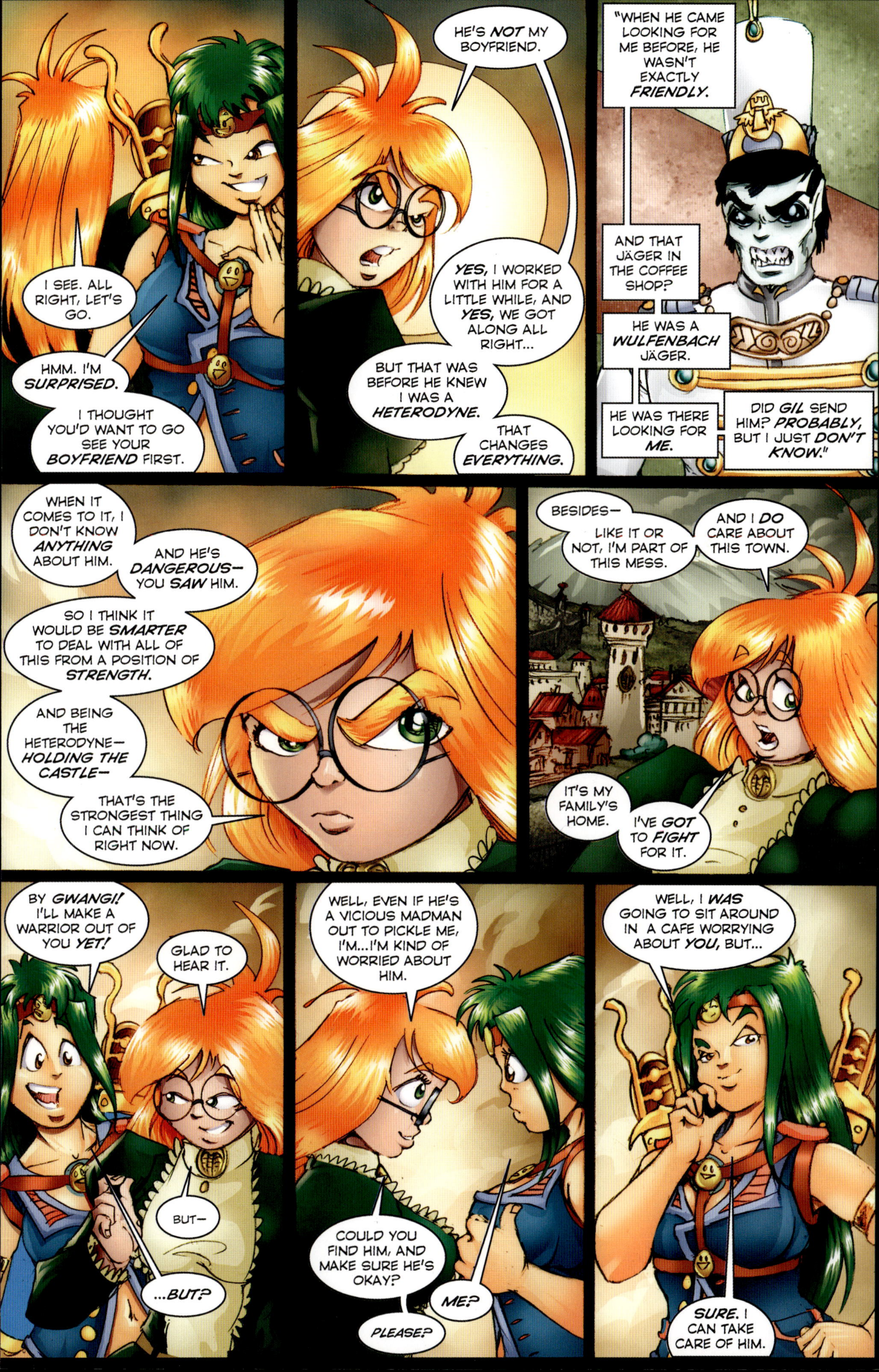
I SEE. ALL RIGHT, LET'S GO.
HMM. I'M SURPRISED.
I THOUGHT YOU'D WANT TO GO SEE YOUR BOYFRIEND FIRST.
HE'S NOT MY BOYFRIEND.
YES, I WORKED WITH HIM FOR A LITTLE WHILE, AND YES, WE GOT ALONG ALL RIGHT...
BUT THAT WAS BEFORE HE KNEW I WAS A HETERODYNE.
THAT CHANGES EVERYTHING.
"WHEN HE CAME LOOKING FOR ME BEFORE, HE WASN'T EXACTLY FRIENDLY.
AND THAT JÄGER IN THE COFFEE SHOP?
HE WAS A WULFENBACH JÄGER.
HE WAS THERE LOOKING FOR ME.
DID GIL SEND HIM? PROBABLY, BUT I JUST DON'T KNOW."
WHEN IT COMES TO IT, I DON'T KNOW ANYTHING ABOUT HIM.
AND HE'S DANGEROUS— YOU SAW HIM.
SO I THINK IT WOULD BE SMARTER TO DEAL WITH ALL OF THIS FROM A POSITION OF STRENGTH.
AND BEING THE HETERODYNE— HOLDING THE CASTLE—
THAT'S THE STRONGEST THING I CAN THINK OF RIGHT NOW.
BESIDES—
LIKE IT OR NOT, I'M PART OF THIS MESS.
AND I DO CARE ABOUT THIS TOWN.
IT'S MY FAMILY'S HOME.
I'VE GOT TO FIGHT FOR IT.
BY GWANGI! I'LL MAKE A WARRIOR OUT OF YOU YET!
GLAD TO HEAR IT.
BUT—
...BUT?
WELL, EVEN IF HE'S A VICIOUS MADMAN OUT TO PICKLE ME, I'M...I'M KIND OF WORRIED ABOUT HIM.
COULD YOU FIND HIM, AND MAKE SURE HE'S OKAY?
ME?
PLEASE?
WELL, I WAS GOING TO SIT AROUND IN A CAFE WORRYING ABOUT YOU, BUT...
SURE. I CAN TAKE CARE OF HIM.

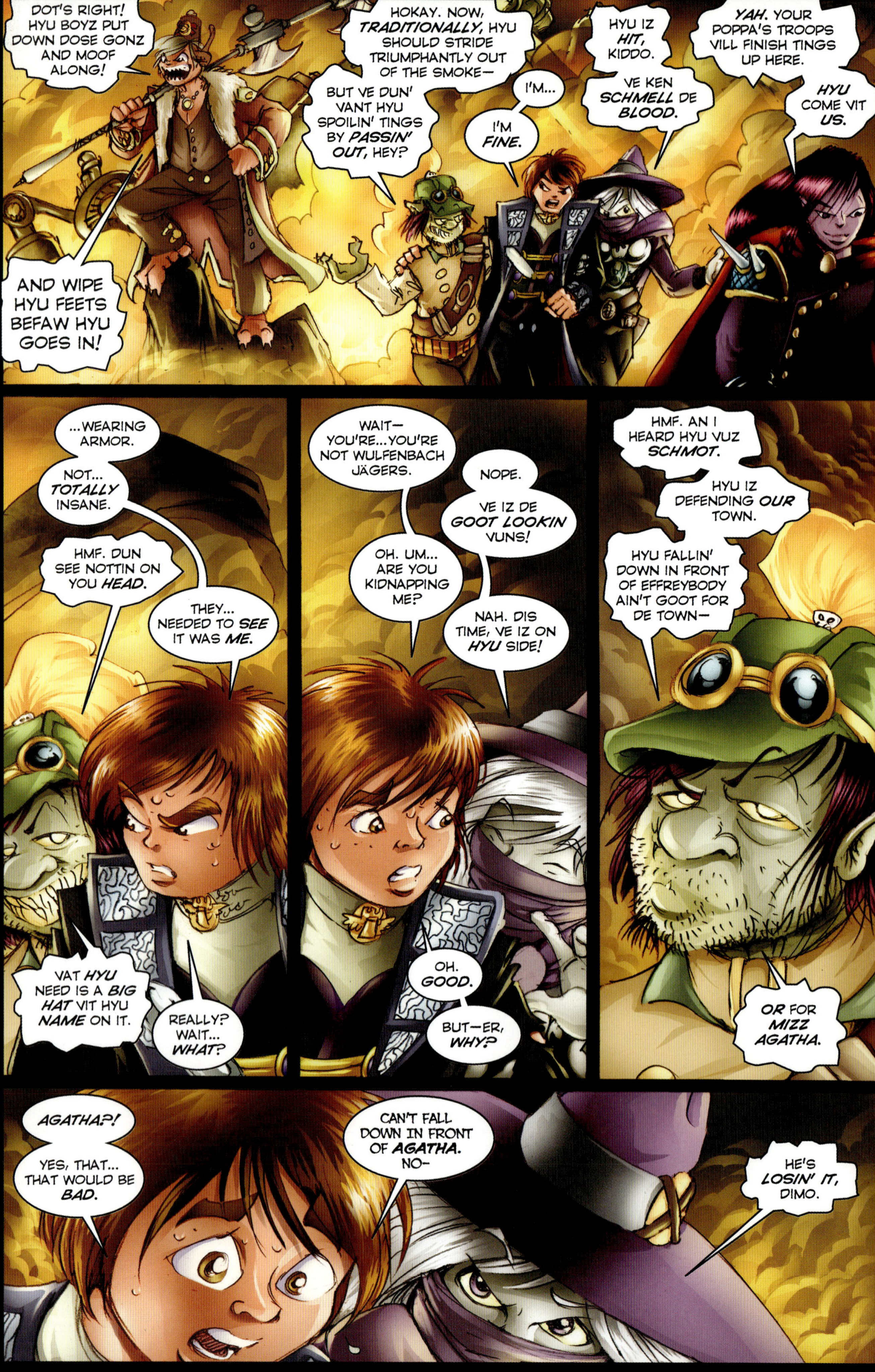

DOT'S RIGHT! HYU BOYZ PUT DOWN DOSE GONZ AND MOOF ALONG!
AND WIPE HYU FEETS BEFAW HYU GOES IN!
HOKAY. NOW, TRADITIONALLY, HYU SHOULD STRIDE TRIUMPHANTLY OUT OF THE SMOKE—
BUT VE DUN' VANT HYU SPOILIN' TINGS BY PASSIN' OUT, HEY?
I'M...
I'M FINE.
HYU IZ HIT, KIDDO.
VE KEN SCHMELL DE BLOOD.
YAH. YOUR POPPA'S TROOPS VILL FINISH TINGS UP HERE.
HYU COME VIT US.
...WEARING ARMOR.
NOT... TOTALLY INSANE.
HMF. DUN SEE NOTTIN ON YOU HEAD.
THEY... NEEDED TO SEE IT WAS ME.
VAT HYU NEED IS A BIG HAT VIT HYU NAME ON IT.
REALLY? WAIT... WHAT?
WAIT— YOU'RE...YOU'RE NOT WULFENBACH JÄGERS.
NOPE.
VE IZ DE GOOT LOOKIN VUNS!
OH. UM... ARE YOU KIDNAPPING ME?
NAH. DIS TIME, VE IZ ON HYU SIDE!
OH. GOOD.
BUT—ER, WHY?
HMF. AN I HEARD HYU VUZ SCHMOT.
HYU IZ DEFENDING OUR TOWN.
HYU FALLIN' DOWN IN FRONT OF EFFREYBODY AIN'T GOOT FOR DE TOWN—
OR FOR MIZZ AGATHA.
AGATHA?!
YES, THAT... THAT WOULD BE BAD.
CAN'T FALL DOWN IN FRONT OF AGATHA. NO-
HE'S LOSIN' IT, DIMO.

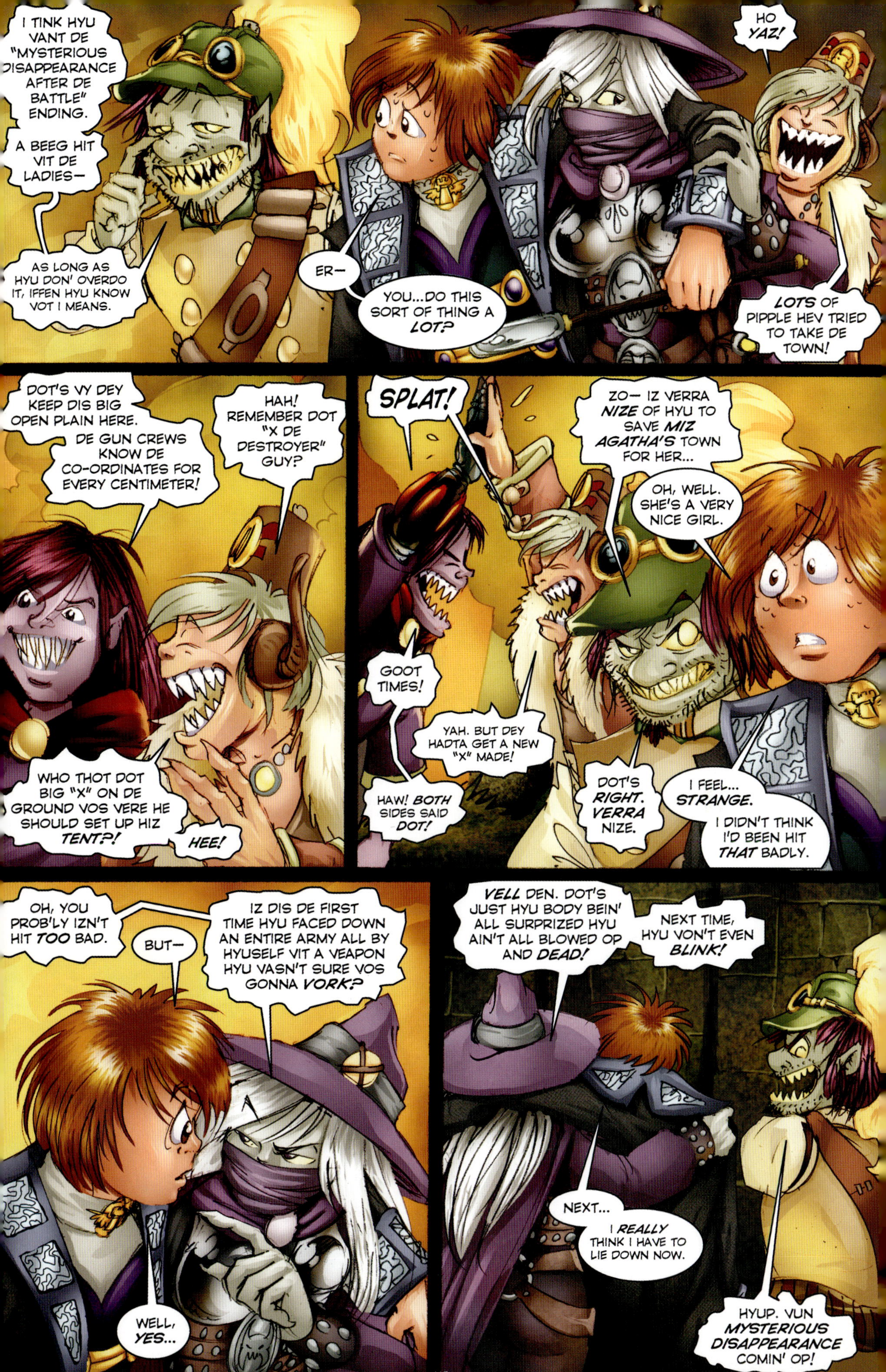
I TINK HYU VANT DE "MYSTERIOUS DISAPPEARANCE AFTER DE BATTLE" ENDING.
A BEEG HIT VIT DE LADIES—
AS LONG AS HYU DON' OVERDO IT, IFFEN HYU KNOW VOT I MEANS.
ER—
YOU...DO THIS SORT OF THING A *LOT?*
HO *YAZ!*
LOTS OF PIPPLE HEV TRIED TO TAKE DE TOWN!
DOT'S VY DEY KEEP DIS BIG OPEN PLAIN HERE.
DE GUN CREWS KNOW DE CO-ORDINATES FOR EVERY CENTIMETER!
HAH! REMEMBER DOT "X DE DESTROYER" GUY?
WHO THOT DOT BIG "X" ON DE GROUND VOS VERE HE SHOULD SET UP HIZ *TENT?!*
HEE!
SPLAT!
GOOT TIMES!
YAH. BUT DEY HADTA GET A NEW "X" MADE!
HAW! *BOTH* SIDES SAID *DOT!*
ZO— IZ VERRA *NIZE* OF HYU TO SAVE *MIZ AGATHA'S* TOWN FOR HER...
OH, WELL. SHE'S A VERY NICE GIRL.
DOT'S *RIGHT. VERRA* NIZE.
I FEEL... *STRANGE.*
I DIDN'T THINK I'D BEEN HIT *THAT* BADLY.
OH, YOU PROB'LY IZN'T HIT *TOO* BAD.
BUT—
IZ DIS DE FIRST TIME HYU FACED DOWN AN ENTIRE ARMY ALL BY HYUSELF VIT A VEAPON HYU VASN'T SURE VOS GONNA *VORK?*
WELL, *YES...*
VELL DEN. DOT'S JUST HYU BODY BEIN' ALL SURPRIZED HYU AIN'T ALL BLOWED OP AND *DEAD!*
NEXT TIME, HYU VON'T EVEN *BLINK!*
NEXT...
I *REALLY* THINK I HAVE TO LIE DOWN NOW.
HYUP. VUN *MYSTERIOUS DISAPPEARANCE* COMIN' OP!

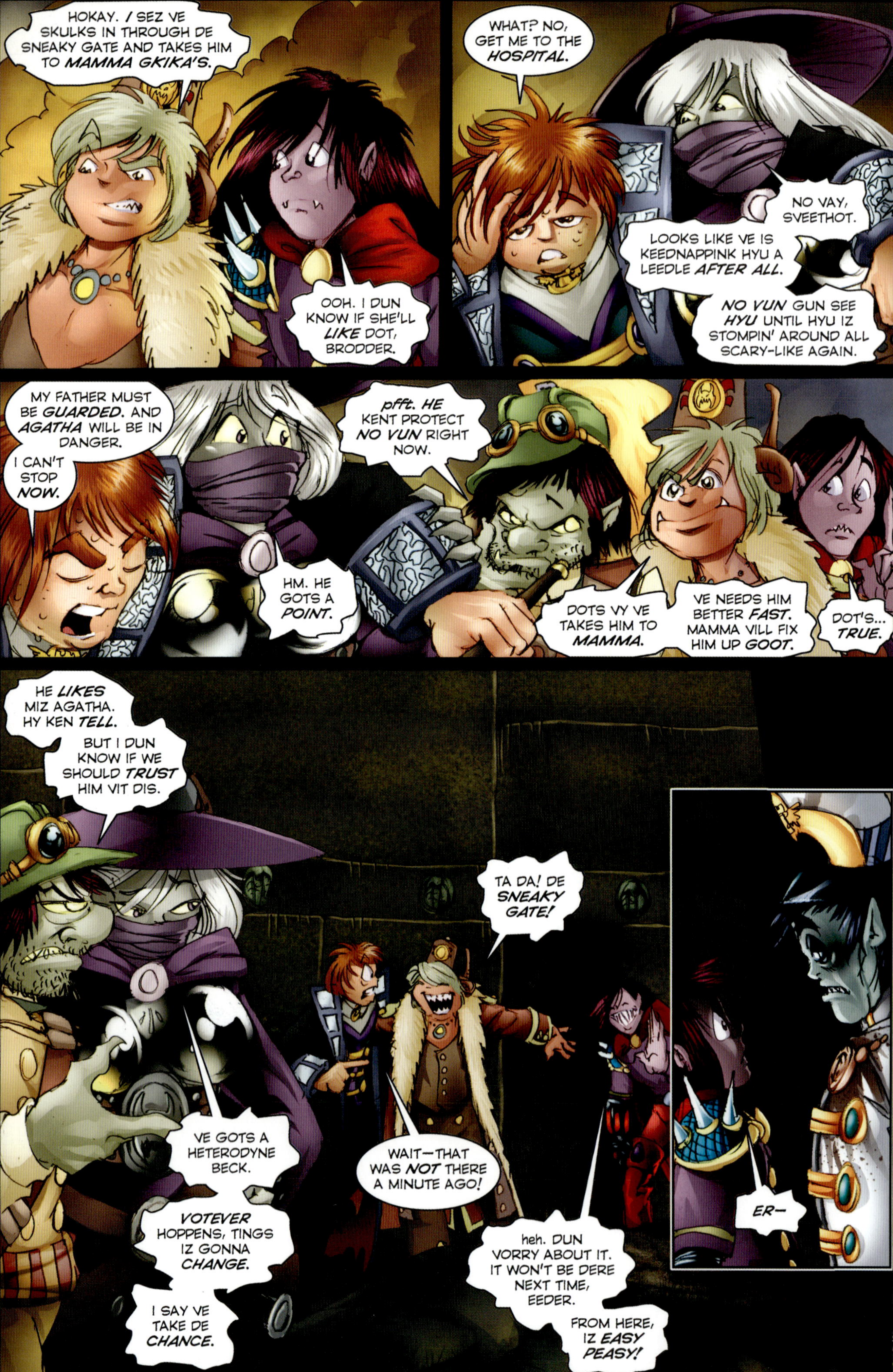
HOKAY. I SEZ VE SKULKS IN THROUGH DE SNEAKY GATE AND TAKES HIM TO MAMMA GKIKA'S.
OOH. I DUN KNOW IF SHE'LL LIKE DOT, BRODDER.
WHAT? NO, GET ME TO THE HOSPITAL.
NO VAY, SVEETHOT.
LOOKS LIKE VE IS KEEDNAPPINK HYU A LEEDLE AFTER ALL.
NO VUN GUN SEE HYU UNTIL HYU IZ STOMPIN' AROUND ALL SCARY-LIKE AGAIN.
MY FATHER MUST BE GUARDED. AND AGATHA WILL BE IN DANGER.
I CAN'T STOP NOW.
HM. HE GOTS A POINT.
pfft. HE KENT PROTECT NO VUN RIGHT NOW.
DOTS VY VE TAKES HIM TO MAMMA.
VE NEEDS HIM BETTER FAST. MAMMA VILL FIX HIM UP GOOT.
DOT'S... TRUE.
HE LIKES MIZ AGATHA. HY KEN TELL.
BUT I DUN KNOW IF WE SHOULD TRUST HIM VIT DIS.
VE GOTS A HETERODYNE BECK.
VOTEVER HOPPENS, TINGS IZ GONNA CHANGE.
I SAY VE TAKE DE CHANCE.
TA DA! DE SNEAKY GATE!
WAIT—THAT WAS NOT THERE A MINUTE AGO!
heh. DUN VORRY ABOUT IT. IT WON'T BE DERE NEXT TIME, EEDER.
FROM HERE, IZ EASY PEASY!
ER—

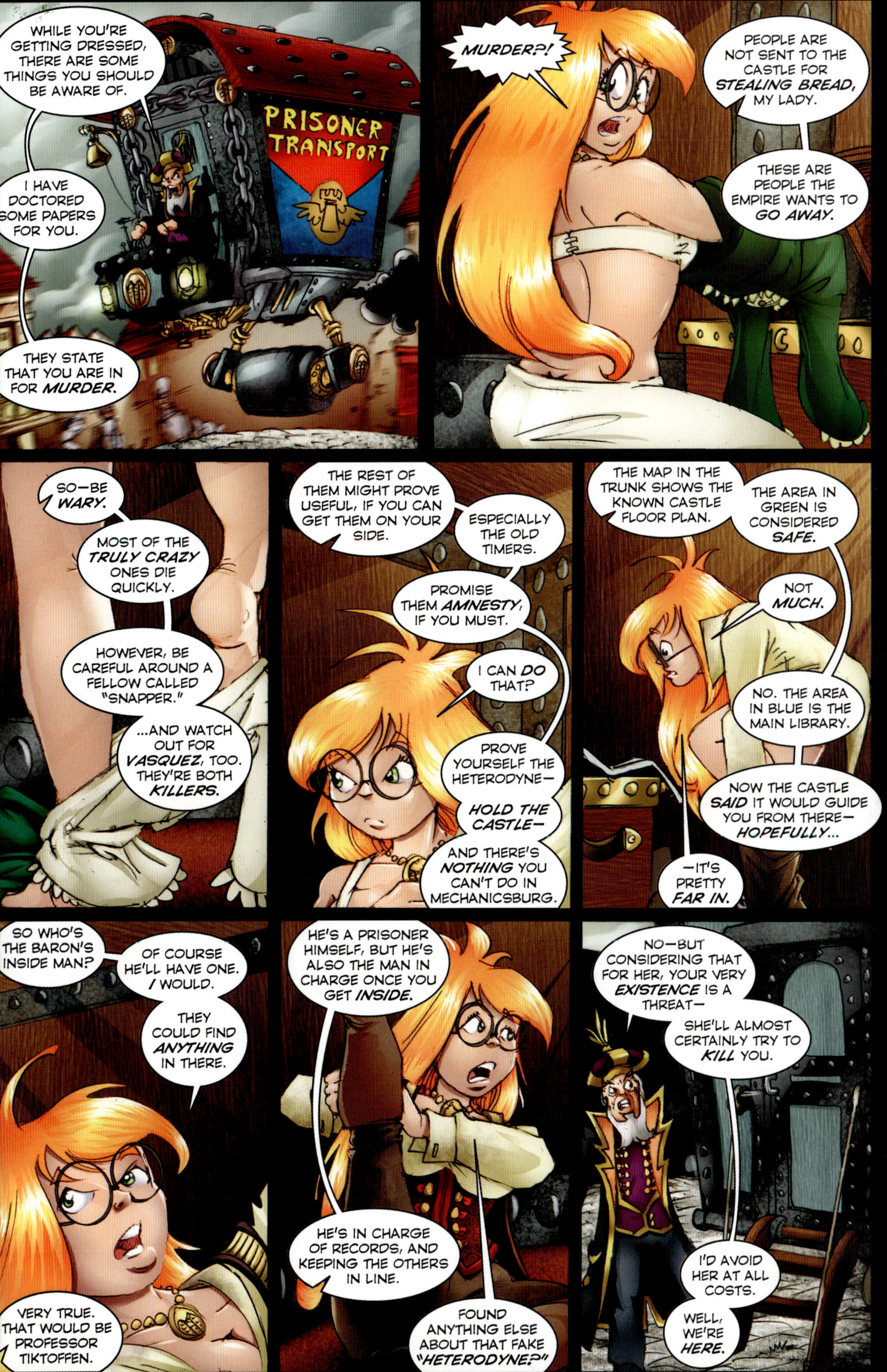
WHILE YOU'RE GETTING DRESSED, THERE ARE SOME THINGS YOU SHOULD BE AWARE OF.
PRISONER TRANSPORT
I HAVE DOCTORED SOME PAPERS FOR YOU.
THEY STATE THAT YOU ARE IN FOR MURDER.
MURDER?!
PEOPLE ARE NOT SENT TO THE CASTLE FOR STEALING BREAD, MY LADY.
THESE ARE PEOPLE THE EMPIRE WANTS TO GO AWAY.
SO—BE WARY.
MOST OF THE TRULY CRAZY ONES DIE QUICKLY.
HOWEVER, BE CAREFUL AROUND A FELLOW CALLED "SNAPPER."
...AND WATCH OUT FOR VASQUEZ, TOO. THEY'RE BOTH KILLERS.
THE REST OF THEM MIGHT PROVE USEFUL, IF YOU CAN GET THEM ON YOUR SIDE.
ESPECIALLY THE OLD TIMERS.
PROMISE THEM AMNESTY, IF YOU MUST.
I CAN DO THAT?
PROVE YOURSELF THE HETERODYNE—
HOLD THE CASTLE—
AND THERE'S NOTHING YOU CAN'T DO IN MECHANICSBURG.
THE MAP IN THE TRUNK SHOWS THE KNOWN CASTLE FLOOR PLAN.
THE AREA IN GREEN IS CONSIDERED SAFE.
NOT MUCH.
NO. THE AREA IN BLUE IS THE MAIN LIBRARY.
NOW THE CASTLE SAID IT WOULD GUIDE YOU FROM THERE—HOPEFULLY...
—IT'S PRETTY FAR IN.
SO WHO'S THE BARON'S INSIDE MAN?
OF COURSE HE'LL HAVE ONE. I WOULD.
THEY COULD FIND ANYTHING IN THERE.
VERY TRUE. THAT WOULD BE PROFESSOR TIKTOFFEN.
HE'S A PRISONER HIMSELF, BUT HE'S ALSO THE MAN IN CHARGE ONCE YOU GET INSIDE.
HE'S IN CHARGE OF RECORDS, AND KEEPING THE OTHERS IN LINE.
FOUND ANYTHING ELSE ABOUT THAT FAKE "HETERODYNE?"
NO—BUT CONSIDERING THAT FOR HER, YOUR VERY EXISTENCE IS A THREAT—
SHE'LL ALMOST CERTAINLY TRY TO KILL YOU.
I'D AVOID HER AT ALL COSTS.
WELL, WE'RE HERE.

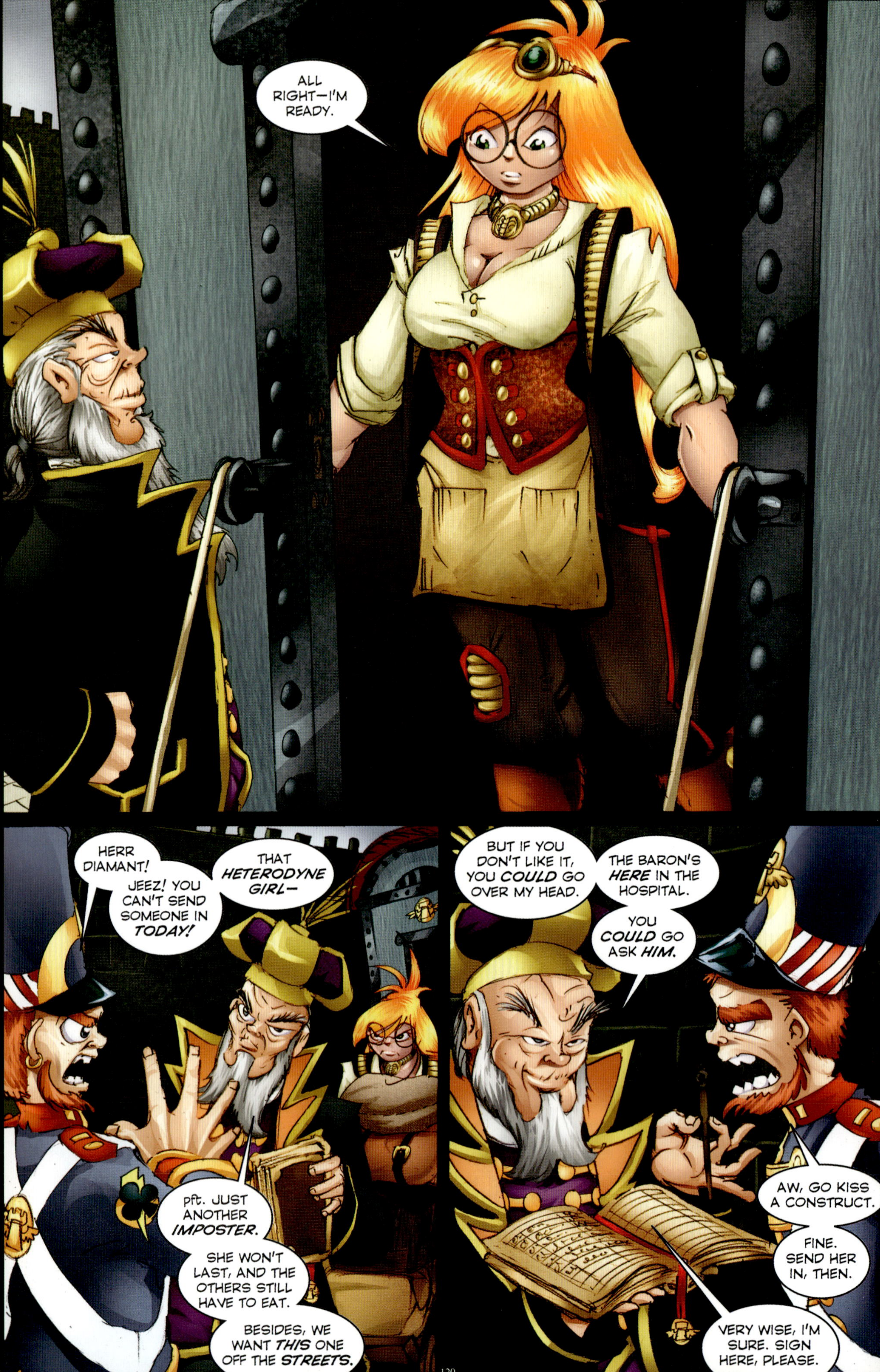
ALL RIGHT—I'M READY.
HERR DIAMANT!
JEEZ! YOU CAN'T SEND SOMEONE IN *TODAY!*
THAT *HETERODYNE GIRL—*
pft. JUST ANOTHER *IMPOSTER*.
SHE WON'T LAST, AND THE OTHERS STILL HAVE TO EAT.
BESIDES, WE WANT *THIS* ONE OFF THE *STREETS*.
BUT IF YOU DON'T LIKE IT, YOU *COULD* GO OVER MY HEAD.
THE BARON'S *HERE* IN THE HOSPITAL.
YOU *COULD* GO ASK *HIM*.
AW, GO KISS A CONSTRUCT.
FINE. SEND HER IN, THEN.
VERY WISE, I'M SURE. SIGN HERE, PLEASE.

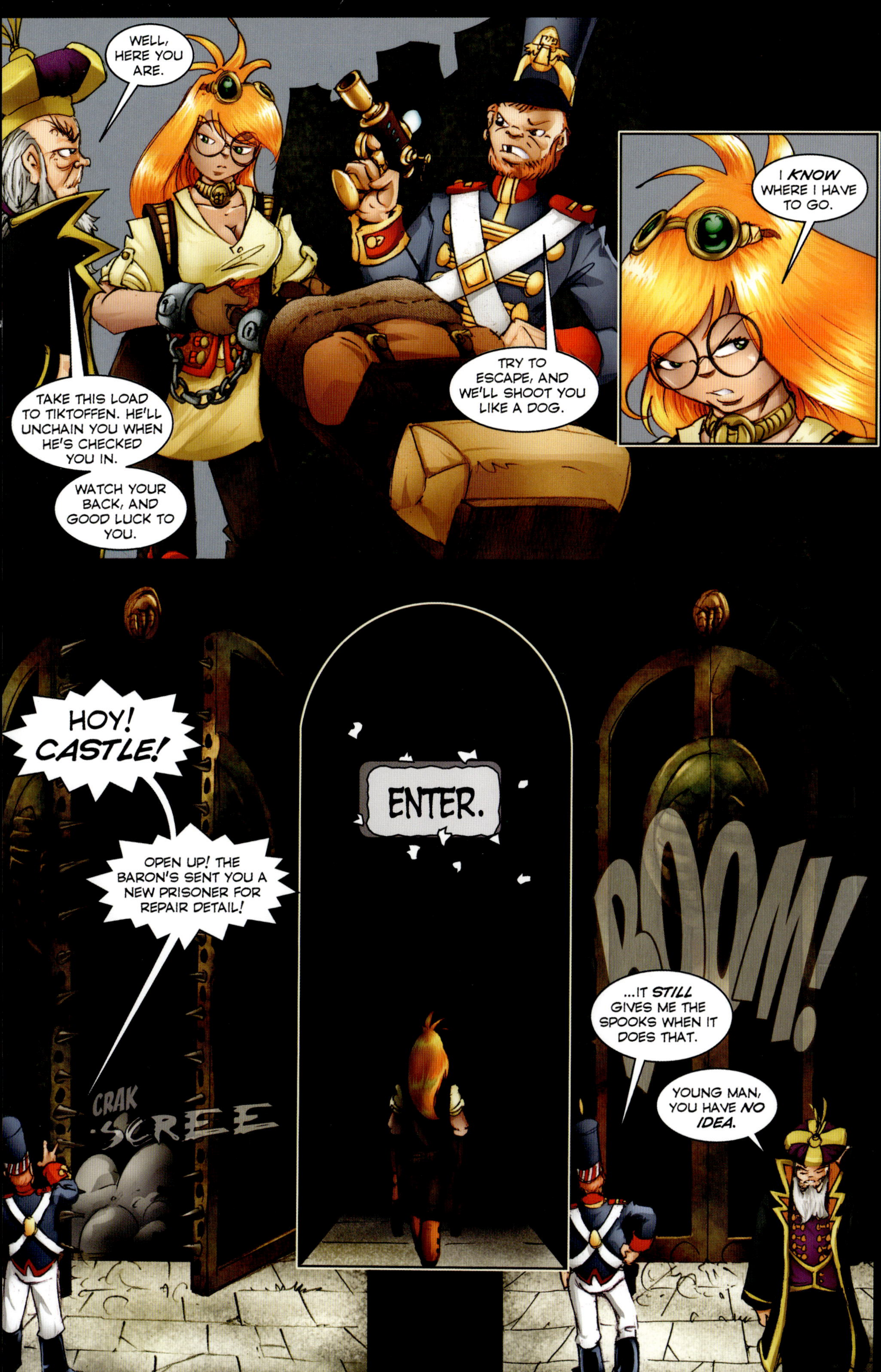
WELL, HERE YOU ARE.
TAKE THIS LOAD TO TIKTOFFEN. HE'LL UNCHAIN YOU WHEN HE'S CHECKED YOU IN.
WATCH YOUR BACK, AND GOOD LUCK TO YOU.
TRY TO ESCAPE, AND WE'LL SHOOT YOU LIKE A DOG.
I KNOW WHERE I HAVE TO GO.
HOY! CASTLE!
OPEN UP! THE BARON'S SENT YOU A NEW PRISONER FOR REPAIR DETAIL!
CRAK
SCREE
ENTER.
BOOM!
...IT STILL GIVES ME THE SPOOKS WHEN IT DOES THAT.
YOUNG MAN, YOU HAVE NO IDEA.

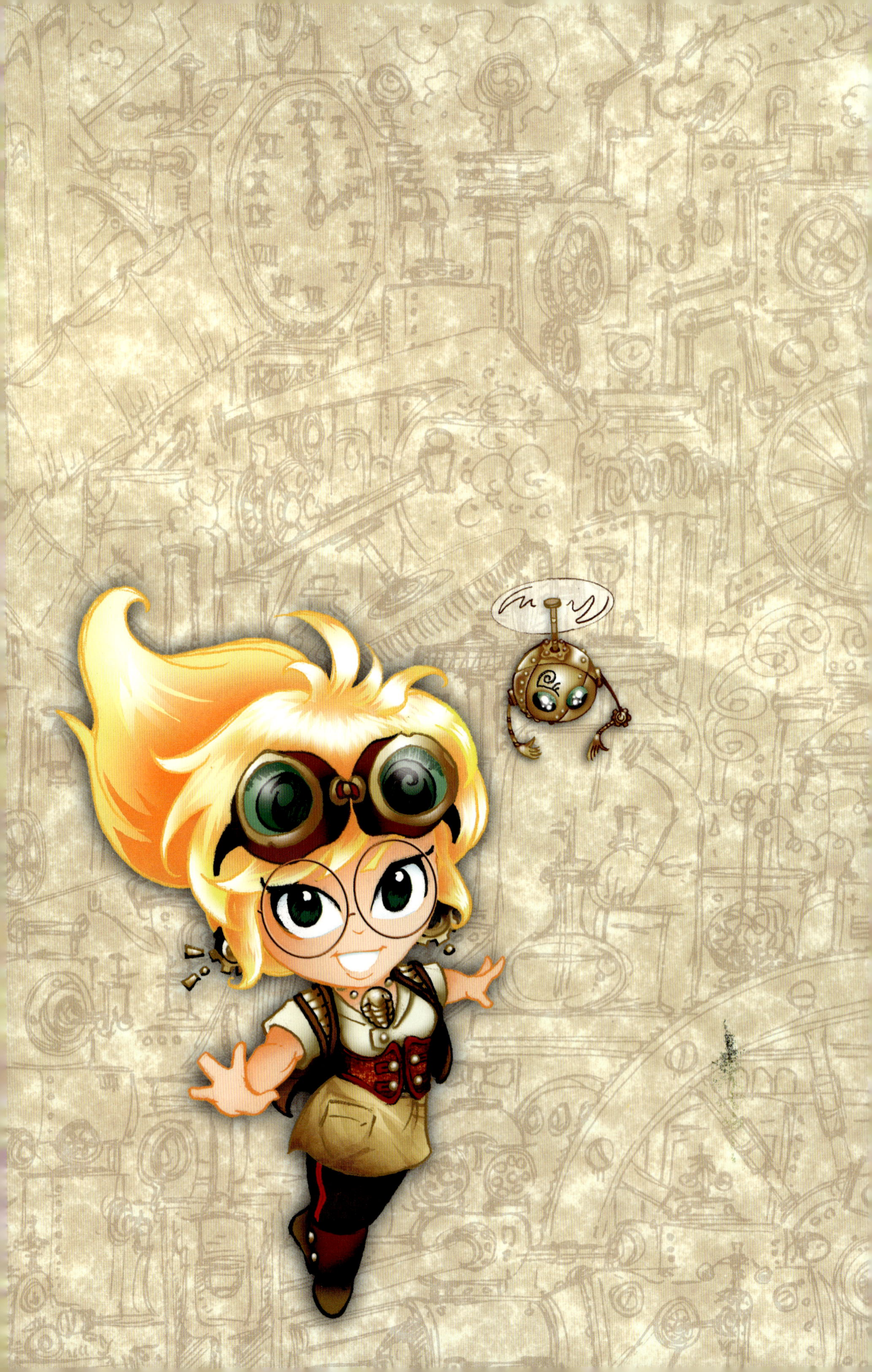

TO BE CONTINUED IN:

GIRL GENIUS® Book EIGHT

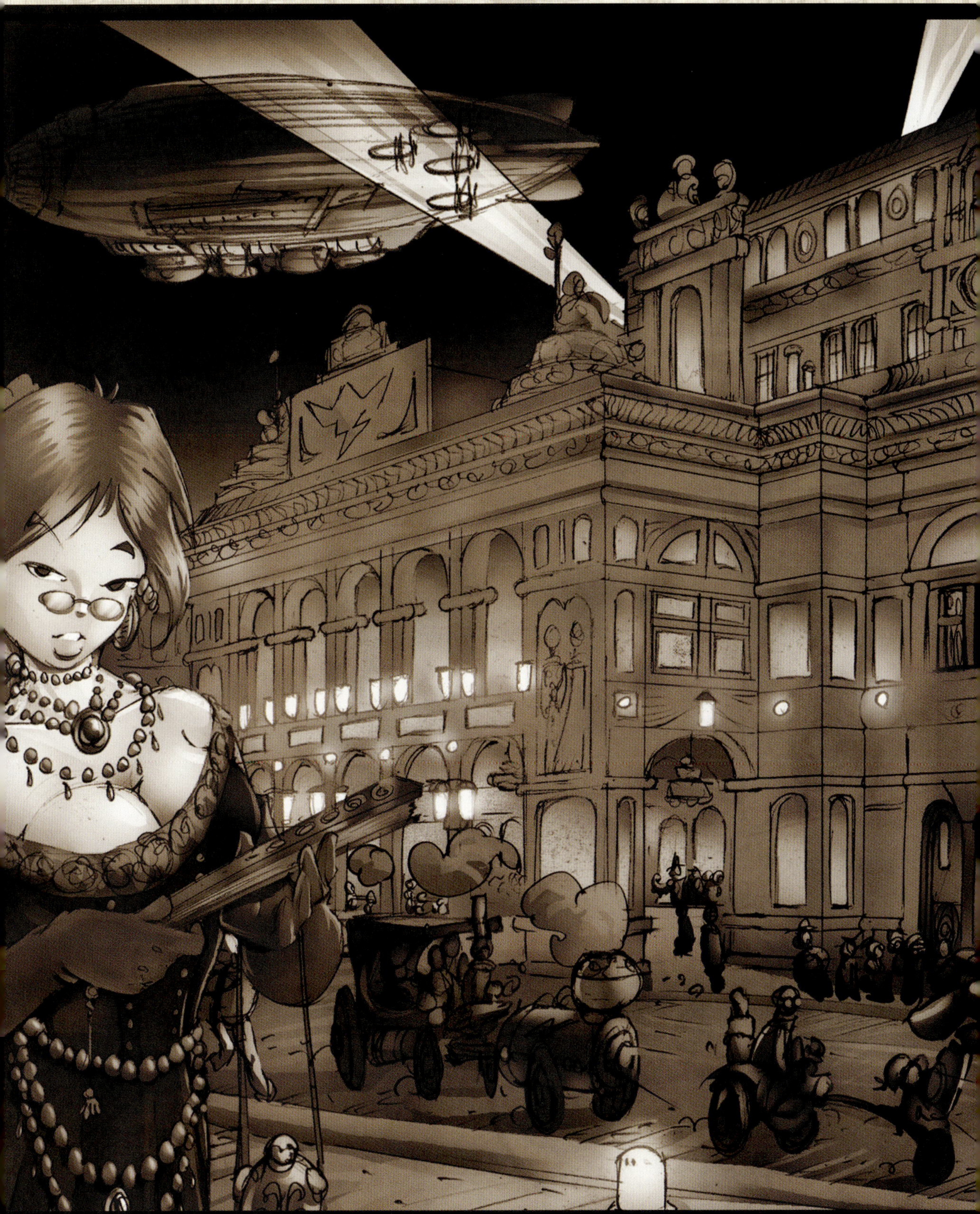

KEEP UP WITH THE STORY! READ NEW COMICS THREE TIMES A WEEK AT:

WWW.GIRLGENIUS.NET

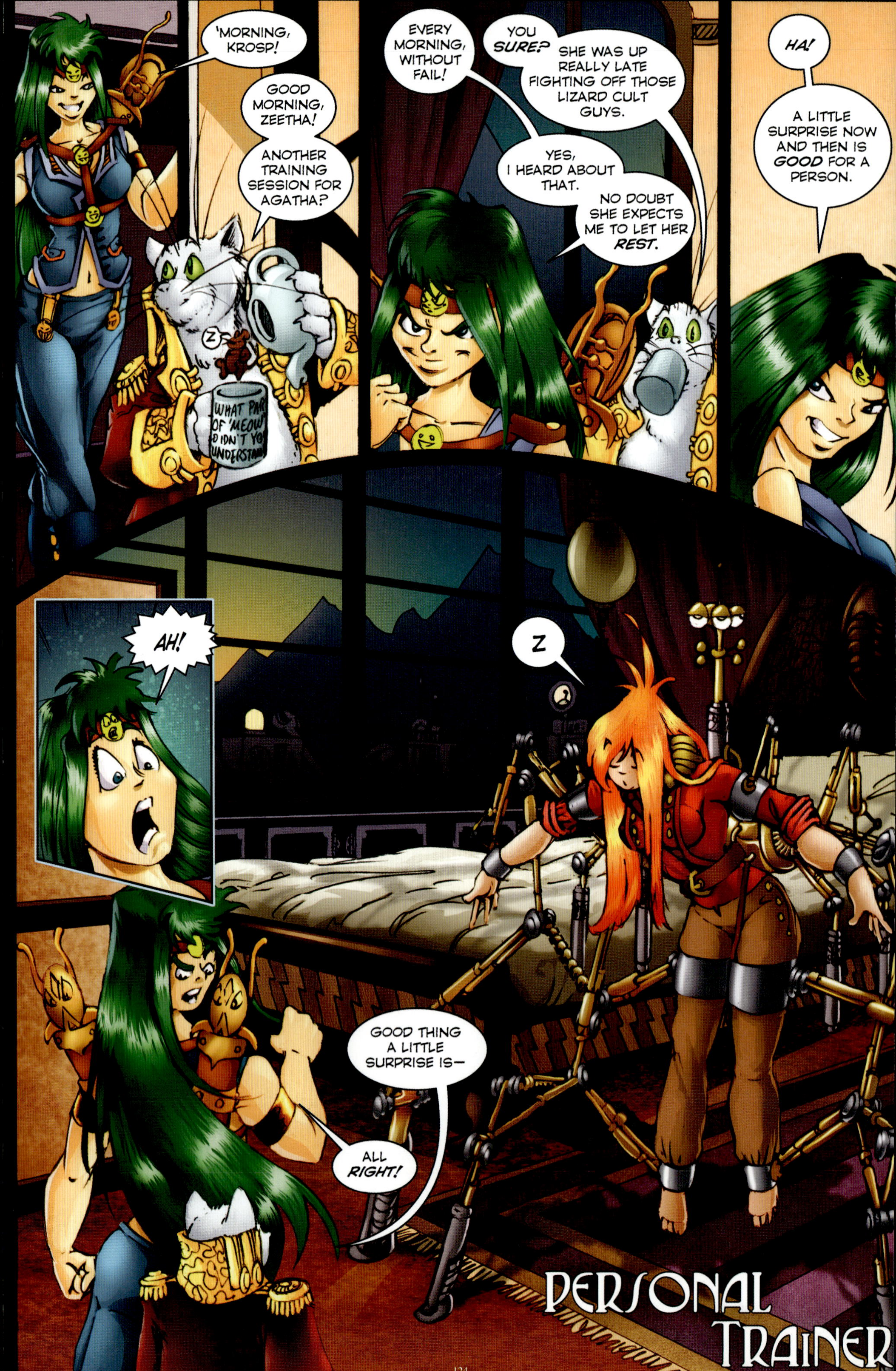
'MORNING, KROSP!
GOOD MORNING, ZEETHA!
ANOTHER TRAINING SESSION FOR AGATHA?
Z
WHAT PART OF 'MEOW' DIDN'T YOU UNDERSTAND
EVERY MORNING, WITHOUT FAIL!
YOU SURE? SHE WAS UP REALLY LATE FIGHTING OFF THOSE LIZARD CULT GUYS.
YES, I HEARD ABOUT THAT.
NO DOUBT SHE EXPECTS ME TO LET HER REST.
HA!
A LITTLE SURPRISE NOW AND THEN IS GOOD FOR A PERSON.
AH!
Z
GOOD THING A LITTLE SURPRISE IS—
ALL RIGHT!
PERSONAL TRAINER

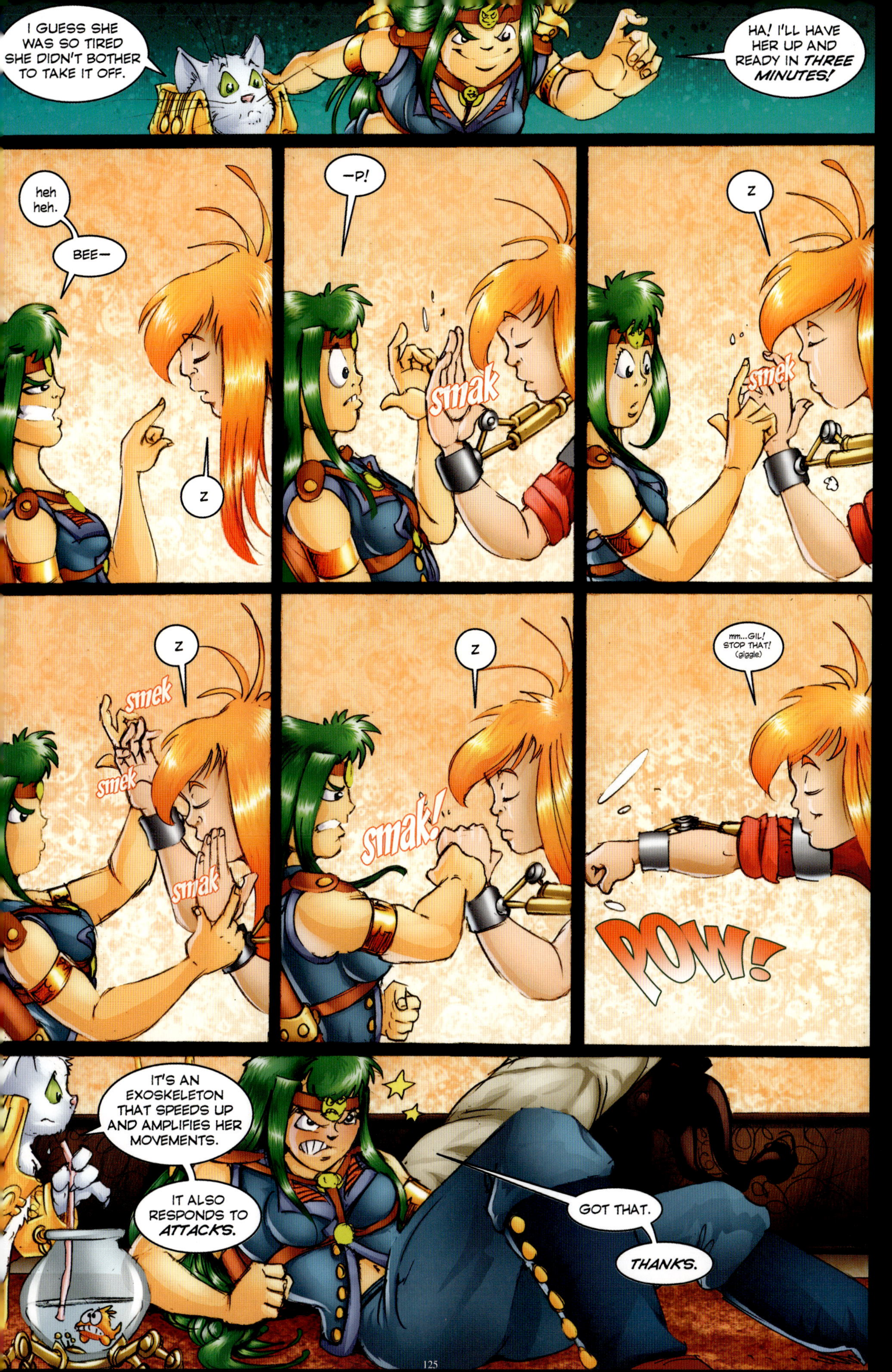

I GUESS SHE WAS SO TIRED SHE DIDN'T BOTHER TO TAKE IT OFF.
HA! I'LL HAVE HER UP AND READY IN *THREE MINUTES!*
heh heh.
BEE—
Z
—P!
smak
Z
smek
Z
smek
smek
smak
Z
smak!
mm...GIL! STOP THAT! (giggle)
POW!
IT'S AN EXOSKELETON THAT SPEEDS UP AND AMPLIFIES HER MOVEMENTS.
IT ALSO RESPONDS TO *ATTACKS.*
GOT THAT.
THANKS.

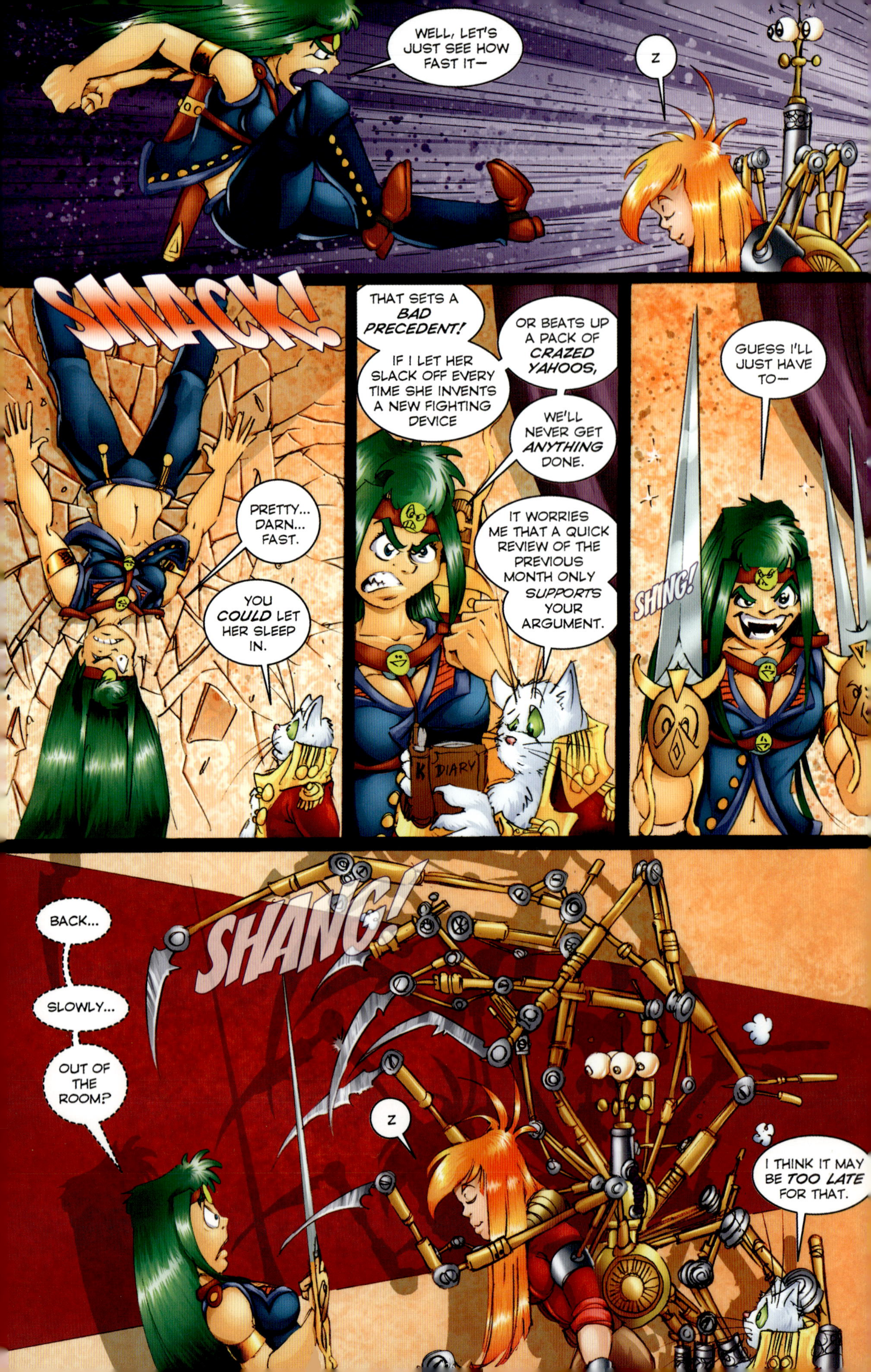
WELL, LET'S JUST SEE HOW FAST IT—
Z
SMACK!
PRETTY... DARN... FAST.
YOU COULD LET HER SLEEP IN.
THAT SETS A BAD PRECEDENT!
IF I LET HER SLACK OFF EVERY TIME SHE INVENTS A NEW FIGHTING DEVICE
OR BEATS UP A PACK OF CRAZED YAHOOS,
WE'LL NEVER GET ANYTHING DONE.
IT WORRIES ME THAT A QUICK REVIEW OF THE PREVIOUS MONTH ONLY SUPPORTS YOUR ARGUMENT.
DIARY
GUESS I'LL JUST HAVE TO—
SHING!
SHANG!
BACK...
SLOWLY...
OUT OF THE ROOM?
Z
I THINK IT MAY BE TOO LATE FOR THAT.

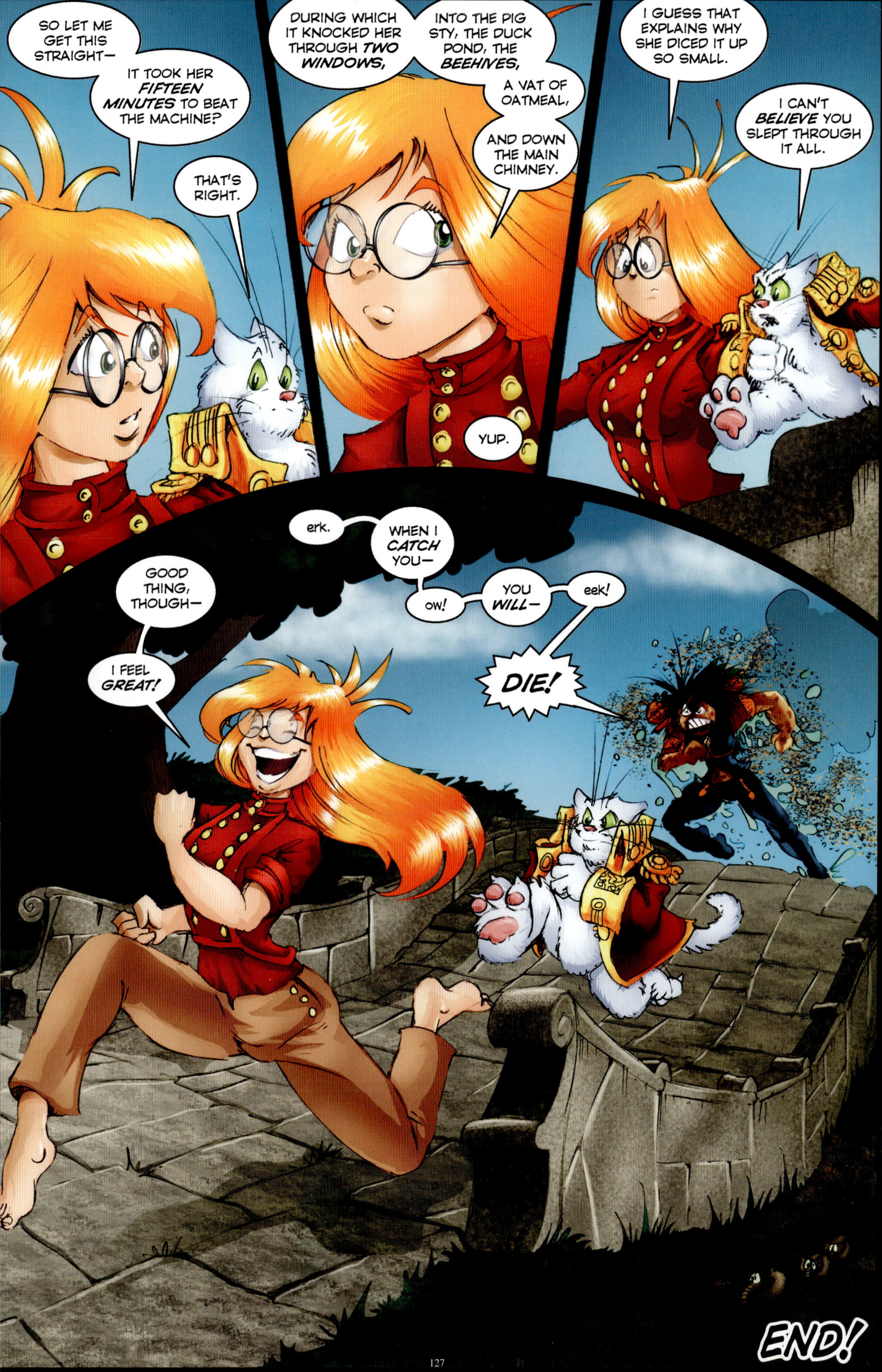
SO LET ME GET THIS STRAIGHT—
IT TOOK HER *FIFTEEN MINUTES* TO BEAT THE MACHINE?
THAT'S RIGHT.
DURING WHICH IT KNOCKED HER THROUGH *TWO WINDOWS*,
INTO THE PIG STY, THE DUCK POND, THE *BEEHIVES*,
A VAT OF OATMEAL,
AND DOWN THE MAIN CHIMNEY.
YUP.
I GUESS THAT EXPLAINS WHY SHE DICED IT UP SO SMALL.
I CAN'T *BELIEVE* YOU SLEPT THROUGH IT ALL.
erk.
WHEN I *CATCH* YOU—
ow!
YOU *WILL*—
eek!
DIE!
GOOD THING, THOUGH—
I FEEL *GREAT!*
END!

READ MORE COMICS ONLINE AT:

WWW.GIRLGENIUS.NET

MONDAY · WEDNESDAY · FRIDAY

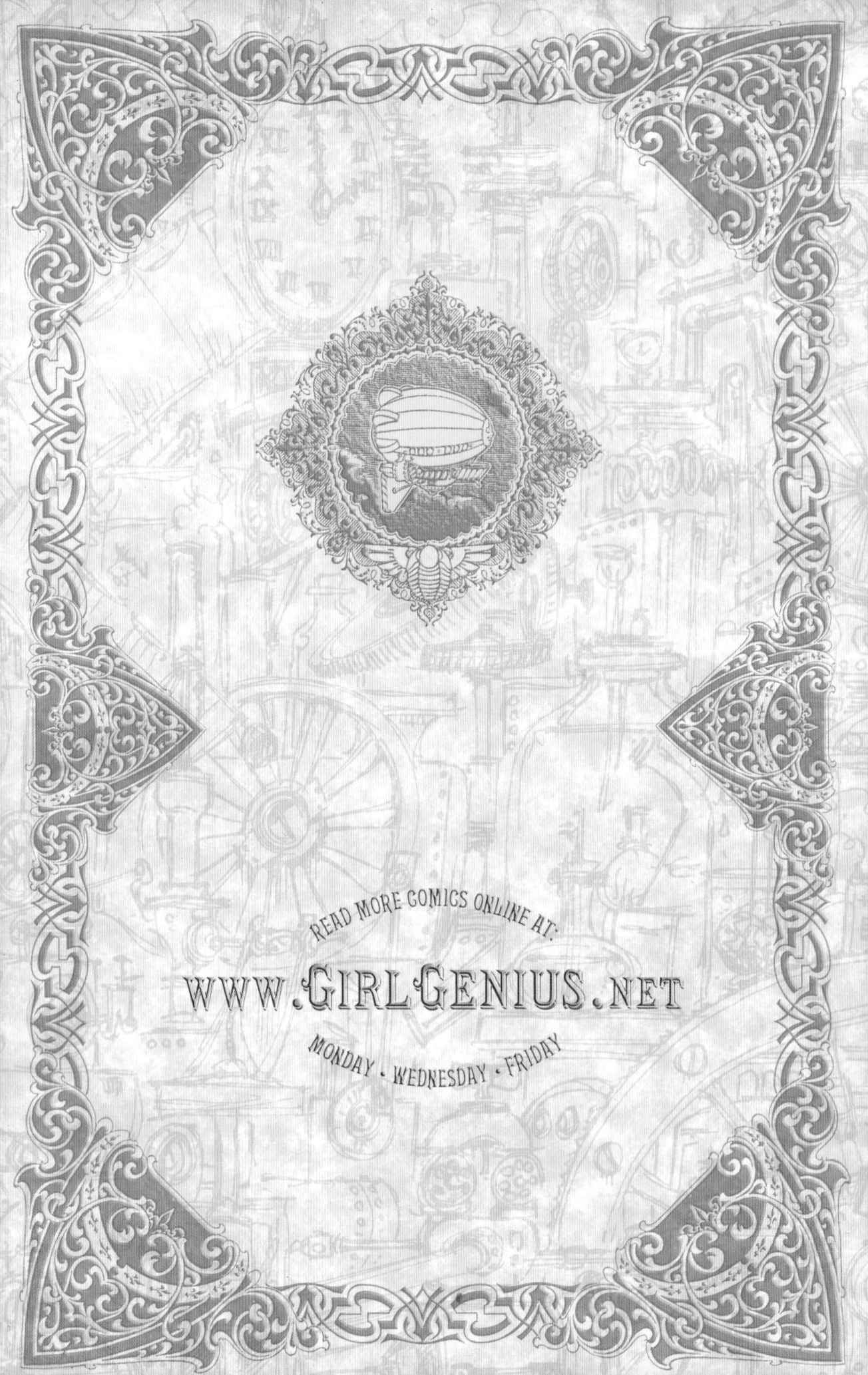